Mike Eller

Brent Ghelfi has served as a clerk on the U.S. Court of Appeals, has been a partner in a Phoenix-headquartered law firm, and now owns and operates several businesses. He has traveled extensively throughout Russia, and lives in Phoenix with his wife, a former prosecutor, and their two sons. He is currently at work on the third book in the Volk series.

Also by **Brent Ghelfi**

Volk's Shadow

Volk's Game

Volk's Game

a novel

Brent Ghelfi

PICADOR

Henry Holt and Company
New York

www.picadorusa.com

Picador® is a U.S. registered trademark and is used by Henry Holt and Company under license from Pan Books Limited.

For information on Picador Reading Group Guides, please contact Picador.
E-mail: readinggroupguides@picadorusa.com

Designed by Meryl Sussman Levavi

Library of Congress Cataloging-in-Publication Data

Ghelfi, Brent.
    Volk's Game : a novel / Brent Ghelfi.
        p. cm.
    ISBN-13: 978-0-312-42784-9
    ISBN-10: 0-312-42784-0
    1. Art thefts—Fiction. 2. Saint Petersburg (Russia)—Fiction. 3. Moscow (Russia)—Fiction. 4. Mafia—Russia (Federation)—Fiction. I. Title.

PS3607.H46V66 2007
813'.6—dc22

                                                              2006049313

First published in the United States by Henry Holt and Company

First Picador Edition: May 2008

10 9 8 7 6 5 4 3 2 1

For Lisa, Brock, and Jake

The line dividing good and evil cuts through the heart of every human being. And who is willing to destroy a piece of his own heart?

—Aleksandr Solzhenitsyn, *The Gulag Archipelago*

Volk's Game

"**What** do you know about art, Volk?"

Maxim Abdullaev hurls the question through the airwaves as if it were an ax, cleaving pretense.

I cram my Nokia cell phone against my ear. Clattering dishes, jostling diners, and raised voices give me an excuse to delay answering his question. "Hold on," I say, then step downstairs to my table in the basement of Vadim's Café near Staraya Street, where I make my office.

Maxim could be anywhere. His headquarters are in the Solsnetskaya neighborhood just a few blocks away, but he changes his personal place of business weekly, sometimes daily, so it is impossible to develop a mental picture of where he is or what he is doing.

Once I've moved away from the din, I take a moment to gather my thoughts. "Art? I have a master's in art history from Moscow University."

I'm sure that Maxim knows enough about my life to catch the sarcasm. Dead mother, disappeared father, late-era Soviet poverty, and five years of killing and worse in Chechnya unsurprisingly failed to harmonize into a world-class education. The things I have learned are not taught in universities. He barks a deep-throated chuckle that offers no comfort. A polar bear probably makes the same sound just before it eats.

"Listen," he says. "You do something for me. Talk to Gromov. Yes?"

"Yes," I say, as if I have a choice, and Maxim disconnects.

Two hours later, nearing midnight, Gromov clumps like a plow horse into my basement office. The flesh on his bald head and puffy face droops like a shar-pei's skin and slits his eyes, which are shifty-nervous, with good cause. Valya lurks hidden among the shelves of café sundries behind him.

"You talked to Maxim?" he says.

I grunt acknowledgment.

He collapses into a padded roller chair that disappears, creaking, beneath his bulk. Even its silvery round feet are covered by the hanging folds of his overcoat, where one hand stays buried in a deep pocket. He likes to show off a chromed Colt .45 Peacemaker, an outdated cannon that rends great holes in bodies, a good weapon for a man whose business is intimidation.

"I got a business opportunity," he begins. "Maxim says you're the guy to help me assess it."

"I don't do partners."

He knows this. My rule is one source of the friction between us. "Yeah, yeah." Scarred leather biker boots twirl the chair as he takes in the surroundings.

There's not much to see here in the basement level. Black slate floor, rows of shelves, exposed raw-wood beams, plaster walls randomly damaged to show the red brick beneath, and dusty '60s-era slot machines. Gromov is looking for Valya, I know, but she won't be seen unless she wants to be. He finishes his survey and grins through crooked yellow teeth ridged black with omnipresent chewing tobacco.

"Maybe you *should* do partners."

"Say what you came to say." I point to the empty tabletop in front of me. "I've got work to do."

"You know diamonds?"

"Maxim says art, you say diamonds. Which is it?"

"Same thing, asshole."

When he yanks his hand from his overcoat pocket, Valya materializes behind him and aims the short barrel of a pistol-grip, 12-gauge Mossberg at the back of his shaved skull. But instead of drawing the Colt, he tosses a crystal rectangle that tumbles sparkling through the air before smacking into my palm.

Valya withdraws.

Gromov leans back, smugly oblivious to the nearness of death, while I examine his prize. The stone is about one centimeter square by three long. One end is broken, jagging up into a ragged half peak. Unreadable inscriptions are etched into its flat sides. The etchings are names written in Persian, I know. I toss it back, and he catches it deftly.

"You're an idiot, Gromov."

His jaw muscles are so big that his face widens into a pyramid when he clenches his teeth. "Fuck you."

I wave toward his hand. "That's a bad imitation of the Shah Diamond. The real one's five blocks up the road in the Kremlin Armory under more security than Putin."

That's a lie. The real one's gone. It was originally a gift to Tsar Nicholas I to atone for a Russian diplomat made dead in 1820s Tehran. Famous, in part, because all the unlucky owners named in the inscriptions died owning it. Damn near ninety carats preserved in uncut form. Three years ago I helped it make a symbolic but unpublicized journey back to Persia, to the rare arts collection of a spoiled Saudi prince, in return for financial considerations benefiting my primary patron, the Russian army. A better fake than this one sits behind glass under twenty-four-hour security in the Kremlin's Diamond Fund.

"See?" he says. "You know about this kind of shit."

"Even the tourists know about the Shah Diamond."

He leans forward as far as his muscle-bound body will allow and settles flying-buttress elbows on my table, which groans but holds. Like much of the older furniture in Moscow, it was sturdily built by cold gulag hands. "What if I told you I could get the real thing, with nobody the wiser?"

"You can't. Don't waste my time."

"Listen." He scrunches his broad face, concentrating. "We got inside guys. Military, pissed off by Putin capitalism. They're like pensioners on the dole while guys like us get rich. They take the diamond, replace it with the fake. Think about it. The fucker's under glass all day, like goddamn Lenin. Who knows if what's under there is real? Who cares? In five years some Swiss prick looks at it under a microscope and raises hell. By then, shit, there's no way to trace who did what and when."

I say it can't be that easy, although it was.

"You just worry about your end," he says.

"What's my end?"

"Work the distribution angle." Gromov's running hot, trembling, obviously excited. "You're tight with that fag, Nigel Bolles." He mouths Nigel's name with curled-lip contempt. "He'll point you to guys in London or New York or wherever and help us find someone with too much money to buy it."

"I'm not your guy."

His jaw drops. "Why not?"

"I told you. I don't do partners. And I think your chances of getting the real thing out of there are zero."

Pounding veins ripple under the five o'clock shadow that darkens his enormous dome. "Why do you make things so fucking hard, Volk? Three times I say let's do business. Three times you tell me to fuck off." He rolls mountainous shoulders, as if to make room under the overcoat. "Business is getting too tight. Every time I turn around you're there. You're in my way."

He's right about our businesses bumping into each other, at least the parts of mine he knows about—drugs, identity theft, pictures, and a Russian brides operation that caters to the middle classes of America and industrialized European and Asian countries. Russia has ten million more women than men, one product of her endless fighting and purging, and she always imports more than she exports. I figure the bride business evens out both imbalances.

Gromov's interests collide with mine in several ways, although he's big into child prostitution and other things that I won't touch. But he's wrong to worry about it, because there's plenty of business for both of us on this little stretch of road below old Lubyanka prison and because the Internet has made us international.

"Don't be so parochial, Gromov."

"What the fuck does that mean?"

"It means we'll get along fine if you concentrate on business instead of territorial bullshit. Steal your diamond. Hump Lyudmilla. Just stay away from me."

He doesn't like my way of rejecting him or the reference to his billowy-breasted girlfriend. He stands so suddenly his chair overturns. Snarls, roars something unintelligible, hauls out his hand cannon, and starts to bear down, slow and amateurish. I don't think he's going to fire. He just wants to make a point. But then the racking slide of a shotgun cracks through everything. He stops dead. His eyes click back and forth like the ones in the plastic clocks that look like tail-wagging pets, but he's careful not to turn around and provoke her.

"It's Valya," I offer, and both of his hands go up slowly until the muzzle of the Colt brushes the bottom of a low beam.

She's behind him, looking amped, ready for anything, almost lost in lace-up boots, cinched parachute pants, and a chrome-colored jacket with its sable-lined hood turned down. The Mossberg rests lightly in her hands. Her white hair sprays backlight like a halo.

"I'm done," he says without turning around.

I nod at him, and he shucks open the overcoat and slots the Colt into a holster made from more than one cow. "I got no choice," he says in the same tone you use to tell a cabdriver to turn right. "I gotta put you out of business, gimp."

The gibe about my foot doesn't bother me. Impending war does, especially given Maxim's newly found interest in the world of art. The General and I had three years to operate freely in that arena. I wish our time wasn't coming to an end.

"Have at it, big man," I say.

He turns fast, but Valya is nowhere to be seen. One last baleful look at me, and then Gromov lumbers away.

Lunch the next day is sliced smoked pork on the sunny side of an outdoor gazebo in grassy Gorky Park. Halfway through, I'm joined by Yuri, a baton-twirling cop. He goes sixty kilos, maybe. He approaches with his spindly chest puffed out, slides his baton into a steel ring attached to his belt, and plops down across from me. The sun glints through the silver birch trees and gambols off the gold double-headed Russian eagle in his cap as I slide an envelope stuffed with American dollars across the plastic tabletop. He plucks the envelope and tucks it under his leg, fast and furtive.

"Shit, Volk!"

His eyes dart, but I'm busy with the pork. I don't care who sees. I stop chewing long enough to say, "There's an extra five hundred for Viktor. And a note."

Viktor commands Yuri's area. He's been on my payroll for two years. The note explains the information I want about Gromov, and the extra money pays for it. Gromov is probably paying for similar reports about me.

Yuri pulls a foil-wrapped sandwich from a brown bag blotched with oil stains, but then he sits and watches me without eating. He sets his cap on the table and licks the down on his upper lip, which has been the same since I met him a year ago, so I suppose it's a mustache.

"Where's Valya?" he asks.

The pork is gone. I suck the fat off my fingers and pat his balding head. He's younger than me, mid-twenties, but the hair gods are fickle.

He's softer than me as well. War and want have hardened my appearance. Military-cut bronze hair, hazel eyes with a feral blaze, stubbled jaw—I look ferocious even when I'm trying not to. Each pat makes his head bounce.

"Don't mess with me, Yuri."

His eyes widen. "God no, Volk."

I leave him to his sandwich. I'm tromping through the high grass of Gorky Park to my Mercedes S-600 when the Nokia buzzes.

"Go."

"It's Nigel."

Bolles. My largest procurer of foreign business. The British expat fop Gromov asked about the day before. I wait.

"Word's out you're in a war, old boy," he says.

His lilting voice is strained, due, no doubt, to a night of hard drinking and no morning Stolichnaya fix. "Business is always tough."

"How can I help?"

Just what I need. "The British are coming," I say, but he apparently misses the negative reference.

"Precisely. I am at your service."

"Just keep finding customers."

"Right." He clears his throat. It sounds like a cold motor coughing to life. "In that regard, you'll be pleased to learn I have an opportunity for tonight. Swiss conventioneers with a common interest."

"Just drugs?"

"Boys and girls, too."

He sounds regretful. He knows my scruple, silly as it is. In the end, what difference who makes the money? The children are pincushions either way.

I stop on a knoll carpeted with flattened grass that shines like wet jade. Even in early May the wind blows chill over the Moscow River and bends the tops of the stately line of birches that march up the embankment toward the towering peaks of the university. Industrial haze blurs the cityscape. The spires of Stalin's other Seven Sisters pierce the haze like upthrust stilettos. Gromov is manageable. I know I can dispatch him with relative ease. But he's one of Maxim's poodles, and as chieftain of the Azeri mafia, Maxim can crush my enterprises on a whim.

"Are you still there, Volk?"

I grit my teeth. "I'll meet you at the National Club at ten to arrange the details." My chest tightens, and suddenly I feel as if I can't take in enough air.

"Well done." He's reenergized, doubtless calculating his twenty percent cut.

I end the call, limp to the Mercedes favoring my newly throbbing stump, and crank the shiny black car into heavy traffic, already ruing my decision. The cell buzzes again.

"Go."

"Volk?"

"Who wants to know?"

"It's Arkady."

Several years have passed since I last heard from Arkady Borodenkov—one of my companions in a foster care facility and, later, at a rehabilitation center for boys situated on the Baltic shore. A childhood friend in places where friends were scarce. And last I heard, an Ecstasy distributor and part-time fence in St. Petersburg. Slightly built, with blond hair worn long, too weak for anything except the fringes.

"What's up?" I say.

"I got a weird one for you. A score that needs muscle and hustle. But mostly it needs brains. I thought of you."

I cut through traffic and outraged pedestrians on Kremlevskaya Street, make an illegal U-turn and then a hard right and rattle over unevenly laid bricks on the edge of Red Square. St. Basil's Cathedral looms on the left, its colorful domes like ice-cream swirls. The bright colors and the crowds lined up around the cathedral seem to be mocking decades of Soviet religious oppression.

"Keep going."

"I'm not even sure how to describe it."

I'm in no mood for stalling, not while the scum of the deal I just made with Nigel still coats the inside of my mouth. "Spit it out."

"What do you know about art, Volk?"

The same question posed by two very different men haunts me for the remainder of the afternoon. Twilight drags on past nine this time of year, making the days seem endless. I fill some of the time with paperwork in the basement of Vadim's Café.

At seven I head out to make my semimonthly rounds, visits to the tiny dwellings of widowed pensioners, women I've selected from a long list of those who have lost loved ones in Russia's wars. Tonight I'm due to make three stops at gray Khrushchev-era buildings, distinguishable from the earlier Stalin-era housing by their shoddy concrete-and-glass construction, low ceilings, and faded green halls. Unlike his successors, Stalin built for cold, rock-hard permanence.

The first two pensioners quake from a pitiful mixture of gratitude and fear. Grateful for the three thousand rubles I press into their trembling hands, a third again more than their monthly pension but only about thirty-six American dollars. Fearful my generosity might end if they say the wrong thing. They murmur, "God bless you, my child," and retreat into their tiny units.

The cramped elevator in the third apartment building is broken. Nine stories later, my stump aches as I push through a scarred-metal fire door into a concrete hall, its floor blotched different tints of brown by decades of scuffing feet. The doors are covered in quilted cloth to dampen noise. Forlorn welcome mats greet visitors. I stop on one made of rubber molded into purple violets and knock softly.

Inside, a shuffling slide is followed by snicking locks. The door creaks open. Masha stands to the side as I wedge myself into her one-room flat.

Thirty-three square meters. Ceiling so low I cringe like a nervous turtle. Hot-plate kitchen, one sink, single bed, thirteen-inch TV capped by a foil-wrapped clothes hanger antenna the shape of an inverted pyramid, and a wicker chair built for a boy. I squeeze into the chair and munch the morsel of cream-frosted ginger cake she can't afford but always has ready in token payment.

She's wearing a billowy, floor-length fuchsia shift, hoop earrings, and a frayed leather necklace adorned with carved ivory figurines. Some are animals, but the rest are more mysterious. She gives me a chipped mug of thick tea. The tremors in her palsied hand ripple the surface of the black liquid.

"Do you want another reading? Maybe this time I will see things more clearly." Her grating voice betrays too many years of unfiltered cigarettes and hard living.

"No. Thank you, Masha."

She always asks, and I almost always say no. Last week I said yes, driven by the kind of crazy impulse to which I rarely surrender. She had dimmed the lights. Settled onto the bed facing me, with our knees touching, taken my right hand between hers like a big slab of meat sandwiched between two dried leaves, and closed her eyes. When she finally raised her head, her eyes were unfocused, so wide they seemed to cover her whole face. "There are two," she said. "Two of everything." She kept stroking my hand with the same faraway look, but that was the end of my reading, no matter how many questions I asked. "I can only tell you what I see," she said later that night.

Now she settles onto the bed and rubs her stump. That's how we met, in a clinic for amputees. My prosthesis is state-of-the-art, titanium in carbon fiber alloy with a rebounding spring. I can run and jump nearly as well as I could before the crushed remains of my foot were removed ten centimeters below the knee, although I pretend otherwise. Hers is brittle leather and cracked wood nearly as old as she is.

Across from the bed the television screen flickers black-and-white images of an inner-city bombing in London, or Jerusalem, or New York, I don't know where, and it doesn't really matter.

"At least the Communists made religion go away," she says, staring at the television. "Now the churches are open, but the schools are closed."

I look again at the shadowy images. The building framed on the screen is a mosque roaring flames in Moscow. The cream from the cake fills my mouth with warm, smooth sweetness.

Her eyelids droop. "The capitalists bring drugs, pornography, and guns. And food, too, but no money to buy it."

Russian women qualify for pension at age fifty-five, men at sixty. Most men die before they collect. The women live on. The pension alone is not enough to survive, so they queue for hours for government stamps, sell homemade trinkets to tourists, eat Chernobyl-glowing fruit, and beg. And suffer.

"Russians are very unlucky in administration," Masha says.

I nod slowly. She has summarized our awful history better than any textbook possibly could.

My Patek Philippe chronometer glows nine o'clock. I swallow the last of the cake and set aside the oily napkin. Move to the edge of her bed, which sags with a surrendering squeak. Cradle her leg and massage the puckered skin at the end. It is calloused and rough, darker where her weight against the prosthesis has worked the grit of the world into the creases. She leans back, closes her eyes, and is asleep in just a few minutes. I can't change her into her nightgown. Even the idea would embarrass her beyond salvage. So I wrap her in a frayed wool comforter, set the money on the countertop, and leave as quietly as I can.

Valya's old enough to drive legally, but she doesn't have a license. Usually that's not a problem, because the police know the Mercedes and leave it alone. But tonight, an hour after I leave Masha's apartment, we're in a battered Lada from my pool, cruising in the twilight glow, so I try without much success to make her slow down.

She pulls to a hard stop in front of the National Hotel. Orange cones separate the crowded street from a line of expensive vehicles bristling with antennae and driven by beefy chauffeurs. The National Club is private, patronized by politicians from the adjacent parliament building, expatriates, hotel guests—easy enough to spot and avoid—and businessmen, some legitimate in the sense that the products or services they peddle are not illegal.

"Be careful," I tell her as I step out, and she gives me big aqua eyes, quirks her lips, and squeals the tires pulling away.

Nigel Bolles has copped a window table for two that offers a nice view of the street, the history museum, and the Kremlin's high, redbrick walls. He is never without an ivory-handled cane, which he uses now to thwack my left leg where the ankle should be. The blow is his traditional greeting, though he seems distracted tonight, fidgeting in his chair, flicking his tongue across his puffy lips. The dark blue lines patterned into his bright red ascot match his navy blazer and the road map of veins in his nose. His mushy, lopsided grin reminds me of a melting wax impression.

"Someday, old boy," he says, "you'll tell me how you lost that thing."

The story of my leg is locked in a vault that hasn't even been opened to Valya, although she was there with me for the last year in Chechnya.

"I don't like this table."

He furrows his gin-blossomed nose. "So this little tiff with Gromov is serious?"

When I stay silent, Nigel levers himself from the padded chair with a huff and signals the maître d'. We meander inland over plush crimson carpet to a table near a baby grand.

"Tell me about the Swiss," I say, and he does, while I listen with half an ear.

The club is bustling with customers. The maître d' immediately seats a fat man and a leaner companion at Nigel's old table. Nigel stops talking while our waiter sets a green-tinged, beaded martini glass of vodka in front of him. He chugs the contents of the glass in two gulps, sighs, licks his lips, and resumes talking about the Swiss.

After we've ordered and he's laid out the deal, I use the Nokia to call Valya. The National Club prizes discretion, so I talk into my cupped hand. "Ecstasy. Coke. Viagra." The conventioneers will powder the drugs into a passé cocktail called a Blue Moon because of the color from the impotence drug. Their choice of poisons dates them to their thirties, maybe forties. Younger clients prefer heroin in one form or another. "And speed." I tell her the quantities.

"Sex?"

The kids will be aged ten to thirteen. Is it fair to call it that? "I'm calling Gromov now."

She grunts at the name. She doesn't like compromise.

I hang up and dial another number. Gromov says, "Is it done?"

Is what done? I wonder. "It's Volk."

He sucks his breath, almost a choke.

"You there?"

"Yeah, I'm here." His words sound forced.

"I have a proposal for you. I need six from your string for a party tonight. All of their action is yours. No cut with me. I want no part of it." I'm already sick just talking about it. I swallow my disgust. "I get any more of these deals, they come your way. I'll carve out the Pig," I say, referring to a slimy east side pederast. I don't do business with him or others like him. Before tonight I've never touched this sort of thing, but Gromov has never believed that. "And I still want nothing to do with the diamond," I finish.

More dead-air silence. "Why couldn't you be this reasonable before?" he says finally. "I gotta make a call. I'll call you back."

He's gone before I can say, *Before what?*

Nigel is florid-faced, at least five vodka gimlets in, but he's developed a high tolerance. The waiter brings appetizers. Half-shell oysters for him, smoked sturgeon for me. Time drags. Conversations buzz the air around us. Russian and English dashed with German, French, Japanese, and, from the bar area, guttural Cantonese. Dinner arrives. I pick at a bloody steak until I feel the time is right to probe further.

"Who do you know who deals in art?" I ask.

This isn't my first foray into paintings. But the times before, I sold impressionists and cubists, working with a moon-faced fence from Munich, now dead. He bought a Picasso sketch stolen from a vengeful Dutch industrialist and ended up chum for the bottom-feeders in a slimy Amsterdam canal. I've never used Nigel for this kind of thing before. Most of my work with Nigel has involved tourists—drugs, prostitution, small-time fencing—with him as the middleman.

He arches an eyebrow and tries a smile, but it seems strained. "Art?"

"Humor me."

He puffs self-importantly. "Sculpture? Painting? What period? There's a great deal of territory here, old boy."

"Paintings." I avoid the topic of my earlier conversation with my foster-care friend Arkady. Misdirection has become a way of life for me. "Impressionists and the like. Cézanne. Degas. Van Gogh. Picasso. Guys like that."

I can almost hear the little calculator in his brain start to whir. "They have quite a variety of such artists displayed at the Hermitage Museum," he says. "Some of it even stolen booty from the war."

I've seen the pieces, including the ones we don't admit to having, and I don't consider any of them stolen, but that doesn't matter now. "Who do you know local who deals in such treasures?"

He makes a show of considering while the waiter clears our table.

To hurry him along I say, "Your cut is five percent. Don't count on anything, though. This is a long shot."

"There is a fine arts dealer with a gallery near Novodevichy Convent. French, so he's, ah . . . flexible. His name is Henri Orlan.

Here's his number." He writes on a napkin and slides it toward me. "If you prefer, I will provide a formal introduction."

"No." I pocket the napkin, shaking my head. I would rather check out Orlan my way.

Nigel nods distractedly and massages his sausage fingers. "There is another. A professor at Moscow University. Tell me, why—"

The outer window explodes in a roar of drumbeating gunshots. Tables overturn. Bodies scatter and shred under a deafening fusillade of bullets.

In the eruption of gunfire, screams, and shattering glass I dive over the table and take Nigel down. A chandelier crashes onto the carpet next to us, blowing shards like tiny knives. Nigel clings to me like I'm a life raft as I drag him through the pandemonium.

By the time we make three meters the firing has ended, leaving only cries of pain and terror, tinkling glass, and the drifting stink of cordite. Huddled with Nigel under a table near the exit, I peer through the smoke. The men at our former table are bloody and tattered. One still belches blood and convulses, but they're both gone. Doors slam shut on a primer-gray panel van jumped onto the sidewalk, and it screeches away from a hail of secondary gunshots—hopelessly belated fire from two ersatz bodyguards crouched behind a black Escalade.

I tow Nigel out of the club, through a door that leads into the shouts and madness of the National Hotel's lobby. Police sirens wail in the distance. I push through the lobby and the adjacent atrium café and out the rear fire exit to a back alley, where the Brit collapses in a dead faint, apparently under the weight of the dawning realization that he was a target, albeit a derivative one. He goes nearly a hundred kilos, and fat makes him unwieldy, but I hoist him onto my shoulder and trudge through the alley to the edge of the tumultuous street.

This near the Kremlin, police and emergency vehicles are everywhere already. Street vendors hurriedly pack their wares and scurry away, hunched with fear, shoving aside dazed tourists and fleeing Muscovites. "Chechen terrorists," one says. "Gangsters," says another. No sign of Valya or the battered Lada she was driving.

Nigel comes to as I unload him against the sooty wall. He seems smaller and lost without his ivory-handled cane. He's a trembling wreck. "He tried to kill me!" he cries.

I assume he's talking about Gromov. "Better to say he was willing to accept your death as a by-product of mine." This does nothing to assuage him, so I grab the wide lapels of his blazer and shake hard to stop his vacant-eyed drift. "What is the name of the man at Moscow University?"

"Woman," he says mechanically. A spray of bystander blood fans his cheek, drying wetly.

"Woman, then. What is her name?"

"Yelena Posnova."

I push him into the street and toward his flat. He wobbles off. He's ruined for the night, and maybe for good. I set off in the other direction. Time to see Gromov now, while the anger is still fresh.

chapter 3

I stomp through three blocks of bedlam amid running citizens, thieves trolling for opportunity in chaos, a ponytailed little girl lost. Then into another firefight.

The car Valya was driving sits crashed through the plate-glass window of Gromov's Jaguar dealership, a profitable front for more nefarious activities. His lieutenants mill about on the street in disarray, apparently confused about what to do.

I work my way to a littered alley in the back. One man stands there, probably told to guard while his betters discuss options out front. They think me dead, or they wouldn't be so lax. I unsheathe my knife from a hidden slot in my prosthesis as I approach the guard from behind. Jerk back his head and pop his windpipe rather than disable him, because he was in league with those who would have killed me, and time is short. The General will just have to understand. I yank down the rusty ladder on the fire escape, climb, break glass, and make the second-floor suite of offices while the erstwhile guard is still twitching.

I find two dead men punched with oozing red holes, then hurry faster down the hallway. Round the corner and there she is, my willowy angel, an apparition in a plush, oak-paneled office. She looms over a supine Gromov with the stubby barrel of an Uzi rammed into his mouth. Her free hand grips a long-bladed knife. I pause at the threshold and listen. She's telling him the things she plans to do to him before he dies, terrible things she learned from me. But then she stiffens, as if sensing something, and snaps her head around.

White hair blowing softly in vented waves of warm air. Enormous aqua eyes, suddenly filled with relief, then joy. "You're alive!" She doesn't remove the gun barrel from Gromov's mouth.

I approach, and then she's in my arms, pressing against me, and her mouth finds mine. Her leaping heart drums against my chest, hitting two beats for every one of mine. I open my eyes to see her gaze angled down at the slowly choking giant on the end of her gun.

I end the kiss with regret and squat next to his head. Saliva curdles at the corners of his straining mouth. The Uzi blow job is so deep he can't swallow. The barrel trails ropy spit when I pull it out and replace it under his right eye.

"I made peace," I say.

His jaw crackles when he talks. "I couldn't call them off in time."

My stump throbs phantom pain. Valya hisses. Crouched as I am, the grip of her Uzi is an inch from the corner of my eye. Her knuckle is white—no slack left in the trigger. Smoked gunpowder from her earlier fire drifts like acrid thunderclouds.

How many like Gromov roam Moscow's underworld? Hungry, smart enough to organize and lead simpler illegal enterprises but incapable of more, the perfect foil for Maxim and the other predators at the top of the criminal food chain. Too many to catalogue. When he dies, another will take his place. I see no profit in killing him.

"How do we make things right?" I say.

Valya sighs at this latest failure of my hatred.

"I'll pay." Gromov looks hopeful. He's talking to her. "In territory or operations. Take the city center. Take drugs. Name the price."

The sirens from the National Club swirl closer. I stand and angle a view out the window at the milling crowd of uncertain Gromov lieutenants and the approaching, strobing lights mounted on Moscow police cars. No military, not yet at least. No matter who is in the two-man cars, they'll be on Gromov's payroll or mine, maybe both. They'll need a plausible story, and money to cover everything up. I decide to let him worry about it.

"Where's your rat hole?" I know he has one. We all have escape hatches.

He's smart enough not to argue. "A tunnel, sometimes used by the FSB." He uses the new name for an old part of the KGB. "I'll show you how to get in. It leads to a food stall near Lubyanka station. The stall's closed now, so no one will bother you."

"You owe me, Gromov. We make peace, but you owe tribute. My price."

He blinks at Valya, at turquoise-eyed death, and gives a shaky sigh of relief. "I owe you," he agrees.

✳

Several hours later, Valya and I are in my loft, six floors up, hidden in a dilapidated industrial building that from the outside looks fit only for heavy machinery and rats, which are what occupy the lower five levels. But the interior of this floor is luxuriously fitted with the finest appointments money can buy.

Lying in bed, after love made more fervid by the near miss of death, I clip, light, and pull on a Cohiba Robusto. I'm still breathing hard from our mutual exertions, glazed with sweat. Valya's alabaster skin glows its self-generated softness. Her aroma fills me, but the warm musk mingles with the bitterness in my heart.

I know where she was tonight, after dropping me at the National. The evidence was in the way she moved her hands and mouth and hips and in the dewy satisfaction of her half-closed eyes. And in an elusive scent, like violets in spring, an aroma that has haunted me for more than two months. But how is it possible to lay sole claim to beauty so sublime?

"You're soft when you should be hard, Alexei," she says gently.

"We had more to gain by letting him live."

She gives me a weary Russian shrug.

"How did you get there so fast?" I say.

"I was in the car, across from the parliament building, watching for you. I saw them shoot into the window. I thought you were dead."

My angel. Failing to protect, and so exacting immediate retribution. "And before?"

Lowered eyelids make the aqua orbs disappear. Evasion is beneath her. "With her."

Now it is my turn to close my eyes, as if the act will blot out the thought of Valya's secret lover—a woman I seem unable to compete against, at least in the ways that are important. I shift to face the far wall.

The flawlessly painted pieces of a *matryoshka,* a Russian nesting doll, rest on a cantilevered ledge under subdued light. But I look through them without really seeing their impeccable beauty, the work of painstaking months by a nameless artisan.

What do I know about art? I know that the greatest works can't be possessed. They belong to the world.

chapter 4

The Mercedes blows past enormous rust-red spikes on the side of the road, carrying Valya and me inside its warm cockpit at a steady one-hundred-and-thirty-kilometer clip, northbound on Leningrad Highway. The spikes are tank stoppers, memorials marking the point of Hitler's deepest incursion. Russia embraces her invaders in a murderous trifecta of bullets, brutal cold, and starvation. Revolutions, civil wars, purges, and other self-flagellations thin the population during the lulls between foreign invasions. Napoleon took Moscow before his decimated rearguard retreat to Poland, but Hitler was stopped here, the hedgehogs seem to say—this far, no farther.

Two days after our confrontation with Gromov, we're headed for a meeting in St. Petersburg with Arkady Borodenkov and his Hermitage Museum mole. The last time I saw Arkady was five years ago, when he used our old friendship and shared orphan history as an excuse to hit me up for a small loan that he never paid back.

"Seventy-four pieces." Valya reads from a paperbound book called *Hidden Treasures Revealed* that she bought from a street vendor.

Her lap is covered with more books and a directory of Hermitage Museum personnel.

I've chosen to ignore her last visit to her unnamed friend. Trying to discuss it has gotten me nowhere in the past. I suppose my reluctance to confront this issue in the same direct manner in which I manage others represents a special brand of cowardice.

"By Cézanne, Degas, Monet, Pissarro, Renoir, Gauguin, Van Gogh, Toulouse-Lautrec, and lots of others," she says, skimming pages of pictures. "Collected from the fallen Weimar Republic by Russian art teams and soldiers, shipped to the Hermitage and the Pushkin State Museum of Fine Arts, stored there while Russia rebuilt after the war. Unacknowledged for half a century. The Germans want them back. The Russians remember the 'Nazis' deliberate, relentless policy not only of robbing and pillaging, but of undertaking the total cultural extermination of the nation—'"

I cut her off with a wave. We know those things now, three years into our operation. Eighty-five pieces were inventoried after the war, not seventy-four. With the General's help, eleven disappeared from the Hermitage, only to be magically discovered in some dusty warehouse or in the attic of a hundred-year-old Frenchwoman claiming to be Van Gogh's pubescent lover or in one of many other plausible, if improbable, places. All of them were auctioned for millions of francs, pounds, or dollars.

"You need artistic rounding, Alexei," she says and laughs like a little girl. Today different contacts make her eyes the color of fired copper.

Thinning stands of weeping birch, poplar, and oak trees blur past, ready to give way to desolate, bleached tundra and then the northern taiga. Clouds block the afternoon sun. Traffic is light. I kick the Mercedes up to a hundred and fifty kilometers per hour, forty more than the speed limit. We should be able to make the trip in less than ten hours. "Western art," I say dismissively. "We should have sold them all. Openly, as legitimate spoils of war."

"The last Van Gogh to sell in public auction went for more than eighty million dollars," she says. "This collection still has four of his works. It's safe to say the total value of what remains is in the billions."

Meanwhile, endlessly suffering Russians starve, and old soldiers die without medicines. Just thinking about it infuriates me. "Let's talk about the value of 'newly discovered' works."

"Assuming they can be properly authenticated and given an ownership history, they would be worth as much as other works of the same quality by that artist."

"Assuming other works by the artist have changed hands in the last five centuries."

"Assuming that, yes. If not, the value is . . ." She playfully pouts a hot pink-painted lower lip. "Speculative." Her smile radiates.

We're traveling the northern path of the tsars. They were transported on golden carriages mounted on runners to glide over the snow. Our way is more mundane, but in profile Valya calls to my mind a glowing, porcelain-doll tsarina. She tucks her sleek legs beneath her body and sits cross-legged.

"Your friend said this is known, but lost? Not hidden war spoils like the others, but truly lost, so it can be given a story?" She looks skeptical. She is wise.

"He says he has a story for it. A true story that will increase its value."

She drops the books onto the floorboard and unfolds a beige chamois on her lap. Removes a .22-caliber semiautomatic Sturm-Ruger from an ankle holster. The pistol looks like a toy, but it's not. It's an assassin's weapon, used for close work. She breaks it down with practiced ease and pushes a bore cleaner through the barrel.

"We will see," she says.

Halfway to St. Petersburg the road is renamed Moscow Highway, which then becomes Moscow Prospect for a straight shot into the city. Compared to Moscow, St. Petersburg seems fresh, western, just as Peter the Great intended when he used the stooped backs and weary legs of serfs and convict laborers to build it on the Baltic's leaden edge three hundred years ago. It's after ten in the evening but still light as we navigate the grid of streets. White nights are beginning their march against darkness. This time in the season and this far north, the sun disappears completely for only a few hours. Within a month the dusk will meet the dawn. Our meeting is set for midnight in an upstairs café overlooking the Neva River from a perch on Vasilevsky Island.

We cross the Dvortsovy Bridge to the Spit. I stop the car on a university side street next to the building where Pavlov trained his dogs. The butt-jointed buildings of the Winter Palace and Hermitage are visible across the river. The view is framed by twin red rostral columns mounted with tripod bowls, which centuries ago were filled with oil and set afire as makeshift lighthouses protecting the St. Petersburg seaport. On the other side of the river, the spire of Peter and Paul Fortress thrusts into the darkling sky.

Valya roars off to establish a position inside the café. I reconnoiter the perimeter streets, slow and purposely hobbling through gaggles of students, see nothing unusual, and an hour later post in a gift shop with a view of the ground-floor front entrance of the aptly named Neva Café. It's nearly dark now, but the foyer is lit a pallid yellow.

Arkady arrives fifteen minutes early. He has aged in the five years since I last saw him. The wind fans back thinning blond hair to reveal a receding hairline. He's still slight, but the paunch riding over his belt gives him a spidery look.

He pauses at the door to look around. He knows me, knows I'm somewhere watching, but gives up without really trying and goes inside. Within the next quarter of an hour he's followed by a pinch-faced babushka in thick-soled shoes that appear to hurt her feet, two bundling couples, a slender boy with a slung messenger bag, and a thick, blue kerchief–clad parishioner from the nearby Orthodox church. None of them looks like an art historian to me.

I cross the street, push in the door of the café, climb steps covered by torn carpet, and stand at the podium to wait for the greeter. Hanging plants and low partitions break up the groups of green-clothed tables. About half are occupied. Valya is reading a book at a window table with a view of the river, which winds past like poured mercury in the washed-out light of moon and stars.

Arkady sits two tables away, not looking at her the way men usually do. He's alone. He sees me and motions, and I make a show of walking with difficulty. He pushes a chair away from the table, but I sit in a different one with my back to Valya, and prop my prosthesis on the chair he had selected.

"Your leg . . . ?"

"Bad. Walking is hard. Running, impossible."

He clucks his tongue, sits, and sips his tea. "Rolf is due shortly."

"Rolf?"

"Dr. Lipman."

The name is familiar from Valya's directory. Arkady's mole is the second assistant director of the State Hermitage Museum and an art restorer. "Tell me about him."

"He's Swiss by birth," Arkady replies. "Mid-thirties. He's been with the museum for several years and—"

"No." I don't want that kind of information. I already have it. "Tell me how you met him and what he wants now."

Arkady squirms and looks uncomfortable. Wispy hair has fallen into his eyes, somehow adding to his nervous demeanor. "He is a . . . friend." He seems to expect a challenge.

I am reminded of a day in our shared history. At a rehabilitation center for boys on the cold Baltic shore north of St. Petersburg, known as Leningrad in those days, we passed bricks in a long line like a fire brigade to the construction crews building a new naval barracks. During a rare break I climbed a hill for an eagle's view of the ant line. Near the top I saw Arkady at the same instant he saw me. He was on his knees on the permafrost, mouth full, one cheek ballooned out, fellating one of the furloughed prison workers. I assumed then that he did it for the money and thought little of it, but now the image connects.

"That confuses things," I say.

"No." He shakes his head like a dog trying to rid itself of water. "That makes it safe. I trust him with my life."

"What does he want?"

Arkady looks surprised. "Money."

"Are art restorers usually so greedy?"

He shrugs. His gaze shifts to a place behind my back. I pretend not to notice, glad for Valya.

"Why me?" I say.

"I told you. We need help with the plans. Guts. Brains. We need your talents, Alexei."

I am not convinced. Those things can be had for less than I charge. "Lay it out," I say.

Just then I hear Valya purr behind me, "Pardon me, do you know the time?"

Arkady watches the little drama unfolding behind me with anxious eyes. I slide my hand into my pocket and grip a Sig-Sauer P226 Navy loaded with exploding 9-millimeter rounds packed with metal shards designed to tear through flesh.

"Just past midnight," a man says. The voice is cultured, the Swiss accent unmistakable.

Valya has done her job. I know he's there, and her cover stands. "Sorry to bother you," she says.

Arkady greets the newcomer with shining eyes and a cheek-to-cheek hug. "This is Dr. Rolf Lipman," he says to me.

He's the messenger bag carrier, older up close. In an odd way he looks like Arkady's frail twin, but I decide the impression derives mostly from his thinning blond hair. His nose is longer and hooked, an angled prop for round John Lennon glasses, and his lips pout over a sandy teardrop soul patch.

I struggle clumsily from the chair, wince, and shake his hand. His grip is firm and dry, not like the dead fish his sallow appearance suggests.

"Are you injured?" he says.

"It's his foot," Arkady answers for me.

Lipman nods as if he's already heard it's gone and frowns. "How will he—"

"He's fine," Arkady says, and Lipman relents.

We settle around the table. Arkady pours tea from a brass samovar. Valya pretends to leave, but I know she'll be nearby. When we're alone in our corner, Lipman pulls a slim leather portfolio from his messenger bag.

"What do you know of the Hidden Treasures?" he asks me.

"Hardly anything."

It is the answer he expects. He smirks and launches into an overly complicated lecture with too many digressions that concludes with, "These paintings, each one worth millions of euros on the open market, languished half a century in a twilight zone of nonexistence." He sips muddy Russian tea and studies the room. His hand trembles when he sets the mug back onto the table. "And there are others," he says in a low voice. "Not from the war. The Hermitage is an underfunded storehouse of art lost in the interstices."

"Who are the artists?"

He leans forward, looking tense, electrified. Whatever comes next, I believe that he believes it with an intensity bordering on fanaticism. "Only one matters," he says.

He hunches over his bag, darts his eyes, pulls out a paper-sized, poorly lit photograph, and hands it to me with a strange, keening moan, as if he can't bear to part with it. All the world roars to a wondrous stop as he chants the name like an incantation.

"Leonardo da Vinci."

chapter 5

We scout the grounds of the Hermitage before lunch the following day. Buy tickets like tourists and surf winding halls of sightseers. Stand at the window in a hallway that overlooks the narrow canal cutting between the Little Hermitage and the Hermitage Theatre. Traverse the museum as Lipman whispers the location of the underground routes that correspond to our path.

The eatery is closed for renovation, so we settle at one of the aluminum tables arranged in a roped space around a slapdash sandwich stand.

"Why not carry it out at night, or under some pretext?" I ask Lipman.

"Employees are searched when they leave the building. Incoming and outgoing shipments are inspected at least twice. And, except for the catacombs, cameras are everywhere."

I allow my gaze to wander over the shifting eddies and winding rivers of people. The crowds mask paranoid layers of Russian security. Camera lenses protrude from high corners like sniffing snouts.

Uniformed guards observe from nooks built into the walls. Other guards are not dressed so obviously. They wear tourist clothes and mingle. Extracting a painting the size of this one will be tricky indeed.

But Leonardo's work is beyond my usual contempt for Western art. Just the idea of it possesses me in an irresistible, amorous embrace. "Tell me how the painting came to be here," I say.

Lipman folds pasty, blue-veined hands in his lap and prigs his lips pedantically. When he wrinkles his nose, his round glasses ride up his forehead. "It was painted in the first decade of the sixteenth century. One of only fifteen paintings Da Vinci created during his lifetime. Fifteen the world knows about, at least."

He looks at me as if he is expecting a challenge, but I don't react.

He exhales in a way that makes him sound relieved. "Today this painting is known only through Da Vinci's studies in chalk and ink, written references, and a number of inferior copies."

"How do we know this isn't another copy?"

"It is signed. And I know his work. Before the Hermitage, I worked in Milan on the restoration of *The Last Supper*. The one on the wall of the refectory," he adds worthlessly, as if it could be anywhere else, and then squints at me, seeming once again to measure my response.

I stare back impassively.

"So I know Da Vinci's work," he repeats. "The oeuvre of the master permeates the essence of this piece. The contrasts of light and dark, the strokes, the symbolism, the similarity to his sketches—I have occupied myself with little else for a year. I know."

I don't, and, like Valya, I'm skeptical. "How is its existence unknown to the rest of the staff?"

He puffs his bony chest and absently strokes his fingers over the back of his other hand. Arkady rests a hand on Lipman's knee, but he jerks away, plainly irritated.

"I discovered it during a routine restoration. Tucked away and covered with lining beneath an inferior painting by Pierre Mignard. The concealment was not professionally done by today's standards, but was exquisite by the conventions of the time. The Mignard was appropriately maintained, even when it was not on display, so *Leda and the Swan* was well preserved with it."

This is the first time he has referred to the painting by name. "When was it hidden?"

"Sixteen ninety-five."

"How—"

He pushes his palm toward my face. "It was last inventoried as part of the French Royal Collection at Fontainebleau in 1694. That much of its provenance is known. In 1700 a number of irreplaceable works were burned on orders of Madame de Maintenon, the mistress of Louis XIV, and many believe to this day that *Leda and the Swan* was lost then, although it was not formally listed among those that she destroyed."

He sips tea. Sets the mug aside and hugs himself, rocking slightly. "Now we know why—because it was already gone from the collection." He pauses for dramatic affect. "Hidden behind *Leda*'s canvas support frame, I found this."

He peers around the café before he eases a yellowed document protected by a plastic sleeve out of his messenger bag and slides it across the tabletop toward me. The document is printed and scripted in French. I can see he's pleased that I can't read French.

"It is a transmittal document from the Fontainebleau," he confides. "An invoice, I suppose we could call it." He uses a shaky finger to point to a barely discernable date written in flowing numbers and letters. "Dated 5 July 1695, five years before Madame ordered the burnings."

"This city did not even exist then."

"No. *Leda* was moved to St. Petersburg later, already secreted behind the Mignard, after its owner died in confinement at Novodevichy Convent. At least that is how I believe it must have happened."

"Who was its owner?"

He drops his finger to a name penned in the same flowing style.

"Princess Sophia Alexeyevna. The sister of Peter the Great. The

woman who ruled the Russian empire as a young girl. The woman
Peter exiled for life in Novodevichy Convent."

Later in the afternoon, Arkady rents an eighteen-foot motorboat. The
sleek hull of the boat planes through the canals of St. Petersburg to
the rougher waters of the Neva as I guide it past a police boat and a
tourist barge. Shadows cast by brooding storm clouds mar the silvery
sheen of the river.

We glide west past the Hermitage, barely above an idle, while
Lipman explains the way we will go inside, pointing out the same
narrow canal cutting between the Little Hermitage and the Hermitage
Theatre that we saw earlier in the day from the hall inside the museum. He looks focused, wired, oblivious to Arkady's smitten gaze.
According to the ancient plans Lipman dredged from dusty files in the
Department of Engineering, the water covers a portcullis that leads to
a warren of catacombs built in the age of Peter the Great, now submerged.

When he is finished, I spin the wheel and surge the motor. The
nose of the motorboat rises to spray polluted water into our unpro-
tected faces. The two lovers cling wordlessly to the wooden seats while
I steer back toward the landing, pondering the possibilities.

Without half trying I can conjure too many problems with the plan.
The one that sticks to me the most later that night and into the
morning is that it suits neither Arkady nor his lover.

"The whole thing is too messy," Valya says, echoing my inner
voice.

She's curled in the crook of my arm, velvet soft in the pleasantly
cool dimness of the third-story bedroom we've rented two blocks off
Nevsky Prospect, a stone's throw from a blue-trimmed Lutheran
church that miraculously survived Nazi bombing.

The old woman who let the place charged a hundred rubles,

about three American dollars. She took the money with clouded eyes, and we understood the reason as soon as we entered the robin-blue room. The bedroom is a shrine to a lost son, stopped in a time when he loved cosmonauts, plastic dinosaurs, and a honey-yellow stuffed bear. I wonder if he's gone dead or gone on. Decide that he must be dead, because no one could willingly abandon such love.

"They're amateurs," I say. "I can clean it up."

"We'll need more people. Nabi and the others are needed where they are, and they're no good for this work anyway."

She's right on both scores. We will need at least two more, by my reckoning. And Nabi Souvorov, my lieutenant, is better engaged running my little empire, especially since his eyes have lately started to flick and jump in the manner of lost souls who lust for the crack pipe. Nabi's addiction is a problem I will need to address, and soon, but in the meantime he is not a good candidate for a heist like this one.

The Nokia vibrates an incoming call. The caller ID shows a Moscow prefix, but I don't recognize the number, so I ignore the persistent buzzing.

"First, let's check out Lipman and see if we can plan our way through this. And we need to investigate authenticity and estimate value." A tricky proposition to do those things and keep our plans secret. I start to mull the options, quickly deciding that Henri Orlan, the gallery owner Nigel Bolles referred to me the night of the shooting at the National, is a good place to start.

Valya sighs, stretches waif-thin across the bed, and props on her elbows to gaze out the window at the lonely church. Her round bottom beckons, but I am distracted by another beauty.

"If the value is there, I'm going to talk to the General," I say.

She nods, still gazing out the window. A red light blinks on the Nokia. She chews a nail while I punch the buttons to retrieve the message.

"You fucked me, Volk." Maxim Abdullaev's recorded voice growls my name like a guttural curse. "Gromov is crying like a girl. And what's going on in Leningrad?" Almost two decades have passed since the Wall crumbled, but Maxim has not yet adapted to the restored name for Peter the Great's city on the Baltic. "Whatever you got going, I want in," he rumbles, then disconnects.

Valya is still staring out the window. I join her, stretched out, leaning on my elbows like her larger shadow. Just past five in the morning. Predawn haze bleaches the church to a grainy black and white tinged a sickly blue.

"We need to talk to Maxim," I say.

She shudders at the name, but doesn't look at me. "Why?"

"He's angry over what happened to Gromov." I consider the tone of his message and amend my words immediately. "At least, he's pretending to be mad about that. He knows something is going on here, and he wants in."

"How could he know about this?"

How does Maxim know anything? "I don't know."

"He is an *almasty*," she says. An abominable snowman, half man, half ape. One of many myths used to terrify Russian children in the night.

I don't like my deepening suspicion that somehow everything is careening out of control. One minute I thought I was the firm hand on the tiller, the next I'm fogged in, locked in, towed in. "I don't think we have a choice," I say.

Valya is wave-pounded, wind-swept granite. The world has done its worst to her—all of the awful things that creep nightmares and leave crawling tendrils of cold dread. But they have only made her stronger. She scoots against me and nuzzles her head into the angle of my arm. White hair like blown cotton candy hides her perfect face.

"He is the only man who scares me more than you do," she says, and shivers.

chapter 6

The next day, Moscow feels gritty after St. Petersburg, as if each chapter of its tortured history layers the city in sediments of suffering. Every one of the millions of souls packed into her crabbed tenements has a story to tell of a place where a father disappeared or a daughter was abducted, or a time when faceless men in a black Volga sapped a passerby to his knees and dragged him away. Stalin purged relentlessly, hundreds of thousands in this city alone, and his successors were good students, so that even today's headlines squawk of newly discovered mass graves. I recall Lipman's description of the *Leda* and decide it has application here. For those able to feel and see such things, the oeuvre of those times and deeds and dead permeates Moscow's essence.

Henri Orlan's gallery fronts a residential street near the pond across from Novodevichy Convent. Hoping the correspondence of the location with Sophia's former prison is a good omen, I dodge bare-chested infantrymen training in the park and angle for a better view of the entrance to the gallery. Stop to pet a scruffy mutt lolling under a tree while I study the area and pretend to admire the gold-and-rust towers and spires of the convent reflected in the still pond.

A slim woman wearing a flowing black chiffon shift and a matching, tilted pillbox hat, from beneath which peeks white hair, wisps over the walk and is buzzed into the gallery. Valya's black clutch holds the .22-caliber Ruger, so I know she's safe.

I sit on a concrete bench and contemplate a family of metal ducks, a gift from the wife of an American president. Some of the ducklings were famously pilfered for the metal years ago, so now they are guarded twenty-four hours a day. This time I watch for real as the reflected convent towers march across the pond, marking time. I wonder from which of the apertures in the towers Sophia Alexeyevna blasted seething hate toward her brother Peter in the Kremlin and, later, in impossibly distant St. Petersburg.

Sophia's name on the transmittal document discovered by Lipman had brought back memories of reform school lessons about Russian history. Years before, I had seen the gilded-gold double throne displayed at the Kremlin, the one with the hole cut out behind a curtain—a hole used by Sophia to whisper wisdom to nine-year-old Peter. A hole that allowed her to rule an empire for eight years, during the time before Peter matured enough to resent her. Before she conspired to kill him and was permanently confined in Novodevichy Convent. Even from the convent she plotted with nobles to take his life. The nobles ended up dead, swinging in trees visible from Sophia's stone-framed window, where Peter ordered they hang ripening for weeks so that the smell would add force to the lesson.

The policeman assigned to the park to prevent further scavenges of the gifted ducks treks past on the hour, but he leaves me be. The late afternoon sun warms me. My eyelids drift closed.

I smell her wafting perfume—part of the costume, because Valya would never stoop to wearing fragrance—before I see or hear her. A light wind has risen to ripple the waters of the pond. The miniature waves dapple reflected sunlight.

"Orlan's not a homosexual," she announces, plopping onto the bench beside me. "Big glasses make him look like a surprised owl, but he has hands like an octopus." The hat is gone. A thin, brown raincoat covers the silly dress.

"Tell me about it," I say.

"He has tickets to *Spartacus* at the Bolshoi Theatre—"

"Be serious."

She pouts. I wait.

"Maybe I should go with him," she says.

I wait some more, wishing I had let her tell it her way, however roundabout, just to speed things along. A cloud crosses the sun, and as though a switch has been thrown the sparkles in the pond wink out. A family passes by us. I wish for a taste of the little girl's ice cream— vanilla swaddled in melting chocolate. She's nine or ten. Maybe nine years younger than my benchmate.

"I'm sorry," I say.

Valya turns to face me. Contact lenses have turned her big eyes a shocking violet. "Assuming the painting is by a known artist, there are several ways to authenticate it." She has apparently decided to accept my apology. "Orlan referred to contemporary or later publications or documents where the work might be referenced, especially catalogues of a particular artist's work."

"Catalogues won't help here."

"He guessed I was asking about an artist from a later period," she explains. "That's why he started there."

"Da Vinci's papers are known and well traveled. Lipman claims they contain early sketches and other references to the piece."

She nods. "That's true. I found a book at the library."

She barely finished six grades of formal schooling before the war and misery of late-'90s Chechnya swept her into their churning currents and made her what she is, but sometimes I joke that the surest position from which to snipe her is on high ground overlooking the steps to the Moscow University library.

"The book is in the loft," she continues. "It shows a charcoal that looks like the painting you described from the picture Lipman showed you."

"That will help, but the Fontainebleau invoice will be the key."

She chews the end of a twist of white hair, nods again. "From Orlan's point of view, the best hope is with laboratory analysis of the paints and the canvas, plus expert study." When she closes her eyes the violet goes away, and her face seems darker. She recites, "Experts study the style. Brushstroke, color scheme, play of light and dark, the overall quality, the 'ambient essence.'" She mimics a French accent at the end, and her dancing tones make me laugh. "Authentication takes many scientific tests as well," she says, and she recounts them while I ponder the *Leda,* wondering what her first glimpse will offer me.

"Where do we find the experts?" I say when she has finished.

Again I'm bathed in the violet glow. "It depends on the artist, *chéri.* And I couldn't name the artist to Orlan."

"No. You couldn't do that."

Back in my basement office that night I reject the idea of contacting Yelena Posnova, the Moscow University art historian Nigel named in the post-shooting hysteria of the National Club. Without giving her any particulars about the painting, I am unlikely to learn anything new. Lipman's credentials check, all the way to the time he spent in Milan working on the never-ending restoration of *The Last Supper.* The *Leda* either exists or it doesn't. It is authentic or it is not. If it is the work of Leonardo da Vinci, it is priceless. More than commensurate with the enormous risk, I decide.

When my work is finished for the night I punch the numbers into the Nokia for Maxim Abdullaev. I have ignored his voice-mail message for too long already. He answers on the first ring, as if he was waiting for the call.

"It's Volk," I say.

"We need to talk."

"When?"

"Tonight."

chapter 7

At two A.M. the streets near the Kremlin are populated by huddled homeless, drunks, a few partyers headed home, night-shift workers and two beat cops walking slowly. None of whom troubles me as I stride through, considering how to best manage the big Azeri. Maxim's control over Moscow's food markets was his initial source of power, and even today it remains the key to his dominance. Since the Gorbachev days, a senior Kremlin administrator—a fellow Azeri—has been Maxim's puppet. Maxim has a say in tax and subsidy policy, agricultural permits, water rights, transportation routes, and fertilizer prices. The whispered claim that he decides whether bread costs five rubles or six is only a slight exaggeration. In the last decade he has parlayed food into a multitentacled distribution network of weapons, drugs, sex, and, if the rumors can be believed, slavery.

This week he maintains an office on the top floor of the newly built Ararat Park Hyatt, near the Lubyanka. Along the way to meet him I pause near the empty hole where the granite-gray Moscow Hotel used to sit on the edge of Red Square, before its recent demolition. The old hotel suited Maxim better than any of the newer ones possibly could. Its schizoid facade of inset and protruding balconies was the result of an architect's fear of challenging Stalin's mistaken approval of two different proposed designs. I know of no one courageous enough to challenge Maxim, either.

The elevator whisks me to the Ararat's penthouse foyer, where two dead-eyed men in dark suits search my body for weapons while another watches. They take the Sig, but miss the blade hidden in my prosthesis because they're too squeamish to handle my stump. They escort me inside the enormous suite to a seating area arranged next to a floor-to-ceiling window. Maxim is there, filling a couch intended for several people.

Valya was right to call him an *almasty*. His powerfully built body is like a mobile chunk of concrete sprouting coarse tangles of black hair sprinkled white, and his oversized head and face and heavy, protruding lips bring to mind a giant ape. But it would be a terrible mistake to underestimate the intellect behind his blunt features.

He greets me with a grunt reminiscent of a faraway landslide. I take a cushioned chair opposite him without waiting for an offer. His mouth yaws open and emits a sonorous sound that I take to be a chuckle at my boldness.

"You're a bastard, Volk."

I wait for him to deliver the punch line.

"Maybe you're mine." He roars laughter. The couch groans under the shifting movement of his tanklike weight. The sycophants standing behind me laugh with him.

I accept the compliment with a tight smile.

He goes suddenly quiet, and all the laughter stops. "Where's the bitch?"

"Busy elsewhere."

He rubs the wiry thicket on his head and considers this. Apparently decides it's just good business for me to leave Valya behind. "Busy making Gromov crawl, maybe."

He laughs again, and I'm reminded that he knows everything.

He dismisses his men to the other side of the room, out of earshot. Pulls a jewel-handled dagger from his shirtsleeve and uses it to clean his fingernails. "Why did you pass on Gromov's diamond?"

"It's bullshit."

"Maybe. But there are buyers for such trinkets."

"He can't get it out of the armory."

"You can?" His eyes burn a fierce iron gray, the color of the Caspian Sea raging on the rocky edges of his hometown of Baku.

I shake my head and lie. "I don't believe the soldiers have the access they claim. They'll pass Gromov a fake. They know the army will protect them if he catches on." This last part is true. The army might not be able to shield its soldiers from Maxim's wrath, but it can from Gromov's. The General retains that much power.

He scowls. "It can work." He points the tip of the knife at my face. "But it needs your brain."

"I don't think so. Anyway, Gromov is wrong for this sort of work."

"Tell me about Leningrad."

Maxim's abrupt change of subject does not signal that I've heard the last of the Shah Diamond, only that he is through discussing it for now. I mentally debate the chances of surviving a lie. Decide they're not good, that whatever the big Azeri knows about my reason for being in St. Petersburg, it is enough to trap me if I try to mislead him. I tell him about the Hermitage and the *Leda* and Lipman.

Maxim's satisfied grunt suggests that the decision to tell the truth was the right one. The knife twinkles in his giant paw, then disappears. "You have the same scheme as Gromov," he says. "Different item, different place, but still the same."

"Except that I can get the painting out."

"Tell me how."

After a few restless hours of sleep I meet up with Valya next to an ice-cream vendor under the high, barreled ceiling of the GUM state department store, a long, three-level building located along the eastern side of Red Square. I tell her about the meeting with Maxim, our new shotgun partner, as we wander in and out of shops displaying American and European products from Nike, Versace, Dior, Levi's, and countless others. The only Russian products available for purchase are trinkets—faux icons, machine-painted pictures of St. Basil's and the Kremlin domes, crude nesting dolls. Russia has lost the wars of commerce as surely as she has been defeated in the wars of conquest.

"He'll work to fence it," I tell her. "And we've got two of his men, whether we like it or not."

"Who?"

"Kamil and Tariq. Brothers. Cutters and burglars. I don't know them except by reputation."

She licks a strawberry cone that matches the color of her lips. "Did you tell him everything?"

"Most. I held back on the second boat and car. If we need them, the omission won't matter."

"What about the General?"

"I'll see him tonight."

Moscow is a city of underground rivers. Most of the rivers are flanked by passages used by service personnel and, nearly as often in these times of underworld capitalism, for trafficking illegal or untaxed cargo. One not-so-secret subterranean passage extends beneath the Kremlin's Tainitskaya Tower to the far bank of the Moscow River. Others, built in different centuries for reasons of war, intrigue, or commerce, remain a mystery to all but the chosen. The passage I go to that night, consisting of several tunnels used for varied purposes, is known to the police and military in the Kremlin.

Stern, green-uniformed soldiers led by a slender captain with square shoulders and a bushy mustache escort me beneath the river to narrower tunnels under the Kremlin complex. Two different passageways lead into the bowels of the arsenal, the home of the

Kremlin Guard. Hand-hewn rock steps carry us deeper until the officer at the front of our caravan bangs on a weathered oak door and we're admitted into a room with walls of crying stone.

The General sits in the shadows behind a gray steel desk. The wintry green light of his eyes pierces the gloom as I stand before him. I'm unarmed. Cold. Achingly aware of how easily I could disappear in this place, lost forever behind river rock and frigid denials.

"Dismissed," he says.

The General's voice makes his malachite eyes seem soft. The captain crunches the door closed behind him. I remain standing at attention. The General requires a different approach from Maxim. This is the first time I have seen him in months, so I have no way to gauge his mood.

"Alexei Volkovoy."

He is reading from a brown file with black binding. My eyes adjust, and he comes into clearer focus. Picture a wax museum depiction of a Neanderthal. Heavy, cantilevered brow looming over a broad, flaring nose and lips that seem to be dragged down by their own weight, rimmed by deep parenthetical furrows.

"Orphaned at birth," he continues without looking at me. "Passed among foster families like unwanted garbage someone hopes to put to use. Expelled from four schools. Fighting, stealing, selling contraband. Three years in the penitentiary."

The gelid eyes lock on me. I'm stiff, still at attention. This exercise of review and contemplation is part of his routine when he believes too much time has passed between visits. Or when he has questions about loyalty.

"A minor in a prison for our worst criminals," he says. "That could hardly have been a pleasant experience."

The General can read between those lines better than most, but he didn't live it, so he can't know the unbearable worst of it. I remain rigid, my eyes steady as he returns his attention to the dossier.

"No criminal convictions as an adult. No doubt a testament to resourcefulness rather than a true reflection of your activities. No known residence." He thumbs to another page and scans it thoughtfully. "What a life, here on these pages. Much of it fiction, of course. But some not. Known to associate with Valya Novaskaya, Vadim Kiselyov, and Nabi Souvorov, all well-known to Moscow-area law enforcement."

He sets the file on the table and pushes it away. His chair squeaks when he leans back to stare at a soggy wooden beam in the claustrophobically close ceiling.

"Other parts are true as well," he says in a softer voice. "Five years military service, most in Chechnya. Special Forces wunderkind. Sniper nonpareil. A fistful of medals that fail to do justice."

He rises and marches around the table to stand before me, caressing the pistol butt at his belt. I stare at a point over his shoulder, which is easy to do. The General is a dwarf. He stands about a meter and a half. His rise to power in the Red Army was no less remarkable than if he had grown wings and circled the Kremlin blowing fire like a dragon. Some are born into power. Some attain it by luck. Others, like the General, claw their way to it through sheer force of will.

We remain standing like that as the seconds drip away.

And then I'm gripped in a bear hug that blows the breath from my body, and he's laughing and, well, emotional. And I realize that I am, too.

I brief the General over the next hour, telling him everything that has happened since Maxim's first call to me at Vadim's Café. His expression tightens when he hears about Maxim's newfound interest in black market art, but other than that he shows no sign of what he is thinking while I talk. He pours himself a glass of chilled vodka without offering me one and then paces restlessly, hearing me out. When I finish, he settles back in his chair, cradling his sweaty glass in both hands.

"I'll take care of Gromov's little diamond scheme," he says, distractedly—Gromov's plan to steal the Shah Diamond is clearly not what is occupying his mind. Nearly a minute passes in silence.

"Could it possibly be true?" he asks, finally, in a half whisper. His gaze is unfocused, almost as though he doesn't see me in front of him. I'm not sure whether he really wants me to answer.

"The invoice appeared to be genuine. And Lipman believes the painting is real."

He seems not to have heard me. Another minute passes. He suddenly slugs down the last of his vodka, clatters the empty glass onto his desk, and stands, his eyes glittering.

"I want the painting, Volk."

I've been sitting in a hard wooden chair facing his desk, but now I rise quickly and snap back to attention. "Yes, sir."

"Do whatever must be done, just get it."

"Yes, sir."

"Don't fail me."

chapter 8

Planning takes on heightened intensity, propelled by the General's order. I push all the players relentlessly. Lipman provides the schematics showing the basement layout and tunnels beneath the Hermitage. Arkady obtains the weapons and an underwater cutting system that fits into a carrying case weighing only thirty kilos fully loaded. Valya handles the details of renting an ancient four-seat Moscvitch, two Lambretta scooters, and a skiff, buying secondhand clothes and scuba gear, and arranging drop points. She also secures the powerboat and the Volga we hope to use if the plan crumbles.

I work out movements and timing. Travel twice more to St. Petersburg, a ten-hour drive each way. Walk the canals with a concealed stopwatch, cruise the Neva eyeing police patrols, study blueprints to memorize burrowing tunnels.

In the end, too many holes remain. Too many unknown people, too many break points, too much reliance on the insider, Lipman. Good sense tells me to walk. But the General commands action and Maxim looms in my subconscious, demanding tribute. And, finally, when I summon the mental vision of the picture Lipman showed me, my mouth goes dry. *Leda* will have to be sold to someone possessing enormous wealth, an appetite for the rarest, most precious art in the world, and the courage of a thief. She will be mine for only a day, perhaps two. But I lust for her beyond reason as I scheme.

One last Moscow plotting session, held on a gloomy morning in a shuttered Tverskoy Boulevard storefront catty-corner from a busy McDonald's restaurant. Maxim procured the room. I'm the first to arrive, but I may be watched, so I limp-shuffle along the boulevard and into the empty back room, where I begin to prepare. Arkady arrives just off the night train from St. Petersburg, looking worn and somehow diminished without his lover at his side. Tonight, if all goes well, he will return on the train with Valya.

Maxim's henchmen are last. Two shadowy, silent men—Kamil and Tariq. Both so thin they appear emaciated. I don't know their last names, only their reputation as quiet killers who can be trusted to obey Maxim like loyal dogs. For now, that is enough.

I show them the linked canals. Explain our path inside through the submerged portcullis and the underwater route we will take once in. Like climbing Everest, the hard part is the return, so I force them to memorize each detail. Tariq, post here with the cutting gear, watch for these things, keep egress open, kill silently if you must. Kamil, go with me into the maw to meet Lipman, who will be waiting in the catacombs beneath the Hermitage to lead us to the painting. Arkady, stay with the boat. We study schematics, time charts, equipment lists. Arkady leaves to buy food. We eat, study some more. The particulars will make or break our operation, and I refuse to lose for want of planning, so we work long into an irritable day.

"We reassemble here." I use a pointer to show the sheltered nook above our submerged entry point. "Back out through the portcullis, into the skiff. We'll drop Arkady here. He can walk to his flat. Kamil and Tariq, here. Take the scooters to the depot, leave separately for Moscow."

Tariq is the talkative brother. He aims a sharp finger tipped with a black-lined fingernail at Valya and says, "What of her?"

"Waiting with the car to pick me up after I leave the boat in the canal." The answer is a half truth. Valya will be positioned near the other drop points so that she can watch each of them get off the boat and cover me if necessary. But her whereabouts should not concern him unless he's crooked.

"What about afterward?" It's Tariq again, challenging me with his tone.

"We'll meet back in Moscow with Maxim within two days."

"I don't like it. You know our movements, but we don't know yours."

"That makes us all safer."

"What about the shit?"

I don't like the way he refers to the art. It soils the beauty. "With me."

His gaze smokes into mine. The brothers are skin and bones, inky behind unshaven, hollowed cheeks and sunken, laired eyes. I saw them eat sturgeon soup less than an hour earlier, but they still look famished. Hunger is coded into their genes. Valya drifts wraithlike to the side, where we will have them in a crossfire.

"Maxim told us to trust you," Kamil says, speaking for the first time in hours. "But if you fuck us, we will kill you both."

Sometimes I forget that in a better world Valya would barely be out of high school. She weighs in foolishly. "That will not be so easy to do."

Kamil turns dead eyes to her. "You, traitor, I will take a long time to kill."

She is going to hurl herself toward him. I know her as well as it is possible to know another, and so I see the rage before the others do. "Stop!" All of them except Valya turn toward the sound of my voice. I can see that she is undecided. I address the brothers. "We may not care for you, but we are partners with Maxim. That is enough."

"We know you, Volkovoy," Kamil says. "From Chechnya. You do your killing from a distance, or in the dark. If you turn against us, I will make you the hunted one, just as I should have then."

It strikes me like a fist in the gut that these two are Chechen separatists. Veterans of the worst kind of guerrilla fighting. Their nationality and political beliefs explain why Kamil used the word *traitor* to describe Valya. Why would Maxim put us together? He knows that part of my history, just as he knows of Valya's Chechen upbringing.

I let Kamil's provocation slide away, unanswered.

"What of the plan?" I say.

Tariq and Kamil trade glances. "It can work," Tariq says.

Arkady is pale, plainly spooked by the undercurrents of hate. He swallows and nods.

After we wrap up and depart separately into the misty twilight, I return to my table at Vadim's and take stock of business. The numbers are off. Nabi needs my attention. He's dipping into the supply, I'm sure of it now as I peruse the books. His new addiction is a problem I won't be able to address for at least another week from today, so I write a laundry list of instructions to give to Vadim for delivery. I consider having a talk with Nabi just to remind him of his priorities, but haven't a moment to spare for him. The problem will have to wait.

Near the bottom of my stack of papers rests an unmarked envelope, waxed shut. I break the seal. The only thing inside is a photograph, the kind that develops by itself. It shows a motorboat roostertailing water. The Hermitage looms in the background. I figure it was taken from the embankment of the Spit on Vasilyevsky Island. Shot two weeks ago, that much is for certain, because although distance and the wheeling prow obscure its passengers, the boat contains Arkady, Lipman, and me.

The picture is a warning. It shakes in my hand, almost as if from the deep vibrations of Maxim's growling voice. *I know everything*, the picture seems to say.

chapter 9

Midnight darkness is almost upon us as we finish loading gear into the skiff. We're sheltered from view beneath the railroad trestles on the embankment of St. Petersburg's Obvodny Canal. The raised walls of the canal capture a chill east wind and funnel it faster through the gap.

The three of us who will go into the Hermitage—Tariq, Kamil, and I—have donned black wetsuits under full-body coveralls and waterproof packs. Tariq loads the case with the cutting gear just in front of the stern section, where Arkady huddles in a black slicker, looking pale, distant. A bead of water, or nervous sweat, trembles on the end of his nose. His job will be to take the skiff to a nearby jetty after we're in the water, so that it won't be seen near the Hermitage while the three of us are inside, wait there, and then pick us up when we return.

In the hours between midnight and two in the morning we will have several windows of eighteen to twenty minutes each between boat patrols. After that the matinal sky will be suffused with pearly phosphorescence, and we risk being seen. When all the gear is on board, the glowing hands on my chronometer point north—dead on midnight. Time to begin.

I yank the cord to start the outboard. Pilot the skiff along the edge of the canal to the Neva, cut north for a time, and then follow the bend in the river west around the gloomed spires of the Smolny Monastery. We're crowded in the small boat, just six meters stem to stern, less than two meters across the beam, four wooden planks for seats.

Ten minutes in. Just in front of my position in the stern, Arkady shifts, and the butt of his suppressed Uzi rings against a steel brace. Kamil muffles a curse from the bow that I can hear from five meters away, while Tariq reaches back and roughly pushes Arkady's gun down into his lap. I throttle back, listening for other engines, but hear nothing. The river is nearly deserted. The big ships heading out to the Baltic are not yet here; the drawbridges won't crack to permit their passage for another two hours.

Thirteen minutes in we pass beneath the arched legs of the Liteynyy Bridge. A yacht froths past, heading in the opposite direction, and for no more than twenty seconds its turbines blot out other sounds. Fifteen minutes in, everything's fine—

And then a hot shaft of white light impales the skiff. An amplified voice like shaking sheet metal commands, "Heave to, immediately!"

The Fontanka Canal is a twist of the throttle away. Jetties punch into the Fontanka's waters at regular intervals. We can race to one, bail out before radioed help is mobilized, disperse, and try again another night. That's what I am thinking, anyway, as I start to turn and pivot the handle—but then another light slashes across our bow. Two police boats are on us now. It is improbable for one to be where none has been before. Two are beyond coincidence.

I kill the engine and raise my hands to the night sky, mentally calculating the betrayal. All my contingencies for trickery considered courses of action after we had the painting, not before, and none involved the local police.

The first police boat holds off our bow as the other one boils to a turning stop that sets it on a drifting course toward the skiff. Oily fumes from its spluttering engine water my eyes. The helmsman peers down at us from his perch in the wheelhouse while his partner swings a grapple from the deck. My co-conspirators huddle forward, in my line of sight. Arkady is a pale apparition hiding his face from the intersecting beams of light. Tariq mimics my hands-high stretch.

Suddenly, Kamil hoists the barrel of his Uzi over the gunwale. It spits jets of orange and white flames, and a stitching of holes stutters up the side of the closing boat, exploding slivers of fiberglass and gobs of torn, bloody flesh. The glass-encased wheelhouse shatters next, and then the boat itself slumps in the water as if to mark the death of the second policeman.

I can't risk a shot for fear of killing the others and crippling the skiff. I fly past Arkady and am almost upon Kamil when Tariq lunges at me. The glittering reflection at the end of his swinging arm warns me of the knife.

I deflect the blow, smash the top of my head into the underside of his jaw in a tooth-shattering crunch, and he's done, eyes-rolled-back unconscious before he crumples. I rush forward, headlong, driving hard across the narrow deck over our stowed equipment.

But I'm too late. Kamil is already firing controlled bursts into the second vessel, expertly braced against the rocking caused by my short fight with his brother. Even as I take him to the deck with an over-the-shoulder throw that leaves the smoking barrel of his own gun under his chin, the second boat begins a rudderless drift, and I know that the crew of that vessel is gone as well.

Arkady hugs his knees to his chest, rocking, and cries, "Oh, no!"

I jab the barrel like a tent pole into the black-stubbled flesh of Kamil's neck. "What the fuck were you thinking?"

He's a pro. He killed the searchlights on the boats, so it's dark again except for the glow of lights from the city. Seconds have passed, not minutes. Wavelets slap the riddled hulls of the police boats, and ripples gurgle against the wooden sides of the skiff. A voice calls out from the riverbank, questioning, concerned.

Kamil's eyes burn hate. "I saved us."

He is a psychopath, I decide, unable to understand that the exchange was far too costly. How am I going to explain four dead cops to the General?

Arkady moans. "Oh, God, oh, God."

I think quickly. We need an hour inside, less than twenty minutes on the canal afterward. That was the original plan. But this section of the Neva will be arc-lit madness in fifteen minutes, tops. Depending on the nature of our betrayal, a greeting party of commandos might wait in the bowels of the Hermitage, but I don't think so. The trap was set to spring here, not there.

I'm returned in spirit to Chechnya's blood-soaked Pankisi Gorge, with everything fucked every possible way. Moments like this one have always seemed to electrify me—to bring out my best, or my worst, depending on one's perspective. Options arrow through my mind. The crazed turmoil of four dead cops will be a distraction, and nothing misdirects so well as a deviation from the expected. I decide that we don't need to leave the subterranean warrens of the Hermitage tonight—we can wait for the window of darkness tomorrow. But can I count on Arkady to pull himself together, understand the changed plan, and hook up with Valya?

The muzzle of the Uzi leaves a rosy blossom on Kamil's throat when I take it away. He's still on his back, propped on his elbows, undecided about how to respond to my attack while I scoot aft to contemplate our weakest link.

"Arkady!" I keep my voice low and urgent.

He stiffens, then turns a wide-eyed stare upon me.

"Can you go on?"

Arkady's jaw drops. Comatose Tariq drools bubbly red saliva onto the deck. Kamil bares fanged teeth and nods with approval.

chapter 10

A narrow canal offshoots the Neva and runs alongside the new Hermitage. A stone recess, an ancient quay with a meter-square step leading to a steel door, provides partial concealment for the skiff while Kamil and I wrestle into scuba gear. Tariq whimpers in slack semiconsciousness. He is no good anymore. Shivering Arkady will have to take him away in the skiff. Meaning that Kamil will have to cut through the portcullis, and we will have nobody to guard the opening while we are inside the Hermitage.

I finish donning my equipment, including a special fin that hooks to my prosthesis to prevent it from detaching, and slip into the water. I dive four meters, stop, and feel a surge of adrenaline. The submerged portcullis is there, just as we had hoped, its ruddy bars descending into holes bored into the bricked bottom. On my signal Kamil dives with the cutting gear—torch, cutting tubes, two-stage oxygen regulator and hose—and sets up in fifteen interminable minutes. The more experienced Tariq could have done it in half the time. Eventually, the water around him boils white phosphorescence as he begins to burn through the metal.

I bob back to the surface to instruct Arkady. Hold his eyes when I'm done. "You understand?"

He gives a shaky nod.

I shoot halfway from the water, reach into the skiff, and grab a fistful of his coveralls. "Make it to the pickup point. Tell Valya we need twenty-four hours. She will know what to do. Tell me you understand."

Stammering with cold and fear, he says, "I understand, Alexei."

I push the skiff into the canal. On the far side of the Hermitage Theatre the bottoms of low clouds glow from colored lights. The destruction on the Neva has been discovered. I adjust my face mask and dive.

I home in on the glare of Kamil's torch. Within five minutes after I arrive, a section of interlocked bars shudders and falls away in slow motion, and we swim through the portcullis. We replace the shorn section so it will pass a cursory inspection, leave the weighted cutting gear in an underwater nook, and enter the tunnels using a water-proofed map I'd had made from the centuries-old drawing provided by Lipman. Algae-coated walls reflect our spots as we kick our way along the expected ducts of water until an unforeseen spit of wall forks the tunnel into two where only one should be.

Twenty seconds of indecision later I jerk my thumb toward the top of the tunnel. We break the surface and splutter in a hand-span pocket of stale air trapped beneath the fungus-slick bottom of the curved, stone ceiling.

"I go," I say. "Stay here with the spot so I can find my way back."

His lips are bluing. "How long?"

It's a good question. We used smaller air tanks because they were lighter and more easily concealed, but we have already wasted valuable time—nearly twenty-five minutes—and precious oxygen. We'll still need to come back out along the same path. "Five minutes. Then I'll try the other way."

We submerge again, and he aims his lamp while I porpoise through the tunnel. Within seconds a subtle bend makes his light wink away. Fifteen meters take me to another fork. I check the map, decide left, kick for less than ten meters, and find a circle of iron the size of a manhole cover. I unsling the pry bar clipped to my harness, wedge its hooked end into a hole in the grate, and slide the cover to a half-open yaw. My beam shines several meters into a murky shaft. It appears to be wide enough. It is almost surely the tunnel we planned to use. I don't have time to rule out the other fork entirely, so this will have to suffice.

The return takes less time. Before rounding the final bend, I snap off the lamp and drift along the wall. I'm early. Kamil still shines the light, but his eyes are not on its beam. He's fiddling with two steel rings. I can't see anything between the rings, but I know that a filament of wire connects them.

The garrote must be for me. The question is, when?

I back away, count to thirty, snap on the light, and kick back. The garrote is gone. He nods at my thumbs-up, and we swim side by side to the open shaft. He's unlikely to try to take me out until we have the painting, so I torpedo into the jagged tube ahead of him, eyeing the depth gauge strapped to my wrist. When we pass six meters, the side wall of the shaft drops away to reveal a wide, upward-sloping entrance—an antiquated loading dock for horse-drawn wagons carrying goods into the tsar's winter palace, used in the days before the rising waters of the Neva made it obsolete.

At my gesture we kill our lights and follow the slant of the underwater dock higher until we see Lipman's water-distorted, flickering candle flame, the signal that he is alone in the catacombs that wind beneath thousands of the world's greatest works of art. Two kicks propel me to the surface. Kamil breaks through next to me. Lipman clutches a bowl that shields the flame from a draft that makes him shiver like his lover.

"What is happening on the river?" The soul patch under his lip quivers.

I'm shedding the wetsuit. "What have you heard?"

"Before I came down there was a commotion. Somebody said drug runners blew up a police boat."

The explanation is as good as any I might have invented. "Then that's what happened."

I unpack. Strap on an ultraviolet wrist light and the Sig, which had been protected in a waterproof pouch. My diving knife detaches from the ankle of my wetsuit and slides into a sheath that hangs down the center of my upper back. Last, I gently stretch out the waterproof carrier and meticulously check it for holes. Satisfied, I carefully dry every centimeter of its surface, using a cloth Lipman has brought for that purpose, reroll it, and slide it into a sling attached to my backpack.

The rest of our equipment we pack into a nylon duffel and store under a water-eroded scarp protruding from the wall a half meter above the level of the encroaching river—a temporary haven that will need to stay dry and hidden for the next twenty-four hours.

I nod to Lipman to tell him we're ready. No more unnecessary talking. We stoop-shuffle through the tight catacombs by the light of his flickering candle—the art historian, then Kamil, and then me last, because this far in the garrote is in play. My stump pounds with drum-beating cold aches, so it isn't difficult to stay in limping, crippled character. Lipman wasn't with us on the skiff, so he has yet to see what I'm capable of. The walls are rust-colored brick spider-webbed with inch-thick black seams of mortar. At each fork I bend and spray an invisible line that will glow green under the black light on my wrist.

Lipman moves with more confidence as we travel farther into the tunnels. Now and then Kamil glances at me over his shoulder. He isn't checking my well-being. Five shuffling minutes later the tunnel widens, the rough stone floor changes to smoother, level concrete, and soon the candle flares against a windowless metal door. Keys jangle loudly in the silence as Lipman finds one, inserts it into the hole for the deadbolt, and cranks open the door. We step into a hall made narrow by slatted wooden boxes and crates, most of them covered with canvas tarps and some sagging forlornly uncovered and rotting, all blanketed by ancient dust that smokes the air as we pass.

Lipman turns into a smaller chamber similarly crowded with packed art detritus. He mounts the candle on a shrouded box while I close the door behind us and click on my hand lamp, bathing the cramped space in grayish light. Rats scurry, dust swirls, stacks loom, water-stained plaster walls curve upward to form a concave ceiling like the unwashed belly of a cupola.

"Help me," Lipman whispers, and then begins unstacking two rows of crates set against the rounded far wall. Kamil wedges in, and within a minute they lug the last of them aside.

We confront double doors mounted on wrought-iron hinges countersunk into the floor like the entrance to a cellar, locked with a hinge-and-clasp mechanism holding a steel bar gripped on either end by a U-bolt. Lipman had told us that he'd installed the lock less than a year before, just days after he discovered this forgotten hideaway, but it already looks old. I squat next to Kamil and watch Lipman work the key, separate the parts, slide the bar from the clasp, and creak open the doors. A rough-hewn staircase like uneven teeth descends into darkness.

"Follow me," I tell Lipman, because I want him right behind me instead of Kamil.

I count ten steps down the gullet to a landing, then another ten that crawl down the side wall of the first flight into what looks like a cave carved from solid rock. We're deep within the substructure of the Hermitage, secreted below the well-lit, wide halls of the museum. Oilcloth covers waist-high, boxy shapes. One tarp drapes tentlike over a smaller object standing alone in the far corner. According to Lipman, *Leda* is sixty-nine point three by seventy-four centimeters, all in one panel, not three as some historians believed. The covered object appears to be the right size.

Lipman approaches it slowly, reverently, as though he is afraid it might bolt or even disappear. He stands still for a moment, inhales deeply, then pulls the cover away like a slow-motion magician.

I stare at the painting, transfixed. The Mignard has been removed. Lipman has placed *Leda* in a glass case, along with a coin-sized temperature gauge that reads twenty degrees Celsius.

But I register those things at a level below the conscious.

The painting is everything. Even in the harsh light cast by my lamp it shimmers opalescent beauty. Time has charged its inevitable impost of tiny cracks and a slightly darkened surface, but Leda's opulent form, wrapped in the snowy-soft embrace of the swan, is a luminescent seashell pink, as are the babes writhing in cracked eggs at her curving calf. She is standing in a phallic bulrush glade, just the way Leonardo's chalk studies showed her. Light and dark perform a chiaroscuro dance choreographed by the magical, five-hundred-year-old brushstrokes of the master.

Any damage caused by handling and the passage of time was apparently minimized by the conscientious staff and the display conditions of the Hermitage—indirect lighting, forty-five percent humidity, twenty-one degrees Celsius. The perfect hiding place, where this masterpiece resided for nearly three hundred years, nestled behind the other canvas—stretched and framed beneath its protective embrace—until finally exposed by a wispy Swiss art restorer.

I snap off the lamp and bathe the painting in UV light from the blacklight bulb on my wrist. The ultraviolet provides a crude test to show corrections on the canvas, often found even in verified originals, I know, but I search for obvious defects. The curve of the swan's neck shows signs of correction, and Leda's thigh looks to be marred by bubbled dimples that I failed to notice in normal light, but no gross irregularities disqualify the painting.

I switch back to the lamp and examine the support frame. It is oak-paneled and bears several fault-line cracks. The oak is a good sign. Valya's research said that such frames were used in early European paintings, and the provenance Lipman provided, as well as the need to keep the canvas properly stretched, suggested that this one would still be in its original frame. The frame is thicker than I expected, by almost double, in fact, but appears to be in good condition. Its panels can be tree-ring dated, with the spacing and number of rings compared to the known tree ring history of a given area to determine where and when the tree was cut. After allowing for drying, construction, and storage, a five- or ten-year window for when the painting was framed can be determined.

That and all the more sophisticated tests, such as pigment analysis, x-ray photos, infrared reflectography, scanning electron microscope examination, and brushstroke comparisons, will need to be done later. I had been working in the dark, potentially on a fool's errand, but now there is an edging of light. Squatting before Leda, I know in my bones that she is the work of the master.

"Come back for us in twenty-four hours," I say to Lipman, continuing to study the painting as he leaves.

chapter 11

Six leech-infested months in a Chechnya mud pit taught many lessons, one of them proving that twenty-four hours of just plain waiting is nothing. An hour spent anticipating the next tied-down assault of rapists, skin-fillet artists, flesh-burning pyromaniacs, and other assorted torturers lasts for weeks.

By comparison this is Astoria Hotel–comfortable. The walls bleed lickable moisture. I eat a protein bar that Kamil eyes ravenously. Other food can be had, but uncooked rats are stringy and oily, not to mention hard to catch and kill, and several are needed to make a meal anyway, so, except for the protein bar, I prefer to pass the hours in hunger. Arkady must have reached Valya without being caught, of that much I'm certain. Otherwise, the pounding jackboots of the palace guards and police would have been heard already.

Twenty-two sleepless hours into our wait, Kamil fingers his left wrist close to where I suspect the garrote is positioned for ready access. I stay backed against the stone wall next to the re-covered painting. The cold wicks through my clothes and skin to find bone.

When only an hour of our wait remains, Kamil says in a gnarled voice, "Tell me the plan in case you die."

The ironic subtext to his question brings a smile to my face, since the most likely cause of my death in the next few hours is the garrote he wields. When she was a child in spirit as well as years, Valya owned a Borzoi, a Russian wolfhound the size of a small pony. It was put down after it mauled her uncle to death at the end of one of his incestuous forages. When I smile the way I do now, she says that I remind her of the blood-splashed Borzoi just after it finished with her uncle.

"No," I say. "I want you to need to keep me alive."

His right hand absently caresses the concealed garrote, and his lips thin into an evil smirk he thinks I don't understand. "We should both know the plan. It's good business."

"No."

Anger boils his cheeks dark red, and his ears seem to flatten against his skull. He stomps to an oilcloth pile, whips off the cover, and busts open the crate beneath, which hatches a painting from the fourteenth or fifteenth century. I don't know the artist. He draws his knife and ribbons the painting in seconds. He cracks another crate and repeats his petty drama, again and again, staring at me, hungry for my pain. The sawing blade sounds like a zipper opening and closing as it slices through canvas. Five paintings later he tires of the sport and sheathes the knife.

"Rest easy," he says. "This is not the place or the time. Tariq and me will work on you together. A little project we can make last for days." Now it is his turn to smile.

Lipman returns, looking even more pale and gaunt, on schedule but without any food. "Arkady told me what happened on the river." His accusing glare tracks me as I load the painting into its waterproof case. "You said nobody would die."

After I glove the case over the painting, I check the seals with a pressure kit and then with my eyes and fingers, painstakingly, because moisture kills paintings as surely as Kamil's blade. When I'm ready I hoist the package onto my shoulder and start for the door.

Lipman blocks my path. "What about it, Volk?"

He is not so much like Arkady, after all. He shows no trace of the softness I thought I saw before. He is cured leather to Arkady's crushed velvet. "Bad things happen, Lipman," I tell him.

I bull past him and climb the cut-rock staircase, hurrying to keep Kamil a safe distance behind me. At the top I follow my precious cargo through the open double doors to the antechamber. Lipman and Kamil have fallen behind, so I lean my burden against a crate and stretch my back. Just then I see and smell the freshly turned dirt of a shallow grave surrounded by an assortment of rearranged boxes.

The Sig leaps unbidden into my hand. I jump into the cellar and take the first flight of stairs in two bounds, turn fast on the landing, raise the muzzle—and then let it droop toward the ground. I've missed all save the dénouement.

One bulging eye is riven with red cracks. Even the pupil is lost in broken capillaries. The other meets my stare with what might be a plea. But he is past perception, contorted in a reverse curve by the fulcrum of the knee driven into his lower back. The garrote buried in the stubbled flesh of his neck is not so fine as the one that wraps his wrist. This one is made of thinly twisted twine attached to wooden dowels, but it is just as effective.

I sag against the wall and watch the last of Kamil's retching spasms. A burp of surrendered air echoes when Lipman loosens the loop and lowers the half-mooned body to the cold, muddy stairs.

"I meant to take him higher," Lipman says, still breathing hard, "but I think he suspected something. Help me drag him up the stairs."

Of course Kamil had a premonition. Psychopaths like Kamil are always suspicious. He had simply underestimated the wiry assistant art director. And so had I.

"No," I tell him. "It's your meat."

"Don't get pissy on me. Whatever you had planned for him, I can do."

Kamil's feet offer Lipman a better grip. I step to the side to make room as he bumps the body up the stairs to the antechamber. Kamil's head thwacks stone with little crunching sounds that become mushier as each staving step softens his skull for the next one.

"Why?" I say.

Lipman looks at me as if I'm a fool. "Why split the profits so many ways?"

"We need his boss to sell it."

"*You* need his boss. I needed—I *need* you to get this out. I can handle the sale myself. I already have a buyer in mind."

"If we cut him out, Maxim will stomp us like cockroaches." I am not trying to convince him of anything. I'm just trying to keep him talking so I can get a belated feel for how his mind works. One thing I know is that he is a different breed of animal than I thought he was.

"You can handle him," he says with the foolish confidence of someone who has never met Maxim.

"This is a mistake."

"What was it you said to me? Bad things happen."

We reach the antechamber at the top of the stairs. Lipman buries Kamil in the pre-dug grave, drags boxes over the freshly turned earth, then slaps his hands together to rid them of damp dirt. "Ready?" he asks, smirking.

We trudge back through the catacombs to the place where the waters of the Neva lick the superannuated dock and recover our equipment. A third wetsuit hides in the nook where we had placed two the day before—another slimy snail track that tells me Lipman had planned this out far in advance. During our dim, wall-scraping trip down to this spot he had confirmed that the shootout on the Neva was being investigated as a firefight with drug runners. I know somebody tipped the police—the coincidence of two waiting boats defies any other explanation—but I'm no closer to filling in that blank than I was when I jammed the hot muzzle of Kamil's gun against his throat.

In some perverse way I liked Kamil better than Lipman. Kamil was direct, predictable in the same way a scorpion can be counted on to sting. The art restorer is something else, like skin-wrapped rocket fuel waiting for a spark. But I can't kill him yet, because his absence would cause a search and invite unacceptable scrutiny at the Hermitage. And because my raised antennae tell me that his plan includes more surprises, that my angel may need me to protect her this time.

We wriggle into the wetsuits. Lipman dons Kamil's air tank, wraps Kamil's fins and mask in the extra wetsuit, and dives with the packet to find an underwater hiding place. As soon as he pops up, I back into the water to prevent tripping over my fins, holding the painting aloft, slowly submerging up to my neck, arms raised. Lipman watches with round eyes, moaning audibly as I lower the painting a centimeter at a time into the water. When it is completely submerged I pull my face mask down and perform a raw-nerved search for bubbles. I see none.

Lipman smiles around his mouthpiece and then dives. We kick through the lower passages. After we pass through the chute to the upper tunnels, I hover while he struggles without leverage to replace the iron manhole cover. When it has been slotted back into its housing, we plow on to the portcullis.

Now I really miss Kamil, because he was going to weld the iron bars of the grating into place again so that our intrusion could be discovered only by close underwater inspection. I know that Lipman can't handle the job, so I have to replace the bars myself, but I don't want to pass him the painting. My anxiety is silly—he has been *Leda*'s sole possessor for several months—but the handoff is still gut-churning. He ascends and disappears into the skiff while I jury-rig the section into place with wire. When it is as secure as I can make it, I surface, bob in the water, and look into the waiting skiff.

Valya smiles her love, but I know something is wrong by the sadness in her smoky gray eyes—*her* eyes. No contacts to hide the real woman behind them now. Arkady sits behind her wearing a triumphant smile and caressing the soft skin of her upper arm with a pistol-grip shotgun. Valya's cheek is bruised, and her wrists are swollen around too-tight bonds.

I make a silent vow to hang Arkady on his Judas tree. Compared to Arkady's, Lipman's betrayal is almost forgivable.

The encased *Leda* rests in the stern. A 9-millimeter pistol lies on the wooden seat next to Lipman while he peels off his wetsuit. Like the shotgun, it is not suppressed. Water drips from his smug lips.

"We kept her alive to make you cooperate," he begins.

They need my cooperation only for as long as it takes to motor to a quiet place where our bodies can be disposed of without discovery. The time to act is now.

I'm still in the canal, forward near the pitching bow. The Sig is packed, safe from the water, unusable. The knife behind my neck is no good for two. Together we might get them both, but if we don't, the water offers our only safety.

Valya knows. Her understanding shows plainly in the upward lilt of the corner of her mouth and the slight tilt of her head. She knows me, and she knows the way out.

In languid half-speed she grasps the barrel of the shotgun in her bound hands, moving so casually that it fails to register on Arkady until she jerks back with surprising strength. The shotgun springs out of his grasp more easily than she had expected. Momentum flings it away to clatter under the planked wooden seats.

All of this registers subconsciously as I use one hand to go for the knife, tighten my grip on the gunwale, and kick myself out of the water as far as I can. I throw the balanced knife at Lipman's white torso emerging like a molting snake from wetsuit skin.

Whether it is the motion of the skiff in the low swells, the timing of my last flippered kick, or just poor work, I can't say. The knife grazes the hanging folds of his wetsuit and spins away. He dives for the pistol.

We've shot our wad. All we can do now is try to get away alive.

Valya cuts the water in a clean dive, and I follow her down, struggling to untie her wrists as we go. I know they won't shoot for fear that the noise will attract attention, but they will shred us with the blades of the motor if they can, so we share the mouthpiece while I undo the wiring on the portcullis. Overhead, the cavitating screw propels the skiff into the canal while we swim rapidly for the safety of the tunnels.

chapter 12

By the time I think it's safe to leave our refuge on the sloping subterranean dock, the long daylight hours are upon us. The interminable
wait for sheltering darkness seems even worse because of the *Leda*'s
loss and Valya's split-skinned bruises. I hold her shivering body
close to mine.

"Tariq?"

"Dead," she says.

"Who killed him?"

"Lipman. Last night." She runs a thumb across her throat. "Like
you drain a trussed chicken of blood."

"How bad was it for you?"

"Arkady was indifferent, and Lipman is an unskilled torturer," is
all she will say.

Later she tells me she's not hungry, that she was able to eat a few scraps
of beef discarded by Arkady and Lipman the night before. Soon I'll

have been without food for almost two days. Feeling as I do about what has happened, it hardly seems to matter.

We follow the path of the glowing-green lines I sprayed the first time through, scouting the passageways for another route out, but find no exit except more locked metal doors like the one Lipman opened on the first night. There is only one way out if we wish to escape without being caught.

When we return to the dock, I dive and bring Kamil's gear to the surface. His air tank is gone, co-opted by Lipman for the trip back to the boat, and his wetsuit and fins are too big for Valya, but we can tighten the face mask to make it work. The gauge on my air tank indicates that we have precious little reserve remaining. Valya will need to use it when we make the dive tomorrow. I'll have to try to inhale a lungful from the mouthpiece when I can, for as long as it lasts.

After sorting through the equipment, we sit pressed together for warmth, talking of insignificant things. Trying to avoid confronting the full magnitude of what was taken from us, and the consequences we may have to face for losing it.

When my chronometer beeps midnight the next day, I strap the nearly exhausted air tank onto Valya's back, hoping it will offer a few metallic breaths. Without a wetsuit, exposure will quickly drive the oxygen from her body, slowing her progress.

We swim out until the ceiling touches her hair. Her lips are teeth-chattering blue already. She presses them icily against mine. She clings. Her steel gray eyes look fiercely determined behind the glass of Kamil's too-big face mask as we take several deep breaths. She nods. We dive and kick hard through the catacombs.

The first ten meters pass too slowly. She offers the mouthpiece and I suck greedily without getting much oxygen, and then push her on. She's ahead of me, so I can't see her face when the air in the tank gives out, but her frantic kicks and the burning in my own lungs tell me that it has happened. She paddles madly through the chute toward the upper tunnels. But she pulls up short with a jerk. I can't see clearly through the murk, but she's flailing wildly. Too many hand-scrabbling, mind-screaming seconds pass before I find that her tank is caught on the edge of the chute and yank it loose.

When she's free again, she struggles furiously beside me, but I know it is a losing battle. Her limbs slow to a ponderous crawl. I grasp a strap. Pull, yank, drag. Our progress is far too slow. My lungs are on fire. The underwater world turns chalky gray. She's deadweight after we finally emerge from the chute.

I kick with everything I have left. Fifteen more meters to go to the air pocket I shared with Kamil. Too far. My lungs are a roaring furnace.

I kick frantically. Ten meters left. Darkness crawls the edges of my vision.

I can't see. I'm not going to make it. *Goddamn it, be strong!* My kicks morph into useless flutters. The murk becomes a swirl of prismatic colors. The water is peaceful, restful, warmly embracing . . .

Last year, at a table in Vadim's Café littered with stacks of used shot glasses and discarded vodka bottles, when Valya was still willing to entertain such questions, Nabi asked her why she used to sell herself for money. Our little party fell silent. I choked the neck of a Gzhelka bottle and considered busting open Nabi's skull. But then Valya answered calmly, "Because I needed to eat." She popped a stuffed olive into her mouth and smiled radiantly around it as she chewed. "And I preferred fucking strangers over fucking my father and his brothers."

For some reason that vignette plays repeating loops in my mind. When it stops, I realize that I'm floating faceup, staring without comprehension at channeled wet stone.

I'm still alive.

I turn my head. Next to me in the water is Valya. Her slicked-back hair and big eyes make her look like a hopeful seal.

"It was my turn to pull," she says.

We navigate the waterway to a nearby jetty where the backup powerboat waits. Observe without approaching for a few minutes to see if it appears to be guarded, but all is quiet. I'm glad we didn't tell Lipman and Arkady about the boat and the Volga.

As soon as it seems safe, we clamber aboard, fire the motor, and gurgle ahead cautiously on the Moyka Canal. She tells me she thinks the air tank gave her one last blow of stale air, just enough to allow both of us to live. I think she is trying to comfort me in my failure.

The waters of the Gulf of Finland carry us to a marina near Kirov stadium. I remain hidden while Valya creeps through alleys to recover the Volga we stashed for an emergency. During the long, empty-handed drive to Moscow, Valya asks whether it was Maxim who betrayed us. It is a good question.

"I don't believe so," I say. "I think Lipman was working for himself, or for a third party."

"Who alerted the police on the Neva?"

Another good question. "I don't know."

"So what will Maxim do when we arrive back in Moscow without the painting?"

"Best case, I'll owe him penance for losing it."

"Worst case?"

"Worst case, we're already supposed to be dead. Meaning I'll have to kill him. Or die trying."

chapter 13

Maxim rages, punctuating each point with a meaty finger thrust into the air like an artillery piece. "You let two fags take the paintings away from you? You're supposed to be a tough guy. A stone fucking killer. What the"—he clenches hamlike fists, casting about for something to crush—"what the *fuck*!"

Less than two days after losing the *Leda,* I'm still tired, and every breath hurts, reminding me of death's icy lick deep inside my lungs. This week, Maxim's office is a basement suite in an incongruously large commercial building that dwarfs the surrounding concentration of churches and other historical structures in the cramped Kitay-Gorod district east of Red Square. He is fanatically focused. The loss of his men means nothing. Only the *Leda* matters, apparently, although he referred to *paintings.* I wonder how he could possibly care about the Mignard when the *Leda* is all-consuming. I wonder how he knows that Arkady and Lipman are lovers.

"How you gonna find those pricks?" he demands.

"I've got a contact in the SVR." I do, through the General. "We can trace their movements if they use a passport or a credit card, get hit with a traffic violation, almost anything. I'll find them."

He growls, low and deep. "The paintings will be gone."

"Then we'll get the money from them."

"Bullshit! Those little fuckers think they can get away with this? Fuck!"

In a monstrous, full-bodied rage he grasps the edge of a drink-laden table and hurls it away. The table, glasses, decanters, and ice bucket crash, shatter, and spray across the wood floor of his suite. When all that's left is the dripping, he stands with his barrel chest heaving and speaks in a low, calm voice.

"Find those motherfuckers. Or pay their price."

Restless days pass with no news. The slightest provocation sends me into a fury. Even Valya and Vadim avoid me. I stalk the streets, day and night, without purpose, itching for conflict that never comes. Two weeks into my self-imposed exile, the General sends a summons. I arrive at the designated spot just after dark. Silently follow the same slender captain with the bushy mustache through the tunnel under the Tainitskaya Tower to the arsenal, where the General waits. No hugs this time.

"Lipman crossed the Ukrainian border at Uzhhorod earlier today," he says. He points to a set of photos spread across his table. "That is what he looked like then."

The stills from the checkpoint security camera are poor quality, but adequate. Lipman is clean-shaven. His jaw appears to be cut from granite. The soul patch is gone. His thin hair is dyed a dark brown, almost black. It looks like a hotel sink job. He sports wraparound mirrored sunglasses, the kind favored by athletes.

The General never lifts his eyes from the table. "I have feelers out. When I know more, you go after him. Live up to your namesake—

hunt him down." In the same way the owner of a special breed is proud of his pet, the General has always liked that my name means *wolf*.

"Yes, sir."

"Meanwhile, Gromov." He spits the name.

"Yes, sir?"

"He is angry that his little diamond plot was foiled."

"Yes?"

"Stop him from doing anything stupid."

During the midnight hour later that same night, the neon lights of Moscow's crowded south side streets offer the illusion of warmth as I walk toward a meeting with Leonid, a discharged artillery major living on a military pension. His flat is three creaky levels up a fourteen-story Stalin building graced with high ceilings and wide halls, but such comforts don't necessarily make for happier homes. This one is a legacy from the deceased mother of Leonid's wife, Lilia. The year-dead mother lives on in the files of Russia's reconstructed bureaucracy, thereby providing cheap fifty-square-meter living for her daughter and her broken son-in-law.

The untrimmed hairs of Leonid's black mustache curl over his upper lip and shape his mouth into a never-ending pout. He checked his heart in an icy ravine on a Chechnya battlefield, and the price of its release was his right arm above the elbow and a gored left eye mercifully concealed behind a black patch. Plus a virus that prowls his blood sniffing for weakness, transfused there when they took his arm and turned him into an unacknowledged victim of HIV, like so many others in this country. Now he is consumed by an endless, fiendish need for antiviral drug therapies he can only intermittently afford.

At least that's the story about how he contracted the disease. HIV rages in the crammed cells of Russia's hellish pretrial detention centers, called SIZOs, where all suspects—guilty and innocent alike—are held pending their trial verdict, sometimes for more than a year. The virus tears unchecked through the SIZO population, because criminals, needle users, and homosexuals are last in line for treatment. Leonid spent a year in Kresty, our largest SIZO, jammed ten to a cell, sleeping in shifts. In the end, he gave Mother Russia an arm, an eye, and a soul, and so he is one of my charges.

I sip from a chipped, pottered mug of Russian tea thick as tar and watch tanks roll across the fuzzy screen of the TV. The scene is somewhere on the jungled outskirts of Jakarta, according to the scroll at the bottom of the screen. Leonid slouches in an armchair that was once white. A clear bottle of vodka etched with a black-lined picture of the old Moscow Hotel rests temporarily next to his left arm. In the bad light I can hardly tell where the faded brown of his crumb-seeded T-shirt ends and the dingy chair begins.

Lilia primps in the corner. Before my tea is half gone, she has artfully applied face paint, eyelashes, and costume jewelry to transform herself from blurrily pretty wife to sharp-eyed, past-prime seductress. She's a saddle-bagged thirty. When she stands, diamonds of pinched flesh bulge between the crisscrossing leather strings that lace a two-inch split fashioned into her faux leather pants. She wobbles on stiletto heels as she brushes her bottle-blond hair.

I drain the dregs of the tea onto the back of my tongue and swallow. Place the mug on the scarred low table in front of my chair. "What news, Leonid?"

He runs a veined hand over his greasy hair, stroking the short ponytail behind his neck. "Gromov has a contract on two Kremlin guards. He doesn't care how it is done. He just wants them dead."

"Why?"

He shrugs and eyes the television, as if its crackling images of yo-yoing strife are more meaningful to him than the sight of his wife cupping her powder-dusted breasts appraisingly in the door mirror. The tops of the cupped mounds quiver as she adjusts her low-cut halter.

"How much is Gromov offering?" I say.

"One thousand American dollars a head."

Nothing comes easy. Gromov should have known at least that much. The soldiers passed him a poorly made fake of the Shah

Diamond, and now he flails in retaliation. He has no idea, of course, that the best they could have done was give him the more artful counterfeit I left behind when I stole the real one. I am responsible for the safety of the soldiers. By revealing the plan to the General I foiled the theft from the Diamond Fund and saved them the pain of *his* wrath, but their greed set them before the enraged bull Gromov. The time has come to call Gromov's marker.

Lilia totters to her husband's side and rests a tremulous hand on his shoulder. Her nails are dark with chipped red paint. He pretends not to notice her. He stares at the TV screen, at nothing really, just talking heads with the sound turned down. Lilia gives up, smiles wanly in my direction, and wobbles to the door and out.

I watch the TV long enough for Lilia to leave the building. To do otherwise would be impolite. Just as I lean forward to go, the image shifts to damask-hued desert rolling under the thrown shadows of the rotors of a speeding helicopter. The scroll beneath the anchor's talking head says that a Russian-built Antonov-32 cargo plane has crashed in the arid Iranian sands west of Tehran. No body count yet, the scroll reads, but at least ten men are believed lost, along with a cargo of heavy armor and other weapons. No mention of why a Russian military transport was ferrying tanks, rocket launchers, and assault rifles to Iran. The aging weapons are part of the Soviet Union's Cold War legacy, I suppose—offal from a dying regime, left behind to become a source of profit for some and the cause of misery to others, many of the victims continents away.

Lilia is long gone by now. I wad an American hundred and toss it onto Leonid's lap. The crumpled green paper pays for the information and, like my visits to the old women pensioners, it salves my conscience. The money Leonid pointedly ignores is about twice again what his wife will earn this evening servicing tourists.

From Leonid's flat I make my regular rounds to the pensioners, stopping to see Masha last. She tells stories of a childhood spent hugging buildings, staying as far as possible from the edge of the street, always alert for black Volgas the way the gazelles at a watering hole watch for lions. I've heard these things from her before. She sometimes forgets what she has already told me. But I let her head rest in my lap and stroke her parched cheeks while she tells me again of the men who laired at the Lubyanka and preyed on young girls. It is nearly midnight before her ragged snores tell me she has fallen asleep. Time to leave and tend to business.

chapter 14

The hours before dawn are a busy time for my porn operation. Most of our images are produced and distributed from a warehouse situated near spiking cranes on the edge of the Moscow River, not far from the Northern River Station. I enter the warehouse through a dented metal door and stump down a dim hallway guarded by a teenage boy with a slung Uzi. I don't know him, but he knows me. He steps aside to give me access to a coded door, which buzzes open when I pass a plastic card key over a glowing electronic reader.

Inside, studio lights glare. Cameras flash. On my orders the images made here do not involve children younger than fourteen, although I suspect the level of care taken to verify age varies, depending on whether I am known to be in the city. The crews film two girls Valya's age having sex with each other and a beatnik-goateed, twenty-something boy. The trio is centered on a mattress set on the concrete floor. Draped blue cloth provides a backdrop. The boy's exhausted member remains flaccid even under their practiced minis- trations, so the girls turn their attention to each other. They're young, not yet used up. Their moans pitch lower, gradually turning into soft mewls that may even be authentic. The cameramen push the lenses closer, blocking my view.

I step over cable lines taped to the floor and stroll along a short hall set on both sides with closed doors. Live video streams originate from each of the rooms, all carried along a complex web of Internet service providers to every corner of the globe. Four of the rooms contain high-tech equipment that allows real-time communication. *Do this, do that,* the Web voyeurs instant-message, and the participants oblige.

The far door opens onto a roomful of glowing computer screens manned by pimpled students, hunched pensioners, cigarette-puffing housewives, tattooed and pierced street kids of both sexes, and Alla, my operations manager—model-thin, blond with black roots, hollow cheeks, tilted green eyes. She looks rapier sharp, and she is. She is also a divine practitioner of the sexual arts we sell to the world.

But Alla's real job is to turn pornography into money, using the Internet's egalitarian distribution capabilities to level the playing field against better-financed operations in L.A., Bangkok, London, and improbable Calcutta, where thousands queue in endless lines for the chance to sell their body for less than two American dollars a day. Our Web sites generate credit card funds and easily stolen identities that turn into more money. Alla's collection of hackers produces an average of twenty-five thousand American dollars a week. Except for the part I shave off for personal use, the rest goes to the General.

I talk quietly with Alla for a few minutes, comparing her numbers with those I've received recently from Nabi, and then head back to the loft for several hours of much needed sleep.

I try Gromov's cell first thing when I wake up, but the number has been changed. I prowl ragged, misty streets without encountering any of his men. Reclaim a banged-up Honda 250cc motorcycle from our pool, new when the Berlin wall tumbled, and weave through cars and pedestrians to his hideout.

The plate-glass window at the Jaguar dealership has been fixed. The curvaceous cars inside attract Russian teens wearing American sneakers. They press their noses to the pane, point, and chatter excitedly. Gromov cultivates a movie gangster reputation, feeds it with calculated attire and practiced mannerisms. With few exceptions, like Valya, the Russian youths of today are more foolish than their predecessors, whose only options were war or grinding labor. Today they are too easily impressed by the surface glamour that hides the reality of short lives spent running drugs, guns, and bodies for men like Gromov and Maxim.

I can't go straight into Gromov's den without warning, so I buy an ice cream and wait, contemplating the sad truth that I use children in the same ways as he does. My reasons may be different, and pictures and petty crimes might not be as horrible as forced prostitution and slavery, but the price of wasted lives is unchanged no matter what they are used to purchase. My enterprises trade their lives and their youth for redistributed wealth, from their generation to the generations of toiling, warring sufferers represented by the General.

Gromov's silver Mercedes SUV sweeps onto the street from an adjacent alleyway and ends my reverie. I kick the Honda to life and follow his winding way south, through miles of clogged streets and neighborhoods that become relentlessly worse. The mist turns to a light, scudding fog. Soon we enter a warren of miniature, hellish worlds—city camps made of stamped tin, wood, cardboard, and mud, built by refugees from recast governments in Belarus, Ukraine, Uzbekistan, Kazakhstan, and too many other places to catalogue, with every ethnicity pressed too close together in too much squalor. I imagine that these awful circumstances are at least superior to the camps created by the industrialized incarcerations of millions of ethnic exiles during Stalin's heyday. In Russia, progress is measured by glacial reductions in the collective misery of society. My Honda slipstreams unobserved in the wake of the Mercedes, which parts the wretched crowds with Moses-like efficiency.

Finally, the paved roads end. The Honda planes mud, spinning madly past hovels and open-air markets of fly-blown meat. By the time the SUV slides to a stop outside a slapdash wooden structure, I am brindled with splattered muck.

I pull off to the side, my foot on the ground, revving the throttle to add the Honda's bark to the cacophony around me. We are in a Muslim district—Tajik refugees, I think. Turbans, colorful caftans, burkas, and downcast female eyes create the illusion that I have been transported to a different world. Gromov's SUV idles in the crowd. A brown boy offers me flat bread carried on a wooden board. His mouth is deformed, his upper lip pulled up in a perpetual snarl. Just as I wave him away, I jolt to see Maxim emerge from the building, surrounded by bodyguards like a battleship among a flotilla of smaller escorts. The SUV lists to the right when he joins Gromov inside. They talk for more than three minutes. Then Maxim levers himself out, and Gromov's driver pulls away, careful not to spray mud at the overlord.

I follow amid a swarm of bicycles, pedestrians, darting scooters and other motorcycles, yet, impossibly, it seems as if Maxim's eyes missile-lock onto the Honda and his thick lips twist to form a secret smile.

Gromov's next destination takes him fifty kilometers farther south, past crops of potatoes and cabbage and cherry trees, and then down a private road too deserted to follow safely. I rattle the Honda through a thin stand of conifers along a bumpy deer path to the base of a hill, park, and struggle up a dripping oak tree.

Set in a clearing several hundred meters away is a dacha the size of a small hotel. The grounds teem with children. I once lived in such a place, so I know what I'm seeing, even if I've trained my mind to forget. The dacha might be innocently termed an orphanage or a halfway house, but in reality it is a farm raising child slaves.

I don't know how long Gromov stays. I let the sights and sounds sink in, and then I motor too fast back to central Moscow to find Valya.

chapter 15

I meet Valya in the square across from the Lubyanka food stall that covers Gromov's tunnel into and out of his dealership, the old FSB rat hole. We get past the proprietor and ensure his silence with a combination of bribes and threats. Inside the tunnel we expect a watch, but Gromov's lazy or stupid or both, so the passageway is unguarded and we make it to his office unseen by any of his men. Valya sits behind his desk while I pace.

Gromov arrives just before six. Stops dead and turns white at the sight of her tilted back in his chair, her thick-soled Doc Martens flaking dried mud onto his desk. He is too slow to react. I am already behind him with the Sig, kneading the barrel into his lower back, shoving him deeper into his office. I shut the door with my foot.

"You owe me," I say.

His head jerks down once without tearing his eyes from the girl. He's probably remembering the dreadful things she said she would do to him before he died.

I shove him into a chair. "Two things, and then we're square."

He's big, maybe only fifteen kilos less than Maxim, but docile under the eye of the pistol.

"I told you," he says, looking at me for the first time. "Tell me what you want, and I'll make things right."

"Take the hit off the soldiers."

A deep line creases his forehead. "Those fuckers lied to me—"

"I don't care."

"I'll lose respect."

"I don't care about that, either."

"What is it with you and the soldiers?"

He never served. He wouldn't know. My face is all the answer he needs.

"Fine. The hit's off." He raises his arms shoulder-high, palms out, and attempts a smile that I don't return.

I need to say other things. But they would be words without consequence. I tell myself what I already know, that it would be easier to try to stop the night. Demand coupled with currency or food or anything else of value will create a supply. Kids will be used and discarded—parentless kids, lost kids, stolen kids, and worst of all, sold kids. Their abandoned souls count for nothing. If not him, another will profit from it, and then another in a sickening line that will never end. Night will always fall.

"You said two things," he says.

"No. Just that one."

When we leave he's still leaning back in the chair, wearing a puzzled expression.

Valya slips her arm in mine on the walk to our loft. "The General wouldn't understand anyway."

She's right. The General is too practical to worry about flesh peddling, or any other criminal activity he knows he can't stop anyway. "He wouldn't have to know. I can divert funds."

"You survived it. So did I."

"We're both broken."

She has no counter for that.

Habit separates us when we arrive at the soot-smudged industrial building that houses the loft. I go first up a fire escape ladder to the flat roof of the adjacent pharmacy, cross a waist-high parapet, and enter through a hinged shutter that appears to block a window in the fourth level of my building. Two rickety flights higher I wait outside a bolted steel door until Valya rejoins me. I key the lock with another coded plastic card, and we're inside.

Home. Concrete floors under Asian throw rugs, glowing maple furniture, vertical, metal-latticed windows, five-meter ceiling, partitioned kitchen with brushed steel appliances, two baths, two bedrooms. All in all, enough space for more than five of Masha's apartments.

Valya watches TV while I grind away for hours on the computer and the phone, fruitlessly searching for something that might reconnect me to Lipman or Arkady.

When we are finally in bed Valya says softly, "The General uses the money we give him for good things. Better to concentrate on our work, not to worry about stopping a man like Gromov."

I consider that for a while, gazing at the *matryoshka* on the ledge next to the bed. "Maybe we are just as wicked as Gromov and Maxim," I say at last, but she is already asleep.

Valya is gone when I wake up, to where I don't know. Radio silence from the General means I'll have some time with Nabi to discuss business. I enter through the back of the café and take the steps down to the basement to my table, where a stack of paper awaits plowing. That occupies me through the lunch hour as the clatter of dishes carries from above. I find no mysterious photos today.

Vadim twitches his hooked nose like a squirrel when he brings my tray. He's rail thin, weighing maybe sixty-five kilos after a big meal, and his arms look skeletal as he sets out the food and plates, but I know from experience that he is deceptively strong. He sees that I'm busy and doesn't speak.

Nabi joins me after I've eaten. I question him about reports showing sales and cash flows, made deliberately cryptic, indecipherable to the uninitiated, but disturbingly clear to me. The numbers fail to jibe in ways that suggest I am under attack, as if competition is springing from nowhere, stealing customers, suppliers, and employees. Like Alla, Nabi has no explanation.

At the end of our meeting I tell him I may have to go out of the country.

His pupils jump and dance crazily when he looks in my direction. "W-w-when will you leave?"

Nabi soldiered in Chechnya. I lost a foot, he acquired a stutter. Somehow the cosmic scales balance. At least they used to balance. "I'm waiting to hear from someone."

"H-h-how long will you b-b-be gone?"

"I don't know. A few days, maybe a week." Depending on how long it takes me to find Lipman and the *Leda*. Nabi is being unusually inquisitive.

"Will V-v-valya go w-w-with you?"

Good question. "I don't know. Concentrate on business, Nabi. The numbers are bad."

"N-n-nigel doesn't have anything. He's still s-s-spooked from the sh-sh-shooting."

"Work others."

He nods jerkily. "K-k-kids?"

Why does it always come back to that? Is Russia so far gone she has nothing else to offer? I flinch inwardly when I remember the compromise the firefight at the National saved me from making.

"No. Not under any circumstances."

I'm summoned that night to the crying-stone room.

"Lipman was in Prague," the General says without preamble. "I don't know his means of transport through Slovakia, but he stayed at the Inter-Continental Hotel last night. Checked out today. Start there."

His fleshy lips curl in disgust. "Prague has become the kind of place a man like him would favor."

He means westernized. I know that he is imagining a time when Red Army tanks rolled through Prague's narrow cobblestone streets, when order was enforced and political dissidents suffered defenestration disguised as suicide.

"Yes, sir."

The General pushes a thin dossier toward me. "This is your contact." His demeanor is like dry ice, far more distant than his usual taciturn coolness. His attitude may reflect my failures at the Hermitage, but I sense that other events are distracting him. "His name is Strahov."

I crack the brown folder. A glossy black-and-white picture shows an acne-scarred man with a head that looks too large for his shoulders. I close the folder and replace it on the top of his table. "Valya?"

The muscles in his jaw ripple. He uses a thumbnail to pick a callus in his palm. I think I know what's going on behind the ridged brow. He is remembering a hole in his calf courtesy of a Chechen sniper, followed by a bouncing ride to safety on my shoulder; the months I spent in a pit after surrendering in order to save the lives of his men; and too many kill shots to count. He owes me, for those things and another that we don't discuss. At least he used to, but perhaps my reserve of favors is exhausted.

"Take her," he grates as he pushes a button set into his desktop.

I stand up to leave.

"One more thing," he says. "Tell Maxim you'll get him the Shah Diamond that Gromov failed to provide."

I struggle to process the request, which represents a fundamental shift in the General's attitude toward Maxim.

"Not the real one, of course," he says. "A fake like the one we used before. To appease him." He stares at me as if he expects a challenge.

My escorts bang the door to signal their return. I nod, salute, and leave.

As soon as I'm outside the Kremlin walls I call Vadim. He arranges a meeting with a diamond merchant, the same fat-cheeked Mongol we used the first time, when we stole the real Shah Diamond and sold it to the Saudi prince. This time we'll be delivering the fake, not leaving the fake behind in a glass case to be discovered years later. No way will it pass muster, but it is still very expensive, even after Vadim finishes haggling. The Mongol will shape the rock and etch the Persian names in a process that will take over a week, so we have to pay half down up front.

After the deal has been made, Vadim walks part of the way back to the loft with me.

"Why are we doing this?" he says.

"I don't know."

"It won't work. Only a fool won't know it's a fake."

"I don't think that matters," I say distractedly. I'm preoccupied, trying to grasp all of the implications of an unholy union between the General and Maxim.

I am in the loft packing for Prague when Valya whisks in. "Henri Orlan has gone missing."

"How do you know?"

"The gallery was closed all day. I found a flat east of the university that his neighbor says he sometimes shares with a woman named Yelena Posnova. The neighbor says they left three days ago with two suitcases that rolled heavy."

I recall Nigel's truncated mention of Posnova at the National Club. I see a heavy, manipulative hand maneuvering unwitting pawns. I remember my decision not to inquire with Posnova about the *Leda*. I chew mental nails. I fume.

"Let's go talk to the Brit."

chapter 16

The National Club has been repaired, as if the firefight never happened. I enter through a side door. Nod to three black-suited bouncers who are obviously hoping for the chance to pound someone. Nigel Bolles is once again gimlet-besotted, facedown on the padded leather bar. I sling the Brit's arm over my shoulder, tuck his new cane under my arm, and stumble him out to the street and into the waiting Mercedes.

Valya drives us back to the café, where I fireman-carry Bolles down to my basement office and unload him on top of a table. I wait impatiently while Valya percs muddy coffee and tries to make him drink. Two hours later he is able to talk in a bleary babble that I am confident holds some measure of truth.

"Two men, unshaved rats," he says. "Brothers, I think." He spills coffee trying to bring the mug to his lips. "Yeeow!" he shrieks girlishly and drops the mug, which shatters on the slate floor.

Valya pat-dries his face with a dishrag.

"Sorry," he says.

"Tell me about the two men," I say.

His hands are shaking too hard to light a cigarette. Valya lights it in her mouth, places it between his quivering lips, and chings his gold Zippo closed. He takes a shuddering drag that burns the paper halfway to the filter. "You're my friend, Alexei. I wouldn't do anything . . . you know, bad. Not if I could help it."

"Tell me."

"Please don't hurt me, Alexei."

"Tell me."

"I can't. They might come back."

"Who?"

His face always reminds me of melting wax. Now it caves completely, like the outer edges of a hot candle. "They had knives, like razors. They sliced off my pants and . . ."

He loses all control, collapses sobbing on the table. Valya queries me with raised eyebrows. I nod and take the steps up to the ground level, where I wait, brooding at a table in the darkened café. An hour later Valya joins me, and we hum away in the Mercedes. Vadim will know what to do with the passed-out Nigel in the morning.

"So?"

"It was Kamil and Tariq," she says, staring out the window. "They sodomized him with a length of rebar. Just for fun, because he would have told them everything anyway."

She's bothered. She must be, because it is unlike her to state the obvious. I wait.

"They threatened to cut off his privates unless he directed you to Orlan and Posnova."

"When?"

"The night before the shooting at the National."

I had met Nigel within hours of the first call from Arkady. Which means I joined the party late. I was a dupe from the start. The timing explains Nigel's blubbery reaction to the botched execution. He mistakenly thought that Maxim had ordered the hit, not Gromov.

"I wondered how Maxim knew Lipman and Arkady were lovers."

"What does it mean?" she says.

Her big eyes are emerald green. *Afraid jade,* I think, and almost laugh at my own foolishness. "I don't know."

I wheel the Mercedes toward Sophia's prison, Novodevichy Convent—toward Henri Orlan's gallery.

The front of the gallery is dark behind the accordion-steel gate. The display window is empty.

"He had two Picasso sketches on exhibit when I was here before," Valya says. We're still inside the purring Mercedes, so we don't have to be quiet, but she whispers anyway.

On the other side of the street is the park with the guarded ducks and the reflecting pond, which on this moonless night looks like an ink-filled crater. Yellow light glows in the window of the watchman's shack.

I have a good idea what we will find inside. Breaking in is a foolish risk to take just to confirm my guess, one of too many risks I have taken of late. But I need to know for sure. And I want the *Leda* back. I make a call. We wait in silence for ten minutes.

Yuri, the baton-twirling cop, arrives on a scooter. He throws a backpack into the backseat of the Mercedes and follows it inside. Streetlights glint off his wispy mustache.

I point to the locked gate. "Can we get in?"

He swings a key made of heavy metal and grins. "Courtesy of Viktor."

The police commander on my payroll. Excessive risk and burned favors. Bad habits.

"The key gets you through the gate and the front door," Yuri says. "Inside is an alarm pad." He tells me the numbers, then looks for a reaction, but I just stare. "It's the corners of the keypad, back to front and back again."

I hand him a torch that fits in his palm. "Flash us when the guard heads east."

He looks at the back of Valya's head and squirms, obviously wanting to say something to her. I motion him out, and he hurriedly exits the Mercedes. He walks north for half a kilometer, crosses the street, and ambles with hands in pockets back toward the park. Valya chews a fingernail. The dashboard glow illuminates her provocative features, reminding me of the way Leda seemed to radiate off the canvas as if she were backlit. I wonder how Leonardo would have captured Valya's ghostly brilliance.

The first time I saw her she was a mud-masked Chechen fighter dwarfed by the smoking Kalashnikov she carried. I came out of a hole too late to stop her from mowing down three careless Russian infantrymen. She heard the sucking of mud on my boots and swiveled to face the new threat. I registered enormous eyes fired gray like electrical storm clouds. Her gun was so big that she needed an extra second to bring it to bear, long enough for me to cover the three meters between us and take her down in a clawing, biting, kicking heap. I had two real feet then. Now I have one, and she wears different masks of ever-changing eyes.

"Forget the *Leda,*" she says.

I track Yuri's progress.

"Business is good," she says in a tight voice I've never heard her use before. "The money is good."

Yuri is within a few meters of the guard shack.

"The General will understand," she says.

"Maxim won't."

"I'll get close and kill him."

She might get close. He likes young girls, and I've seen how he eyes her. But killing Maxim would be hard work. Maybe impossible work. "Even if you did, we'd live our lives running."

She starts to protest, but I end it. "There is more to this than the *Leda.* Somebody is behind it all, and I want him. Or them. And Arkady and Lipman need to die."

"We're not in the revenge business, Alexei."

And she thought *I* was going soft? "Sometimes we are."

Yuri blinks the torch. We step out on the street. Valya unlocks the gate, and I slide it open on steel grooves set into the concrete sidewalk. She works the door lock and pushes in. While she enters the numbers into the blinking alarm pad I take a last check of the funereally quiet boulevard. Yuri has resumed his round-shouldered ramble. A car chugs the cross street two blocks away. A breeze rustles a candy wrapper over asphalt. We are unobserved.

The foyer is empty save for a curved reception desk made from blond wood and burnished chrome. No chairs, no magazines, no wall art. We approach double swinging doors to the left of the desk, and that's when the rancid air stops us. It is a days-old battlefield smell.

Valya wrinkles her nose. "Orlan?"

"I don't think so."

She juts her chin, as if to ask, *Who then?* But I take a deep breath and stride through the swinging doors and into the main gallery without responding.

The room is dim, almost hazy from low, hidden lights—except for the very back, where the spots are on full display high. Here in the front, the tops of the walls are fitted with track lights angled for an indirect glow, but their subdued beams wash blank space. Ceiling-mounted wires drift down like fishing lines without fish. All of the works of art are gone.

Except the one captured in the cone of light at the back.

Valya trails wordlessly as I approach the far wall with a sense of sick fascination. The back of the gallery is the place meant for the centerpiece. That much is obvious from the way the room funnels and the spotlights softly caress. The taut wires holding the freshly hung centerpiece disappear in darkness. The body below them seems locked in a suspended, endless plummet toward Earth.

"What was there before?" I ask.

She is covering her mouth to block the smell. "A Monet. The gardens at Giverny. Orlan was very proud of it."

The new piece hangs by its feet over a river of dried blood at least two meters in diameter that waterfalls down three marble steps to the viewing area. It turns and sways gently in the stream of air from the cooling ducts. Wispy blond hairs turned dark from gore float like jellyfish tentacles beneath a face bloated by purplish blood. Whatever fluids the slash in the neck failed to drain have collected there.

I want to lower him to the ground, if only for the sake of our shared orphan history, but I don't. Arkady Borodenkov will remain a work of representational art until the smell prompts a call to the police and a disinterested junior medical examiner pulleys him down and carts him away.

"I can start to make things right," I tell Maxim.

Within hours of discovering flying Arkady I'm back in Maxim's basement suite in the Kitay-Gorod district, playing the role of supplicant—a role that does not suit me very well. The General's demand is taking the full measure of my loyalty to the towering dwarf.

"How?" Maxim growls in a tone that carries like the sound of an angry bear in a dark cave.

He is reclined on a couch that looks more like a chair because of his massive bulk. His hairy knees are spread wide to accommodate a rail-thin girl younger than Valya diligently servicing his member. Her fanned auburn hair veils the view. The usual coterie of watchful guards is on the other side of the room, out of earshot.

"I'll pay," I tell him.

"You don't have enough."

"How much for the Shah Diamond?"

Maybe the General is right about that much. What difference to steal it twice? A spoiled Saudi prince may find the authenticity of his prize questioned, but the new buyer will own the fake, and whoever it is will be in no position to seek satisfaction from the giant ejaculating into the girl's mouth in front of me. But I still don't understand why the General believes Maxim is owed anything.

While the girl is still wiping her chin, Maxim says, "You said it was not possible to get it out of the armory."

He does not seem surprised by my change of heart about the diamond. "I've made a new contact there."

The girl collects herself, prepares to slink off.

"Wait," Maxim says, and she stops, facing me with her back to him. Her cheek is scratched and one of her eyes is raccooned black. "You want one?" Maxim asks me, nodding toward the girl.

Her eyes implore no. I shake my head, and she patters away in a restrained run.

Maxim snorts at my foolishness, but returns to the topic. "You steal, I sell?"

"Yes. Then you'll owe me, since you gave me Kamil and Tariq and they let themselves be killed so easily."

He throws back his head and bellows at my gall. "Now I am sure," he says when his laughter rumbles to a stop. "You are my bastard son!" He appraises me. His stormy eyes gleam with the light from a hidden thought I can't decipher. Mockery? "Okay. Two hundred thousand for you. American. When the job is done. And I still want my piece of Da Vinci."

chapter 17

Valya and I barely catch Aeroflot's early morning flight from Moscow to Prague after rushing to the airport directly from my meeting with Maxim. The plane carrying us is a rattletrap Tupolev built before Valya was born. Passengers are crammed together in two rows of cloth-covered seats on each side of an aisle too narrow for drink carts. Smokers haze the interior. A baby coughs and cries. Stewardesses balance plastic trays and smile through cracked lipstick, crooked teeth, and coffee breath. Except for the knife ingeniously built into my prosthesis, we're unarmed. Naked.

The plane scuds in low over firs and slaps the tarmac with a whiplash jolt. We unload behind a one-armed vet who struggles to negotiate the mobile stairs pressed against the side of the plane. Take a packed bus to the terminal. Inside, a Czech military officer with a bobbing head like a soccer ball on a broomstick holds a placard that says *Volkovoy* in frowning black letters. He is the man from the picture the General showed me in the dossier.

I nod at him.

He looks from Valya to me. "I am Captain Strahov," he says in Russian. He tries a smile that crinkles his pitted cheeks.

We wait.

He shrugs, turns, and leads the way down tiled corridors. Prague's Ruzyne airport is cleaner than Sheremetevo-2, Moscow's international terminal, but more crowded. More colorful as well, showing the advancing front of Western influence on style. A wall mural depicts a misty forest glade instead of one of the celebrations of wars past that are ubiquitous in Moscow's public places. Advertisements crowd into every bit of available space, not haphazardly the way they do throughout most of Russia. Sadly, Russia has felt just the first exploratory thrust of the advancing army. She is next for a full-blown invasion she can't hope to repel. Tank stoppers cannot turn back culture.

Sliding glass doors open onto a crowded loading area. Strahov takes the front seat of a white Toyota van, next to a driver whose ears stick out like wings. We race out of the terminal and onto the main road leading to central Prague. Ten bumpy minutes pass in silence.

"We need guns," I tell Strahov.

He swivels his big head to watch the soaring spires of Prague Castle fly past some distance away. "I know your reputation, Volkovoy," he says after a moment.

"Then you know that I will need a semiautomatic pistol loaded with hollow points and extra magazines. So will my partner. Make hers a smaller caliber. She likes to work in close."

The van drumbeats over cobblestones. Makes tight turns in the warren of busy Old Town streets while Strahov's head jiggles like a balloon on the end of a plucked string. The effect makes him appear childlike, simple-minded. The appearance is a lie I don't buy. Valya is like coiled steel on the seat beside me. She isn't buying his act either. Strahov is stalling, but I can't figure why. Before I have time to work things out in my mind, he reaches a silenced Beretta over the back of the seat and points it negligently in my direction.

"First," he says, head bouncing, "we need to establish your bona fides."

We can take them. The constricted streets packed with pedestrians preoccupy the driver. Valya will distract while I finger-lock, wrist-lock, pop out his shoulder. I'll have the gun before his big head finishes three more bobs—

The driver swerves the van to a lurching stop halfway onto a wide sidewalk. The door slides open. Two blue-suited commandos leap inside and prod handheld machine guns into our ribs.

Strahov nods sagely. "You took the wrong ride."

Within minutes the van rolls through an arch cut into the side of a yellow limestone building equipped with bars caging in the first-floor windows. The building hulks forebodingly. It reminds me of Lubyanka.

We unload in an inner courtyard bustling with soldiers and civilians with hooded eyes. Intelligence agents everywhere look the same—clinically detached, emotionally dead.

They push me face first into the side of the van. Zip cuffs made of plastic click tight on my wrists, locking my hands behind my back. Another series of clicks indicate that Valya has been similarly restrained. I crane my head around to see her. She looks small and lost between two jackbooted soldiers. Her gaze finds mine. Colored aquamarine again today. She quirks her lips in a playful smile that melts my heart. *I love you,* she mouths, and then Strahov jerks me around and hustles me away.

We pass through an opening leading to a stone-floored hall, and head to the right down stairs along a passage that ends at a metal door. Strahov shoves me into a cell outfitted with a metal bed and nothing else. The bed has flat steel straps for a nonexistent mattress and flanged legs bolted to the floor. The sound of the door crashing shut behind me is followed by the clang of the steel slide covering the door's view port, known to Russian prisoners as the Judas hole. Nobody has bothered to remove the cuffs.

The cell has a familiar Russian feel. I'm struck by the irony that it was probably built in the 1940s by Red Army engineers on the orders of the NKVD—a part of the Soviet plan to instill occupation discipline among the Czech populace. Now it is where Czechs hold Russians.

Twenty hours pass without food or a visit. I learned to be good at counting time without sun or moon in a place far worse than this one. But there I worried only for myself. Here I imagine the things they might be doing to Valya, and it requires all the willpower I can muster to choke back my boiling frustration and rage. And to concentrate on the true nature of the problem I'm facing.

The General directed me to Strahov. Either the General was misled or I have been badly betrayed.

The steel slide rattles across the Judas hole. I sense more than see peering eyes.

"Stand back, please," says a voice I recognize as Strahov's.

I press my butt and cuffed hands against the back wall. The door slams open, and he rolls through, head bobbing. He prods my ribs with a rod tipped with a metal ball, directing me past guard stations outside a line of doors marking other cells. The door to one of the cells hangs open. A guard stands in the doorway holding a thick hose, his feet planted wide against the reverse thrust of the blowing water. Strahov slows as we approach. I realize that he intends for me to see whatever is inside.

Pink water swirls around the guard's boots and laps against the coiled hose on the ground. Red-laced offal, like chunks of meat in thin tomato soup, ride the eddying waves. The guard steps back and directs the nozzle downward, sending the awful concoction into scuppers lining the floor at the base of the walls. We come to a halt at a point where I can see the center of the cell. A man lies facedown on the concrete floor. Marbled flesh streaked with jagged canyons of red makes the body appear sculpted, like a horizontal statue slashed by red crayons. His legs are splayed wide to reveal crushed testicles—a bloom of welling scarlet laced with pearly tendrils.

Strahov puts his mouth next to my ear. "You see? Better to answer questions from the start."

He shoves me forward. We round a corner to an empty hallway. Two uniformed men wait. One holds circular manacles connected by a half-step length of chain.

"I can put you down," Strahov says and slaps my thigh with the cudgel. "Or you can behave."

I stay on my feet, but just barely, pretending the pain doesn't exist. "I'll behave."

One of the men approaches and kneels. When he puts his head down, I recognize him as the driver of the van. Elephant Ears. He smoothes my pant cuffs before he clamps one of the manacles around my ankle—a small, surprising gesture of kindness. He starts to crunch the other around my prosthesis, but hesitates when he feels the unexpected rigidity. My Czech captors have bad intelligence, or maybe dated intelligence, because he obviously thought that I had two real legs. After his initial uncertainty, he continues to fasten the circle of steel.

Behind me comes the sound of rustling fabric.

"Stand still, Volkovoy," Strahov says into my ear.

He slips an executioner's hood over my head and cinches it around my neck. The hood is made of leather. It is damp, rancid from the hot breath of its prior inhabitants.

A rough hand grasps my arm just above the elbow and leads me down stairs. I count from habit, trying to account for my shortened strides. Forty-five shuffling steps, and then four flights, all below street level, by my reckoning. Even through the stench of the hood the smells become progressively worse until unwashed bodies, untended toilet buckets, and moldy walls meld into a physical presence like an oily mist. Our steps boom echoing thuds. The number of treads indicates that three guards accompany me. The hand on my arm jerks me to an abrupt stop. Keys jangle, a creaking steel door opens, and brightness glows through the hood.

I'm shoved forward into cool, antiseptic air. Our shoes tap a staccato beat on the smooth tile of a different passageway that smells medicinal, like a hospital ward. We walk for a long time, more than two hundred steps and three turns—right, left, then right again before I'm nudged to a stop.

Another door opens, this one whispery smooth. I am directed inside by a prodding shove in my back. The metered thump and hiss of what sounds like a ventilator cuts the silence. Someone—Strahov I assume—jerks me around and pushes me back until my knees buckle against the hard seat of a chair. As soon as I'm seated, the chains are clipped to the chair.

My three escorts clomp away. The door sighs closed behind them. The room is dead still except for rhythmic mechanical breathing coming from a few feet to my left and the chirp of what I presume is a heart monitor. I am not alone. But whoever is in the room with me says nothing—is probably in no condition to say anything.

I wait. Track almost an hour in my head, counting my companion's breaths at a metronomic fifteen per minute. And then the air seems to shift, and I know that someone new has entered the room.

chapter 18

Deprived of sight, my other senses are heightened. The new man drinks chicory coffee and smokes Cuban cigars—Romeo y Julietas, by their smell.

"So. Colonel Alexei Volkovoy. A pleasure to make your acquaintance, even under such difficult circumstances."

He has a voice fit for radio. Rich and smooth like mocha ice cream. I'm glad that the hood conceals my surprise. It is possible for him to know my rank only if he is with the Russian government in an important capacity. As far as the rest of the world knows, I was discharged as an invalid three years ago.

"Our files on you are quite interesting," he says in a mocking tone. "Not a dull character at all, by any means."

Chicory coffee, Romeos, and perfect Russian with an oddly familiar northern accent—I sear every sensation into my brain so that I'll know him by voice and smell.

"What should I call you?" I say.

He makes a little clicking noise with his lips. I sense that the question pleases him. He likes the attention, the strokes to his ego, like a cat licking his own fur.

"Call me Peter. I like the sound of the name of a tsar. I think it is appropriate."

Peter the Great, Sophia Alexeyevna's brother. I wonder if his choice of pseudonyms is coincidence.

"The girl is a remarkable specimen," he says. "You know that, of course. Stronger in some ways than you are, Alexei. I'll call you that, hmm? Perhaps you prefer it to *colonel*."

I do my best not to stiffen at his reference to Valya. He waits for a response, but I give him nothing.

"Where was I?" he says after a moment. "Oh, yes. The girl. Put her in a woman's clothes, take away the ridiculous eye lenses, why, she would make an exquisite courtesan."

Again he pauses for a reaction. Maybe he thinks calling Valya a prostitute will offend me. He sighs, no doubt thinking I've missed the insult. My heightened perceptions lead me to think that he is strangely self-conscious in the way that very intelligent people tend to be, as if he is measuring each of his words for just the right tone.

"As I said, she is stronger than you are. We've already had a demonstration of that. She laughed when I told her we were prepared to carve you up and make you eat the pieces." He pauses again to lend weight to his threat. "You won't laugh when I tell you that I'm prepared to do the same and worse to her. You won't laugh, will you, Alexei?"

"No. I'll tell you whatever you want to know."

"Of course you will," he purrs. "But . . . how should I say this? I feel you might be inclined to dissemble. It is a part of your training, you see. Training sprinkled with a dash of natural aptitude."

He scrapes a chair closer to mine and settles into it.

"Surprise me," he says.

Through the hood, I tell him about the *Leda*, and about the betrayal of Lipman and Arkady. My interrogator seems to be fascinated by the history of the painting, its connection to Sophia, and its value in a way that leads me to believe that he is not toying with me, not about this. But something about the way he asks his questions suggests that his true interests lie elsewhere.

"Your friend was right to think its provenance will make the painting even more valuable," he says. "Sophia Alexeyevna is a source of fascination, even today. Such brilliance and ambition confined for life in a nunnery. How she must have seethed away the interminable years."

I don't bother to tell him that Lipman is no friend of mine, so he persists in using the description.

"How did your friend propose to explain how it came to be in his possession?"

"He intended to buy a work from the late seventeenth century, hide the *Leda* behind it, and then claim to discover it during restoration of the inferior piece, just as he did when he found it the first time behind the Mignard."

"Before or after he sold it?"

"Either way. The buyer will have to be in on the deception from the start. Most will want him to make his charade discovery first, so he assumes the full risk of the theft. Others might like the element of intrigue involved in making the discovery themselves."

"It is a good plan," Peter says. His mocha voice drips syrupy greed, and something more as well. An odd longing mixed with suppressed anger comes to mind, but that makes no sense. "It might actually work."

The hood itches, but I can't scratch, so I focus on my invisible adversary. Peter is from the Baltic region, I think. Maybe a former high-ranking Communist. Possibly military or KGB, although he seems too smooth for those roles. The more I think about him the more I lean toward the political angle. I need to keep him talking. Every word gives me more to work with.

"You mean it *could* have worked," I say.

"I mean it *can* work. Why are you here?"

"I'm hunting Lipman."

"What about the other one? Arkady Borodenkov?"

"Dead in a Moscow art gallery."

"Which gallery?"

"It was owned by a man named Henri Orlan."

He makes a guttural sound. Whatever he knows of Orlan he doesn't like.

"Is Orlan dead as well?" he says.

"I don't know."

"Tell me what you suspect."

"Orlan and Lipman were in league from the start. Arkady was a shill to get to me, a planner who could also execute. Someone who could take the fall, if need be."

I leave out Maxim and the General. And I say nothing of Yelena Posnova, which is easy to do because I don't know her role anyway.

"Who else was involved?"

The tone of his question triggers associations in my mind. Suddenly, I know in a flash of insight that this is where Peter's true interest lies. "Orlan left Moscow with a woman named Yelena Posnova," I tell him, and then I concentrate all my available senses on his reaction.

He sucks his breath, ever so slightly. I might have missed the sibilant hiss if I wasn't waiting for just such a sign. "What do you know of her?" he asks casually, in the same tone he has used for his other questions.

I recall the way Nigel Bolles referred me to her, just as he pointed me toward Orlan. Alternate paths set before me—each leading to the same result, I'm sure. I wonder how Posnova connects to all that has happened since Maxim asked me what I knew about art. "She is in the art world. A professor at the university, or so I was told. Other than that, I know nothing about her."

Peter's chair scrapes back. His padded footfalls mark his pacing. The floor is tile. His shoes are soled with soft material, maybe rubber like sneakers, but I think them more likely to be expensive loafers with rubberized soles. When he stops in front of me I picture a tall man in tailored, casual clothing contemplating me with his hands clasped behind his back. I might be wrong, but that is what I see in my mind's eye, and I trust the image.

He drops his voice an octave. "I know about you and the midget general, Alexei."

I remain perfectly still except for unchanged breathing. Maybe he *is* military.

"He uses you, like Lipman did. Except he still needs you, so he pretends loyalty. Now I do not expect to convince you of that. I know your breed. You think loyalty counts for something. To put it another way, you are too stupid to see the truth."

Although my doubts about the General haven't been completely erased, I no longer believe he set me up. Not for this, anyway. He pointed me to Strahov, but I don't think he knew about Strahov's connection to Peter. Peter is a wild card.

He is closer now, his face just inches from mine, separated by the leathery barrier of the hood. I have become acclimated to the smell of the hood, so other scents penetrate. The wafting smell of coffee and cigars rides the barest whiff of subtle cologne.

He whispers, "Meaning you can't be trusted to work with me. Fine. I'll give you an incentive."

The footfalls pad away. He bangs the door. A muted buzzer sounds, and it opens quietly.

"I'm keeping the girl," he says, and my heart starts a heavy thud. "In pieces," he adds, and the thudding threatens to explode my chest. "Two to be exact. I wanted a matched pair—bookends, you and your little trollop."

I'm lost. Blood swirls and roars in my head. The buzzing in my ears seems to vibrate down my spine. The best I can manage is a croak that sounds foreign even to me, like another person using my vocal cords and tongue and mouth to form words.

"What are you saying?"

His chuckle sounds like a glacier moving over ribbed granite. "I'll let you see for yourself. Remember, one week. You have that long and no more to find the painting. I'll trade for it. The *Leda* for your little pet, minus her foot. Straight up."

The closing door cuts off the sound of his laughter.

chapter 19

After Peter has gone I try to scrape my chair closer to her, but it is bolted to the floor. I fall back, breathing heavily, listening to the sounds of the medical equipment I can now only assume is connected to Valya. I try not to imagine what they did and how it was done.

The door opens. Steel wheels roll across tile. Something thumps to the floor. The unmistakable sound of hands rummaging through ice is followed by clinking snicks. The hood comes off.

I'm in a hospital room. White tile and dazzling lights momentarily blind me. As my vision slowly returns I see matte-gray machinery, a hospital bed too high to peer over the edge, and a blue ice chest yawning open on the floor. Strahov and a round man wearing white surgical scrubs with a stethoscope roped around his neck are standing together next to the chest.

I observe these things all at once, like a still-life photograph, without really seeing them. I can't tear my eyes away from the tripod-mounted, stainless steel apparition set directly in front of me. It is an IV carrier, with one long jutting arm. It looks like a sinister metal scarecrow. The arm holds a clear plastic bag. Rivulets of water make glistening trails on the outside of the bag and drip onto the tile. The bag holds an alabaster foot attached to a gleaming ankle and the beginnings of an achingly curved calf that ends in three metal clamps.

Strahov smiles at my reaction. He unclips my chains from the chair, pulls me to my feet, and pushes me closer to the bed, to a point where I am able to see over the edge. I tear my eyes away from Valya's foot to peer at her bone-white, drawn features. My beloved is surrounded by beeping, clicking, thumping devices. I have a view of her in profile between the heart monitor and another machine that I assume is used to help regulate her breathing.

The skin of her eyelids is translucent, webbed red and light blue. An errant puff of white hair wafts in the circulating air like the leaves of an underwater plant. A tube erupts from her mouth and snakes over her terribly small form to the ventilator. Electric wires and IV tubes sprout from her chest and arms. She's lost inside a wire-and-metal womb. I'm grateful for her unconsciousness. She hasn't always been so lucky.

After Valya's family was slaughtered for being Muslims in the wrong place, she was systematically raped and sodomized for weeks before she was accidentally loosed long enough to grab a rifle and turn it on her tormentors. Two weeks of hiding out and moving only in the night brought her to a band of Chechen fighters. They fed her. Offered a protected place to sleep. Thinking she was safe, she dropped her guard and fell into a deep sleep that ended with the prod of a rifle, more ropes, and more abuse. The only difference between the two groups of men, she told me later, was the way they smelled.

She has shared other stories as well, not uncommon in a place like Chechnya, echoes of deeds done in war throughout time, but as I stand in chains gazing upon her waxen face I think that chopping off a healthy limb from her body might be the worst violation she has experienced.

"How long does she have before it can no longer be reattached?" My voice still does not sound like my own.

The round man dressed like a surgeon blinks and clears his throat. But it is Strahov who answers.

"You heard the man. You have one week. Longer than that makes no difference to you or her."

The doctor shifts his weight. "The nerves may be damaged in a matter of hours. They won't survive—"

The surgeon stops mid-sentence when Strahov shoots him a look like daggers. The surgeon risked much to say what he did. I wonder what compulsion forces him to ply his trade under these circumstances.

"Shut up." Strahov's big head is angled down at the doctor.

"What is the truth of it, Strahov?" I say.

"Finish the job early," he grates.

"I won't be able to find the painting in time."

"Too bad."

"Put her foot back. Keep her to ensure my cooperation. I will do whatever you ask of me."

"You will do whatever we ask anyway."

I want to bury him to his neck and use a steel-toed boot to kick off his bobbing head, to tear it off with his spine still attached like a bloody root.

He snaps his fingers and the guards reappear. I stare down at my love until he jerks me around and leads me blindfolded back to the courtyard, where he removes the hood and cuffs. It is late afternoon. Low clouds the color of worn slate threaten rain. He shoves me into the same van that met us at the airport. Elephant Ears drives out through the arch and rattles through the winding streets.

"Who is he?" I say.

Instead of answering, Strahov stares at spires.

We enter a tourist-packed cobblestone square. Crowds and honking cars bring us to a stop. I have less than one week to find Lipman and the *Leda*. I don't know if it can be done. I realize that I have been unconsciously digging a hole in the upholstery of the van.

"The girl," Strahov says, bobbing his head. "Valya. Save her. Do that, don't waste your time worrying about him."

He means my interrogator. This is his way of answering my question about Peter's real identity. The people in the square look up at the same time, collectively. Huge glittering hands on a clock mounted on the wall of the tower looming over the square strike four P.M. Filigreed wheels spin interlinked mechanisms. A golden astronomical dial decorated with symbols of the zodiac flashes light from the angled sun. Windows fly open, mechanical apostles and skeletons begin a clanking dance of destiny, and the leering figure of Death tolls the bell four times.

The crowded tourists who were waiting for the show at the top of the hour begin to disperse. The younger ones look disappointed. Movies and video games with graphics so real you see splattered brains are stiff competition for fifteenth-century relics.

I draw a deep, shuddering breath. "If Valya is harmed further, or if she can't be made whole again, I will kill everyone connected to this." I'm lying, of course. I plan to kill them all anyway.

Elephant Ears pops the clutch and pulls ahead through the thinning crowd. Strahov goes back to staring at distant spires.

"That is your reputation," he says, and yawns.

They drop me in the square on Kaprova Street near a secondhand store. I buy an old jacket with patches, gold-wired spectacles with clear lenses, and a silly fedora, then hurry outside through the labyrinth of narrow roads and alleys.

The Inter-Continental Hotel rises just off the Vltava River. It sits at the junction of streets lined with shops featuring designer clothes and jewelry from Italy, France, and America, the perfect funnel for a hotel catering to rich European and American tourists.

A white-gloved doorman admits me to a marbled foyer, which opens to a reception desk and sweeps left to a sitting area, a bar sparkling with bottled spirits, and a ground-floor restaurant nearly empty in the late-afternoon somnolence. A flashy, auburn-haired girl behind the counter greets me like an arriving guest. She speaks in English, the international language. Mine is good, or so I've been told.

I have already donned my props. Now I adopt a professorial attitude. "I am here to meet one of your guests. Dr. Rolf Lipman."

Purple-painted nails rattle the keyboard. She regards the monitor. Her smile droops into knit-browed confusion, and she stiffens her spine, seemingly girding for another argument with a spoiled hotel guest. "Dr. Lipman checked out two days ago, sir. But his associate is still with us."

I feign surprise. Make a show of checking my watch, wondering if the associate is Henri Orlan or Yelena Posnova.

"I'm sure our meeting was for today."

She bites her lower lip, looking hopeful I'll not blame her for the snafu. "I'm sorry, sir. Perhaps the manager—"

I stop her with my upheld palm. The manager is the last person I want to see. "That won't be necessary. Dr. Lipman must have had a change in plans. I've been incommunicado on a flight from New York."

Something about the mention of the city causes her to glance back at the monitor. I wonder if New York was listed as a destination for one of the guests I'm asking about.

"Did he leave any messages?"

She shakes her head. "No. But perhaps his associate can help you."

"Dr. Posnova?"

"Nooo." She appears suspicious for the first time, apparently remembering her training about the privacy of hotel guests.

Posnova might have used a different name. "Well, it must be one of the techs. What does she look like?"

Worry lines scrunch the girl's forehead. I've guessed wrong on the gender. The associate must be Orlan, not Posnova. "Let me get the manager."

She hurries off through the door leading to the frosted-glass room behind her. I take a slow walk into the bar, removing the glasses and fedora, throwing the jacket over my arm as I settle onto a bar stool. The reception desk is reflected in the sitting area mirror across the lobby. The auburn-haired girl returns, towing a chunky Czech squeezed into a black suit. He looks around while she tries to explain, then snaps at her for wasting his time and disappears. She slumps crestfallen, twisting a finger in her hair. Then a couple approaches the counter, and she's back to work.

I nurse a glass of Polish vodka and try to remember how Valya described Orlan.

When the auburn-haired girl goes off duty I move to the sitting room and pretend to read an American newspaper. At nine I pick a table in the restaurant that offers a partial view of the lobby and choke down a tasteless meal, my first in nearly two days. I linger over coffee until the waiter's hover tells me it is time to leave, then drift back to the bar for more coffee, dead tired but unwilling to waste a night, needing progress. I'm scheming for a way to obtain access to the hotel's computer when a lanky man in owlish glasses steps from the elevator, slings on a jacket, and strides into the night.

Orlan is just as Valya described him—an owl with octopus limbs. I trail him like a stalking cat. Elephant Ears thinks I don't see him as he sneaks into position behind me.

Narrow sidewalks carry our trio through swirls of blown fog to a five-story Gothic edifice abutting the Charles Bridge. The first three levels are a chest-thumping techno club. Drunk and drugged youths swarm on the littered street and the bridge. Others hang from open windows like colorful laundry. Orlan pushes through shirtless boys and makeup-smeared girls with a look of distaste. He is an easy man to follow—no backward glances, only a preoccupied press forward. Fifty paces past the bouncer-protected entrance to the club, Orlan turns into one of the shadowed canyons shunted away from the neon lights.

I approach cautiously and peer around the corner, still pretending not to see Elephant Ears lurking behind me. Halfway along a gun-slot alley Orlan steps over a passed-out lump with his pockets turned out and hurries to a door under a rusted metal awning. I pull back behind the wall just as he gives his first backward glance. When I look again, he has disappeared inside.

I trot around to the back of the building. Seeing no obvious way out, I return to the front and follow Orlan's path down the alley. The sign on the awning over a dented gray steel door announces the Smetanovo Place Casino.

The smarter course is to wait and then follow the Frenchman to a quieter place when he leaves. But those things take time and a partner to watch other possible exits. My partner is in pieces, and every second ticks her closer to some new horror.

The dimpled door opens into a square room. Straight ahead is a wall with a cut for a window covered by steel mesh. A pasty woman wearing a shocking red wig mans the cage. In front of it stands a uniformed guard armed with an MP5 submachine gun slung by a strap over his shoulder. He looks me over, rolling a wad of chewing tobacco under his lip. I know what he sees. Cellblock-hard Russian, street-fighter mean, glistening bronze stubble, and feral eyes—gangster resonance.

He tilts the barrel of the MP5 in my direction and nudges his chin. My jacket wings open when I hold out my arms. His pat is thorough but as courteous as it can be, considering that he carefully feels me ankle to crotch to armpit. Russian gangsters are good business, not to be needlessly offended.

While he does his work a wall-mounted camera whirs to zoom tighter on my face. I suspect Orlan is merely a patron, not one of the owners of the place, but even if he sits in a control room at the other end of the camera my face shouldn't mean anything to him. The knife in my prosthesis survives another search.

The guard steps back. I lean on the cage counter and convert rubles to chips worth five hundred American dollars. When the cage woman smiles, the draping rouged folds of flesh on her face remind me of a circus elephant's swaying behind. The chips are made from heavy clay, painted brick red with a circle of green. The guard holds open a smoked glass door and I step inside a dark anteroom.

As soon as the door closes behind me I sense a presence, but pretend not to. Out of the darkness a voice says in Russian, "Welcome."

I make a show of being surprised as I turn to face a man wearing a black suit over a chalk silk shirt. He motions for me to follow and then leads the way up spiraling mesh-metal steps.

"What is your game?"

"Roulette." Orlan strikes me as a roulette player.

"That infernal silver ball."

We reach the top of the spiral staircase. He leads me down a carpeted hall past another guard station into the casino. Rows of slot machines ping coins and burp electronic chuckles. One side of the room is dominated by blackjack tables, the other by a long bar. Roulette, craps, and baccarat occupy the center. An elevated dais in the back hosts poker. Unsmiling men dressed like my companion oversee the table games. The dealers look grim. The cocktail waitresses have the high butts and jutting breasts of youth. One of them balances her tray on her shoulder while she stands hips forward at the bar talking to Orlan.

"You're right," I say. "The ball is evil." I head for the bar. "I need a few shots of courage before I brave it."

"I'll have drinks brought to your table."

"No, thanks."

He looks disappointed, bordering on angry, but he leaves me two stools away from the Frenchman. The bartender slides over, takes my order for vodka rocks. I hear snippets of conversation. Orlan is talking about money without using the word—his fabulous hotel, his Thai massage, the exquisite room service. The waitress is coy, negotiating while pretending not to. The casino must earn a cut of her after-hours income; otherwise, the prowling casino men wouldn't tolerate her wasting so much time talking to a customer.

On closer inspection Orlan looks like an overdressed ornithologist, a bird-watcher without khaki shorts and binoculars. The owlish glasses make him appear inquisitive as he transparently attempts to be charming.

"I'm off at three," she says.

"I'll wait for you." It is not a question, but his face makes it look like it is.

"Okay. Or I can call you from the lobby. Room six-eighteen, right?" Her back is to me, but I can still hear the smiling reassurance in her tone.

"I'll wait," he says.

He keeps badgering her for a firmer commitment, but I've heard enough. Fifteen minutes and half of my chips later I am able to leave without raising suspicion. An honest roulette wheel favors the house five points. I'm new and unlikely to return, so management wastes no time letting the odds take their course. My guess is that a dealer-operated foot pedal imperceptibly tilted the wheel, but there are lots of other ways to rig a roulette game.

Elephant Ears follows me back to the Inter-Continental. It is a weeknight, so the hotel has a room available for a late-arriving traveler. Once inside the room I dial housekeeping and request more towels. The rumpled Korean maid who brings them wears her master key card on a flexible cord pushed high on her forearm. She is unable to hold my gaze as I stand aside to allow her to pass. I know why. The passing years have taught me to temper my appearance somewhat, to make my face softer, my eyes less ferocious, but right now the familiar look is back with renewed wrath.

As uneasy as she is, it is still a simple matter to bump her and relieve her of the key on the cord. Easier even than stealing a tourist's watch. With luck she won't notice it's missing for several hours. She sets the towels on the bed and hurries from the room, doubtless glad to be away from me.

I check my chronometer. Just past one in the morning. Plenty of time before Orlan returns with his date. I roll confidently down the deserted sixth-floor hallway. The key works, and I'm inside Orlan's room unobserved in seconds. His suite is nicer than mine. Inlaid teak, leather settee and coffee table in a small sitting room, bathroom big enough for jumping jacks.

I start in the closet, where the door to the hotel safe swings freely—nothing inside. Wooden hangers with brass hooks hold neatly hung slacks, two suits, olive and navy, and several bright shirts. His clothes are nicer than mine are as well, made of better fabrics cut in a more modern style.

The crackle of paper under my groping hand leads to a shipping manifest folded into the inside pocket of the navy jacket. The form is printed with the name and logo of a company called Golden Egg

Shipping. The blurb beneath the logo claims that the company specializes in the shipping and handling of "valuable antiquities."

The package referenced in the manifest is one-fifty by one-fifty by ten centimeters. Large for the *Leda,* but I imagine the protective packaging would be substantial. It was labeled "Extremely Fragile." The packaging charge was an additional $500 above the shipping fee. It was sent via airfreight two days earlier to Ms. Yelena Posnova in care of the Medici Gallery in New York City.

My original plan was to question Orlan. The idea still makes sense. I am overwhelmed by unanswered questions. The General, Maxim, and Peter, each playing his own game, with Valya's life in the balance. The odds in the rigged casino were better by far. But the problem with questioning Orlan is that in the end he will need to die or disappear. Either alternative will alert Lipman.

I copy the address to the Medici Gallery, replace the manifest, slip back to my room, and work the phone. Ten hours later I'm chasing the sun to New York in a Lufthansa 747. Judging from his blithe manner, Elephant Ears thinks I don't notice him sitting ten rows behind me.

chapter 21

I take a room at a moldy hotel on Manhattan's West Side. Fuzzed carpet surrounds island patches where tramping feet have worn through to the pad; scuffed furniture, chipped paint, and a stained bedspread mark the mishaps of visitors past. The hotel room is larger than Masha's Moscow flat, and it may have fewer rats, but it feels unpleasantly colder.

I stow my tiny bag and drift along the busy streets, using the concrete miles and sunset hours of the same day I left Prague to acclimate. Eavesdrop conversations, one of them in my native language. Brush shoulders with hustlers, hurriers, vendors, tourists, pickpockets, cops, diners, theatergoers, Johns and their targets—Third World and First braided together, locked in an uncomfortable embrace. I suck fumes, the smell of cooked meat, and body odor. I can feel New York's labored breaths like gusts of air from a massive bellows.

The last time I was here was in '03, when the General sent me to be fitted for my advanced prosthesis. He said he needed me whole.

Much has changed since then. The slow descent into JFK framed a plane-window snapshot of a missile battery parked to guard the approach, the product, I assume, of yet another surge in terrorist chatter. My cabbie distanced himself from his nationality, gravely informing me that he was *Persian.* The city lists slightly, maybe even imperceptibly to those who live here, but noticeably to a visitor from a place of suffering. The streets thrum with an undercurrent of sadness, of fatality maybe, an almost Russian sense of inevitable sorrow, coated in swagger but still palpable. In a strange way the changes accentuate New York's quintessential resilience. The skyline may be diminished, but the spirit is not. It is still all hustle and bustle and uniquely American purpose and certitude.

The Medici Gallery is in the Midtown arts district. By early evening I'm standing across the street from it, but there is little to see. The gallery is housed in a five-story brownstone veined green and red by climbing bougainvillea. Darkness falls while I wait, watching for activity, but nothing happens. More hours drag past. I cross the street for a closer look.

Shallow concrete steps lead to a wooden door that looks fit to withstand a battering ram. Next to the door is an inset bronze plaque discreetly cast with the name of the gallery and the words *By Appointment Only.* A camera noses out through the vines.

I recon the perimeter. The walls on one side and the back abut other buildings. A fire escape crawls up the other side above a Dumpster in an asphalt alley that ends in a chain-link fence. A gate made from steel tubes and wires blocks the entrance to the brownstone's underground garage. All of the windows are covered on the inside by metal shutters, the kind that scroll down from the ceiling with the push of a button. The Medici Gallery is serious about security.

I'm without a vehicle in which to sit and watch the entrance all night. I am already three days behind the *Leda* and nearly the same into Peter's artificial deadline. The possibility that the package designated on the manifest doesn't hold the painting is too awful to consider.

Walking back to the front of the Medici building, I decide that it is time for a confrontation. At the first opportunity I duck around a corner and then hurry across the street and backtrack to the other side to hug a wall and wait for Elephant Ears. He has done a workmanlike job trailing me this far. He was KGB-trained in the bad days, is my guess, and now he's with the FSB or works freelance for Peter.

He follows the KGB book. Instead of rushing headlong around a blind corner he crosses the street first. But I read the same book, so I'm waiting, and he is in my grasp before he knows what's happened.

I push his arm up his back until his wrist tops his chicken-wing shoulder blade, and then whisper against the translucent back of his jutting ear. "For right now we're on the same team. Don't do anything stupid. Yes?"

His ear waggles. As if on signal, his head jolts up and down.

I propel him into an alleyway, quick-frisking him as we move. Everything happens so quickly and subtly that the few pedestrians around us pay us no mind. Elephant Ears is not armed anywhere obvious.

"Why are you here?" I ask.

"I was ordered to follow you and report your movements."

"By who?"

"Strahov."

"Bullshit." I push his wrist higher until joints pop.

He's tough. He barely whimpers. "I don't know who's pulling Strahov's string." His breaths are so shallow that it's hard for him to force the words out.

"Who pulls yours?"

"I'm FSB out of St. Petersburg."

"Who did you take me to meet in Prague?"

"Don't know," he gasps when I ratchet up his arm. "I swear it. Whoever it was came and left in a limo with windows like black ice. I never got a look at him."

I spin him around. He's older than I thought from seeing the back of his head. Early to mid-thirties, with thin lips centered in a narrow, pale face decorated with two large moles, one on his temple and the other next to his nose, and mournful brown eyes. I remember the gentle hands that placed the manacles on my legs. I switch to English.

"Did your orders say not to help me?"

His faltering smile reveals bucked teeth, all of them yellow except for one that's dingy white. The unmatched one is false, of course; except for the very rich, Russian dentistry is too practical to concern itself with cosmetics.

"No," he says.

"Let's talk."

I grasp his uninjured arm and tow him along the street to a throbbing basement club I passed earlier in my ramble. The light outside the barrelhouse is tubed, sapphire neon spelling *The Rhythm Room*. Forty dollars pays the cover for two. A bouncer admits us into a smoky, sauna-close bar. We work our way around a crowded dance floor so small that it makes me think of angels dancing on the head of a pin. A table in the back offers a view of a blues band heavy on horns. They call themselves the HooDoo Kings.

My new friend is mesmerized by the spectacle of the gyrating crowd and the pumping resonance of the music. The band mixes primitive rhythms with soulful sensuality. The first time I heard raw Delta blues was in the American capital. I was there for a joint intelligence exercise described as a "cooperative sharing" of information deemed in the "common interest of the U.S. and the Russian Federation." The process was not so pure, but it was symbolic of the historic relationship between the two countries. The Americans instructed, and the Russians dissembled. The NSA operative who took me to the D.C. club late one night after another mind-numbing briefing session, a man named Matthews, watched my reaction just as I watch Elephant Ears's now.

Matthews said to me then, "What do you think?" and I repeat the question to Elephant Ears when the band takes a break.

His sad eyes regard me. He sees a blunt instrument incapable of appreciating his observations. But he wants to talk about the way the music made him feel, I can see the desire in him, so I wait him out.

"I've listened to this music," he says finally. "On bootleg CDs."

Popular music is available in Moscow stores and at stands in the subway tunnels. More creativity, usually in the form of Internet downloads, is needed to find music like this. I nod encouragement.

"The recordings are not the same as seeing this." He points to the stage.

"No, they are not."

"It is very—how do they say it? Black America."

I nod again, waiting.

"But the loneliness and . . . the hunger." He looks away. He seems embarrassed, probably remembering that he knows me only from a thick file. One filled with horrors, I'm sure.

"Go on," I prompt him.

"It's so damned Russian."

I settle back into the hard chair, somehow satisfied even though it means nothing. His answer is the same one I gave Matthews years ago.

It is just past two A.M. when I leave Elephant Ears at his hotel with plans to meet for breakfast, trundle back to my hotel room, and climb into a bed that is too small for me. Thrown red neon burns through the closed shade, alternating on and off. Roaches scuttle on the walls, but don't bother me. A rebel I interrogated in Grozny told me between sessions that he once lived on the tiny beasts for a month, even grew to favor the taste. "Like overcooked bacon" was the way he described it. He was a poet from the shabby Volga River town of Uglich, famous as the site of the murder of Ivan the Terrible's son Dmitry. He was soft and a Christian, not Muslim like most of the rebel fighters, not even a fighter at all, really. Skinny, afraid, and naively hopeful for humanity, he was in that barbarous place because he believed in the cause of Chechen independence. My job was to question and then kill him. After the first part was done, I left him trussed and gagged. Radioed my superiors what I had learned about a secret supply route, one of hundreds of such insurgents' ant trails, then huddled with Valya over a tiny fire on top of a shelled-out building. The flames fired her eyes into molten pewter.

"You can't kill this one," she said.

"Why not?"

"It would make you evil."

She was barely more than a child then, elfishly small next to the Kalashnikov leaning against the parapet wall behind her. Even so, she had the gravity of a woman three times her age. Her glowing gray eyes were enormous, soulful, but no match for what was inside her heart.

The poet lived.

And that was the night Valya and I made love for the first time.

First thing in the morning I place a call from my hotel room to my NSA acquaintance, Matthews, using a special number he had given to me at the D.C. conference. When he gave it to me I never expected to use it. I was sure that he had been assigned to befriend me, to work me for information. Today I'm willing to be worked. I give the person who answers my real name. It takes more than ten minutes for him to come on the line.

"Volkovoy?" he says in a wary tone.

"I caught a blues act last night," I say. "It was just my second time."

He laughs. Some of the tension drains away now that he knows it's really me. "What are you doing in New York City, Volk?"

"Do you still have all those fancy computers at Langley?"

"Yeah. And guess what? They don't say a damned thing about you being in the States."

I can tell from his tone that he's serious, cloaked in post-9/11 paranoia. "When was the last time you were officially in Russia?" I say, knowing he'll get the point that a certain amount of comity works both ways.

Silence stretches. I picture him raising an eyebrow in the direction of a grim-faced superior. "What name did you use?" he says finally.

I give him the false name on my passport.

"Hold on."

My palm goes sweaty on the handset while I wait for his response. The possibility of Homeland Security agents snaking through the grubby lobby of the hotel below is slight but real, even during these relatively friendly times in Russian-American relations.

Matthews comes back on the line. "You want something off the computer, huh? What's in it for me?"

It's always the same with Americans, forever selling. He probably thinks that it's always the same with the Russians, forever asking for something for nothing. We are like two squared-off children trying to make a simultaneous exchange, except that in this case one of us really has nothing to offer.

"I'll owe you a favor," I say.

"And?" He knows my favors don't count for much. He is also trying to confirm whether my actions are sanctioned.

"So will the General," I say, without adding that the man who calls himself Peter might be a preferable debtor and therefore a better bargaining partner for men like Matthews and his handlers.

"Tell me what you need. Then I'll decide."

This is an enormous risk. If I give him a name that causes his computer to scream, I'll have inadvertently invited another player, the NSA, into the game.

"Yelena Posnova. The Medici Gallery. And Dr. Rolf Lipman."

"How deep do you want me to go?"

It is a good question asked too late. I'm already so deep I'm choking. "Whatever you've got."

"You'll know in an hour."

I tell him how to contact me. And then I wait. Wishing she was here with me.

chapter 22

"They like dead Italians at the Medici Gallery," Matthews says a few hours later. He sounds more at ease, almost bored now that the strangeness of hearing from me has worn off. Maybe I haven't triggered the computers. "It was established in 1990 by its current owner," he adds. "Marc Pappalardo. He's out of Jersey. Mobbed up, but not family. They gave him his start, so they own him. You'll like him."

"What do you mean?"

"He's missing a piece, just like you are. Get it?"

Some Americans have a way of saying hurtful things in a casual, backhanded way. Cultural narcissism, I think—a kind of self-absorption that blinds them to the wells of emotional pain in others. I plow ahead. "Is the business legitimate?"

"He lost his left hand. We're not sure how. The file says it might have been chopped off as punishment. You know, a lesson, don't steal from us."

"So the business isn't legitimate?"

"Actually, we thought it was. Figured maybe Pappalardo made a partial break and started operating the art store as a money laundry. Now we're not so sure."

"Why not?"

"Because you're asking questions about it. What are you chasing? Drugs? Flesh?"

The best way to sidetrack him is to come as close to the truth as I can. "A package was sent there. We think it might contain stolen Russian artifacts."

"Yeah? So that's the Lipman connection. I was wondering about that."

"What's his story?"

Matthews gives me the same chaff I already know about Lipman's background. I tell him so.

"Then you know about him and Posnova," he says.

"What about them?"

He chuckles. "I didn't think you knew."

"Knew what?"

"He's fucking her."

Poor Arkady. "So what?"

"Well, that brings us to the good part. The name Yelena Posnova is an alias. Her real name is Kasia Anfimova—at least that's her maiden name. She's a real patron of the arts over there."

Matthews keeps blathering, but I'm busy making unpleasant connections. Now that I know who Yelena Posnova is, I also know who Peter is. When I pay attention again Matthews is winding down.

"—she's the wife of Russia's foreign minister, Peter Vyugin. They've been separated for about a year. Word is he's searching high and low to find her. My guess is he's probably more than a little pissed off that an art restorer is fucking his bride." He gives a laugh, superior and small at the same time. "Jesus fucking Christ, Volk, sometimes I think you guys ask these questions just to make us think you're stupid."

After hanging up with Matthews, I let my thoughts wander to an earlier confrontation with my Prague captor, Peter Vyugin, to a time when I was still whole, but already broken. As far as I know, we had crossed paths just that once, in 2001, at Smolny Institute, the Communist Party headquarters in St. Petersburg, where I had been dispatched to brief party leaders on the progress of the Chechnya mop-up—the same grim mop-up that continues today.

An aide led me to a conference room that housed a glossy marble table and two dozen leather wingback chairs, each one costing more than an army captain like me made in a month slaughtering the enemies of Russia.

I had to wait for two hours before the politicos filed in, slapping rust-colored files on top of the table, murmuring gossip and family stories, stoking pipes and cigarettes until the air was hazed with smoke. Assistant foreign minister Peter Vyugin arrived last. The other men quieted and stood when he entered the room. He wore a fluid, chrome-colored European suit and a white shirt that contrasted with his tan and blended nicely with the flecks of gray sprinkled in his black hair. He settled at the head of the table and took his time reading my report. Then he raised his head and regarded me as if I were a waiter who had just spilled coffee in his lap.

"This is shameful," he said in smooth, rich tones that belied the iron in his black eyes.

I thought so, too, but for different reasons.

The sides of his aquiline nose sucked in. "We are being overrun by rabble. I remember a time when Russians were fighters, not cowards."

The Chechnya conflict has been a war of soldiers and civilians coupled in unquenchable grief. Street fighting and carpet bombing reduced the city of Grozny from nearly half a million people to a virtual ghost town. Some men refused to fight at all. Some fought for a time and then did everything in their power to quit the horror. But I refused to call any of them cowards.

I stood stiffly at attention, focused on the far wall over his head.

He snorted and leaned back in his chair to stare contemptuously at me. "So what do you have to say for yourself?"

"The Chechens fight for their homeland. They're well armed by their Muslim brothers in other countries, they know the ground, and their spies are everywhere. Our men fight for a cause they don't understand in a country they hate."

"What are you trying to say?"

"If the government stays committed we will grind them into submission, but it will cost men and time."

He sat back, sucked in his cheeks, and blew a gust of air that fluttered my report on the table in front of him. Disgust wrinkled his features.

"You're a coward like the rest of them."

I was armed with a Browning .40-caliber semiautomatic pistol loaded with ten rounds in the clip and another in the chamber. Another clip was attached to my belt next to a combat knife. Eighteen men circled the table centered in the room. I was supremely confident that I could seal the door with my body and kill them all before the guards could break through to save them. The idea warmed me so much that I toyed with the details in my mind while I let the silence drag out to insolent proportions. Peter held my gaze steadily, glinting amusement and wearing a private smile that made me want to take a shower. It was almost as if he could read my thoughts, as if in some strange way he could see into the hidden places in my mind where hunting was sport and killing was sensual. As if we were connected by an evil current.

I looked away first. "Yes, sir," I said finally.

When I arrive at the Medici Gallery after my talk with Matthews, Elephant Ears is waiting on the corner across the street, chain-smoking

Yava cigarettes, leaning against a squared-off column. It's overcast, not hot, but the back of his hand swipes his forehead as he pushes away from the column at my approach.

"You told them I broke your cover," I say, and he startles.

"How—"

"It's in your face."

He sets his jaw. "They had to know," he says defensively.

His report to Peter or Strahov doesn't matter. My useless subterfuges mean nothing as long as they have Valya carved into pieces.

"Have you picked up a weapon?" I ask.

His eyes widen. He drops his gaze.

"I know the FSB has contacts here."

His face runs a gamut of emotions before he seems to reach a decision. He pulls out a Glock and hands it to me. I pop the clip, check the chamber, and slot the magazine back into place. The gun slips easily into the pocket of my jacket. I like the feel of its swinging weight at my side.

"Anything so far?" I ask, pointing in the direction of the gallery.

"A delivery boy at seven."

We settle between two buildings to wait. "How'd you lose the foot?" he asks half an hour later. "OZM?"

If only it had happened as fast as an exploding mine. "No." My tone precludes further inquiry.

An hour passes. I itch everywhere.

"What's the story on the girl?" he asks.

"Wait here while I check the back," I tell him. "Come for me if you see anything strange."

The side alley is graced with rats bigger than toy poodles and four battered Dumpsters. The two on the side away from the gallery doubtless serve the adjacent building, but I take no chances and dive all four of them. Wet fast-food wrappings stick to my jacket. A sticky clump of dissolving tissue catches in my hair. Every piece of garbage is uniformly damp. Effluvium rises in eye-watering waves.

All of the papers that are still intact refer to a lawyer or a ream-generating accounting firm. The remaining documents are in shredded, curlicue strips. I'm down to the sediment-covered bottom of the last Dumpster when I find a torn half-page of what looks like a memorandum. The document is an order of consignment for a work by Paul Mignard, called *Clio*. Delivered yesterday from Prague by Golden Egg Shipping on behalf of customer Henri Orlan care of Yelena Posnova.

The reverberating bang of a fist on the side of the Dumpster startles me. I tug out the Glock and lunge over the edge, grab a fistful of hair, and pull—but it's only Elephant Ears, his face twisted in pain.

"Let go," he gasps, and I do.

"Why aren't you watching the front?"

"A car is coming," he says.

I lean out, grab on to his jacket and yank, just as he jumps. He lands hard and sprawls in the grunge on the bottom of the Dumpster as I peer over the side. The hum of a heavy motor is accompanied by the sound of tires crunching asphalt. A black stretch limo turns into the alley and heads in our direction. I drop back into the dank container. Elephant Ears has drawn a snub-nosed revolver that looks like a water pistol. It's bigger than Valya's .22, but it looks smaller in his hand.

"Wait out front after I'm gone," I tell him.

"Where—"

"I'm going to follow the limo inside."

The car passes us, slows to turn into an underground garage, and then stops to wait for the wire gate to scroll higher. I roll over the edge of the Dumpster, keeping low, crouch behind the limo's right bumper in the driver's blind spot, then follow bent over at the waist as it turns in and heads down the ramp. Once inside the garage, I hunker behind a support column as the car roars ahead at a pace too fast to follow. The gate starts down behind me. I'm committed.

chapter 23

The limo circles a concrete pillar and screeches to a stop. The driver stays inside. Two men wearing untucked white shirts and loafers crack the doors and stand waiting while the most beautiful woman I have ever seen emerges from the vehicle, leading with long, slender legs. A second before I was sweating, ketchup-stained, pissed off. Now I'm mesmerized.

Valya is big-eyed, heart-faced allure. Her boyish body brims inner-strength beautiful. The only magazine cover she might grace would be one featuring teen runaways, and if she ever did her image would haunt the memories of all those who saw it. She tantalizes, drifts the ethereal currents of your mind until you're like Yuri the cop or one of hundreds of others in her orbit—edgy, chewing on cotton, trying to swallow a lump in your throat that won't go away, needing her in ways she can't be had.

This woman stops the mental currents altogether. She unfolds sinuously from the limo wearing a tailored white suit that flows over the curves of her body, catching all the right parts in a clingingly choreographed minuet. Jet-black hair sweeps away from finely honed olive features that remind me of the perfect faces of the pixeled girl-women created by computer programmers for the games played by lusting teenagers. She is *Cosmo*-ready.

Her companions are obviously smitten. I have to shake myself mentally to remember that this is the woman I will always think of as Yelena Posnova. Lipman's lover, Peter's wife. Whatever game she is playing, she is one of my enemies.

The unlikely troupe enters an elevator. I rush over to the closed doors, careful to stay out of the sight of the driver, and watch the indicator lights. The elevator stops on the fourth floor, then starts down again. I circle over to the limo, keeping low. The driver is silhouetted in the dashboard lights. He's talking on a cell phone. His window is open.

I approach the car from the side. He's too absorbed by his conversation to notice me until it's too late. I lean in and crunch an elbow into his temple. He's quicker than I expected, so the blow glances off his skull and only stuns him. I don't want him dead, not yet at least, and I don't want blood on his uniform, so I lunge halfway through the open window, catch his throat in my hands, and choke him, riding his thrashes until he goes slack.

I wriggle back out of the car and scan the garage. Nobody is about. I open the door and push him aside so I can get into the front seat next to him. Slam the barrel of the Glock into the back of his head to make sure he stays unconscious. Remove his hat and blue uniform jacket, which is hard to do in the close confines of the front seat of the car. The garage is still quiet, so I haul him out and stuff him into the trunk. Then I ride the elevator up to the fourth floor.

The doors open onto an unmanned reception area finished in fabricated stone cut by a tinkling waterfall set amid plastic trees and plants. It is as if I've been teleported to a carpeted jungle. Ignoring the designated hallway, I pass beneath hanging fronds, using decorative rocks as stepping-stones to navigate the carved concrete river, hugging the wall until I hear voices.

"They're fakes."

Posnova is talking. I don't need to see around the wall to know that, because her voice is a perfectly matched musical caress of her body.

The scratch and flare of a match covers whatever noise I make settling below the faux foliage into a position where I can see into the room. It is an open sitting area, with a low table flanked by leather settees and a long window that overlooks the man-made canyon of the street below. Posnova is pacing. Each step sheaths a leg in the accentuating white silk of her skirt. Her escorts sway like palm fronds each time she passes by.

"How do you know they're fakes until you've seen them?"

The speaker puffs a cigarette. Tight gray curls cling to his head like a skullcap. A matching beard follows the line of his prominent jaw like a horseshoe; without an accompanying mustache, it makes him look as if he's leaning forward even when he's standing straight. He's wearing a long, black jacket with a Mandarin collar. Thin black gloves cover his hands.

Posnova glides to a stop and turns to face him. Without seeming to move, she's suddenly in close, her face almost touching his.

"The provenance won't work, Marc," she says.

She's talking to Marc Pappalardo, the gallery owner owned by the mob. The gloves must be worn to hide his false left hand.

"No such works have ever been in the Hermitage," Posnova adds.

"You people denied the existence of the Hidden Treasures for fifty years." The closeness of her body has turned his voice husky. "Make a new discovery. What's two more pieces?"

"Two more Pissarros?" she asks dryly.

"Two more from his summer in Dieppe. His letters to his son suggest their existence."

"It won't work."

"Yes, it will, at least for long enough for us to make a nice profit. Have your trained bunny, Lipman, find them in a secret catacomb."

Lipman's name startles me. My recoil causes the covering of plastic fronds to shimmy. Pappalardo turns his chin like a pointer, but I'm huddled low, out of sight. He snuffs out the butt of his cigarette in a shiny black onyx ashtray resting on the table. Lights another.

Posnova watches his routine and then says through tight lips, "I'll consider it."

His smile reveals perfect white teeth—caps no doubt, strikingly offset against his tanning-bed bronze skin. "Tell me about your latest, ah, project," he says.

"It is not a project. This is the most important art find of the past five hundred years."

Pappalardo gives a wrist-flicking wave. "Of course it is," he says dismissively. "Just like my Pissarros."

Posnova stiffens. Her breasts rise and fall, and patches of red grow on her cheeks. "Don't you dare patronize me, Marc. This is real. If you're acting this way to negotiate, stop it now, or I'll cut you out."

Her escorts shift their pointy feet and stand straighter.

The gallery owner shows his capped teeth. "Of course, my dear. No need to be so touchy."

He waits for a response without getting one. She's still breathing hard, staring at him through narrowed eyes that look like gleaming cobalt slits.

He sucks his cigarette down to the filter and crunches it into the onyx dish. "So where is Leonardo's lost masterpiece?"

She hesitates. "We think it's in Moscow."

Fuck! It is all I can do not to scream in frustration. I've wasted three days. Prague was useless, Valya's abduction avoidable, New York a waste. The *Leda* was in my backyard the whole time. I've heard enough. I start to back out.

"You think?"

"We've run into some problems. We're going to have to do some searching."

"Searching? Well, by all means, let's have a treasure hunt, shall we?" Pappalardo says, the sound of his voice fading as I round the corner into the reception area. "I'll have you dropped at your hotel. We'll leave tomorrow. Dinner tonight, my dear, will be . . ."

I ease through a door that leads to an interior stairwell. Bound down the steel steps three at a time back to the garage. Don the driver's cap and wait inside the limo. His jacket is too small for me, but I don't think the men will notice that mine is darker.

The elevator dings. The bodyguards follow Posnova like trained hippos into the back of the limo. One of them raps the window that separates passengers from the driver's compartment. "The Peninsula Hotel," he says.

I don't know where that is, but it won't matter anyway. I need only to create a diversion to rid myself of the goons and get Posnova alone. This isn't the place to do it, though, so I wheel the limo around and up the ramp. The garage door starts to roll up automatically. I check the rearview mirror. Posnova's blue eyes are staring back into mine. She's tense. She knows I'm wrong.

I gun ahead into the alley and crank the wheel hard right—and then have to slam the brakes to avoid plowing over Elephant Ears. He is in a shooter's crouch, pointing through the windshield with his snub-nosed pistol, suddenly confused when he sees that it's me behind the wheel.

The guards may have appeared plodding, but they're well trained, and they react reflexively. The jolting stop throws us all forward. My hand finds the Glock, but I can't disentangle from the wheel and find the door latch before the men in back, propelled toward the rear doors by our forward momentum, roll out. Elephant Ears hesitates, apparently unsure if they are friends or foes.

The delay costs him. His whole body jerks, and then his leg buckles and he goes down at the same time as I hear the cracking shots. One of the bodyguards sidles toward his downed form for the denouement while the other holds his pistol aloft in two hands and searches with his eyes for more threats in the alley and the windows and the fire escape landings.

I check the rearview and do a double take. Posnova is watching me in the mirror. She knows I'm a danger to her. That much is written plainly on her remarkable face, but she seems more curious than afraid.

The doors are open. She can run if she wishes. I have to eliminate the most immediate threat. I step out of the car, rack the slide on the Glock, and walk toward the bodyguards. The first is poised over Elephant Ears, readying for the kill, close enough that one hand is raised to block the spray of blood from the head shot. I press the barrel into the small of his back and loose three rounds that fold him backward nearly in half. Each discharge sounds like a small explosion that reverberates in the enclosed alley. The second guard whirls at the roar of the shots, just in time for my fourth bullet to slam him in the mouth and rip away his face.

I kick their guns across the alley and squat down next to Elephant Ears. He's drowning in blood. A big red bubble pops wet mist over his nose. His eyes are wide. Frightened. I think he knows that it's me squatting above him, but whether he does or not, I owe him comfort. So I cradle his head and put my mouth down by one of his big ears to warm it with my breath and hold him close until the shuddering stops.

I gently set his head on the asphalt. Turn on my haunches to look toward the limo. Yelena Posnova is gone, vanished in the minute it took Elephant Ears to die.

chapter 24

I close Elephant Ears's wide, staring eyes. His bucked teeth are rimmed with rusty blood. His slack jaw won't stay shut.

The squeal of braking tires fires me back into action. Three dead men are strewn over the asphalt grime in front of the limo, which sits with its doors winged open, empty. On the street end of the alley a knot of people stand staring, their voices growing louder in a rising swell, pointing me out to a hurrying cop. The gate into the brownstone housing the gallery never closed, so I suspect Posnova hightailed back to Pappalardo and that they are even now scheming how to answer police questions. Just then the gate begins to roll down, cutting off one potential avenue of escape.

The novelist Aleksandr Solzhenitsyn compared the Soviet legal system to a sewer ridding society of human waste. The things I know about America's reconstituted system of justice for foreigners suggest that it traps suspected human garbage like insects in amber, suspending them in seeming perpetuity. No charges, no hearings, just everlasting incarceration and interrogations in a Guantánamo prison

or someplace else even more secretive. My chest tightens at the suffo-
cating prospect of a cramped prison cell, daily rations, and timed visits
to the latrine. It is past time to leave if I want to avoid becoming
trapped in the sticky maw of the American judicial system.

A quick pat-down locates a cell phone in Elephant Ears's breast
pocket. His toy revolver lies unfired nearby. I grab it quickly and stuff
it along with his cell phone into the pocket of my jacket. Wailing sirens
and the running approach of one of New York City's finest mean I have
no time to search the dead bodyguards.

I sprint away. Jump the chain-link fence at the other end of the
alley just as a bright-eyed cop whose courage is outstripped by his
foolhardiness rattles the metal links to follow. He is nearly over, fingers
intertwined in wire, clinging like a cat, when I take a running start and
jackknife my good foot into the fence where his chest is. The force of
the blow sends him windmilling off the fence to land with a grunt. I
chug off, running hard. The alley on the other side of the fence leads to
a narrow path behind another brownstone, which I follow, tossing the
Glock into the trash wind-piled against a wall as I go. I'm not worried
about a trace on the gun. Elephant Ears obtained and loaded it. If it
leads anywhere it will be to him.

Three blocks later I slow to a walk. Step into the shroud of a
crowded street somewhere along the West Sixties. The sounds
of pursuit fade in the distance. Within seconds, I'm lost in the herds of
people and buried deep inside my own thoughts.

I'm back in my hotel room before an hour has passed. The bed groans,
and cockroaches scuttle as I settle in to examine Elephant Ears's phone.
It is a satellite phone. Instructions describing its use have been typed in
Cyrillic onto a cut piece of paper taped to the inside of the foldout
earpiece. I check the call history and hit pay dirt. Early in the morning,
before he met me, Elephant Ears had made a call to an international
number. The last incoming call had been logged just two hours before
from the same number. I punch it in and wait for the connection.

"Yes?" I recognize Peter's mocha voice. He sounds relieved.

"This is Volk. Your man is dead."

Silence stretches while I listen to him breathe. The connection is so good that I can hear the wet clicks in his mouth, like the sound of his mind working.

"You killed him?" he says.

"No."

"What happened?"

"We staked an art gallery owned by the mob. The old mob—the Italians. I thought it was where the *Leda* would pass. I was wrong. Things went bad."

"Your little girlfriend is dead, Volk." For the first time his ice-cream-smooth voice rasps, metal on metal, confirming my feeling that his interest in this affair is deeply personal.

"Fuck you."

My response is not the one he expects. His mouth clicks a wary beat. "That attitude will make me kill her slowly," he says after a moment's hesitation.

"Then you'll never see the *Leda*."

"So what."

Now I am nearly certain that the *Leda* is secondary to him, but I administer another test. "And I'll kill you."

He laughs.

I play my last card, sure that it is an ace. "I'll kill you," I amend slowly, "just after I kill Yelena Posnova."

It is as if one of those dusty sound dampeners on the outside of the doors in Masha's building has been shoved into his mouth. His muffled breathing carries over a continent and an ocean. I like the sound of his suffering.

"Why would I care about her?" he asks hoarsely, trying to sound casual, but he's already given away his secret, and he knows it.

"Because she's your wife, Peter."

Choking sounds like gurgles float across the line. He is so sick with love that it's eating him worse than a cancer.

"Where is she?" he manages to say.

"Here. In New York."

This time I interpret his silence as uncertainty.

"I'll work with you, Peter," I tell him.

"How?"

I'm sleep-deprived woozy, probably hallucinating when I visualize Valya, pale like a drained corpse, fading into herself, disappearing from this awful, undeserving world. The round surgeon in Prague warned of nerve damage within hours, and it has already been nearly three days. Peter is sick with love. I am sick from fear.

"Put Valya's foot back."

"How do you propose to bring my wife to me?"

The truth is that I don't know, especially if the dead bodies outside the Medici Gallery have already wreaked cyber havoc on the NSA's computers. Recovering Yelena Posnova is one of many problems flitting around me like drunken butterflies. I figure to swat them one at a time and see what happens. "Let me worry about that."

"Call me when you have her," he says, and hangs up.

chapter 25

Midnight finds me pacing Fifty-fifth Street, outside looking into the gilded foyer of the Peninsula Hotel, three hours into a watch for Posnova or Pappalardo or Lipman. More machine-gun-toting police can be seen on the streets of New York City than in Moscow. The deeper meaning of this paramilitary transference is beyond me. Maybe it is a case of Gresham's Law applied to societies—bad driving out good. But to whatever it is attributed, the cowed acceptance of the Americans to armed commandos and missile launchers in their cities suggests a frightening permanence, perhaps the product of too little suffering and too much comfort for too long.

After he hung up on me, I tried repeatedly to raise Peter again on the cell, but he never answered. I am dying to send him severed shreds of his wife, but I can't. Not yet, at least. He called my bluff and won because I won't risk Valya.

I continue to pace, shoulder-bumping pedestrians. The brightly lit entrance to the hotel waters my gritty eyes. A triple shot of espresso from a nearby Starbucks helps to keep me awake as the hours creep past. A passing car illuminates the interior of an American SUV, back-lighting two silhouettes that look like the human shapes painted on gun-range targets. The men from America's intelligence services are here, watching.

At six in the morning a shuffling lady in a faded shawl emerges from the Peninsula lobby, trailing a bellhop wheeling a brass cart loaded with a leather duffel bag he could easily carry. Her head hangs so low that her ropey gray hair hides her face. The bottom of her lavender skirt brushes the sidewalk. From a distance she reminds me of Masha. Right up to the moment she catches her foot on a lip in the concrete and gracefully regains her balance.

I palm a hundred-dollar bill I had placed in the pocket of the threadbare jacket I bought at the secondhand store in Prague. Cross the street to the covered drive, alert for movement in the parked SUV but seeing none. Posnova's disguise seems to have worked so far. Her bag has been loaded into the back of a cab by the time I arrive. The bellhop takes her arm and helps her inside. He straightens, wearing a look of disappointment at no tip. I clap him on the back and say, "Thanks." He steps to the side as I slide into the seat next to Posnova, stick the hundred through the slot in the glass partition, and tell the driver, "The Shea Hotel on West Fifty-ninth, please." He roars off.

Posnova stiffens. Her indigo eyes narrow and then suddenly flare with apprehension at the pointed press of the barrel of Elephant Ears's little revolver into her side.

"Who are you?" she says.

"You already know that."

The cabbie cranks rap music. The hundred has purchased his indifference to his charges.

"I saw you yesterday, but that doesn't mean I know who you are or what you want."

I don't like her patronizing tone. She is used to men treating her with deference, apparently, accustomed to a scraping approach. I suppress the welling fury that threatens to explode. "You know both of those things."

She pouts out a sultry lower lip. "I think you have me confused with another." She molts out of the shawl, twisting and turning so that her breasts thrust against the silky blue blouse that matches her eyes, playing the seductress.

I press the pistol harder into her flank and stare out the window at the passing buildings, willing them to move faster.

"Where are you taking me?"

"To a quiet place where you can tell your husband to do what I say."

She ducks her head and pulls off the wig. Inky hair cascades over her shoulders as she raises her arms and arches her back. An evocative scent wafts up, fighting the stale cab smells of musty carpeting and unwashed bodies.

"Don't. Let's talk things over. Just you and me."

"No."

Her jaw hardens. "So you're his lap dog now, is that it?"

"At least I didn't marry him."

Her eyes grow cold, and her lips twist bitterly. "What do you know about anything?"

I know enough. She's the queen—the manipulating cause of Valya's misery. This creature thinks I can be worked on the grindstone of her beauty like Lipman or Pappalardo or Peter, and the time has come for her to learn how wrong she is.

I punch the barrel into her ribs so hard that it blows the breath from her body. A crackling sound tells me that one of her ribs is broken. She collapses into a gasping ball. The cabbie has angled the mirror down, pointing away from us, and is performing a seated jig to the beat of the music.

I pull Posnova close. Press her face into my jacket. Lock her right pinkie in my free hand and snap it back. The sound and sensation is like breaking a thick twig. I squeeze her tightly against my body to dampen her screams and bridle her thrashings. Four times I repeat the process, until all four fingers have been bent to impossible angles and she's quiet and still, passed out from pain.

I settle back into the ripped vinyl seat. My heart thuds slowly, heavily. My senses are heightened to the point where I seem able to feel the powerful surge of blood in my arteries carrying a rush of adrenaline. And something else—something deliciously awful, like an exotic drug.

I close my eyes as the familiar demon worms inside my soul, gripping like a millipede with talons for feet, whispering hate and hideous madness I thought had been left for dead in burned-out Grozny subbasements.

chapter 26

"This is Peter."

I grip Elephant Ears's cell phone like it's the head of a deadly snake. Posnova is splayed on the stained, fuzzy carpet of my hotel room, one among many cockroaches. My boot is pressed against her neck, pinning her in place. Ragged breaths rasp my throat like saw blades.

"Listen," I say, then lift my boot from her throat and lean to place the phone next to her mouth.

"Oh, God, help me, Peter. Oh, please, take this animal away—"

When I press my boot down she gurgles to a stop. By the time the phone reaches my ear he is breathing so hard that he sounds like a bellows.

"I like this, Peter," I say through clenched teeth. "I'm good at it."

His silence is all the answer I need. He has read my file. He knows the truth of it.

"Reattach Valya's foot. Make her better." Posnova's eyes are bulging. I ease up on my boot, and she inhales a sharp whistle of air.

"I will," he says hoarsely.

"How long?"

"I don't know. Six hours, maybe longer—"

"Get moving! Call me when it's done."

"Don't hurt her anymore."

I set the open phone on the floor next to Posnova. Press my hand to her mouth to muffle the impending scream. Twist a finger on her other hand until it snaps into the phone. Let her gagged howls of anguish provide his answer.

✠

Posnova remains unconscious for an hour. I use the time to lash her to a chair, tied with the twisted lengths of her own clothes. She is already beginning to bruise around the eyes, probably from the force of my arm pressing her face into my chest to dampen her screams. Her pupils are shock-dilated. She stares at me like I'm the devil.

"Tell me about Lipman."

When she moves her lips they crack thin red lines of blood. She hasn't had anything to eat or drink since I picked her up. I don't need water or food, and her comfort means less than nothing to me.

"I met him in Zurich. Three years ago. Can I please have water?"

Maybe I'm better than I once was. Or maybe I've been softened by hopefulness for Valya. The old me would have broken teeth to teach a lesson in responsiveness. "No. Tell me more about Lipman."

"I needed help developing believable provenances for forged works of art, usually by obscure artists. Rolf agreed."

"Leonardo da Vinci is not obscure. Nor is Pissarro."

Blue sparks of defiance leap from her eyes. "*Leda and the Swan* is no forgery!"

We're in agreement about that much. "How long have you been doing this?"

"Forging art?"

I nod.

"Four years. The Communists confiscated private collections—from the time of the revolution through both world wars. They confused provenance, sometimes deliberately, other times through sheer mismanagement. And the history of works going in and out of the Soviet Union is, well . . ." A glimmer of her magazine smile peeks through the pain and fear. She tweaks an eyebrow and uses a word I remember Lipman using. "Murky."

It is a wonder that our paths haven't crossed before. The General's cadre started with forgeries, then quickly moved on to the real thing after we decided that was the only way to build long-haul profits. We put Russia's artistic history on the auction block to aid her regeneration. Even supported by our other illicit machinations, our profits have been laughably insufficient. Maybe if all the black market profits in Russia could be harnessed the country might be restored to the path of prosperity, but as it is we erect paper parapets against hurricane winds.

"I moved Rolf to St. Petersburg and secured his job at the Hermitage," she continues.

"How did he discover the *Leda*?"

Something flickers in her eyes, as if she's accessed a mental file.

"Just as he told you. Hidden beneath the Mignard."

"Where is Lipman now?"

She takes too long to answer.

I offer no warning. Just grab a fistful of luxuriant hair and pull so hard that she and the chair lift off the floor. The skin on her face sucks so tightly she can't mouth a scream, only a low moan.

"When you think, you lie," I say, then drop her onto the floor.

Head down, she hiccups like a beaten child. I pace like a hungry lion in a small cage. More than a minute later she's still shaking.

"Where's Lipman?" I repeat.

"I don't know." She cowers, anticipating another attack. "I think he's back in Moscow, but except for a message sent from Prague a few days ago he has been incommunicado for over two weeks, since early June."

Shit! I've been chasing a Trojan horse. "Why was he in Prague?"

"To ship a painting by Mignard called *Clio* to me here in New York."

"What happened to *Leda and the Swan*?"

"I don't know—wait! Please don't hurt me anymore. I'm telling the truth. Rolf turned it over to someone while he tried to find a buyer—I think he was ordered to turn it over. Whoever Rolf gave the painting to betrayed all of us."

"Who ordered Lipman to turn over the paintings?"

"I don't know. All he would tell me about them is that they were government officials."

"Not your husband—not Peter Vyugin?"

"No. Peter only knew what he could surmise from having me watched. I think Rolf was talking about high-level politicians. Elected politicians."

"Who did Lipman give the paintings to?"

"I don't know, and he isn't telling. He's hiding. From you, from everybody."

How could Lipman possibly have lost the *Leda*? What politician would have had enough control over him to make him surrender the treasure of a lifetime, even temporarily? The very idea is ludicrous, but I believe that Posnova is telling the truth, at least as she knows it.

Maxim, the General, Peter, and now another group with the power of office behind them—I am beginning to think that I'm out of my league, that there are too many powerful players for a man like me to prevail. And too many connected points, far too many for me to decipher.

Posnova interrupts my thoughts. "Valya," she says. The name cascades off her tongue like softly flowing water. "Who is she?"

My back is to her. I watch a roach skitter up the wall in an antennae-waving search for food. "How did you leave it with Pappalardo?"

"You've got fat mobsters from Jersey looking all over the city for you. They took your picture pummeling the driver and sneaking in the halls."

The men I killed at the Medici Gallery were tame, like zoo animals, not the rabid predators and scavengers I'm used to dealing with in Russia and Southeast Asia. The problem with the Italian mob isn't trifling, but I doubt that it will follow me out of New York.

"What of Pappalardo?"

"He's booked a flight to Moscow tomorrow—I mean later today."

I ask for details, and she rushes to provide them. She has seen the demon inside me. I call the airline and book both of us on the four P.M. Delta flight out of JFK. I pace. I ponder. "What went wrong on the river in St. Petersburg?"

"Peter learned of the plan. I—well, I made a mistake, and he found out about the theft. He didn't know *what* we intended to steal, just that something was planned for that night. He tried to foil it by calling in a tip to the police about drug runners."

"What of Lipman and Arkady?"

She sneers, then winces when the movement opens a new line of blood on her lower lip. "Rolf only pretended to care for him."

Poor Arkady, I think again.

Just before noon, the satellite phone buzzes. I hit Talk and wait, too dry-mouthed to speak.

"She made it," says Peter.

"Let me talk to the doctor."

"What?" he says stupidly.

Posnova lolls unconscious on the floor, still tied but no longer sitting up in the chair. I still haven't given her food or water. All I have to do is squeeze her ruined hand to make her whimper loudly enough for him to hear. She comes to in dazed slo-mo, groaning.

"Stop," Peter says. "I'll get him."

Posnova writhes on the filthy carpet while I watch indifferently, marking time. More than five minutes pass, too long if all Peter needed to do was summon the doctor. I try not to think about what that probably implies.

"Hello?"

The voice on the phone rides a quavering tremolo. I can't remember how the round doctor sounded that gloomy day in Prague. The hissing, thumping machines keeping Valya alive distracted me too much. "Is this Valya's doctor?"

"Uh, yes."

I don't like the hesitation. It means he is looking to someone else to help with his answers. "Tell me how she's doing."

"She'll recover."

"What of her foot?"

He coughs. "The reattachment may or may not take. Even if it does, she'll walk with a limp for the rest of her life."

"What are the chances?"

He hesitates.

"Tell me the truth!"

"Slim at best."

I deliberately slow my breathing, trying to ratchet down my pounding heart. "How long before she can leave?"

"Two weeks minimum, if it takes. If not . . . sooner."

"What do they have on you?"

Six thousand miles away and I can still hear his breath catch. I give it a moment, until it becomes clear that he is not going to answer.

"Is it your family?"

The doctor's cutoff sob answers my question and tells me that I don't need to kill him. Then Peter comes back on the line.

"Let me talk to my wife," he demands.

"Keep Valya safe."

"Don't hurt her anymore!"

This time I am the one to hang up the phone to cut off his pleas.

chapter 27

The remainder of the time before the flight passes slowly. I just have to look at her hands, and Posnova babbles, but I don't care to talk very much. At one point during the long wait I ask her whom Pappalardo might be traveling with.

"I don't know." She catches my hardened eyes, moans, and starts pushing against the dirty carpet with her feet to try to scoot away from me. "I swear."

"Where in Moscow is he going?"

"I don't know that, either. But I think he knows how to contact Rolf."

Every fiber of my body thrills with the hope that I might be given the chance to square the debt with the art restorer.

When the time to leave finally arrives I swaddle Posnova in sunglasses and a bulky overcoat with a high collar for the trip to JFK. "Keep your hands in the pockets," I tell her.

Her mangled, blood-ballooning fingers need medical attention they won't get anytime soon. She is thoroughly cowed, sloshed in Percocet from my private stash. Head bowed, she shakes with an unrelenting ague as she follows me to the terminal and docilely submits to security checks. Once we've checked in, I drag her to a bank of phones and call Vadim using a calling card I purchased at a gift shop in the airport. No answer, and no voice mail, either. Vadim loathes that kind of technology. So I call Nabi and leave him a voice mail with our flight information and instructions on where to meet us at the airport in Moscow.

Pappalardo boards first class, his haughty chin like the leading edge of an icebreaker cutting through the wadded crowd in front of the gate. Looking dazzling in lavender felt with a matching fedora, he bumps his shoulder-slung duffel through those waiting for coach. He's '60s chic, an antimobster, far removed from the gallery owner dressed in inescapable black. I'm familiar with the breed. Moscow is a playground to him, a place where meaningless amounts of money will buy anything he desires, where he's free to act out forbidden impulses. He's traveling alone, apparently unconcerned by Posnova's absence, reclining and sipping white wine, and he fails to notice the huddled couple passing him in the aisle on the way to the back of the plane.

The DC-10 buzzes the Arctic, so close we seem enveloped in white. Lights out, movie over, Posnova and most of the other passengers fall asleep. If anyone is awake they pay no attention when I slip past the curtain into the first-class cabin, open the overhead compartment above Pappalardo's sleeping form and remove his duffel. It's leather with gold-zippered compartments.

Back in my seat, I systematically search the contents. Neatly folded beige linen suit, powder blue shirt, silk underwear—obviously a change of clothes to get by in case his checked luggage is lost. Toiletry bag loaded with multicolored pills in sufficient quantity to make a pharmacist proud. Some I know. Viagra, Prozac, Valium. Others I don't recognize. A slim laptop computer resides in a separate pouch.

I set it on my knees and pop the top. He's a fool. The default setting automatically reads his password. I'm inside in three clicks, only to learn instantly why he was so lax about security. The laptop holds almost nothing. Spreadsheeted financial statements for the gallery, undoubtedly cooked to show more earnings than it has. Dirty money in, clean out, another one of many mob laundries. A half-finished memorandum discussing a delayed shipment of a Kandinsky oil painting. Pass-coded e-mail files I can't access.

Then I click the Pictures icon, and there she is, Leda in all of her uncovered beauty, shown in a studio-quality photo. The painting is propped against a light blue background. The light from Leda's curved thighs, the swan's belly, and the babes emerging from the eggs contrasts with the stiffening darkness of the valley of bulrushes to make her appear three-dimensional, almost jumping off the canvas and through the screen. Pappalardo's trip is about more than two forged Pissarros.

Another picture shows Da Vinci's *Last Supper,* hopelessly lost in decayed tempura but still beautiful nonetheless. The photo appears to have been taken from a slight angle by someone standing in the back of the Santa Marie refectory. It is not a stock photo. A portion of the railing that separates the painting from the throngs of visitors that view it daily is visible in the bottom-right corner. I wonder how the picture was taken despite the security on site to ensure no flashes that might accelerate the deterioration of the painting.

Posnova stirs, groans unconscious agony. I replace the computer, swipe four Valiums, and return the bag to the bin above Pappalardo. Two hours left. Sleep is hopeless.

chapter 28

As soon as the plane lands at the Sheremetevo-2 airport in a mid-morning drizzle, I push Posnova ahead through the crowded aisles, working to stay close to my prey in the first-class area. Pappalardo disembarks onto the gangway a dozen people ahead of us. By the time we reach the customs queue the gap has narrowed to three. Standing in the line for foreign visitors, he glances back once, casually. We are in the shorter line for nationals, less than five meters away from him, but his gaze sweeps past the hooded Posnova without a hint of recognition.

We clear customs. Pappalardo winds through the crowd to the baggage claim while Posnova and I hurry past him through two sets of sliding doors to mingle with the crowds in the main terminal area. He strides through the doors a few minutes later, pushing a cart loaded with luggage, heading for the taxi line.

We follow him outside. Nabi is waiting in the Mercedes under the shelter of a concrete awning next to loading cars, honking taxis, and buses belching yellow smoke. The drizzling rain patters overhead. Runoff from the awning forms oil-slicked puddles that I splash

Posnova through to shove her into the backseat ahead of me. Nabi spies her in the rearview and twists suddenly for a better look. He's clearly surprised, but not by her beauty, which shines even through the concealing glasses and hood. Something else has drawn his attention. He turns to face forward before I can discern what it is.

I slide into the backseat beside her and toss Elephant Ears's cell phone on the seat next to him. "Charge it and bring it to me at the loft."

He nods jerkily. His eye ticks. He starts to ask about the woman next to me, but wisely holds his tongue.

Ahead, Pappalardo is loading his bags into a cab. I point him out through the rain-beaded front window. "Stay close."

We follow Pappalardo's cab past the tank stoppers into the city center, where he takes up residence in the National Hotel.

"Get out," I tell Nabi. "Watch him. Call me if he moves."

"S-s-sure, b-b-boss."

I drag Posnova into the front seat with me. She follows my lead without protest when I glance at her hands to ensure compliance. Nabi looks back into the car. He again appears ready to say something, but I speed off with my wounded hostage before he can.

During daylight hours the lower levels of the building that houses the loft are operating businesses, with enough people coming and going that we're safely anonymous when I use my card key to ride the elevator to the supposedly abandoned sixth floor. I handcuff Posnova to the radiator grill in the main room, feed her three of Pappalardo's Valium, and retire to my bedroom.

Lying in bed, I key the number for Peter into the Nokia.

"Hello?"

"It's Volk."

He clears his throat. That's all, a common enough sound, but it tells me everything I need to know. "I'm going to kill this bitch, you motherfucker."

"Wait a minute! It's not that bad, Volk! You live without a foot. We tried, goddammit!"

"Let me talk to the doctor."

"Don't you fucking kill her!"

"Give me the doctor."

Several minutes pass. I'm dizzy, nauseous, near tears for Valya's lost limb.

"Hello?"

"How long before she can be moved?"

"Several days, maybe, with help."

"Give her drugs for the pain. Help her, please."

"I'll do my best," the doctor says quietly.

I swallow two Ambien and settle back into the bed, filled with hate, and bitterness, and more hate.

✦

Valya cries in agony, "Help me! Oh, God, please help me!" It is so unlike her to show fear, let alone such agonized terror, that the sound bolts me upright. I'm covered in cold sweat, my heart races, my palm slaps the reassuring grip of the Sig—

And then the high ceilings and gunmetal gray steel of the loft blanket me in familiar safety. I'm home. Ten hours have passed. The whimpering cries are coming from the woman chained to the radiator in the main room. A shrill whistle warning me that someone is riding the elevator up to my floor punctuates her sobs.

I jump off the sweat-dampened sheets and hop without my prosthesis into the main room, passing Posnova without sparing her a glance. A monitor in the kitchen offers various views of the outside of the loft. In one, Nabi's scruffy face stares bug-eyed up at the camera. I buzz him in.

I'm dressed only in shorts. His eyes fasten on my uncovered stump—a shocking sight to the uninitiated, graced as it is with abraded scars jagging all the way up the muscles of my thigh.

"J-j-just checking in," he says. "The g-g-guy hasn't moved. I th-th-think he's jet-lagged. One of my m-m-men is on it."

Nabi hands me the cell phone, breaks his gaze from my stump, and cranes his neck to ogle Posnova. Through what must be unremitting agony her eyes squint a communiqué I can't identify, but the meaningful look is there, impossible to ignore, like a turd in a crystal punchbowl. Even slowed as I am by oversleeping and drugs, the implications of the exchange start crawling the pathways of my mind.

"Meet me in the café in an hour," I tell him.

He tears his gaze away from the wounded woman. "S-s-sure. Okay, boss," he says, then backs out the door.

I fill a bowl with water and place it within Posnova's reach. Her wrists are cuffed around the radiator, so she'll have to lap like a dog if she wants to drink. I dial the number in Prague.

Peter picks up on the first ring.

"Volkovoy?" he says. He sounds out of breath.

"How is Valya?"

"When can we make the exchange?"

"No exchange. I'll let Posnova go when I get Valya back."

"That's not fair. We are trading equal value."

"Valya is not a goddamn horse, Peter. And you carved her up, you fucker. You'll do it my way or this goes to the General, first thing. What did you call him—the midget general? My guess is that he could cause serious problems for you in St. Petersburg. How would you like Putin's boys on your ass, poking around in your business?"

"I should have killed you in Prague."

"That's true, because the second thing is that if I ever get you alive I'm going to tie you down and set you on fire."

"You're psychotic, you know that?"

"Put Valya on Aeroflot flight seven-twelve from Prague three days from now. Make sure she has whatever help she needs. Yes?"

"Yes," he says in a voice that is so tight it sounds as if he is choking.

"Let me talk to her."

He starts to say more, but stops. I hear the rustling sound of the phone transferring hands.

"My love," she says.

My good leg buckles, and I collapse on the floor in a rush of emotion so powerful I can't feel anything else. The molded plastic of the phone creaks. I have to release the pressure of my grip to prevent it from shattering. I am unable to contain my relief, even as Posnova's gaze stays glued to me and a private smile plays at the corners of her crusty lips.

✦

Nabi nervously digs his toe into the slate floor of my basement office while Vadim serves black coffee thick as tar and stands wordlessly off to the side, the kind of man who fades into the background when he wants to. I gulp the scalding liquid, trying to drown my rage and sorrow.

"The w-w-woman you b-b-brought. She's in b-b-bad shape. We should t-t-take her t-t-to a d-d-doctor."

Nabi is concerned about Posnova, of all things. I try without success to recall an instance when he cared for the well-being of another person. "Revenue is off fifty percent," I tell him.

"I t-t-told you, Nigel B-b-bolles is n-n-no good anymore."

He is days past a shave. The uneven stubble of his beard tracks too high on his cheekbones, all the way to the crisscrossing wrinkles beneath his eyes. Age and too many parties have mixed gray in with the black. When his left eye ticks, the gray hairs flash reflected light from the uncovered bulb above my table.

"Bring Bolles to me tomorrow afternoon," I tell him, then wave him out.

He shrugs into a jacket and leaves just as the Nokia buzzes an incoming number I don't recognize. "What?"

"Two soldiers are dead," says the General.

A moment ticks past while I gather my thoughts, recalling Gromov's contract to kill the two soldiers who tried to pass him a fake Shah Diamond, the contract Leonid the broken soldier had told me about. "Gromov's soldiers?"

"No. Two others."

I must be obtuse. I can't make a connection.

"They were the two I sent to Uzhhorod in the Ukraine," he says. "They photographed Lipman passing through the checkpoint into Slovakia."

I still don't see a connection that makes them worthy of killing, except that they are part of the General's corps of men. Another link starts to nibble at the corners of my mind—there, then gone, like a gossamer strand in a spider's web, visible only in the light cast from certain angles.

"Are the police involved yet?" I ask.

"Not yet. The bodies were discovered in the arsenal barracks. They are still there. You need to investigate."

"I'll be right over."

"Captain Dubinin will bring you through the tunnels," he says, then hangs up before I can ask him who Dubinin is.

Before leaving for the arsenal, I spend a moment at the table in the café with Vadim. "Tell me about Nabi," I say.

He settles into the chair across from me. Imagine a hungry mouse, but don't be deceived by looks. Vadim is a Gypsy. Somewhere in his fifties, I think, but it's hard to tell. He spent the decade of the '80s surviving in an Arkhangelsk work camp, outliving far more impressive physical specimens. The Communists learned to be relentless persecutors under the tutelage of Stalin and his henchmen. Vadim takes pride in outlasting them.

His gaze holds mine steadily. "Nabi's not right," he says in his usual blunt way. He rolls Jian Shen balls in his right hand, making the muscles of his forearm ripple beneath the washed-out blue numbers branded into his skin. "He's been to see Maxim, I think."

Nabi doesn't know enough to reveal anything truly sensitive to Maxim, or at least I don't believe so. But he can slowly destroy my business by stealing my leads or tipping my competitors to my plans. Worse, he might have divulged my travel plans and placed Valya in harm's way. I inquire for more with raised eyebrows.

Vadim's lips thin. The balls stop circling in his palm. "He sold out."

Valya says I'm soft at the wrong times, and maybe she's right. All I can think is that Nabi is an ex-soldier. He ate the same mud and shit as me in Chechnya. Besides, I pay him enough to stay loyal.

"I need proof," I say.

Vadim rolls the balls and offers a barely perceptible shrug. "Pictures?"

"No. Just hard evidence, from your eyes or mine."

"Okay."

I follow him up the stairs. He heads for the kitchen. I stride out the door to take a look at two dead soldiers.

chapter 29

Captain Dubinin has square shoulders and a bushy mustache that seems poised to leap off his stony face. As he leads me through the Tainitskaya Tower tunnel and across the Kremlin grounds I recognize him as my familiar escort by the stiff way he carries his back.

The arsenal barracks are painted gray wood and steel, built with Stalin permanency. Dubinin heads for one of the hangarlike buildings that has been designated *D-230* in stenciled paint. Two guards flanking the outer door salute as we pass through.

The entryway is curled linoleum, walled off from the main sleeping area. The walls are coffee brown marred by darker water stains. Another guard blocks the inner door, holding a Kalashnikov across the front of his body. He stands aside after giving Dubinin a grim-faced salute.

We step into an open room, maybe fifteen meters wide by twenty long, cut by two parallel lines of steel support beams. The powerful musk of many men living together in close quarters thickens the air. Neatly made cots and gunmetal gray lockers line the walls. Green woolen blankets stretch tightly across each cot. On the other side of the room, two more soldiers stand rigidly at attention, partially obstructing the view through an open doorway behind them. The squared opening and the room beyond are coated with small tiles the color of stale mustard. I have spent enough years in such places to know that the door leads into a communal head. Our boots boom hollow echoes as we cross the raised steel floor decking.

Dubinin's gesture sends the guards scurrying aside to let us pass. I follow him inside.

The tiled floor slopes to a centered drain. The far wall is lined with stainless steel sinks below a long mirror that has been rubbed dull. Another tiled opening with a raised curb leads to a communal shower room with nozzles projecting from the walls every meter or so. The floor along the shower walls drops to form a moatlike drain.

Before us, looking like dead jellyfish, sprawl two naked bodies gleaming under the harsh overhead lights. Legs splayed wide, backs propped against the walls, ass-first in the drainage channel. The mustard wall behind them is sprayed with twin peacock tails of shiny body fluids. The smell of blood and feces fouls the air. One soldier's head is pitched down. A bib of drained blood covers his hairy chest. The other soldier's head is cocked to one side, as if he is waiting for the answer to an important question. Lines of grout carry tributaries of fluids away from the thickening pools around the bodies.

Dubinin points out each soldier as he says their names, which I immediately forget. They were killed for something they did or saw, not for who they were.

"He stuck the gun barrel down their throats," Dubinin says.

Maybe he knows more than I do. "Who did?"

The captain stares blankly at me, obviously confused by the question. Blinks. "That's what we're here to find out," he says finally.

I squat next to the questioning soldier, pulling powdery surgeon's gloves over my hands. In life he had cheeks sprayed with blackheads and soft fuzz. "When did this happen?"

"This morning, between six and seven hundred hours. Before

and after those times the barracks were busy. Too busy for this." He points down at the bodies and waggles his mustache. "Even with a silencer."

Someone made the soldiers swallow bullets. That much is certain from the nature of the wounds. The two broken holes in the tile behind them are low on the wall, so they were already seated when the shots were fired. I pull the knife from the sheath buried in my prosthesis, ignoring Dubinin's appraising glance at the sudden appearance of the blade, and use it to probe the holes. The tile was set over concrete. The tip of the blade dislodges both mutilated bullets. The rounds appear large enough to have come from Gromov's .45-caliber hand cannon. But how could Gromov have entered the barracks? Still squatting, I hand the rounds to Dubinin.

"Do you have access to a lab?"

He nods.

"Caliber and make. Check for matches." The last part is a long shot. Russia's criminal justice system is antiquated at best, so he won't have many records to match against. Information is gathered haphazardly and rarely shared among law enforcement agencies—one of many legacies of a post-revolutionary police force designed to apprehend selected enemies of the state rather than locate and arrest mere criminals.

He nods again.

"Were these men assigned to guard the treasures in the armory?"

He takes a step back. "Why do you ask that?"

His surprise seems genuine. I don't think he knows of the theft of the Shah Diamond or of Gromov's foiled plan to steal it again. The General has not revealed all of his secrets to his prized captain. "Just answer the question," I tell him.

"No. The armory guards are housed elsewhere."

Even if the General is right about their deaths being related to their role as spies watching for Lipman in Uzhhorod, why kill them now, after they photographed Lipman and ended their role in the affair? "Who has access to this place?"

He shrugs. "Too many to count. It is not a tightly controlled area. Not anymore."

"Are civilians allowed here?"

He shakes his head. "Only military visitors. And they are logged."

"Get me the logs."

He makes a note in a palm-sized spiral notebook like a reporter.

"Get me copies of their orders, going back two months." The soldiers' assignments might tell me something about why they were killed. Or they might not.

Dubinin writes another note in his little book.

More can be done here, I know. A good forensics team would have a field day with the evidence—sifting, scraping, probing, measuring, marking, bagging, testing. But I believe that I already know the who of it, if not the why. And, once again, I feel the familiar tightness across my chest, like a cinched steel band that tells me that a master puppeteer is manipulating the strings.

Just after dusk that same day I wait in the alleyway behind Gromov's Jaguar dealership. A wobbly prostitute with demented eyes approaches me. Crazily applied lipstick turns her leer into a bloody slash. I push her on her way and then slide back into a nook in the wall. She's still staggering down the alley when Gromov's Mercedes SUV rounds the corner and growls toward my hiding place. The prostitute lurches to the side to avoid its onrushing grill. It stops less than a meter away from me. Gromov opens the door and starts to get out. One step and I'm on him, poking the barrel of the Sig into his ribs, pushing him back until I'm next to him inside the vehicle. His whole body grows rigid. The driver sees me in the rearview mirror, grunts, and starts to turn around.

"Tell him to keep driving," I say.

"Keep driving," Gromov says hoarsely, and the driver edges the SUV ahead.

"Give me your gun."

Gromov struggles to shift his weight to free his overcoat and reach his hand underneath. He fetches a .40-caliber Glock and hands it to me.

"Not that one. The Colt."

"I don't have it."

"Where is it?"

His brows knit together. He licks his lips. "I don't know." He holds out his palms against my scowl. "Swear, Volk. I came home a couple of days ago, and it wasn't in the holster. Maybe it was picked. I don't know."

I used to think I was good at separating lies from truth. I am no longer delusional about such things, but in this instance my gut tells me that Gromov is telling the truth. I pocket the Glock. Prod the driver in the back of the head with the muzzle of the Sig. "Stop here."

Gromov looks confused as I step from the vehicle and trudge away, dialing Dubinin as I go.

Dubinin meets me a short while later at the Botkin Hospital morgue, wearing a black overcoat with silver epaulettes and a dour expression. He hands me a file.

I raise an eyebrow.

"You asked for copies of the soldiers' orders and the barracks logs, remember?"

The soupy reek of cadavers, drained blood, and pungent formaldehyde coats the place like a mad scientist's blanket. The icy sterility of the corpses on the autopsy tables sickens me in a way that the freshly dead never have.

Dubinin aims his mustache in the direction of a white-smocked medical examiner preparing a saw blade for the next skull while his assistant busily snaps pictures. "The M.E. tells me the cause of death in both cases was gunshot wounds to the head. Remarkably insightful, don't you think?"

The M.E. sniffs, flips a switch on the side of the saw, and presses the whining blade into the skull of the corpse. I'm not sure which of the two soldiers is lying on the slab. A red tag blossoming on the big toe would tell me, if I cared to look.

"What about the bullets?" I have to raise my voice to be heard over the screech of the saw.

"Forty-five caliber."

Not the Glock I just took from Gromov, then. The Glock is a .40-caliber, meaning it leads nowhere, or to another corpse I don't care about. The saw grinds to a stop. The M.E. splits the skull. He looks happier now, absorbed in his work. Fluids drain from the decapitated skull through holes in the metal table and accumulate in a basin, where they are routed through a polyurethane tube into a stainless steel collections tank. A small-parts dissection table with matching drainage holes awaits the brain, which the M.E. is studying in place the same way a child might examine a new toy before playing with it.

Dubinin wrinkles his nose. "We'll know more when ballistics is finished."

I leave them together—the dour captain, the newly cheery M.E., and the industrious assistant. Head for the loft with my hands thrust into the deep pockets of my overcoat. Brooding.

Back in the loft Posnova lies passed out on the painted concrete floor next to the radiator. I go to my bedroom and study the files Dubinin gave me. The dead soldiers worked together most of the time, probably one of many special teams maintained by the General. Their assignment to Uzhhorod to look for Lipman crossing the border was described only as "ongoing surveillance for suspected smuggling activity."

A few days before that, they were briefly transferred to a unit stationed at an air force base near Vladikavkaz in the south, where they were assigned to an unspecified "transport operation." Something about the date—within a few weeks after I lost the *Leda*—and the nature of the operation triggers an elusive association in my mind, but I can't figure out what it is until I read the barracks logs. They show a five A.M. visit by discharged artillery major Leonid Gribakin on the morning the soldiers were shot. He logged out just over an hour later.

The dead soldiers' assignment in Vladikavkaz, combined with Leonid's name in the log book, has reminded me of the Antonov-32 cargo plane that crashed in the Iranian desert while ferrying heavy armor and other weapons from Russia to Tehran. But the only connection I can make among those events is that I saw the news of the plane crash while sitting in Leonid's flat.

I close Dubinin's file. Technically, the murder investigation is over. I still don't know *why* the soldiers were killed, but now I know *who* killed them.

The insistently buzzing Nokia wakens me later that night. The sound repeats itself until it threatens to saw my brain in half. I answer without saying anything.

"Volk?"

I don't recognize the voice. "Who's this?"

"Yuri," says the baton-twirling cop. "I'm outside that gallery. You know, the one where you found the body on hooks."

"And?"

"A light's on."

The digital clock next to the bed glows 2:54 A.M. "Wait for me there," I tell him and end the call.

chapter 30

The Mercedes glides over wet streets, carrying me to the park across from Novodevichy Convent in minutes. Yuri waits in the shadows on Luzhnetsky Street, slapping his nightstick against his overcoat. He clambers into the rolling car. I kill the lights and coast around the corner to a stop behind a dark delivery truck parked against the curb across the street from the gallery.

Yuri was right. On the other side of the metal gate the display window of the gallery glows diffused amber. "Key?"

He extends the big iron key we used before. "Do you remember the alarm code?"

I take the key and quietly press the door closed without answering such a foolish question. He follows me out just as silently.

"Wait here," I whisper. "Be careful."

He looks around at the empty streets. "Of what?"

"Of whoever is in there," I tell him, pointing toward the gallery.

I leave him and approach the entrance. The key twists, I press, and the gate inches open with hardly a squeak. Then I'm inside, squatting to present a smaller target. The light on the alarm pad glows green. It is unarmed.

I pause to take stock of the situation. Draw the Sig. Pull the knife from the cavity in my prosthesis. Its sharkskin grip is reassuring, even as the feel of it takes me back to times when we had to root rebels out of their burrows in bombed-out Grozny buildings. Most of the gutted shells were occupied by innocents as well as by the guerrillas we sought. The fighting was close, deadly work, dreadful in unfamiliar confines that concealed waiting blades, trip wire shotguns, suicidal machine gunners, land mines, and, worst of all, fighters holding child shields.

I clench the knife in my teeth and slide forward on my haunches, the Sig held ready. Pass through the lit chromed reception area to a nook outside the double-swinging doors. The display area behind the doors is dark.

I listen hard for noise, sensitive to every shifting current of air that might signal a moving body. Nothing moves or makes a sound.

I wait.

A horn honks in the distance. A car or truck rumbles along the street. Someone sniffs, just the tiniest intake of air, but enough. The sniffer is on the other side of the doors, on the left.

Time to go. Fast or slow, downside either way. It's a personal thing. I go fast. Roll through. Pop up hard and leap to the side. Roll again as I hear the singing thwack of a silenced bullet hitting the wall beside me. Lead with the thrown knife into a scrambling ball of terrified man, who drops his gun in the face of my bull rush.

He says, "No!" as I ram the Sig into his belly to muffle the discharge and cut loose two quick rounds. He grunts and collapses in a gurgling heap. I twist to face the main gallery—too late. The swinging doors mark the passage of the gutshot man's partner. I hope that Yuri was ready.

The dying man is choking blood, thrashing. I wrap my fist in his hair and twist his head so that I can study his face. Fleshy chin covered in blood, flared nostrils, panicky eyes—impossible to tell the color in the darkness. Nobody I know. I don't know what the right thing to do is. Who really does in these cases? So I choose the way I would prefer and blow a round through his head to end it fast.

I yank a torch from my overcoat pocket and shine it around. The gallery is mostly the same as it was on the night when Valya and I found Arkady in his eternal dive. He is long gone. Only the dried stain of whatever poured out of his body remains. Crumpled police tape, discarded plastic bags, and chalky fingerprint powder have replaced the rest of him. On the floor next to a wall is a blocky piece of machinery. When I get closer I see that it is a power generator, still shiny and new. Next to it is a saw with a gleaming circular blade. The writing on the side of the blade claims it is edged in diamonds capable of cutting through concrete.

I pick up my knife, snap off the torch, and rush outside. My cursory search lasted for less than thirty seconds—too long, perhaps—but I don't think the difference mattered. Yuri was unprepared at the fatal moment when the door burst open and he came face-to-face with whoever ran from the gallery wielding a silenced pistol.

The little cop is a crumpled pile in the wet street. Russet rainwater beads his overcoat. I kneel at his side and rip open the clothes covering his chest. Probe. Find a hole, high on his left side, pumping crimson trails of blood. A radio is attached to his belt. I key it on and position it under his body to keep the channel open, all the while scanning the street. It's quiet. Just one chugging car. But then a shadow darts through the trees in the park, and I'm back up, running hard.

I chase the runner through the park to Luzhnetsky Street. I'm closing in when he suddenly jets into and over the shrubs lining the high wall that separates the street from Novodevichy Cemetery. I follow. Hit the wall running, slice open my palm on one of the glass shards embedded in the cement top, and land awkwardly on the other side, torquing my right knee. Resting amid the underbrush, I listen for movement, trying to control the pounding of my racing heart while I stanch the flow of blood with the fabric of my overcoat.

Thickets rustle and drip sooty Moscow rain. In the distance a train blows a forlorn song. I scrape along the wall behind mounds of flowers that bury the gravestone of Raisa Gorbachev. Listening, hearing nothing save the pattering drizzle and chirping crickets. Famed sculpted figures loom larger than life. Icons to the dead, shifting in the waving shadows of oak and birch, beckoning me deeper, closer to Russia's past—science, medicine, war, all overlaid by art and politics, represented here in sarcophagal splendor. Chekhov is buried a worm's crawl away from a diplomat, a symbolic linkage of Russian art and politics, in death as in life. The maggots and moldering flesh and faded finery inside the caskets are nothing to me, not after the brutality of Chechnya. The tombstone memorials—representational art romanticizing lives terrible and noble—are far more unsettling.

A twig cracks, rifle-shot loud. The sound is followed by running steps and huffing breaths. It may be a ploy to lure me into a trap, but I can't afford to wait, so I push away from the wall and follow. Past the two-faced diplomat, past the surgeon's hands holding the throbbing ruby heartstone, deeper, past the sublime ballerina frozen in her forever pirouette, around the miniature rocket ship and the scaled tank, and finally, there, I glimpse a running man with trailing tails from an overcoat born aloft by air and speed. As the surrounding trees thin out I can see him more clearly, turning now, moonlight glinting on round glasses, but he's not looking toward me. His head is rotating to the side instead, and then he's plucked by an unseen hand and tossed into a clump under Eisenstein's brooding tomb. I skid to a stop and crouch behind a wiry bush.

He fell ten long paces away, but I can see that Henri Orlan is still alive. His right hand flutters as he cries out weakly. But then he jerks strangely as two misty mushroom clouds fountain from his wet coat where it covers his chest, and he slumps quietly still.

I hug the ground, crab hard left, knowing what is coming next. Sure enough, leaves and severed branches shower down upon me as the killer loosens round after silenced round in a patterned grid. Firing back blindly would be a waste of time, so I crouch behind an oak. When the whizzing bullets stop, I shift as quietly as I can to press my ear hard to the ground. The vibrating thud of footsteps tells me that my new adversary is running away.

I creep stealthily through the brush to Orlan's body, hoping against reality, but he's dead. A quick search finds nothing, so I'm off at careful speed, tracking new prey. He left a wet trail in the grass, which I follow slowly for fear of ambush. Soon I arrive at another wall and scramble over, out of the cemetery and into a narrow alley. I see no sign of my quarry. In the distance, spuming lights and squawking police radios say that Yuri's body has been found. I head away from the sound, hurrying between two apartment buildings, then past closed eateries and a store peddling cell phones.

I cover several blocks before deciding it is fruitless to keep going. I change direction suddenly, just in time to see a big form turn quickly away. Cursing my own foolishness for not thinking he could follow me even more easily than I him, I pound after the fleeing shape, which never looks back, only straight ahead, running at least as fast as I am, and then it dives left through what looks to be a wall.

At the place where he disappeared, driving techno beats heavy on hammering bass thrum a metal door built into a brick wall at street level. Crisscrossing tire irons grace the front of the door. Crimson neon lights above the door announce *CrowBar*. I push through the door into a stairwell so narrow I have to turn my shoulders to the side to fit. Ten steps down, a bouncer looms on a landing. He's a bare-chested Buddha with hoop earrings, a devil tattoo starting on his neck and crawling down his fat-ringed torso, rouged lips, and running purple eye shadow.

"Hello, sweetie," he greets me.

I push past him without a word and clop down more metal-lattice steps into strobing colored lights, like a movie made of stills flipped one after the other to reveal a roiling sea of upturned faces. The faces wear expressions of drugged ecstasy, anger, lust, jealousy, rhapsody, and—there off center stage to the right a slash of purple light reveals the silhouette of a bulky man pushing his way purposefully through the heaving throng.

I plow partyers, heedless of the flying bodies in my wake. Faces materialize and then disappear, frightened by whatever they see in my face. Someone blocks my way with a forearm wrapped in a leather bracelet sprouting silver spikes. Finger lock, wrist lock, a shiver of snapping bone more felt than heard over the pounding beat of the music, and he falls away.

The back consists of a short hall and doorless unisex bathrooms. The music and revelry are still loud, but the noise is muted somewhat here, the difference between a shrieking jet engine ten meters away and another that is fifty. Ignoring offended shouts, I shoulder-twist urinal users to check faces, sending sprays of arcing piss into the queue; open wooden stalls with my crashing boot, startling a kissing couple; slam into the next bathroom to find a girl on her knees puking into a shit-filled bowl. Howling rage I push back into a hallway that's become even more crowded, jammed with ogling drunks waiting to see the spectacle—waiting to see me beaten into submission.

The Buddha bouncer wields a sap, wearing a scowl instead of a leer. On the steps above and behind him a thin man in an oversized orange suit points a pistol. He is the owner, I assume, here to cover while the hired help does the dirty work.

I am enraged beyond reason. Valya is in pieces. Baton-twirling Yuri is dead on my watch. Orlan is dog food in Novodevichy Cemetery, no good to me anymore, unable to tell me where he intended to use the diamond-coated blade to cut through concrete. Whoever killed them is gone, and I don't have any fucking answers.

I use a straight kick, no fancy roundhouse or sideways movement, just up and out, that fast. My steel-toed boot crunches Buddha's nose, splashing gory red petals like a blooming rose. As he falls away I leap and grab a length of exposed pipe, hoping it holds. Jackknife over dazed clubbers to land on the same step as the orange-suited man, who stares outright astonishment, as if I am a magically appeared apparition. The gun wrenches easily from his grasp. I put it to use pummeling his face and, when he's down fetal, to pound his exposed neck and back.

When I'm finished, when some of my rage has been dissipated, I toss the gun clattering down the stairs. The crowd appears to be at the end of a long, roaring tunnel, cowered back, pressing the walls, seeming to look at me through white orbs instead of eyes. *Good.* Let the lesson sink home. Let them experience the tiniest taste of reality, let them see what manner of animal delivers the drugs, the whores, the guns, and the cheap liquor and cigarettes without labels. I stare them all down before trooping off through the blaring music and oblivious ravers on the main floor. Only when I'm on the last set of stairs leading up to the street does my gaze fall on the camera suspended from the ceiling, red light burning.

Outside, two police cars pull to a squealing stop, radios squawking. A girl with a face full of metal piercings points me out. The cops slap cuffs onto my wrists and roughly shove me into the back of a squad car. One of them works the radio as we pull away. He tells the dispatcher they've got a cop killer in the car.

chapter 31

Viktor, dead Yuri's commander, slams his fists on his desk. "He was my nephew, goddamn you, Volk! How the fuck am I going to explain this to my sister?"

I am not unsympathetic. I liked Yuri, too. But time is my enemy. Already an hour has passed since my arrest outside the bar. "I need the tapes from the cameras at the CrowBar."

His jaw drops. "You gotta be kidding me. I got dead people everywhere, one of them a cop. I got a respectable businessman turned to pulp in front of about two dozen witnesses. I'm running paraffin tests on you right now."

"I wasn't the shooter. Get the videotape."

"Fuck you, Volk! You don't pay me enough to cover up this much shit."

I pull out the Nokia and dial a special number for the General. It is after four in the morning, but I don't think he sleeps.

"Yes?" the General says after the first ring.

"I need help with the local police."

Viktor can only hear my side of the conversation, of course. He's staring at me with a dumbfounded look on his face. I want to reach over and shut his hanging jaw.

"They think I was involved in a shooting," I say to the General. "They've got it wrong. And I need them to get a videotape for me."

"Where are you, and where is the tape?"

I tell him.

Viktor narrows his eyes. I can see the wheels spinning in his mind. He is reassessing who I am and dying to know who is on the other end of the line.

"The videotape is important," I finish.

The line goes dead. I slip the Nokia back into my pocket.

"Who the fuck was that?" Viktor says.

I sit on the edge of his desk to take pressure off my stump. Check my watch while Viktor seethes at my silence. Several minutes pass that way.

"Get the fuck out of here, Volk," he says. "Get out before I throw you in jail on charges of murder and accessory to murder."

A knock sounds at the door.

"What?" Viktor shouts.

A timid head pokes in. "You have a phone call, sir. From the assistant chief."

An hour later I'm sitting in an unused interrogation room studying videotape of the scene in the CrowBar hallway before I burst in and started tossing bodies like potato sacks. Frame by frame—a series of pictures captured in color by the camera in the short hall, pictures showing how my Novodevichy Cemetery assailant had gotten away.

He shed his overcoat. Donned a rainbow-colored sweater he ripped off a comatose partyer huddled in a corner. Let me burst past him into the bathroom. Slipped away behind me. Simple, the sort of thing I would have done, which makes sense because I am the person who taught my assailant, Nabi Souvorov, how to do such things.

Nabi's flat looks tossed before Vadim and I start. The sun is up, it is nearly nine in the morning, but it still feels like nighttime to me, not as if six hours have passed since Yuri's call woke me. Remnants from meals past are scattered from floor to tiled countertop, the latter a sickly green except where the grime in the grout runs to speckled purple. Vadim works the living area with a tire iron while I wade through dirty clothes and old newspapers to the shuttered bedroom and click on the light. The sudden brightness reveals sleep-tousled Lilia, ex-soldier Leonid's prostitute wife.

She startles awake and then settles back when she sees it's me, making no move to cover her breasts, which ride heavily down on her ample belly.

"Nabi's not here," she slurs.

If she is surprised by my presence she hides it well. In the front room Vadim smashes furniture into kindling, but she makes no remark on the sound. The bed sighs when I settle my weight upon it. "Why are you here?"

"Why do you think?" She tries a sexy smile, but the fog of drugs and sleep turns it into a squinting frown.

"What time did he leave last night?"

"I don't know. We went to bed together, but . . ." She shrugs. "You people keep strange hours."

I sweep a hand over the bed. "How long, you and him?"

"A month. Maybe two. Who cares?"

"Where does Nabi keep his files?"

Calculation glints her eyes. "What is that worth?"

I don't hurt for Leonid, especially not if he was the triggerman who killed the two soldiers, as I suspect. In some ways his desperation to hold the virus at bay forced his hand, but he had alternatives, maybe. He chose to work for the wrong side, and his choice helped to make her into this. The knife slides into my palm. I shimmy it in the lamplight, letting the bouncing gleam stab her eyes. An artery on the underside of her pendulous left breast throbs. She points straight down. "Under a floorboard."

I call out to Vadim. We push the bed aside with her still in it. He wedges the forked end of the tire iron between two tightly placed planks and splinters them apart. Hidden beneath is a metal box with a combination made from three spinning dials.

Vadim cracks the box, and it's all there—money, jewels, account statements, and other papers that show deception going back more than a year. And a sheaf of photographs, all of me. In the park with Yuri, giving money to pensioners, scouting routes in St. Petersburg, holding hands with Valya on a predawn walk to the loft.

Vadim sits on his heels, awaiting orders. Lilia takes position on the far edge of the bed, eyeing the knife in my hand. They both seem far away.

I hear Maxim's growling laugh echoing in my mind. I feel the Azeri's hot breath on the back of my neck, so real I twist away. He is everywhere, moving pieces on a chessboard. I feel like a rook sacrificed to capture the queen.

"Can I go now?" Lilia says. "There's something I need to do."

"Replace the box as it was and cover it back up with the bed," I tell Vadim. "Then get her dressed and bring her with us."

chapter 32

Nabi drives a lightning-quick Audi. He parks it on the second underground level of a garage beneath his building. That night it takes twenty minutes for Vadim to fit a device to the bottom of the car under the driver's seat. Afterward, we return to an untraceable dusty red Mitsubishi van parked where we can see the Audi and wait.

Nabi slides behind the wheel of the Audi at six in the morning. He casts his gaze all around, no doubt nervous after finding his apartment in such a state. He likely blames the mess on Lilia and one of her thieving boyfriends. He doesn't know I've blown his cover. If he did he would be long gone already.

I dial the number to his car phone and watch him hit the button to connect the call.

"H-h-hello?" he says warily.

"It's me," I say.

"W-w-what's up?"

"I've got something. Big money on blow. For you only. A misdirected shipment is being stored in a warehouse down south. Don't say anything to anybody."

"W-w-what d-d-do you need me to do?"

"Meet me there." I give him an address and hang up.

We watch in silence as he dials a number on his mobile phone and talks for a few minutes, and then we follow him out of the garage. I'm driving, stone cold, remembering another time different from this one but not unlike it in one important way.

I was holed up in the jagged rubble of a bombed-out apartment on Grozny's east-side killing zone. Caked in dried mud. Hunting a targeted Chechen distinguished by a ruby-bellied black widow tattooed over his carotid. Waiting, three days in, when a ragtag band of rebels cruised past planting toe-poppers. Five men, easily killed with the dual advantages of surprise and position, but my target was not among them, so I just watched.

The next day a Russian recon platoon crept through the area, bent low, clutching new machine guns—justly afraid, poorly trained, lacking experience. Impossible to warn without breaking cover, I decided, subconsciously aware of the flawed stewardship with which I wielded my godlike power.

The boy on point was bolder than the others. He looked young, still a teenager, probably, but whippet-wiry and peasant-tough. He stubbed a mine, popped into the air, floated dazed in the crunching well of sound from the explosion, thumped the ground screaming next to his smoking leg.

In the echoing cries of the young soldier's death throes, it came to me that we all have our toe-poppers. One is out there, waiting for each of us. Maybe it is the iron that will be forged into the steel bumper that cleaves your skull one stormy night on a curving street. Maybe it's a bad cell not yet mutated or a virus nurtured in the blood of another person. Whatever form it might take, it is out there, waiting.

Two days later my Chechen target proved the point. He met his toe-popper in the form of a high-velocity bullet that ripped away the ruby belly of the black widow tattoo, along with the rest of his throat.

We follow Nabi's Audi as it winds down narrow streets to a squat office building, where he's greeted by one of Maxim's underlings. Vadim grunts confirmation of Nabi's guilty association with the Azeri. Nabi and the man talk for several minutes, and then two men I don't know join them, and the new arrivals crawl into the Audi with Nabi and drive off. I pilot the Mitsubishi twenty car lengths back, thinking that a direct confrontation would be better. I prefer face-to-face showdowns with betrayers. But this needs to be staged to look like one of many enemies could be the source, so it will have to be done from a distance.

Several kilometers later, on a deserted street flanked by brick warehouses, I incline my head. A click signals that Vadim has pressed the button to detonate the plastic explosive he molded under the Audi the night before. The blast sends the fragmented car off the ground. Even from a distance of forty meters the shock waves rock the Mitsubishi on its chassis.

"What should I do about Lilia?" Vadim asks on the drive away from the explosion.

I'd forgotten about her. By now she's spent nearly twenty-four hours locked up in a storeroom beneath Vadim's café. There's nobody left to warn.

"Cut her loose."

Vadim drops me at the loft and I spend the rest of that day and most of the next there, sleeping intermittently, missing Valya. She's due back in less than two days, the soonest she'll be able to travel. Time seems to crawl. I feed Posnova when the thought comes to me, the way you feed a dog you don't care for. She kneels in front of her bowl with her ruined hands wrapped around the radiator grill and presses her face into the food, snorting piglike. She is more than a week without a shower. She is no longer *Cosmo*-ready.

I leave her late in the afternoon, headed for the café. Three-day stubble scratches my palm when I rub my tired face. My eyes feel gritty, dragged down at the edges. The basement is hot and close. Upstairs is noisy. It is a Friday, I realize, a busy day for Vadim. He pokes his head down the stairs and nods to acknowledge that he sees me.

A few minutes later he comes down with a tray of coffee. He pours, and we sit in silence, drinking in sips. The rows of dusty slot machines march toward the darkness in the back of the basement. They remind me of the terra-cotta soldiers in Xian, China, lonely sentinels waiting for a call to battle that will never come. I can't bring myself to tell him about Valya's foot.

"A captain is looking for you," Vadim says after a time.

Dubinin. I had almost forgotten about the dead soldiers in the arsenal barracks.

"He says to call him at this number," Vadim says, sliding a strip of paper across the table in front of me. He collects the mugs on his tray. He mistakenly believes my depression is from killing Nabi. "Nabi chose the wrong path," he says matter-of-factly as he leaves. "He gave you no choice."

I call the number on the paper. Dubinin answers with a grunt.

"What do you want?" I say.

"Where have you been?"

"Go fuck yourself, Dubinin." I don't like having to explain my business to anybody, but especially not to someone I am not indebted to.

A long silence follows. Dubinin's rank is misleading, I realize. He is unaccustomed to being talked to in that manner. I wonder what he's thinking. Perhaps he's trying to decide whether he outranks me, either officially or in the unofficial pathways of the General's mind.

"We have a lead," he says, choosing to get to the point rather than argue with me. "Ballistics tied the bullets to one of the guns used to kill an arms merchant several years back. The gun that administered the coup de grâce."

I remember the shooting, although I was in Chechnya at the time, so I heard of it secondhand. The arms merchant was a mobster from Tajikistan with a military background. When the wall crumbled he used his contacts to form an export company, supplying armor and heavy weapons to peacekeepers in Somalia and later to both the Afghani Northern Alliance and its enemy the Taliban. But then he got greedy and attempted to tackle the lucrative African markets—Angola, Liberia, Rwanda, Sudan, Swaziland, Congo, and many others. A good idea flawed by one bad problem—the African arms market already belonged to Maxim. So the merchant was spectacularly slaughtered along with two unfortunate prostitutes and a bodyguard in a high-ceilinged suite in the Hotel Baltschug Kempinski. I am not surprised that Gromov was Maxim's messenger on that day.

"So what?" I ask Dubinin.

"We found the gun, and we've got prints."

"Gromov," I say.

His surprise is so palpable that it seems to bleed through the earpiece of the cell phone. "How the fuck did you know that?" he says.

"A lucky guess."

He mutters something under his breath. Finally, he says, "We're sweating Gromov now, at the Kosygnia station. I'll meet you there."

I disconnect, considering whether the best course is to let Gromov swing for a crime he didn't commit.

The police station on Kosygnia Street contains an interrogation room with a one-way window. A police lieutenant with whiskey breath leads me there. Dubinin is already in front of the window watching the proceedings.

Gromov is chained to a steel chair bolted to the floor behind a wooden table etched by the digging fingernails of prisoners past. His battered face signals that he's been here for a while already.

"Murder, Gromov," Viktor the police commander says. He's resting one butt cheek on the table next to a blackjack. His hands are folded in his lap, making it hard to see the gleam from the brass knuckles on his right fist. "You'll hang, or maybe just spend the rest of your days at a work farm breaking rocks and fucking hairy assholes." He grins widely.

"Someone stole my gun." Gromov's defiant tone is belied by the fear that coats his face.

"Before or after you killed the soldiers? You see? It doesn't matter, you stupid fuck, because we got the gun, and we got you for the arms merchant." The commander triumphantly holds up Gromov's Colt .45 Peacemaker.

"How did you get the gun?" I ask Dubinin.

"It was turned in by a hooker, if you can believe that. Yesterday. Said she found it behind a Dumpster in an alley not far from the Kremlin. Wonder what she was doing behind a Dumpster in an alley," he smirks. "Anyway, ballistics matched, we ran the prints and came up with Gromov, then turned everything over to him." He jerks a thumb toward the inside of the interrogation room, where Viktor is lustily sapping Gromov's shins with the blackjack, varying the force and the timing between blows. To Gromov's credit, he cries out only a little.

"What was her name?"

Dubinin scowls. "Whose name?"

"The hooker's."

"I don't know, Lilia something."

I may be off on the particulars, but I don't think I'm missing anything important about how it was done. Lilia stole the gun. Leonid used it to kill the soldiers, then gave it back to Lilia, who turned it in to the police to frame Gromov. That was the *something* she said she needed to do. Lilia, I realize, is a better woman—and wife—than I gave her credit for.

All of which, of course, still leaves open the question of *why* the soldiers had to die.

chapter 33

The cloud-covered sun glows low on the horizon by the time I leave the Kosygnia Street police station. The same slow drizzle that has been going for days captures the smog and deposits it like a sludgy coat covering the city. I'll need to watch my American prey myself now that Nabi is no more.

I straddle a backfiring Vespa through misty rain to the National Hotel. Park and lock the scooter to the base of a lamppost next to a small river of polluted water coursing through the gutter, knowing the Vespa will disappear if left untended for more than a few hours, but not caring. I stand in the shelter of an awning, studying the passersby—innocents and evildoers mingling in a bubbling soup of black umbrellas and the musty smell of dirty rain.

Tourists wearing clothes unsuited for the weather eye the Kremlin's domes and dog-eared guidebooks. Locals move purposefully under heavy rain gear. Predators prowl. Russia's new-breed capitalists, hungry for Moscow's needy. Darting pickpockets. Scheming scam artists. Cooing HIV hookers. "Come on, baby," and then you dip your dick in poison, and she kills you slowly with your own blood, or she takes you to a shabby room and her steroid-pumped boyfriend cracks your skull for your wallet. Edgy boys kneading grubby plastic bags filled with bulging white rocks like hard candy cut with rat poison. Armani suits with slicked hair and slicker business plans, ready to exploit the greed of trolling Westerners for cheap labor or plentiful oil or limitless timber or whatever else the resource du jour might be.

Night falls. The drizzle slows to a patter, then temporarily stops. I buy dinner from a vendor working a wheeled cart, who cuts strips from a rotating side of beef under glass. Eating these reminds me of Valya, who likes to tilt back her head and dangle the strips into her mouth in a way she knows I find amusing. But those thoughts soon turn murderous as I contemplate her sad state and the preordained path that I am now certain led her there.

Pappalardo sashays out of the National wearing leather pants tucked into boots that clasp his calves and a cropped, metal-studded jacket. He takes the stairs down to the tunnels leading to Revolutionary Station. I ditch my greasy plate and follow him past hawkers, grimy street musicians, teen wolf packs. On the platform he ignores the life-size bronze statues celebrating Russian workers, choosing instead to stare at the digital clock counting down the seconds to the next train, tapping the toe of his boot.

The train trundles to a stop, the doors slide open, and he pushes in and rides to Komsomolskaya Station. I follow him out. He bumps through the throngs in the station without looking at the ceiling mosaics memorializing Russia's great wars against invading armies— German crusaders, Tartars, Poles, Austrians, French, and then the Germans again. The bloody past of the motherland, all depicted in stylized tiles turning black with grime. The dead, the dying, and the forever wounded clumped in wasted piles, spent to preserve . . . what? The privilege of oblivious foreigners like Pappalardo to cruise the city's nightlife sewers, culling her weakest sons and daughters.

He emerges from the station and heads south, winding along wet streets and beneath dripping underpasses until we're shrouded in pulsing magma neon from flashing signs. He pauses, taking stock, then continues on. Two blocks away the lights are lower, the music is louder, and the crowd coarser. Pappalardo seems to fit here, mixing in the packed street with mostly men and boys in leather. Dog collars and chains and pierced nipples abound. One muscular specimen plants himself in Pappalardo's path, turns his back, and grabs his ankles to expose a long slit in his pants that gapes to reveal hairy butt cheeks cracked wide. He's laughing, trying to get a reaction for the amusement of his friends. Pappalardo nods warily, attempting to avoid a confrontation, and edges past.

I'm behind him, taking care to remain unobserved. Some in the press of people recognize me for what I am, so I'm not bothered as I trail him into a squalid Khrushchev building. A handful of its inhabitants lean from open windows, shouting, cursing, chatting, or just observing the swirling masses below. The foyer floors are sticky with goop. A naked infant cries and squirms in a damp corner it shares with a crumpled can of Red Bull and a sodden newspaper. The door bumps flesh when I push into a stairwell.

"Go away," a hard voice says.

I slide inside and swing the door closed to reveal a ponytailed man in a denim vest coupling from behind with a woman bracing herself against the wall. Her head hangs low and tangled black hair veils her face. Her skirt is hiked to her waist, and her long legs are planted firmly against his thrusts. She doesn't acknowledge my presence, but he does. He blinks into my face and finds no comfort. He drops his gaze to the drawn Sig.

"I didn't see nothing," he says.

"Whose baby is that?"

Silence. I push the barrel of the Sig into his hooked nose. He stares cross-eyed down the oiled chrome of the barrel.

"Mine," the woman says, raising her head.

Her eyes are shocking blue set against the coal black of her hair. I am practiced at recognizing contacts, but the color strikes me as real. She might be beautiful except that drugs and hard living seem to have wasted her into a dried-out husk. "Finish up fast," I tell him. "The kid needs attention."

His jaw drops, but I'm gone, following Pappalardo's footfalls up the concrete steps slowly and quietly. He exits on the fifth floor. I follow him into a hall similar to the one in Masha's building except that long-tailed rats haunt this one. Up ahead, his retreating form slips into a room.

A silencer screws neatly onto the barrel of the Sig as I approach the door. It would be safer to wait, to give him time to disrobe and start in with whatever his poison is—sex, drugs, or both. But that approach does not fit my mood, just as I have no desire to use the lock-picking tools secured in a pouch attached to my belt. My boot splinters open the door with a single practiced kick.

Pappalardo is already on his knees with his face buried between straddling, doughy, varicose thighs. The lashes of a whip caress his bare shoulders. A potbellied Arabian woman in thigh-high stockings and a bra made of two pointed cones stands pressing her bushy crotch against his mouth. She lurches back onto a bed covered with stained sheets as I follow the splintered door inside. Whips, ball gags, clamps, and harnesses grace the far wall. Pappalardo's choice of partners is different, but not remarkable. Variegated human sexual needs ceased to surprise me a long time ago.

Pappalardo is still on his knees. "Who are you?"

I shut the broken door as far as it will go and move closer until I'm standing over him with the Sig dangling next to his eye. His erstwhile dominatrix is bug-eyed, pressing as far into the wall as she can go, trying her best to be invisible, like two hundred pounds of nothing. She knows a nonnegotiable problem when she sees one.

Pappalardo leans away from the gun, frightened, taking his cue from her. "Do you want money? Is that what you want?"

I consider whether to shoot the dominatrix's foot. I know the sound and the sight it will create, down to the keening pitch of her screams and the cauliflower eruption of blood. It is one of the best ways I can think of to get fast answers. Except this time I stay my hand. I don't know why.

"I want Lipman," I say as calmly as I'm able.

"I don't know—"

My nice guy persona vanishes. I slam the silencer into his cheek, a sharp blow that drops him to the floor holding his face.

"I want Lipman," I repeat.

He spits blood and cowers, but he fails to speak quickly enough, so I jam the head of the silencer into his gloved left hand and pull the trigger. His whole body spins from the force of the bullet as his false hand rips away, smoking.

"Oh, shit!" he screams. "Shit!"

The Arabian woman whimpers and hugs the wall.

"The next one takes off your real hand, Pappalardo." I take aim.

"Wait! All I have for him is a phone number."

He recites from memory while I key the numbers into the Nokia. The prefix indicates it is a Moscow-area phone. If the number connects to a land line, I'll be able to find Lipman using the General's access to various computer databases. If it's a cell phone it may or may not be enough. The General might be able to triangulate outgoing calls. I know the Americans can do it, but our technology is sadly lacking in many ways, and this might be one of them. Either way, I don't believe Pappalardo has any more information about Lipman to offer.

I pocket the phone and look down at the American. He is wide-eyed, obviously hopeful the ordeal is over. His garter-clad girlfriend is squished hard into the corner on the bed, spilling fleshy rolls, her eyes squeezed shut.

"What do you know of the painting Lipman's peddling?"

His eyes turn calculating. I raise the pistol.

"Nothing definitive," he says quickly. "I haven't seen it, and now it looks like I never will. But it has to be a forgery. How could it possibly be real? Still, it's worth a great deal of money if it dates to that era, or even close to it."

I mull over his words without agreeing. He is a waste of a man, an implement for other, harder men. Not really worth killing. "I'm going to let you live. Maybe someday we'll do business. But I'll find you again if Lipman is warned."

He swipes his cheek with the back of his hand, smearing the blood on his face, and tries to compose his features into something approaching dignity. "I understand."

I backtrack down the stairs. The coupling pair is gone. The baby is still on its back in the corner, wailing and flailing in an invisible wafting cloud of pea-green baby-shit stench. I squat next to it. It's a girl. She has blue eyes like her prostitute mother's. The pupils are wild, jerky, dilated. She is suffering from withdrawal.

I strip to the waist and wrap her in my shirt. Shrug back into my overcoat, tuck her under my arm like a soccer ball, and head for Komsomolskaya Station in the same soft drizzle that suddenly feels a little bit cleaner. The swaying train and the warmth of my body stills her cries. I feel as if all the eyes in the compartment are on me as I nuzzle her soft cheeks, but I know that nobody cares if the wolf grips a lamb in his canines, not really. Not unless the lamb belongs to them. I wish I knew a lullaby. I've heard snippets of them on the television shows, but nothing comes to mind at the moment, so I content myself with a low tuneless hum while watching her little hands rhythmically clench and open as she falls asleep.

Masha answers my gentle knock. She holds the baby while I drink the tea she already had boiling and tell her what I want. It is too much to ask, but I do anyway. "Can you find a home for her?" I feel like I am discussing a stray cat.

"Yes," Masha says. The contrast of her parchmentlike flesh against the glowing softness of the infant's skin is disconcerting, as if they are separated by more than mere generations. "Last week a woman I know lost her husband and son in a fire. This child will take their place."

✗

Somewhere in grieving Chechnya I lost the capacity for joy, and every other deep emotion except for hate. I cruise life meanly, grind through good times and bad with a ferocious sameness, repelled by the depths of Russia's failures, sometimes compelled by the abiding strength of her simplest people. Contributing to both halves in unequal measures, favoring failure.

But today I feel love in all of its overwhelming power. Pressing my face to glass at the Sheremetevo-2 terminal, I see pale, radiant Valya being helped off the bus that carried her from Aeroflot flight 712, a wisp of her former, twisted steel self, but more than sufficient sustenance for my craving eyes. I race through the tiled halls, wait heart-pounding minutes for her to pass the checkpoint, the last seconds the hardest of all, seeing her crutch the final meters through the security portal. Her left leg is heavily wrapped. It appears to be folded and tied back, but that is only an illusion. She leans stiffly on the crutches as I take her into my trembling arms. Her body does not melt into mine the way it usually does.

We make our way slowly out of the terminal. She needs help climbing into Vadim's van. Once she's settled into the passenger seat we drive away.

"Tell me about it."

"What's to tell?" She's tracking traffic through the window with smoky eyes. Her hair is its natural white. She's ghostly. "Strapped to a bed in a hospital room. Helpless. Chopped up. They told me what they were going to do before they did it. That made it worse. That and then not knowing if I would ever be made whole." Her lips are dry. Cracked waxen lines disappear when she runs her tongue over them. "At first I felt hate. For everybody. Peter. The doctors. Slimy Strahov. You."

Even though I suspected my name would be on the list, hearing her say it cuts me to the bone. Her gaze still has not yet met mine. We leave the terminal lanes and merge with heavier traffic on the M10. I take my eyes off the road for occasional glances in her direction, but she continues to stare pensively out the window.

"I can't comfort you, Valya. I know the feeling of loss, and I know that words can't make it better."

She nods and squeezes her eyes shut. "I saw it when they changed the bandages. It is very ugly."

"Is my leg ugly?"

She blinks several times and nods vigorously. "Yes," she says, sniffing. The corners of her mouth tweak up, showing a shadow of her old humor.

"But it never made you love me any less."

"You're a man."

"And you are still the most beautiful woman in the world."

"Wait until you see it," she says, but her tone is less grim.

"We'll send you to America for a prosthesis like mine, or better."

She nods distractedly. Her gaze has returned to the window view. "They never even tried to put it back, you know. The doctor told me how you demanded it, but by then it was too late. Nerve damage, he said."

My grip tightens on the wheel even though I had suspected as much.

"At least I was able to leave that place sooner," she says, but there is a catch in her voice.

"What of Peter Vyugin?"

"So that is his full name? He is terrified that you are going to kill the woman he loves."

"What should I do with her?"

Valya has been my friend and lover for more than four years. More than that, she's been my anchor windward, helping me to hold the demons prowling my mind at bay, preventing the full-blown unleashing of my unholy brand of terror on the world. "Things are accepted in war that would never be permitted in any other time or place," she once told me, rightly, and I have tried to keep firm rein on my worst impulses ever since.

She takes several pained seconds to rotate her body to face me squarely. I pull my gaze from the road to meet hers. Fires of hate burn brightly there.

"Peel the skin off of her body one strip at a time. Take a blow-torch to her. Make it last forever. And then kill him the same way."

chapter 34

At the loft I struggle getting Valya to the service elevator and down the short hall to the door. The card key beeps the lock. The door clicks open. I walk ahead of her into the main room. Each thump of her crutches makes me wince. We approach Posnova, who is huddled on the floor with her back to us. As we draw closer she shifts to face us by rotating her lower body. Her arms are still wrapped around the radiator, cuffed at the wrists. She looks pained, haggard, wretchedly lying in her own shit. But an evil light gleams in her electric blue eyes. I need an extra heartbeat to recognize the expression.

Expectant. The wicked spark in her eyes comes from anticipation. Posnova has been waiting for this moment.

I know it then. All of a sudden I see that part of the puzzle clearly for the first time. I turn to stop Valya from seeing it, but I'm too late. She stops dead. Color flares in her cheeks.

"Hello, Valya," Posnova says.

Valya's eyes roll back, and she falls limply into my arms as her crutches clatter to the floor. I carry her into our bedroom. Gently place her burning body between cool sheets. Set water and medicines within reach on the nightstand. Kiss her hot brow. Shut the door behind me and walk across the main room until I stand towering over Yelena Posnova, my lover's lover. The woman she wouldn't give up for me.

"I should kill you now."

"Don't you think you should wait to hear what Valya says first?"

"You used her," I say stupidly.

"Not entirely in the way you think," she says, and she runs her tongue over her bloody lips.

If I stay I will kill her, so I leave the loft, burning with hate and jealousy and more hate.

I am still wandering the streets two hours later when the General calls with the address he obtained from the phone number Pappalardo had given to me. East side luxury building, number 804. Moscow's soggy streets have been carried in shaken umbrellas and the soles of countless shoes into the trains, which now smell like wet cotton and body odor. Two transfers and a short walk take me to the arching facade of a showy high-rise built after the Soviet Union collapsed. I speed-dial Vadim on the Nokia and tell him what I want him to do.

The doorman takes a hundred American dollars to look the other way. Money has purchased working lifts in this building. I ride one to the eighth floor, glad to avoid another climb. The hallways are wide and clean, carpeted in plush red. Even the textured ivory wallpaper seems to bleed wealth. The lock works with an old-fashioned key, not a card. I angle my back to the security camera even though the odds of anyone actually watching me are only slightly above zero, because most security is invariably an expensive joke. I select tiny tools from the pouch around my waist, pick the lock in under a minute, and drift inside like windblown vapor.

The travertine foyer is dark. To my right a stainless steel kitchen reflects green light from the glowing digital numbers on an oven-mounted clock. Travertine gives way to hardwood floors, which sweep away from me into a short hall that opens onto a wide living room with doors to the left. One of the doors is cracked ajar, leaking soft white light and an unidentifiable sound. The living room smells of new leather, varnish, and spicy chicken. The whole apartment is pathologically clean. I edge toward the light, and the sound resolves into moans and fleshy thwacks. I draw the Sig and slip into the room.

Lipman is mounted, thrusting into a redhead, who sees me and says "Rolf" quietly, as if I can't be permitted to hear. When he fails to respond, she pounds his ridged back. But he mistakes the blows for ardor and thrusts harder. I rack the slide on the Sig, and he stops in midthrust. He doesn't look behind him, but his ears seem to swivel back like a cat's.

I lock eyes with the redhead. "Call girl?"

"Y-y-yes."

"Who runs you?"

Her eyes widen. "Huh?"

"You heard me."

She names a pimp on the payroll of a mustachioed mobster I know, which is good enough for me to know she's no one Lipman cares about. Her clothes are piled at the foot of the bed. I toss them to her. "Dress, leave, shut your mouth. Yes?"

She jerks her head in consent. Lipman's penis flops flaccidly out of her as she rolls away. He still hasn't turned to face me. She takes several shaking minutes getting dressed, risks one last glance in my direction, and then she's gone.

Lipman finally rolls onto his back and shakes a cigarette free from a pack on the nightstand. He makes no effort to cover himself.

"Alexei Volkovoy," he says for no reason.

"Why did you do Arkady that way?" I keep my tone level and mild, moving closer to the foot of the bed.

Just as it did in the pictures the General showed me of him crossing the Ukrainian border, his face appears harder than before, edged with a cruelty I failed to recognize at the Neva Café. His face thins even further as he lights and puffs on a long cigarette.

"Why did I kill him that way? For fun," he replies, curling his lip.

He thinks I'm slow. He's seen the way I limp. He's heard from Arkady and maybe others how the Chechens took my foot. And so he is unprepared for the explosion that launches me across the bed to land knees first on his hairless chest. The barrel of the Sig cracks his teeth when I jam it into his mouth so deeply he is unable to cry out.

Holding him pinned that way, I pick up his fallen cigarette and take a long pull, watching the realization of the coming horror bloom in his eyes. When the tip glows crackling copper I push it into the soft flesh of his throat. Ride out his thrashings. And then I do the same thing again and again, until pungent piss sops the sheets and he passes out.

I flip him off the bed and cuff his wrists over his head to the frame. While he's unconscious I pull out the knife and toss the place, slicing cushions, cracking furniture, hacking tailored suits, pulling floorboards.

Halfway through the job Lipman moans back to consciousness.

The pack of cigarettes on the nightstand is nearly full. I light another and, when he is fully aware, I do it all again. I stick to his chest and belly because that area is easiest to reach while holding the gun crammed into his mouth. Except for choked moans and the thud of his kicking heels the procedure causes little noise, but I turn up the music on the sound system anyway, just in case a scream escapes. This time I'm careful to dispense the pain more evenly so it takes him longer to pass out.

He is still unconscious while I finish tossing his apartment. I find nothing significant. No papers, no personal touches at all. I think it's a fuck pad. I kick him once to be sure he's not faking, then I remove the cuffs and wait.

"Dress," I tell him when he comes to for the second time.

He dons black underwear, slacks, sweater, and shoes with three-inch soles, wincing whenever an item of clothing touches blistering flesh. He keeps his face averted and his mouth shut. Once he's dressed I cuff his hands again, this time in front of his body, and fold his overcoat over them.

"We're going to walk out of the building through the lobby to the street," I tell him. "We're going to hail a cab and ride it without a word to where I tell it to go. You're not going to do anything to upset me."

He does what I say. We reach the street. The Sig hidden under my windbreaker propels him into the rain. Across the street, Vadim lurks in the shadows. I signal with a small shake of my head for him to wait.

The doorman whistles, and a cab splashes water and lurches to a stop in front of us. I'm pushing Lipman inside when he slams his forehead into my face. The attack catches me unprepared. The man has a well of inner strength that I keep failing to appreciate. His forehead clips me high on the cheekbone, snapping my head back into the door frame of the cab. I drop to the wet pavement, dizzy, bloody, almost out. His pumping legs churn away from me jerkily, as if I'm watching a reel of ancient film. I grab the open door of the cab and lever to my feet.

The cabbie and the doorman are frozen in place, uncertain about how to respond. When I push between them I catch a glimpse of a darting form as lean and hard as angle iron cutting off the street to the left—it's Vadim, in hot pursuit. I charge after him, weaving, catching my balance on a newspaper kiosk as I round the corner, plunge into an alley, and chug into the darkness.

Only to pull up short, breathing hard, shaky.

Vadim is standing over Lipman with a foot on his back. He doesn't say anything, he just looks at me and raises an eyebrow.

I bend at the waist and grab my knees while I try to catch my breath. "Maybe I'm losing my edge."

"Maybe."

The side of Lipman's face plowed pavement when Vadim took him down. It drips blood and scraps of flesh. I draw the Sig and smack the barrel into his head. His eyes roll back and he spasms into a fetal position, but he's not all the way out, so I have to clout him again.

Vadim's laugh sounds like metal scraping metal in a hollow tube. "You're definitely losing it, Alexei," he rasps.

✦

We load Lipman into Vadim's van and head toward the Kremlin, where the General is waiting for us. I want answers, and I want Leda, and now that I appear to be so close to both the drive seems to last forever. I spend the time brooding in silence, considering the depth of my greed and hubris.

My desire for the *Leda* goes far deeper than money. Money is the shell covering the things that are truly important, just as the eggshells at Leda's feet have cracked open to reveal the luminescent pink babes beneath. I long to discover the meaning beneath the surface, and the sin of my pride is to believe that I can, to believe that I am worthy of such revelation. Maybe the best I can hope for now is to prove that the price that was paid was well spent. The best way to start is to get answers from Lipman, even if I have to reach my arm down his throat and tear them from his very soul.

I sit up straighter as Vadim steers onto a side street near Red Square. The time is now.

chapter 35

"**Leda** is grand beyond words," Lipman intones. "But *The Last Supper* is nonpareil."

Four hours have passed since I knocked Lipman out in the alley. His eyes are glazed from sodium thiopental dripping into the IV tube from a bag suspended on a bright steel carriage, the same kind of device used to display Valya's severed foot in Prague. His wrists and ankles are restrained against the metal posts of a bed suited for a hospital room, but this place is not a hospital.

The drug has caused an increase in the same pedantry Lipman displayed at the Neva Café, when he first described the *Leda* to me. We are far removed from there, on the underground banks of the Moscow River now, not the Neva, several meters below the earthworks buttressing the walls of the Kremlin. The General watches and listens from a shadowed corner as Lipman gushes rivers of words in response to my simple questions, encouraged by the chemicals cruising his bloodstream—and by the lit cigar between my fingers. At times he seems to wander, as he just did then, confusing the past with the present, and inexplicably talking about *The Last Supper* when I asked him where we could find *Leda and the Swan*.

Sodium thiopental suppresses higher brain functions, making Lipman more likely to talk freely and less likely to fabricate, but it is no truth serum. No such drug exists, although the Americans are rumored to be experimenting with various chemical mixtures in their secret prisons. The Chechens injected me several times with a similar drug, scopolamine, during the months when they had me in their clutches. Although my memory of it is hazy, I know that my silence was broken—I remember talking like an addled babushka. But I also recall attempting to mislead my interrogators. Whatever Lipman says, fact will have to be harvested from fiction.

"I spent two years at the refectory in the Santa Marie delle Grazie Monastery in Milan," he prattles on. "Helping to restore *The Last Supper*. Even as we uncovered layer after layer we saw more of the beauty and grace of the original, but it was only a distant shadow of what it had been. I know that now."

I raise an eyebrow at the General. Lipman's career is of no interest to us. The General motions, *Let him talk*.

"Leonardo was experimenting with paint techniques," Lipman continues. "He used oil and tempera on dry plaster. Not durable at all. So much was lost—color and nuance and detail beyond compare. Legends have arisen. St. Thaddeus was Leonardo's self-portrait. The apostle described as St. John was really a carefully drawn Mary Magdalene. Leonardo left Christ's face deliberately opaque. All of this everyone knows."

Lipman falls silent. He is bare-chested. Salve glistens over the raw magenta sores dotting his torso, slow-leaking puss. I drag hard on the cigar, considering whether to apply the fiery ash to more places. He sees the glowing tip, turns his face away from me, and keeps talking.

"The brilliant groupings of the disciples lent balance and tension to the scene. Standing alone, the arrangement dramatized the moment when Christ told of his betrayal and distinguished this painting from all contemporary efforts to depict the occasion. But the magic, the majesty, was in the intimate portrayal of gesture and facial expression. Leonardo conducted intense physiognomic studies for the faces of James, Philip, and Judas, and he employed hand models for added realism."

I'm bored, pacing, wondering why he's blathering about *The Last Supper* when what matters is *Leda and the Swan*. The General shifts his weight. His heavy lips twist into the closest he can come to a smile. He knows what's coming next, apparently, although I have no idea how he could. I still can't see where Lipman's heading.

"The painting was already beginning to decay in the sixteenth century," Lipman says. "Some of the older copies by lesser-known artists, made when the damage to the original plaster was less grotesque, reveal details no longer visible on the wall painting and they are inestimably valuable for that reason alone."

His voice lurches to a stop. The silence stretches to nearly a minute. Lipman's eyes are closed. Maybe the drugs have put him down. I query the General with a look, but once again he signals me to stand quiet. Just then, Lipman starts up again, back on the same topic, talking rhapsodically.

"Even before Leonardo departed Milan for Mantua, the French king inquired whether he could buy the entire wall of the refectory and move it to France. He was the first to truly understand the genius of the work, you see."

"What does this have to do with now?" I ask the General, but he shushes me again as Lipman continues with his story.

"After Leonardo left Milan, there followed a two-year gap in his creative output. Historians have attributed this to his wanderings and his fluid interests in science and medicine and war and so many other things, all of which is true in some respects. You see, Leonardo left Milan a rich man, able to indulge his genius however he saw fit, at least for a time."

"How do you know that?" I ask, harshly, tired of the digression.

"When King Louis the Twelfth was told that it would not be possible for him to acquire the wall, he must have approached Leonardo directly and purchased a comparable work."

"What did he purchase?"

"*The Last Supper.*"

I give the General an exasperated look. "He's wasted."

The General clicks his tongue to silence me.

I approach the bed and talk into Lipman's fuzzy ear, holding the lit cigar over his face for added emphasis. "*The Last Supper* is in Milan. On a *wall,* goddamn it. Tell me about the painting acquired by the French king."

"The king purchased *The Last Supper.* A preparatory work—on canvas."

The room seems to reel. I feel as though I've just opened the last piece of a *matryoshka,* only to find a completely unexpected treasure inside.

I lunge across Lipman's chest, grab the hair on the back of his head, and jerk back hard to hold his face steady. Suck on the cigar until I can feel the heat of it on my nose, then crush the blazing ashes into the skin directly under his eye. He shrieks so loudly it hurts my ears.

"Bullshit, Lipman! Where the fuck is *Leda!*"

I pull the cigar away, but he keeps screaming, a long wail that seems like it will never end. I give him less than thirty seconds before taking another slow drag.

"No! Stop!"

"The next one takes out your eye, Lipman. I'm through fucking around with you."

"*The Last Supper* was hidden with the *Leda,* beneath the Mignard!" He's talking so fast that spit sprays into my face. "Sophia purchased them both. And when it was time to conceal them, she hid them together."

"Where are the paintings now?"

Lipman is transfixed by the cigar. He's lost any ability he still had to concentrate—a good thing, because I'm sure that he's not lying, not now at least. Knowing that *he* believes it to be true, the vast importance of his words crashes down upon me. Leonardo painted *The Last Supper* twice. The implications are so profound I can hardly breathe, and my heart seems to be hammering audibly.

"St. Petersburg. They never left St. Petersburg."

"Where in St. Petersburg?"

"The man with the terrible scars hid them. Felix hid them."

"Who is Felix?"

"He's dead."

I restrain myself from burying the tip of the cigar into his eye. It won't help. The drugs and the pain are doing their work well, almost too well, because now he is becoming incoherent.

"Who is dead?" I say.

"Felix is dead."

"Who *was* Felix, then?"

"Nobody. Just a caretaker at St. Isaac's Cathedral. He's dead."

"How did Felix the caretaker die?"

"He fell. Maybe he was pushed."

"Who pushed him?"

I didn't think it was possible for his eyes to widen even further, but they do. "I don't know, I swear."

"Speculate."

"Maxim," he says, as if he's answering a question he has asked himself over and over again. "I think Maxim threw Felix off the dome of St. Isaac's when Felix wouldn't tell him where the paintings were hidden."

"Where *are* the paintings hidden?"

"I don't know that, either."

"How did Felix come to acquire them?"

"Right after we left you in the canal we gave the paintings to a man we were told to trust. He left them with Felix for safekeeping, and Felix learned what was inside. He wasn't supposed to. He overheard that fool Arkady talking."

"What happened then?"

"He went crazy. 'Sacrilege,' he said. 'You cannot defile this.' He hid them, and he refused to answer questions about where except to say they were secreted somewhere in the church. I've been on the run ever since."

"Who is the man you first gave the paintings to?"

"I don't know. I didn't want to give them to anybody."

"So why did you?"

"I was ordered to."

"By who?"

The General shifts his weight behind me, as if he doesn't like the direction of my questions. "By Maxim, of course," the General says. "Ask him about Maxim."

It is so unlike the General to interrupt a line of questioning in this situation that all I can do is stare at him, stupefied. After a moment I push myself off Lipman's chest to stand next to the bed.

"Ask him," the General says again.

"How did Maxim get involved?" I ask mechanically.

"Maxim learned of our plan when we inquired with Henri Orlan. Maxim forced us to work with you. We had no choice. He told us to be careful because you are much smarter than you appear."

Another connection is firmed up. Maxim learned of the existence of the paintings from Orlan—and Orlan's part-time flatmate at the university, Posnova. He then conscripted Lipman and Arkady, or at least he thought he had, before Lipman proved to have another agenda. Maxim used Arkady to hook me in, and he had Gromov and Nigel Bolles steer me to Orlan and Posnova to make sure the circle stayed as tight as possible. He also employed Nabi for some reason, although I'm not sure for what purpose, unless it was to keep tabs on me or interfere with my business.

But that is only one part of the story. A different trail must lead to whoever ordered Lipman to turn over the paintings to the man who then gave them to Felix the caretaker. Because Maxim lost the paintings at the same time I did—when Lipman motored away in the skiff on the canal, leaving me and Valya to wait another day beneath the Hermitage. Posnova told me in New York that Lipman was ordered to turn over the paintings by high-ranking government officials, and I believe her. But that is a trail the General clearly does not want me to go down.

"What has Maxim done to try to find the paintings?" I ask Lipman.

"Even Maxim could not make Felix reveal his secret."

In the end, silence cost the caretaker his life. God only knows what it cost him in the hours leading up to his death.

The General gestures toward the door and leads me out of the room, even though there are countless more questions to ask and it is doubtful we can ever force Lipman to be this cooperative again. As soon as the guard bangs the steel door shut behind us, I wheel upon him.

"What was that all about?"

"We learned what we needed to learn."

"I have more questions—"

"Your job is to find answers, not to look for things that don't exist. Go find the paintings."

"You'll keep him here for me?"

The General pulls on an overcoat. His heavy features appear to be carved from the river-rock walls of his subterranean headquarters. "We'll see," he says as he treads past me.

I'm still angry at the General hours later, walking the streets aimlessly, trying to figure out his motives, but I can only seem to concentrate on one thing. The most important thing—the staggering possibility that there might be two Da Vincis, and that one of them could be a canvas duplicate of the most momentous and least understood works of art in the history of the world.

chapter 36

"**Maxim** will know it's a fake," I say.

"He won't test it," the General says confidently.

We're back in his room made of crying stone, less than twelve hours after leaving Lipman in his cell, studying the ersatz Shah Diamond fashioned by the fat-cheeked Mongol that Vadim and I met with before, when Valya had a real foot. Looking at the diamond in the dim overhead light in the General's subterranean office, I find it hard to believe it will pass muster.

"Why won't he test it?"

"Because he doesn't care. And once he has the money, the buyer can cry all he wants. You think Maxim does refunds?"

I don't need to answer.

The General swivels his chair to turn his back to me. "By the way, I have another job for you." His voice crackles, as if he has something lodged in his throat. "A politician needs to die."

"Who?"

"Dudayev," he says. "A member of the Duma."

I know the name but not the man. He is a representative of the Liberal Russia Party, one of its co-chairs, and an outspoken critic of President Vladimir Putin. "Why?"

The General doesn't answer for long seconds. He doesn't like questions. "He is interfering with Putin's business," he says finally, not really answering at all.

Putin ran covert operations for the KGB during the bad days, when the Iron Curtain prevented outside scrutiny. He has a stable of men like me at his disposal if he wants Dudayev dead.

"When?" I say.

"Soon. Before the end of the week." He rotates his chair back around and hands me a glossy eight-by-ten photo. It shows a paunchy man in orange running shorts leaving the lobby of a residential building. The photo was shot from higher ground. The stringy strands of Dudayev's combed-over hair do little to hide his shiny pate. "He lives across from Sokolniki Park in that awful Luzhkov edifice," the General says.

Luzhkov, Moscow's mayor, has pissed all over the city in the form of tasteless projects financed by shaken-down investors. An ugly, cantilevered, high-rise apartment building is probably one of the least of his architectural transgressions.

"He runs in the afternoon," the General adds. "Every day except Sunday."

"Yes, sir."

"Work from a distance."

My throat tightens. More than three years have passed since my last sniper shot, and that was in burned-out Grozny, where things just didn't seem to count the same. "Yes, sir."

"Use caution."

"Yes, sir," I tell him.

I pass the fake Shah Diamond to the big Azeri that same afternoon at his office in the Solsnetskaya district. The diamond rests in a carved wooden box that he doesn't bother to open before handing it to one of his lieutenants, a heavy-lidded Ukrainian with a sloping forehead.

"What about the Da Vinci?" Maxim growls. He uses the singular, not slipping up this time the way he has before.

"Still looking."

His big lips flap when he blows out air to show his exasperation. He watches the flat-screen television. The screen is nearly as large as a wall in Masha's flat. It shows a red-haired American girl performing aerobics on a beach. He pulls out his shiny dagger and picks under a nail with the tip. Looks me full on, suddenly. "You killed Nabi?"

I hold my gaze on his slate-gray eyes. "Why would I kill my own man?"

He twirls the knife and points it at my face. "You. You're smart, Volk. You joke and pretend not to know things, but I think you have lots of secrets."

He shifts his gaze back to the television girl. She's doing splits, bouncing her taut butt up and down, humping sand. "You owe me," he says after a time.

I wonder how many times I will be obliged to repay the same debt.

He hoists himself to his feet and lumbers to an aluminum briefcase lying on the tabletop near the window. He thumbs the combination and cracks open the case. Without looking back he tosses a spinning revolver over his shoulder.

I pluck the gun out of the air. It is a Colt, like Gromov's, except that at .38 calibers it looks to be about half the size of that cannon. The walnut grip is cracked, and the blued-steel barrel bears numerous dents and scratches. The serial number has been filed into a furrowed, silver canyon that gleams against the darker surface of the barrel. The weight tells me the gun is loaded, but I pop the cylinder anyway to be sure, then snap it back into place and give it a spin. Out of balance, but it'll have to do.

"Who?" I ask.

"Yakovenko."

The name chills me. Two in one day. Yakovenko is another member of the Duma's Liberal Russia Party.

"Why?" I ask, even though I already know.

Maxim clips a Partagas. Takes his time lighting it for an even burn, puffs appreciatively, then regards the perfect ash with satisfaction.

"He looks too hard at the tables," the big Azeri lies. "This percent, that percent—what difference do a few points make? They lose faster, that's all." His rolling thunder of laughter seems to emanate from the cavernous depths of his barrel chest. He breaks the laugh in half and narrows his iron-hard eyes to slits. "Do it soon. Make it public—make it a lesson." He drags hard on his cigar, just as I did last night while working on Lipman. Wreaths of smoke obscure his blunt features. "And I want the gun back."

That night when I return to the loft, intending to use the computer to e-mail the General, I stop dead in my tracks at the entrance. Posnova is gone. The radiator seems naked without her chained body lying next to it.

My blood boils. I stalk over to the doorway of the bedroom. Valya is passed out on the bed, knocked out by the drugs. She is being watched over by Alla, my lissome porn queen and manager, who has been sitting next to the bed reading a book, but sets it open on her lap when she hears me and regards me from wide green eyes.

"She wants you," Valya had confided to me months before, standing by my side behind a one-way mirror, watching as Alla stretched her long body across a canopied bed, arching, masturbating for an adoring camera that was streaming video into the hard drives of voyeurs all over the world. Alla's spread legs framed her dancing pink fingernails, above which her glistening gaze honed onto the mirror, seeming to find my face. Then the girl typing on the keyboard next to Alla read new directions keyed by one of the real-time cyberviewers, and Alla twisted onto her belly and hoisted her perfect bottom high into the air and angled it toward the camera to offer the requested view.

"No, she doesn't," I had answered, but Valya simply snorted and walked away from the window.

"What happened to the woman?" I ask Alla.

She raises her plucked eyebrows. "Valya told me to bring a doctor to her this morning. I did, and then I left for the warehouse. When I returned, she was gone."

I look away, trying to conceal my anger. Freeing Posnova, if that is what Valya did, is the same as pointing a gun at my head. I want to shake her awake, but she is in no position to talk, not yet, at least.

I e-mail the General to alert him to Maxim's latest demand, so similar to his own, then head back out to the café to pick up Vadim. I walk quickly, breathing hard, feeling terribly alone. Feeling betrayed, again. After everything that has happened, Valya has put her part-time lover ahead of me.

✠

While awaiting a reply from the General, Vadim and I scout central-city locations for Yakovenko, puttering through the night in the Mitsubishi van. To make the killing public, per Maxim's order, we'll need daylight and crowds. The best time and place, we decide, will be on the lawmaker's way to work on the busy Novy Arbat.

We find a spot behind a billboard depicting a bulimic blond model draped over a red sports car that appears to be parked on turquoise water. After we agree on the location, Vadim pilots the van down alternate routes, marking times and distances. I would prefer to recheck the routes again in the morning, under the same traffic conditions as those that will exist at the time of the shooting, but time is short, and these runs will at least give us an idea of what to expect.

The operation is simple, really, but we spend the extra hours perfecting the timing in the hope that I won't have to kill any bodyguards or bystanders. All the while I do my best to throttle back my frustration

212 / Brent Ghelfi

at being held back from the things that really matter—Valya, *Leda,* and, if it truly exists, *The Last Supper.*

✦

I'm up at three the next morning, working at my desk in a corner of the loft. The General's e-mailed response to my query about Yakovenko is one word: *Acknowledged.*

The lawmaker found no safe haven with the General.

I snap my laptop closed. Check in on Valya, but she is still sleeping. Pace to a window overlooking an alley strewn with the detritus of Moscow's drug culture. The exposed bulb of the streetlight casts its jaundiced glow over a used foil wrapper, cracked syringes, cigarette butts, beer cans, wine bottles, a dull orange pool of drying vomit, and a passed-out whore whose hiked skirt reveals a folded white leg gleaming like cold ivory against the black tar.

I turn away from the window and use the speed dial to call Vadim.

"Ready?" I ask.

chapter 37

We meet at the gate of a taxi storage lot near Novospassky Monastery. Use bolt cutters to snap the chain. Steal a taxi. Cruise the route one more time, then take up our position, where we wait together in silence.

Just before six in the morning Vadim cranks the engine. We idle, waiting some more. Fissures in the ominous clouds admit traces of predawn phosphorescence. The neon lights of the casinos on heavily patrolled Novy Arbat flicker off. Early morning traffic crawls.

I study the .38 Maxim gave me, wondering whether it already connects to another murder or whether this is intended to be its first. The answer doesn't really matter. I pocket the gun, pull on gloves, and check the rounds of a different gun, a .38 Special from Vadim's stock of throw-downs.

Vadim grunts as Yakovenko's limo rolls into sight.

I step out of the taxi. Begin a slow walk toward the sidewalk where he will be dropped off. Behind me, the gears grind on the taxi as Vadim maneuvers it into position for our getaway. I slip through the crowds, head lowered, shapelessly anonymous in a long, dingy-gray overcoat. The limo closes the gap, meeting me halfway. It stops in perfect position, nearly bisected by the terminus of the alley we will use for our escape.

Yakovenko hops out. He must be a morning person, because his fleshy cheeks are glowing rosily and he's smiling. He steps forward, looking confident, on familiar turf, leaving his bodyguard behind in the idling limo. He expects the crowd to part for him, and it does, forming an impromptu tunnel between him and me. His gaze catches mine. His step falters. Recognition dawns in his eyes. I am sure that he does not know *who* I am. He has never seen me before. But he knows *what* I am.

A shrug sends the front of my overcoat flapping away from my rising gun arm. His eyes go big, like porcelain dinner plates dabbed in their centers with circles of brown paint. The barrel of the throw-down probably looks enormous to him, big enough to swallow him whole. He falls back, wind-milling his arms to speed his retreat, but he is already far too late.

I close in tight. Press the barrel against his forehead. Squeeze off a shot that sends a jet of blood and gore against the tinted window of the limo behind him. His feet fly out from under his body as he's propelled backward to thump the ground ass first with his back propped against the tire of the limo. His mouth is moving, but no words escape—just reflex, I'm sure.

The crowd erupts in screams. The people who can see what has happened claw to escape.

I look inside the limo to check on the bodyguard. He's against the far door, pointedly not looking in my direction. I am glad he won't have to die today.

I pump two more rounds into Yakovenko's face. Roll him over to be sure that the back of his skull has been blown away to show the stirred maroon soup beneath.

Then I melt into the roiling crowd, pocketing the pistol. Those closest during the initial shot keep scrambling away. Others press forward to see what happened, squeezing me aside in their rush for a better view. I slide around a lamppost. Once I am past the first wave of gawkers, I've already faded away into the muddled masses.

Ten steps later I jump into the rear of the taxi. Vadim pulls away from the curb slowly and carefully, signaling as we cross lanes through crawling morning traffic into the alley. I remove the rubber surgeon's gloves and stuff them into my pocket. Two blocks, another turn, a slow mile, and then Vadim parks the taxi in an alley near the storage lot.

We take a leisurely walk along Nozhovy Lane across from the Church of the Grand Ascension. My stomach growls.

"You want to stop for breakfast?"

He bobs his head. "Sure."

He leads the way to a shop owned by a Tatar with walnut skin and a wispy beard, a Sunni Muslim Vadim befriended in the days following the first of many waves of terrorist bomb explosions that ripped through Moscow to protest the government's Chechnya policies. As preferred customers, we are given an isolated corner table. Vadim asks the Tatar for a paper bag, and I scrunch Maxim's .38 into it. After we order breakfast I phone Maxim on the Nokia. He answers on the first ring.

"It's done," I tell him.

"Listen," he rumbles. The excited baritone of a news anchor comes over the line, describing chaos and confusion on the Novy Arbat. Maxim's heavy breaths provide a sonorous backbeat to the anchor's babblings about contract killings and gangsters. Then the television sounds fade, apparently as he lowers the volume. "Where are you, Volk?"

"On Nozhovy." I give him the name of the café.

"My man will meet you there. To get the gun."

All other sounds save his huffs and the thudding in my chest fade away. Nothing good can come of Maxim's insistence that I use his gun and return it to him. "I'll be here," I say, and Maxim disconnects.

Maxim's man, the Ukrainian, arrives within an hour. His protruding eyes and high forehead make him look like an aging frog. He refuses to meet my gaze, and he hurries off without a word as soon as I hand him the bag.

I'm tired after breakfast, not yet ready to begin preparations for Dudayev. "I'll be by the café later."

Vadim shrugs indifferently.

I trudge home alone.

When I arrive, Valya is awake, watching the televised bedlam on the Novy Arbat. "You?" she asks.

"Yes. And there will be another in a day or so."

She grimaces, then points the remote, and the television snaps off. "They say he was a good man for Russia."

"What did you do with Posnova?"

"Kasia. Her name is Kasia."

"Whatever. What did you do with her?"

She looks away. "I had Alla bring a doctor. Then, well . . . she won't bother us anymore."

"How the fuck do you know that?"

She bites her lower lip and squeezes her eyes closed. "I don't know if I can live this way," she says.

Posnova was in the mix from the beginning. I can't think of anything that would make her stop searching for the paintings or prevent her from seeking revenge against me. Valya's decision to release her was either hopelessly naive or fundamentally disloyal.

I leave without saying another word. I keep an apartment off Solyanka Street, not far from the loft. I spend the rest of the morning and early afternoon sleeping there.

I pilot the Mercedes toward the northern part of the city later that afternoon. Stalin's impassive neoclassical structures mingle with later drab block constructions—designed by impressed Soviet architects to avoid Western excesses—and with more modern, hastily erected Lego buildings with gaudy colors and reflective glass, the infantile vision of Moscow's self-aggrandizing Mayor Luzhkov. The disjointed montage is a microcosm of Moscow's economic spasms leading to nowhere. Old Moscow is perishing in plain sight.

Dudayev resides in one of the hideous Lego buildings, little more than stacks of blued glass rising imperiously over Sokolniki Park across from Resurrection Church. The General's distaste for the monstrosity is understandable. The doorway leading to the lobby is set back beneath the cantilevered ledge of the upper stories. The covered outdoor foyer opens on a wide sidewalk across the street from the church. It is the same sidewalk captured in the picture given to me by the General.

I limp along the pavement, moving slowly west into a slight breeze. The front door is manned by a sour-looking doorman. Resurrection Church looms over my right shoulder. Behind the church, Sokolniki Park stretches out like a beautiful green blanket. The walkway is busy. Not chockablock, just bustling. The concrete path leads to Sokolnichesky Rampart, which overlooks the park.

I stop and rest my elbows on a cinder-block parapet wall, pretending to gaze at the colorful foliage for a time before turning to lean back against the wall. Mid-rise apartments, shops, and restaurants edge the street on the other side of the rampart. Several windows in the apartments overlooking the park are boarded over. They would be good spots for a stationary target. I could use a cordless electrical drill to bore a loophole, make the shot, then withdraw without haste. But Dudayev will be moving, so the rifle barrel will need to pivot.

The setting sun reflects oddly off the glass of one of the apartments. I step closer for a better view. Several windows are broken but not yet boarded over. I key in on one with an expansive view of the rampart and the park. Four stories high. Slightly more than a hundred meters from the center of the rampart. Clean sight lines.

When the location has been fixed firmly in my mind I sit on a bench. It is nearly six o'clock. A light haze makes the late afternoon sky seem brighter, brings out the Kodachrome colors. Day workers bustle past. A family of Japanese tourists snaps pictures, then the mother leads the way into the park followed by her gaggle of children, reminding me of the metal ducks marching along the edge of the pond in the shadow of Novodevichy Convent.

Dudayev slaps by me, running smoothly and easily in Nike joggers, blue tank top, and yellow shorts at a pace that belies his paunch. His shiny dome stays on a level plane, hardly bouncing at all.

The basement of the café is quiet, even though it is not yet midnight. Muffled sounds from the diners on the floor above seem distant, almost as if they are happening in another world. Vadim's pen scratches across paper as I describe the equipment I'll need to assassinate Dudayev.

"Mk 11. Twenty-inch barrel, custom stock, black-matte finish all around." The shorter barrel and stock will reduce weight and make the rifle easier and quicker to handle. Loaded, mounted with scope and bipod, the gun will weigh slightly more than ten kilos. Black is best for city work; the matted finish will absorb light like spilled ink. The rifle is what I need for a close shot in an urban setting.

"Optics?" Vadim asks without looking up from his notes.

"Leupold Vari-7, three point five, ten by forty millimeter, long-range M-1 with a variable power scope."

"Distance?"

"Just over a hundred meters."

He arches a bushy eyebrow, his way of saying that the scope seems too powerful for such a close shot. But all he says out loud is, "How soon?"

A year? Ten years? Never? I shake my head to rid my brain of fanciful notions. Valya might have the luxury of such thoughts, but I do not. "By the end of the day tomorrow." I stand to leave. "Tomorrow night I'll take two cold-bore shots to zero it."

The day after tomorrow will be the time for the shot.

chapter 38

The two days that follow are filled with news of the public death of Yakovenko on the crowded Novy Arbat and talk of his elaborate funeral ceremony at Moscow's Vagankovo Cemetery. His parliamentary colleagues eulogize the lawmaker as an honest and idealistic man. I don't know how true the accolades really are, but the possibility that the politicians' motives for stealing the paintings were at least as noble as the General's is not lost on me. The leader of Yakovenko's party summed up the state of Russia's affairs best, I think, as I read through the latest ITAR-Tass news stories. "We live in a country where base actions go unpunished," he said. Setting the paper aside, preparing to leave the café to kill Dudayev, I am forced by an insufferable voice inside my head to reflect on the wretched reality of his words.

The Sokolnichesky Rampart feels the same as it did two afternoons earlier, when I scouted the shot. Hazy light, good angles offering clean sight lines through a well-spaced dusting of pedestrians. I'm wearing the same shapeless gray overcoat I wore to kill the other politician. The Mk 11 rifle is slung over my shoulder underneath the coat. A rucksack worn outside the jacket lends my burden an unrecognizable, roundish shape. Taking my time, alert for any unexpected activity but seeing none, I cross the rampart to the buildings to the north.

The apartment building with the broken window dates from the Khrushchev era. A quick look behind as I enter seems to confirm that nobody is interested in what I'm doing. A sprawled skeleton of a man wearing filthy rags and reeking of expelled vodka blocks the path to the elevator. Spittle trails from his mouth and flows into the patchy forest of his scruffy white beard. The naval blue of his faded, grimed jacket causes my step to falter.

I stoop down, cursing my own weakness under my breath, roll him to the side, and straighten the crud-crusted sleeve of his jacket until a submarine insignia becomes visible. The stitching underneath reads *Kursk*. The hundred and eighteen crewmen of the *Kursk* are all dead, and this specimen is too old to have served on her anyway. Suspecting that the jacket belonged to a son or nephew, I stuff ten one-hundred-ruble notes into the lost submariner's tunic. Reposition him more comfortably against the wall, out of the way of heedless feet. Press the elevator call button and wait. Nothing happens, of course.

I hike four flights of stairs to a narrow, green hallway. Count to the sixth door on the left of the stairwell, then press my ear against the padding to listen for unexpected sounds in case I miscounted.

Hearing nothing, I slide a set of small keys from a pouch at my waist. The second one clicks the tumblers, and then I'm inside, closing and relocking the door softly behind me. The flat is empty, lit by the horizontal rays of dust motes dancing in the late-afternoon sun. I set my equipment on the peeling linoleum floor. Unzip my rucksack near the broken window and remove a tarp splashed with broken camouflage colors of black, brown, and olive, careful to stay back out of sight from below. Using folded cloth to absorb the sound of my Lilliputian hammer, I nail the tarp to the ceiling just above the window. Once it has been tacked up and spread out, the tarp forms a sniper's hide under which my dark shape will blend without silhouetting. That done, I examine what is left of the windowpane, then quietly break out enough glass to allow lateral movement of the barrel as I track Dudayev. After the window has been prepped I study the view outside. The rampart is laid out before me. The windowsill is under a meter high, perfect for a kneeling shot. The location is good.

I squat in front of the window behind the sill and free-fall into the moment, my temporary lapse with the submariner forgotten. I zone.

Range. Windage. Angle.

I take a Bushnell rangefinder from my rucksack. Zero in on a sign mounted on the parapet I leaned against two days ago. Laser the distance—one hundred and twelve point two meters. Shift to point at the bench closer to the center of the rampart. Ninety-seven point four meters. I am reasonably sure that Dudayev will jog between those two points.

I set the rangefinder aside, turn on a palm-sized radio, the kind with a range of a few kilometers, make sure the sound is low, put it on the floor below the sill, then inspect the rifle one part at a time. When I am confident that the rifle was unaffected by the trip to the apartment, I screw in the sound suppressor. Load the magazine with ten 7.62-millimeter Winchester rounds and rack one into the chamber. Turn back to the window. Place the empty rucksack on the sill to use as a base to slide with the bipod as I move the barrel. Settle into position on one knee, tight, bone on bone. Shrink my world down to the crosshairs centered in the deadly circle of the scope.

I dial in the optics dead center between the parapet wall and the bench. Raise the scope to study the motion of swaying leaves in the park, then aim over the horizon and scrutinize the wind-bended waves of the dancing mirage. Together those things tell me the wind is from the east at about five kilometers per hour, not gusting.

Back to the rampart to calculate mils and minutes of angle, using inches, feet, and yards with this optics system. Mil dots built into the optics make the calculations simple—a few clicks on the scope, and

I'm dialed in. Ingrained facts line up inside my head. Average distance from a person's head to waist is thirty inches, the same as the distance from deck to turret top of a Russian tank. Top of head to groin, thirty-nine inches . . .

My chronometer beeps. It is 5:55 P.M. My breaths come slowly and steadily. I close my eyes. Concentrate on the blood coursing through my veins and arteries, on the deliberate beat of my heart. Firm my position.

The radio clicks. "He's moving," Vadim says in a static-filled voice.

I aim for the eastern edge of the rampart, locked in and supple at the same time, like flowing marble. Dudayev rounds the corner and leaps into the crosshairs. I can see the fine hairs on his ear.

I feel at one with him. Nikes slapping concrete; light sweat breaking; muscles beginning to warm; blurred emerald foliage rushing past. Feeling good, at peace, alone, able to think without interruption— about politics or business or the woman he hopes to love later that evening.

The barrel pivots, tracking him. Ideal line of sight. Solid body, at one with the rifle. Natural respiratory pause. Easy press on the trigger. For the first time in three months there are no thoughts of *Leda* in my mind. Dudayev's head sprays misty red, like soundless crimson fireworks against the verdant shades of the colorful park.

He drops.

I rack another round into the chamber, still staring through the scope.

The people nearest him don't react for long seconds. When they do, they move slowly, as if they are puzzled. The body is face up, so the gore is masked somewhat. A woman flops him onto his side. The insides of his exploded skull pour onto the concrete, and she screams so loudly that I can hear her from the apartment.

A second shot is unnecessary. Dudayev is dead.

I pick up the spent casing. Ease away from the window. Repack my gear, the olive-drab tarp last. Sling the rifle, put on the overcoat, settle under the rucksack, tromp back down the stairs. The submariner is still where I placed him. I check the pocket of his jacket. The money is gone.

A scraping sound near the elevator startles me. I whirl around, straightening quickly, reaching for the Sig buried in the pocket of my overcoat.

Before I can draw the gun a little girl steps from the shadows in the corner of the lobby. She is no more than eight. A startling purplish and turquoise bruise on her cheek mars her creamy skin. She stares solemnly at me from caramel eyes as big as saucers. I step backward, never dropping my gaze from hers. Here I am again, out of the moment, worse than a rank amateur.

"What are you doing to my uncle?" she asks in a near whisper.

"Helping him."

"Why?"

Good question. "Because he fought for the motherland."

She poofs her lips while she considers this. "He has bad scars on his back," she says a moment later. "Did he get them from fighting?"

Without seeing the scars I can't know for sure, but I suspect that his superiors lashed her uncle. Perhaps with justification—maybe he was a deserter or a coward. Maybe not.

"Yes," I answer.

She nods solemnly. We stand that way as the seconds tick past and the risk that I will be seen increases exponentially.

"Did you take the money out of his pocket?"

She looks down at her scuffed shoes without answering.

"Why?"

"My momma needs the money."

"So does your uncle."

She shakes her head. "Only for vodka."

Here I am, being taught by a child. My pathetic attempts to help lost soldiers are wasted—probably more harmful than helpful. I need to go. The police will cordon the area soon. The apartment building will be searched even before the experts have triangulated the shot and know for sure that this was the place it came from.

"What will your momma use the money for?"

"Food. And a new tooth."

"A tooth?"

She nods.

"What is your name?"

"Ella."

"Then the money is for you and your momma, Ella. Good-bye, little one."

Even with a broken front tooth her smile lights her face so brightly it almost hides the bruise that I suspect came courtesy of her passed-out uncle.

"Good-bye," she says, then dashes away up the stairs.

chapter 39

The night train from Moscow to St. Petersburg takes seven and a half hours. Most people sleep when they take this train, and a part of me wants to join them. I have slept poorly in the five nights since the first politician, Yakovenko, died. But I figure the cozy, soft-class compartment is perfect for a forced confrontation. Valya and me, two broken pieces, two scorpions in a corked bottle, with time to confront our differences before renewing our search for the paintings hidden by scarred Felix, the caretaker of St. Isaac's Cathedral.

Valya stares into the darkness sweeping past the window. She's stronger now, still nowhere near her racehorse norm, but moving better on the crutches. She's wearing loose black yoga pants with the left leg tied back to her upper calf, one black, slip-on Capezio shoe, and an oversized red sweater.

She suddenly turns to face me. "Why didn't you bring the baby to me?"

I think she's truly hurt. Valya has met Masha only once, as far as I know. News of this sort must be transmitted on some secret network that exists beyond my frequency. I don't know how to answer her except with the truth as I see it. "You haven't yet had the chance to live your own life. You shouldn't have to give it up for a child, or for anybody else." Meaning *me,* of course, as painful as that is.

She bites her lower lip.

I plow relentlessly ahead. "You're too young to be tied down. You need to discover life on your own. The evil witch I had chained to the radiator is evidence enough of that."

A vibrating growl escapes her throat, like the warning an angry sable might give. "You are a thickheaded mule!"

"Maybe. But I was a faithful one."

"I never lied to you about anything."

"No, you never lied. You just did whatever you wanted to do, with whomever you wanted to do it with. Exactly how the fuck do you explain Posnova?"

She flushes. A vein pounds in her pale neck like the racing heart of a dove. "I knew her as Kasia. I thought she was a teacher at the university." Tears spring into her eyes. "I didn't know she was a part of all this." Her waved hand takes in everything that's happened during the past three months.

"How did it happen?" This is a question I've asked before, without getting an answer. I can see that it bothers her to reply even now.

"Nabi introduced us. In a club one night, drinking, having fun. It was nothing. Then we met again in the library." She squares her shoulders. "You've seen the way she looks. You can guess how it might have started."

I recall Lipman's drug-hazed ramble. He found the paintings but made the mistake of discussing them with Orlan. Orlan and Posnova took the information to Maxim, who started pulling strings. Including the string attached to my lieutenant, Nabi. Now I know at least one of the reasons why Maxim employed Nabi.

"It might have started that way for me, maybe, or for another man. Not for a girl."

"Don't act so damned naive, Alexei."

Rising bile threatens to choke me. I can't restrain myself. "You were enough for me, Valya! I didn't fuck every upturned ass that caught my eye, and I goddamn well didn't start fucking men!"

Her eyes narrow into a fearsome look I know well, so I'm prepared when her fist lashes out at my head, quick as a striking snake. I parry. Dodge the second fist that comes from nowhere and thumps the seatback behind me. Pull my face away from raking nails. Then I am left to slump dejectedly into the upholstery as she struggles in the narrow confines of the cabin to open the door and leave me behind.

After she is gone I pass the time watching for an occasional light beyond the window. I had vowed not to lose my temper. So much for that. So much for a great many things. Three rocking hours later the door slides open, and she settles slowly into her seat. Her narrowed eyes tell me she's still angry.

"She made me feel things you can't," she says. Her eyes smolder as she gauges my reaction to this opening gambit, hoping, I think, to hurt me the way I hurt her.

I know that what I am about to say is not the right response, but it is as if I have no choice. "Then you should be with her. You made your choice when you let her go."

Lightning flashes in the storm clouds in her eyes. "You're a vicious man, Alexei. You know why I like you better when you fight? Because you like it so much. Because it helps you live when you make other people suffer and die." She stands on one foot, one hand gripping her crutches and the other held stiffly in a fist at her side, breathing as if she had just finished a race. "Sometimes I think you like fighting more than you like fucking," she says, and she leaves me again.

Her words were a lie, I think, intended to hurt, but they do their job.

This time she does not return. The hours slide wastefully away like the blacked-out tundra on the other side of the frosted window. When we reach Moscow Station in St. Petersburg, I hunt Valya down in the crowd waiting to disembark onto the platform.

"I need to know some things," I say into her rigid back.

"What?" She doesn't turn around.

"When did it start with Posnova?"

"March. A few months or so before we met with Arkady and Lipman in St. Petersburg."

"Did Posnova know about the loft?"

"No." Sharp, angry that I think so little of her. She doesn't have enough information to make all the connections. She doesn't realize that Posnova *certainly* knew everything she wanted to know about us, through Nabi or Maxim. My questions are designed to discover why Posnova compromised Valya. What was she trying to gain?

"What did you tell Posnova about me?"

"Nothing. She knew of you in the abstract. My boyfriend."

"What did you tell her I did for money?"

"Drugs."

"What did you tell her about the *Leda*?"

"Nothing!"

So what was Posnova's motive? I wonder.

Valya apparently senses the direction of my thoughts, even with her back turned to me. "Maybe she liked me."

"She targeted you, Valya. She knew you were coming when I brought you back to the loft. You were surprised, but she was not."

The muscles in her curved neck tighten. "I don't know, then."

Perhaps the answer is simple. "She could keep tabs on you, and on me. She gave Maxim a different window into our activities." I recall Maxim's voice mail when we were in the house with the bedroom that was a shrine to a lost son—*"What's going on in Leningrad?"* I think of the photo of the wheeling prow of the powerboat on the Neva River. "She knew when we went to St. Petersburg. She knew the timing. She was probably able to learn other things as well."

Valya says nothing.

A beefy woman bumps me, curses. Other people swirl around us, me and Valya, seemingly inseparable only a few weeks ago. Now, standing in cool Baltic air lit by the magnesium brightness of St. Petersburg's summer sun, I feel a well of emptiness so deep that I fear I'm about to be lost in it forever, as if a boring bit has cored a great hole in the middle of my soul.

"You were right when you said you can't live this way anymore, Valya. Russia is sick. I am sick. You need to go to a place where things are better."

Her whole body tightens. She stands that way, leaning on her crutches with her back to me, for a long time. "Okay," she says finally. And then she hops off the platform with one hand against the building for balance and her crutches in the other, and leaves me forlornly alone, watching her lithe form swing away through the crowd before she disappears in the crush of travelers. I don't know where she's going or even if she plans to return to Moscow later today. She's just gone.

chapter 40

The depot platform hums with rush-hour activity, but passengers and blaring announcements and screaming advertisements tide-pool around me in a dull roar that registers only on the outer limits of my consciousness.

Somehow during the hours that follow I trek out and onto ruler-straight Nevsky Prospect, head pitched down, past the soot-covered Kazan Cathedral. I pause under the awning of a nondescript brick building with hanging globular lights and a placard announcing it is the home of the original Fabergé factory, where the Imperial Easter Eggs were made for the long-dead tsars of yesteryear—

Oh, shit! Oh, fuck! What have I done? How could I let her walk away?

I collapse into a squat right there on Morskaya Street, my face buried in my hands, like a shuddering rock splitting a river of people flowing over the sidewalk. A faraway voice says, "Are you all right? Do you need help?" And it takes all my strength to stand straight, to pitch forward, to walk away without answering, because the answer is unbearable.

Yes, I need help.

What I had with her was utterly unique in my experience, and I don't believe it will ever come back to me again. The only way I can force myself to move past the unthinkable loss is to focus on the task at hand.

So that is what I do. I cross the sparkling Neva without looking toward the Hermitage or the spire of Peter and Paul Fortress and wend through busloads of tourists to the university library. Once inside, I leaf through the archived newspapers, starting at the end of May on the day after Lipman and Arkady motored away on the canal in the skiff.

I find what I'm looking for buried in a back-page article dated June 10. Felix Kuvaldin, a caretaker hired to maintain the cathedral grounds, plunged to his death over the balcony railing wrapped around St. Isaac's dome. Preliminary indications suggested the fall was a tragic accident, although suicide was not ruled out. A follow-up two days later said that he had been despondent over the recent death of his mother. A picture shows a man with scarred, drooping skin that seems to pull down the left side of his face, as if it had liquefied and then frozen in place.

I lean back and cross my arms in front of my body, suddenly cold at the sight of Kuvaldin's ruined face and the memories it has brought to life. My missing foot begins its phantom throbbing. The periodicals and dingy walls of the library fade, replaced by a shroud of hazed whiteness broken by the leafless branches of the trees in the forests of Ingushetia.

After a two-mile chase by Chechen rebels I had the high ground, a decades-old Mosin-Nagant 7.62-caliber sniper rifle, and enough ammunition to fight for longer than it would have taken for the cold to kill me. And three confirmed kills already, maybe two others—the rebels had dragged off the bodies before I had the chance to turn the scope back on them to see the impact of my shots. I estimated that at least twenty and maybe as many as fifty rebel fighters were hunkered in the valleys and depressions that surrounded my makeshift redoubt atop a wooded knoll. If it was my time to die, I decided, I would make it last for as long as I could, like a starving man savoring his last crust of bread.

The wind moaned a sad song. A kestrel wheeled in the darkening sky, signaling nightfall and the time for hunting. I bit off the end of a stick of jerky. It was as hard as iron and would last for a long time in my working jaw. Chewing was good because it kept my teeth from chattering.

A shriek rose out over the crusted snow. It was the sound a wounded animal might make. I swept the forest through the scope, but there was nothing unusual to see. The cry rose through the air again, piercing, agonized, almost inhuman. The hairs on the back of my neck bristled. I wondered whether it was Corporal Kuvaldin or Lieutenant Passky being tortured. Both men had been captured less than two hours earlier, when their truck caught a rocket-propelled grenade just minutes before I had been spotted in the hills above them and chased here. I felt worse because I knew they had been dispatched to this terrible place to search for me. *What a waste.*

"Volkovoy!" The shout came from the woods below me. "Come out now, or your friends will suffer!"

Another scream, this one pitched even higher.

Movement on the edge of the scope's circle caught my eye. The cracked leather toe of a boot was peeking out from behind a tree trunk two hundred meters away. Dirty cotton wrappings, used in place of socks, had pushed through the hole in the toe. I adjusted the scope, aimed, pressed the trigger, and watched the toe explode, feeling warmer as the wounded man's screams joined those of my tortured comrade.

Suddenly, a figure appeared from nowhere, as if it had risen from a dark patch of ground beneath a tree. Corporal Kuvaldin walked toward my position with short jerky steps. His left ankle was manacled. A length of chain attached to the manacle trailed snakelike behind him before falling away into the low ground of a riverbed. His unlined, youthful face was pale, with round eyes the color of honey and bloodless lips. He jerked to a sudden stop as he reached the end of his iron tether.

"Watch, Volkovoy!" the same voice shouted.

And then a tongue of fire from a flamethrower rose from the low ground and licked him, climbing along his legs and back before wrapping his entire body in its hungry slurp. He screamed, and tried to run, but was jerked to the ground by someone pulling on the hidden end of the chain. He clawed snow and dirt, howling for what seemed like forever before the flames stopped. Through the scope I saw that the back of his uniform had burned away in places to reveal cooked flesh, and that the nylon webbing of his harness had melted into the skin of his back. His face was buried in the snow, mercifully hiding the damage done to it.

Another man appeared and limped to the end of the same kind of tether. Lieutenant Passky stood stiffly erect, but his throat was constricted and his fright showed plainly in his wide eyes.

"Throw down your weapon, Volkovoy!" the rebel leader commanded again from his unseen post. "Come out with your hands held high!"

The crash of a heavy book dropping onto the library table next to me shatters my nightmarish visions. I shake my head, trying to rid it of memories, but even now I still wonder why I did what I did. Maybe if the soldiers hadn't been captured while searching for me I would have let them die that way. Maybe I was just ready to die myself. Whatever the reason, I threw out the rifle, put my hands behind my head, and walked into the arms of my Chechen enemies.

I put aside the newspaper with Kuvaldin's picture and make my way to the nearest pay phone. The St. Petersburg phonebook gives a number for Mikhail Passky. He answers after many rings.

"Yes?" He voice trembles. I wonder what he fears.

"This is Volkovoy," I say.

A long silence follows. I listen to him breathing. "What do you want?"

"I want to talk about Kuvaldin."

"Are you working for Maxim Abdullaev?" he asks.

"Meet me at the Astoria in an hour," I say.

He doesn't answer.

"You owe me, Lieutenant."

"I'll be there," he says finally. "Of course I'll be there. But you won't like what I have to say."

chapter 41

I make my way back across the Dvortsovy Bridge. The enormous dome of St. Isaac's Cathedral launching golden rays into a cobalt blue sky dominates the view heading south. The cathedral fills the skyline as I approach along the front of the Admiralty building, which is large and grand, in contrast to Russia's navy, which is neither, at least not anymore. I tromp amid the grass of Isaakievskaya Square to regard the dome. Useless schoolboy facts buzz my brain. Constructed over a period of forty years, progress on the massive edifice was slowed by ineptitude and the superstition that the Romanov dynasty would fall with the completion of the cathedral. The Romanovs did fall, some sixty years later. Close enough in Russian time. But still, Nicholas II rides his steed in perpetual glory high on his pedestal in the middle of the square.

The Astoria Hotel is catty-corner from the cathedral. Its lobby is Old World beautiful, but all of the grandeur is lost on me. I find a niche off the lobby and order tea, then drink slowly, gnawing everything over in my mind while I wait for the lieutenant.

A short time later I'm still drinking tea, but now I'm regarding the frightened lieutenant without pity. He's told me his story of how Lipman and Arkady made a hasty handoff of stolen artwork on the banks of the Fontanka Canal the night Valya and I spent shivering on the ancient dock beneath the Hermitage Museum. The next night he gave the paintings to his wartime comrade Kuvaldin for safekeeping.

"I didn't even know you were involved until later," he finishes. "I only did what I was told."

"By whom?"

"My bosses in the party."

"Which party?"

"Liberal Russia."

"Who are your bosses?" I ask, to confirm what I already know.

"Yakovenko and Dudayev. They're both dead now. I think Maxim killed them, just like he killed Felix." He jerks a thumb over his shoulder, in the direction of the shining dome of St. Isaac's.

I sip tea, letting the pieces settle more firmly into place. By the time I became involved, the politicians and Maxim were already separately pursuing the paintings. The General joined the action when I did and, I suspect, merged his interest with Maxim's sometime after the debacle the night of the theft in the Hermitage, although I have no idea why. Peter is linked through Posnova to either the politicians or Maxim. I suspect Maxim, because Maxim used the General to send me to Prague, where Peter and Strahov waited. All of that fits except that Peter has seemed strangely disinterested in the paintings from the beginning.

"Where did Felix live while he was the caretaker?" I ask after a time.

"On the cathedral grounds. I don't know where exactly."

I stand without warning. "Good-bye, Lieutenant."

"Volk, wait!"

I pause.

"You did a brave thing for us. I was never able to say thank you. I guess I knew that whatever I said wouldn't be enough."

I raise my hand good-bye as I'm walking away. He only held the paintings for a night, and he is unlikely to have known the value of what he had, so I hope that I will not have to kill him for the same reason I was told to kill his politician bosses.

A doorman holds open the door as I step out of the hotel into the early afternoon sunshine. The plaza is more crowded than it was in the morning. I ignore the street vendors selling T-shirts, nesting dolls, phony jewelry, prisoner-carved chess sets, and candies. Study the main building and her four smaller sister domes. Consider whether an obvious protrusion marks a likely hiding spot for two of the world's most valuable works of art.

Concrete steps sweep up to an entryway topped by giant columns that bring to mind the weathered trunks of ancient trees. Tourists enter to the right, paying one toll to visit the church and another to ascend to the balcony encircling the outside of the dome more than fifty meters high. Sunshine bounces off leaded-glass windows mounted high in the stone walls. From somewhere on the balcony of that curving gilded carapace Maxim flung the battered caretaker, in a regretted fit of pique, no doubt, because Maxim is wise enough not to kill his source of information without learning answers first.

I loop around the building. Past the Admiralty building. Through Dekabristov Square with its famous statue of Peter the Great, the Bronze Horseman rearing over the snake of treason on the bank of the Neva. And then back to the grass in Isaakievskaya Square, no closer to learning the secret of the caretaker Kuvaldin and his hiding place.

A guard shack made of plywood stands on the eastern edge of the cathedral grounds, manned by bored local police. A shawl-draped pensioner the cops are too lazy to move along sits cross-legged on concrete, an empty basket beside her. I drop a thousand-ruble note into her basket when I pass her on my way around the back of the church for a second time about an hour later. I still see nothing worthwhile. The clumps of pedestrians have thinned. Instinct prompts me to check my back. Darting movement catches my eye, but whatever it was is lost in the shifting streetscape. An ice-cream cart rolls past. A Greek family chatters excitedly. I move on, scouring with my eyes.

A flash of color grabs my attention, but it is gone so fast that I think for a moment it might have been my imagination. Then the wind blows a gap in the rustling shrubs interwoven through a wrought-iron fence, revealing a fluttering strip of yellow tape beneath a low, sloping roof covered by tar paper—an odd break in the cracked, girded wall of the church. I push through the bushes to the fence to take a closer look. On the other side of the hedge beneath the roof a gnarled wooden door stands slightly ajar on iron hinges. A broken strip of police tape dangles in the wind.

I take a quick look all around. Nobody appears to be paying me any attention. I climb the fence and drop into a grass-carpeted sanctuary bordered with well-tended, wind-rippled violets. Everything seems suddenly quieter, as if I've entered a place where the world hums several decibels below its usual howl. Pigeons gurgle. A hand spade rests in a dried bed of turned earth. The revving buses on the surrounding streets seem to growl less aggressively.

I approach the door and peer through the crack into the darkness inside. Wooden steps fall away, leading to a room of no more than twenty square meters. It contains a neatly made cot with an open footlocker at the far end, a thick clay washbowl pushed into a corner next to a leafy fern turned brown, and an armoire. An Orthodox cross hangs on the plaster wall over the cot, seeming to watch over everything. Another wooden door is set in the opposite wall. It is similar to the one I'm leaning through but less weathered, and it is closed tightly. It appears to lead into the bowels of the cathedral. The small room looks like the quarters for a caretaker.

I step inside. The first thing that hits me is the familiar smell of roasted chicory and expensive cigars, just as a sudden movement catches the corner of my eye. I pivot, crouch, aim a straight punch—

too late. The inside of my skull explodes incandescence. The room reels while I strike weakly at unseen foes, swimming in a viscous haze. I crack to my knees onto unyielding stone. The walls whirl, rainbow colors spin and flash, and I hear a creamy voice say, "Finish him." Then everything goes black.

chapter 42

I gradually come to my senses, feeling as if I've been encased in heavy oil. Trapped, eyes glued shut, mouth clogged—no, gagged. I struggle mightily to free my bound limbs, gasping, choking, willing my eyes to open, but to no avail.

"He's awake," says a vaguely familiar voice.

"Make him able to talk," says another voice, this one like smooth mocha, a voice I've branded into my memory. Peter.

"I doubt that he's coherent," says the first voice, which I now recognize as that of Big Head. *Strahov*, I remember. Strahov was the name of my Czech captor.

"He is made of stern stock," says Peter.

He's right. I've been smacked on the head so many times that I've developed a high tolerance. Rough hands jostle my head as they untie the blindfold and yank out the gag. Whatever bindings lash my hands and feet stay in place.

I make a show of being punch-drunk, lolling my tongue and moaning. Force my eyes open to the merest slits, which is a mistake because when I do I no longer have to pretend to be in pain as aluminum rays pierce my retinas like needles. I squint through the stinging glare to take in what I can.

I am still in the square little room. I'm lying faceup on the cot. When my eyes focus, the Orthodox cross shimmers into being, seeming to emanate from a fog until the wall behind it hardens into cracked, faded plaster.

Peter is mostly as I remembered him from the Smolny Institute conference room six years before—the one where I longed to kill him and his coterie of armchair military experts—slender, but starting to paunch. He has the same oiled hair, except that it is thinner and grayer now. Wrinkles spiderweb the corners of his eyes, which on reflection seem smaller than before, more piggish. He is holding a pistol, a Tokarev semiautomatic, well polished but still a relic. One can die just as easily from a bullet delivered by an antique, I reflect.

"So we meet again, Colonel Volkovoy," Peter says. "On my terms."

I spit blood, aiming for his alligator-skin shoes. Miss.

His face tightens. He strokes his thumb on the trigger guard of the Tokarev. Strahov shifts his weight. I can't decide whether his fidgeting is a sign of discomfort or anticipation.

"Always the barbarian, Volk," Peter says, but this time his tone is rougher, as if the mocha coffee is full of gritty grounds.

"Fuck yourself," I tell him. "Hard and rough, just like I fucked your wife."

He launches himself at my face, pummeling me with the pistol. In his anger and eagerness to inflict the most damage the blows are wild, uncalculated, sparing major damage to my face. A cheekbone crunches, blood jets inside my mouth, and a strip of skin peels away near my temple, but I'm conscious enough to know when Strahov drags Peter back, bear-hugging the enraged man's arms to his sides.

"Your wife hit harder than that." I do my best to speak clearly through the blood. "At least she did in the beginning, before she started to like it."

His eyes bulge, and he renews his struggles. "Let me go!" he bellows, but Strahov clamps down even more tightly.

"No!" Strahov says in a low, urgent tone. "He *wants* you to knock him senseless, don't you see?"

Strahov is right. My desire to antagonize Peter is only a part of what drives me to goad him. Another part of me craves oblivion.

Peter takes a deep breath, shrugs Strahov off his back, and straightens the knot in his bloodred tie. "Where is she?" he says hoarsely.

Valya released Posnova almost a week ago. Apparently she has not seen fit to contact her husband. I smile my Borzoi smile. "Dead," I answer, reveling in the agony that surges into his eyes.

Strahov jumps between us. "That's not true," he says, more to Peter than to me.

"Bullshit!" I'm enjoying the moment, playing it, taking out a loan against the pain I know Peter will soon deliver. "A friend of mine works at the Moscow Zoo. He opened it for me in the night. After I tired of fucking her, I carved her up a little at a time and fed her to the hyenas like table scraps. She's hyena shit now, Peter."

His face turns ashen. The pistol falls from his hand, and he drops down to his knees, moaning "Oh, no, oh, no, oh, no."

Strahov wheels on me furiously and slams a big fist into my vulnerable solar plexus. I lie there gasping as Strahov tries to comfort the shattered man. It almost saddens me to see how deeply Peter loves his treacherous wife.

"It's not true," Strahov is telling him when my breath returns.

"You should be glad she's dead," I wheeze. "She's the one who got you into this mess. Trust me, it'll be harder to get out than it was to get in."

Peter turns his shell-shocked eyes to me. "What are you saying?"

Strahov's face twists in fury. "Shut up!" he screams at me. "Shut the fuck up!"

The framework I've built in my mind creaks, groans, tilts dangerously to one side. "She brought Maxim to you," I say to Peter slowly, because the truth is just beginning to dawn on me.

"What are you talking about?"

Peter seems to be genuinely puzzled, and now I have no doubt that he is simply a lovesick husband with too much power, not part of Maxim's scheme with Posnova, not even in league with the dead politicians. I don't doubt that he was the one who sicced the Neva police boats on us, but he must have been acting on limited information, trying to foil a plot he knew virtually nothing about. Even in Prague he was driven by desire for his estranged wife—he knew she would come to whomever had the *Leda,* and so he sent me out to find it, and to find Posnova in the process. He didn't know just what he was getting himself in for, however, or with whom he was getting involved. Maxim is far beyond his power to control. His face goes through a gamut of emotions. Confusion. Growing realization. Resignation.

My own bashed features must be going through a similar transformation. "You came to the party late, didn't you, Peter?"

He nods wanly, still considering the implications. The last dot takes him too long to connect. His erstwhile partner acts before he is able to come to grips with the newly exposed reality.

Strahov draws a silenced Heckler & Koch from his shoulder holster and uses it to splat bits of Peter's skull and brains all over the far wall beneath the hanging cross. Peter doesn't even change expression; one minute he's dejectedly connecting mental dots, the next his head distorts and explodes into fragments. The body has barely crumpled to the floor when the gun presses against the underside of my nose. I don't know what Strahov's hurry is. Lashed down as I am, I'm going nowhere.

"Okay, wise-ass. Start talking." His big head is doing its familiar bounce. His eyes are doe-brown and hopping.

"What do you want to talk about?"

"The fucking paintings! What do you think? Where are the fucking paintings?"

"How long have you been working for Maxim, Strahov? Do you really think he's going to give you a piece of the action? As soon as you find the paintings he'll turn you into fertilizer."

He scowls. Jams the muzzle against my nose so hard that it scrapes off skin. Shifts his body to reach behind his back and produces a black, formed-plastic handle with metal prongs at the end. "Know what this is, Volk? A fucking Taser. Know what it feels like? This."

He replaces the pistol under my nose with the Taser. His fist contracts. Lightning bolts crash through my skull. My entire body convulses. The pain is so disabling that I can't even scream. All that comes out is an agonized "Aaaargh!" The lightning bolts stop. The smell of singed flesh fills my nose. My limbs twitch uncontrollably, for how long I don't even know.

"I ask, you answer. Yes?" Strahov's voice seems to come from a great distance.

Electric currents crackle every nerve ending in my body. Drool dribbles off my chin. The air smells metallic. Why lie when I don't know the truth anyway? The effort to speak is nearly too much to bear.

"That's why I'm here, Strahov." I try to talk slowly to delay the next racking dose of electricity. No matter what I say, it's coming. Strahov likes this sort of thing. I know the signs of that sickness well. "I'm trying to find the paintings just like you are."

"What do you know?" he says.

"They were hidden by the caretaker who lived here. He's dead."

"I know that, damn you!"

Strahov jams the Taser into my belly and blasts another screaming shock wave through my body. It blows the breath out of me. I can't even cry out. I can only groan and perform a tied-down jiggling dance that lasts a long time after he removes the device.

"You look funny," Strahov says and giggles.

I remember the bloody gristle being hosed off the concrete floor in the limestone building in Prague. At the time I didn't picture Strahov as the man who put it there, but now I know that I was wrong.

"Next time it's your balls, Volk," he says, big head bouncing, grinning. "Where did Kuvaldin hide them?"

"I don't know," I tell him truthfully, and then steel myself against the pain to follow.

He presses his toy into my crotch.

I bite down so hard I taste ground enamel, but the anticipated explosion of agony fails to come. When I open my eyes I think I have fallen into a dream.

Above me, hovering ghostly over my clenched face, is my beautiful guardian angel. White hair fans out to frame the smoky brilliance of her gray eyes. Kuvaldin's cross floats over her head, a blurred chiaroscuro slash against the eggshell background of the wall.

chapter 43

Valya's left hand looks like a child's against Strahov's big forehead, wrenching it hard against her shoulder. Her right hand grapples with the heaving handle of Kuvaldin's spade, the business end of which is buried in Strahov's gaping mouth. He flails in her arms, but his rolled-back eyes look like white marbles, and the blood from his mouth covers his chest. He is dying in installments. Each time Valya grinds the spade deeper into his throat he cuts loose a wet, choking scream that dies inside him. She rides him down to the throw rug next to Peter, still cranking on the spade handle as if it were a motorcycle throttle, corkscrewing past his Adam's apple. She braces herself on her good leg as he gurgles and kicks. Dying that way takes a long time.

When Strahov is finally gone she uses his shirttail to wipe the blood from her hands. "You're such a fool, Alexei," she says, concentrating on her cleaning. "I knew you would need my help."

"You looked ill when you left the station," Valya says later, when I've recovered somewhat.

I'm sitting up in the cot, massaging my wrists. Valya has unclasped the restraints—the same kind of plastic ties they used in Prague. The silver fillings in my back teeth spike jolts of pain and leak a metallic taste.

"I wanted to be close to you," she continues, "but I knew it wasn't the time to talk, so I followed you. That's when I saw the one with the big head. You would have seen him as well, except you were feeling sorry for yourself."

I'm still jumpy from the electricity. The ends of my toes and fingers tingle.

"Your nose looks like a giant strawberry," she says.

"Thank you, Valya."

She looks away to hide the moisture in her eyes. Shrugs.

I rub my chafed wrists. Strahov's leg spasms. A fly—the first of many, I'm sure—lands on the metal flange of the spade and delicately picks its way into his yawning mouth.

"What can we do, Alexei? About us?"

She has taken a seat on the edge of the bed next to me and is digging a chewed nail into the foam of Kuvaldin's thin mattress. The translucent skin on the side of her neck flutters.

She deserves a better life. She has brains and beauty and an impossible-to-quantify depth of character that makes her more precious than the rarest diamond and the most sublime painting. She is a symphony of granite and grace. I am Russian. Fatalistic. Broken. My heart pumps icy vodka. The greatest gift I can give her is freedom from me and my kind. It is, I know, a gift that will have to be forced upon her in stronger terms than I used on the night train.

"You know Leonid? The soldier with HIV?"

She turns to face me with a nod.

"His wife, Lilia, loves him. I think she would do anything for him. One of the things she does is fuck for money. I don't think she likes whoring, but she likes the money. Some of it goes for the drugs to fight the virus inside him. Some of it goes to buy fake Manolo Blahnik shoes and Gucci handbags."

Her brow furrows. A fresh blast of pain shimmies up my nose to my eyeballs. Her set jaw makes clear that she sees where I'm heading.

"Leonid has accepted the trade-off, because in his mind he has no choice. He gave up his bond with Lilia to stay alive. Despite it all she has kept her bond with him, and it's killing her just as certainly as the virus is killing him—killing her spirit, at least, and her self-respect."

"Just say it, Alexei."

Every part of me hurts, but the worst is my heart. It feels as if it's fracturing into a million pieces of shrapnel. I plow ahead, because if I don't I won't be able to live with myself. "When you were with Posnova it was a betrayal. Even though you told me about it. Even though it was not with another man. And you made it worse when you let her go. Those things severed our bond in a way that I won't get over. Jealousy ruins a man, Valya."

"It's over with her."

Tears brim in her wide eyes. They are like acid burning into my soul, because I know they are there because she believes I am telling her the truth about why things have to end between us. I want to take her into my arms and hold her close, feel her heart beating, smell her soapy skin, let her flaxen hair tickle my face while I tell her that I can forgive her affair with Posnova. But the price, the price of her future, is too high.

"I can't forget," I say, wishing I were dead at the end of Strahov's electric prod.

Her mouth works. She swallows hard and jerks her head sharply up and down. "Okay, Alexei." She rises and hops around the bodies to the doorway. Reaches through and grabs her crutches. "Okay," she says again. And then she struggles up the two steps and disappears.

I don't think she'll be back, not this time.

For a while after she leaves I just sit on Kuvaldin's bed, telling myself that nothing is forever. Scar tissue will develop over this wound, too, just as it has over others. I realize that I have been rocking in place, but for how long I don't know. I steady myself with great effort. It is time to move on.

I take a deep breath. Regard the bodies on the floor with distaste. Kuvaldin's room is just over a stone's throw from Maryinsky Palace City Hall and enough policemen for a small army. Traffic churns less than forty meters away. On the other side of the wall, inside St. Isaac's, tourists are craning their necks to gaze at the high, domed vault. What to do with two dead bodies?

I finger the flap of skin hanging from my temple. Wash the blood from my face and mouth in the stale water at the bottom of Kuvaldin's clay bowl. Pour the pink water into the private garden outside the door, refill the bowl from a wall spigot five steps away, and return to the confines of the room.

The activity does me good, helps to get my mind working again. I decide that no one can make any connection between Peter and me. He was not acting within his authority as a political appointee or a member of the FSB or whichever of the alphabet soup of secret service agencies he might have worked for. Neither was Strahov. I doubt they were even here to try to find me. I think Maxim set Strahov to watch Kuvaldin's quarters, and Peter happened to be with him when I blundered in. They can be left behind, and the ensuing uproar won't be traced back to me.

The open chest at the foot of the cot has already been rifled through—by the police, by Peter before I arrived, and before all others, by Maxim and his henchmen. The main compartment contains clothes, a Bible, slippers, a folder of notes referencing biblical text, a plastic-wrapped half loaf of banana bread turned to mold, a Snickers candy bar, a used bar of soap, a frayed toothbrush, and a rolled-up tube of toothpaste. A small interior chamber has been cleverly built into the corner. The locking mechanism consisted of a metal strap held in place by tumblers released by a key, but none of that matters anymore. The entire mechanism has been fractured. Nothing is left inside the chamber except for a faded icon on a piece of wood the size of my palm. Whatever else used to be in the chest has disappeared into opportunistic pockets and evidence lockers.

I collapse wearily to the floor with my back to the chest, still holding the icon. The coppery smell of spilled blood wrinkles my nose. I try to recall Lipman's exact words, rambling and drug-induced as they were. Felix hid the paintings in the church, Lipman said, referring to St. Isaac's, or so I thought. Doubtless Maxim has searched every inch of the place, with help from the local authorities, but he has come up empty. Maybe Felix *did* hide the paintings in a church, but *which church?* The icon seems to burn my palm. A film of cold sweat coats me as I study it more closely.

It shows Mary kneeling before an angel at the moment of the Annunciation of Immaculate Conception.

My heart falters, skips a whole beat, then races to catch up.

I mind-plow old lessons about the Russian Orthodox Church, trying to recall the significance of the positioning of the images on the icon stand in a church. Remember that hard left of the altar is Mother Mary, hard right is Christ, and the icon second from the right of the altar identifies the church. One more connection—the church in Novodevichy Convent is a church of Annunciation.

I use my front teeth to pull up the antennae on the Nokia. Speed-dial my special number for the General. He picks up without saying anything.

"It's Volk," I say.

He grunts.

"I need you to find out whether a man named Felix Kuvaldin traveled to Moscow sometime during early June. Probably by train, but we should check flights as well."

"How soon do you need to know?" the General says.

"We're already too far behind."

He hangs up.

I return to the washbasin and reclean my wounds. The water stings where Peter's pistol scraped skin, but my face feels better when

I'm finished. The fecal smell of death wafts up from the bodies. One at a time I grab their heels and drag them into the far corner, meaning they're now three steps away from the cot instead of one. Then I lie down. The cot is soft, indented by many sleeping forms. My eyes are heavy. I put the Nokia on vibrate and rest it between my cheek and the mattress. Close my eyes.

Later, the Nokia's vibrations startle me into wakefulness. Its clock tells me that I slept for more than two hours.

"Go," I say into the phone.

"Kuvaldin rode the night train to Moscow on the third of June."

His trip would have been similar to the one Valya and I just made. Rocking through the darkness that seems to hold the tundra and taiga at bay. Except that he would have been clutching a precious package, probably trembling from fear.

"You think he hid the paintings in Moscow?" the General asks.

"I think he returned them to Sophia Alexeyevna."

Static crackles while the General considers this, probably thinking I'm crazy.

"I'm going to need after-hours access to Novodevichy Convent," I tell him.

"Call me when you're back in Moscow," he says.

This time I disconnect first, and then I'm up and out of there in seconds. Rushing. Because if I've figured out the significance of Kuvaldin's icon, someone else may have too.

chapter 44

A cab drops me on the corner across the street from Novodevichy Convent. Twelve hours have passed since I left the dead caretaker's quarters in St. Isaac's Cathedral, but I have not slept or changed clothes. I spent the lonely ride back to Leningrad Station mentally cataloging my many failures over the past two months. I wait impatiently until a nun with a twitching nose like a mole's opens a small wooden door set into the wall several paces away from the main entry, the baroque Transfiguration Gate-Church. She is acting on orders filtered down by the General through his underground network, and is clearly displeased by the nature of her task.

"How many more are coming?" she sniffs.

I assume she is referring to the soldiers who are due to arrive soon, probably within minutes, and don't answer. She stands aside as I pass by, then closes the door behind me and hurries away. I begin traipsing around the convent grounds, not knowing what to look for, really, just walking and thinking. As I enter, the Monk's Quarters are on my right. A small ticket office is on the left in front of an exhibition room. I meander along a pathway of broken bricks, past scattered tombstones and the tiny Prokhorov Chapel, until I am standing beneath the lit domes of Smolensk Cathedral. I bury my hands in the deep pockets of my overcoat and sigh. I have no idea where to start my search.

Shards of exploded red brick razor my face just as the reverberating echo of the shot cracks the stillness of the night. I am instantly down, cranking blasts from the Sig in the general direction of the shooter as I roll heedlessly through shrubs for the cover of a tombstone. Exploding green mushrooms in the high grass near my arm mark the impact of more bullets. The next instant I'm jamming my back into the tombstone, breathing hard, assessing the situation.

Troops from the General's special forces are probably already approaching the main gate. The prudent course is to wait, but I don't feel like waiting. The shooter is no pro, or I would already be leaking brains all over the grass. The angle of the misses tells me that he has the high ground—probably a window in the bell tower, which overlooks the cathedral grounds and my meager shelter behind the weathered headstone.

I crab over to the shelter of a sarcophagus built on a concrete support stand about a meter high. Bolt without hesitation to another headstone topped by an Orthodox cross, which clangs from the impact of another shot just as I thud to the ground behind it. The momentum of my running slide carries me past the safety of the new headstone, and another shot rips the fleshy part of my calf above the prosthesis, slamming my leg to the ground like the wing of a butterfly under a needle. I scramble desperately to fold my limbs behind the narrow cover of stone.

Sweat waterfalls off my chin and forehead as I huddle there panting, trying to ignore the tearing pain shooting up my leg. The shooter might not be a pro, but with the high ground in his favor all he has to do is shift position for a better angle and I'm dead. I need to make the refuge of the nearby wall of the tiny chapel. My probing fingers determine that the bullet has torn flesh, not bone. My prosthesis moves when my mind wills it—the combination of muscles and mechanisms works through pain. Thinking more about it will get me nowhere, so I bound up and over the stone and fling my body against the chapel wall just as my ears register new shots.

Crouching against the wall, I take stock. My lower leg is soaked in blood, and my boot is squishy, but I'm mobile. Only one shooter is up there. He may have company with him in the tower, but whoever is with him does not have a high-powered rifle. I wasn't ready, the shooter had the high ground, but I'm still alive. I can take him, even in this state.

Twenty paces to my right is the ivy-covered wall of an exhibition room. A short dash from there will take me to a wooden ticket office that will offer concealment but not protection from high-velocity bullets.

I push away from the chapel. Run madly for the ivy wall. Bullets zing as I hit the concrete behind the ivy. I bounce away instantly to keep surprise as my ally and dive toward the ticket office. A bullet shatters wood, sending splinters whizzing into and past my face. Most people, even trained soldiers, would wait here, then gather for a final charge. He'll expect that, so I don't. I dive, roll once, and dive again headfirst into the shelter at the base of the high wall, where bullets from the bell tower can't reach.

Behind me comes the pounding sound of men at the front entrance. The General's men have arrived. Together we can storm the tower. Best case, the shooter will be done in minutes. Worst case, we will have to endure a siege with an inevitable favorable conclusion. My blood lust is up. *Fuck waiting.*

Stone steps lead up to a wooden door that cracks open under my ramming boot. I charge up more steps recklessly, heedless of the possibility the shooter might be waiting. Shouts behind me indicate that the soldiers are in the courtyard. Movement flashes in the corner of my eye just as I round another corner. Bricks explode into flintlike pieces next to my ear as a thunder-cracking shot booms. I drop, wheel, fire into a sulfurous haze—*Bam! Bam! Bam!*

A man clothed in black slams back, then slumps. My fourth shot thuds his skull against the rock wall behind him. His head leaves a lustrous trail of gore glistening on the wall as he slides to the floor. I scoot toward the body. Roll him over so that the moonlight from the cutout window shows what is left of his face. The dead man is Maxim's Ukrainian, the aging frog. A revolver has fallen to the ground next to his body. He must have left the rifle upstairs.

My injured leg sears with fiery licks. I settle onto the gritty floor on one haunch, my bad leg stretched out in front of me. The corpse means that Maxim is here in spirit, haunting me.

Suddenly, a hot ring of steel burns into the back of my neck. Pressure forces my chin toward my chest. Too late I realize the Ukrainian was not the shooter. He was merely an accomplice.

"You bastard," Yelena Posnova says. "My only regret is that I won't be able to make it last forever, the same way you hurt me."

No wonder the shots were wild. She must have found it nearly impossible to hold and fire the rifle with her fingers so badly mangled. So consuming was her hatred that she must have been unable to surrender the rifle and let the Ukrainian take the shots. She needed to kill me herself. The barrel digs deeper into the back of my neck as she shifts her weight to prepare for the recoil.

I react with snarling fury. She is unskilled in this kind of fighting—easy to take. I'm already leaning back on my left hand, so it is a simple matter to sweep my right arm in a rigid arc into her ankles. Her feet fly out from under her. The barrel flings away from my neck as her arms flail in an instinctive reaction. The momentum from my sweep carries me around in time to catch the dislodged rifle—a Kalashnikov—and swipe the butt across her face. Her head snaps back. She collapses into a heap next to me. A canyon of blood wells below her cheekbone, and lines of red rim the teeth in her open mouth, but she is still conscious. Tears of frustration mingle with the blood in rosy trickles.

I point the barrel at her left eye. "Peter is dead," I tell her, and then wait for a reaction.

Nothing. Her face may as well have been made of forged steel.

Steps pound on the stairs behind me. Her eyes flicker over my shoulder and then shine with relief. I don't have to turn around to know that the soldiers have arrived.

"Put down the weapon!" one of them shouts. The others stamp the floor, positioning themselves for better angles from which to cover me.

Posnova gives me a crimson lip curl that I suppose signifies victory. She was never straight with Peter, so she has no way of knowing I'm still military.

"I am Colonel Alexei Volkovoy," I say without turning around.

Behind me, gravelly crunches provide evidence that the soldiers have grounded the butts of their rifles. "Yes, sir," says the same man, only now his voice is strained. He's probably saluting.

Posnova's eyes widen in shock. They shift back and forth from the soldiers to me.

I lever painfully to my feet. "What was it between you and Valya?"

Posnova is still too surprised by the soldiers' reaction to manage a hateful lie. But, as usual, truth cuts more deeply than deceit. "She's young. She thought I cared for her." Posnova leers. Apparently she has regained enough of her wits to want to hurt me. "Maybe I was the momma she never had."

I feel as though I'm being consumed by the memory of the man I was before, by the killer inside me, unable to alter my preordained path and become someone better. Rationalization comes easily—she tried to kill me; her evil schemes led to Valya's mutilation; she is beyond redemption. But the simple truth is that compassion and forgiveness are beyond me now.

The barrel of the Kalashnikov cracks her teeth when I shove it into her mouth. I let a moment tick past to allow the horrible realization to dawn in her eyes, which are wide and wet like watery blue globes. When I can see that she knows what's coming I pull the trigger and shower brains and bone all over the chamber.

chapter 45

Shadows lean and dance. Sounds fade and boom unpredictably. The convent gardens reel beneath me. Somehow I manage to stagger out of the bell tower and onto the grounds of the courtyard. I blink away blood only to see captain's bars gleaming reflected moonlight from a black cutout figure standing before me.

"Captain Dubinin reporting, sir," the cutout bellows. The captain squares his broad shoulders. His bristling mustache threatens to scrub my face, but I know the sensation is only an illusion created by my addled senses. He is standing a good three feet away. He salutes, staying rigid until I give a halfhearted wave that he apparently chooses to consider an acknowledgment. "At your service, sir," he says.

I wince and turn my head in a failed attempt to dodge the noise. "Don't be so goddamned formal, Dubinin." I squint at him for a better view.

"Yes, sir," he says, ending the salute.

Priests, nuns, groundskeepers, and police mill about us, chattering in the way people do when they're frightened. "Clear away the spectators."

Dubinin barks loud orders that ricochet in my pounding skull. Soldiers prod, herd, shove. The gathering dissipates.

"See that the cathedral is emptied."

More thunderous orders. Three men jog away. I drop to the base of an oak. My leg has gone blessedly numb. I wish I could fall asleep, wake up hours later in the loft with Valya warm beside me . . .

The next time I look up the crowd is gone. I don't know how much time has passed. Dubinin looms over me. His mustache hangs in a concerned frown. "Do you need medical attention, sir?"

"The cathedral?"

He looks at me strangely. "All clear."

I hoist myself to my feet. The world lurches. Dubinin grips my arm near the shoulder. "I can make it on my own, Captain," I tell him.

"Yes, sir."

An arc light explodes behind me. I cringe as if I've been shot. Turn around to regard the roped section of dirt where part of the Ukrainian's skull landed after my bullet blew it through the stone aperture, then march through a line of soldiers toward the entryway.

The soldiers stand at attention while I pass through the towering doors of the Cathedral of the Smolensk. Ornamental cast-iron plates form the floor. They echo a reverberating gong from my heavy boots as I approach the fiery gold iconostasis. I stop beneath an enormous golden chandelier, bonfire bright, the light like razors slicing my eyes. Pull Kuvaldin's icon from my overcoat pocket and compare it to the icon second from the right of the altar. They match. Blood slides down my forearm when I return the icon to my coat. I didn't even know I was cut there. The weight of the Sig in my other pocket feels disproportionate, threatening to tilt my entire body to one side.

Where? Where would a frightened, determined man like Kuvaldin hide the paintings? I shuffle through the interior, passing over the tombs of Sophia and two of her sisters without coming any closer to the answer.

On my orders Dubinin rousts a quaking priest and drags him

away from a huddled flock of convent residents. He is bald except for tufts of whitish hair standing straight out from his head over his ears, which stick out at an odd angle, reminding me of Elephant Ears. It saddens me that I never even knew his real name. We trudge down stone steps into the burial vault in the basement. Cobwebbed tombs. Musty-smelling pathways leading nowhere except to more of the convent's famous dead and then to a short hall ending at a cracked door. Dubinin scrapes it open, and I push past.

"Please," the little gnome says from behind me. "There is nothing in the sacristy."

Dubinin muzzles him with a look.

Ferocious pain eats at my leg. I lean against the wall and scan the cluttered room, only to see the expected tools of the religious trade. Candelabra, dog-eared lectionaries, psalm books, brocaded, gold-threaded vestments, a row of Orthodox crosses, a dulled-silver chalice, discarded icons that would grace museum walls in most countries, ancient texts. Nothing. No sign of any recent disturbance. No strange boxes or shrouded piles or concealed compartments.

My frustrated growl causes Dubinin and the wizened priest to startle backward. The priest nervously pulls at the ropey cord of the cincture circling his waist as we tread back up the steps and out to the grounds. Soldiers are still swarming around the bell tower, which has become a brightly lit crime scene that won't be connected to me, not officially at least.

"Where did Sophia live?"

The priest looks at me like I'm crazy. "Sophia Alexeyevna died over three hundred years ago."

Dubinin grabs his arm. "Just answer the man's question."

"In the convent. I can only guess at the precise room."

"Take me there."

The priest leads the way into the convent, shuffling ahead of us through tight halls and up more nearly impossible steps. Everyone waits for me when I pause to gather myself on each landing as we wind higher.

Finally, the priest tugs open a heavy door. Dubinin and I follow him into a cramped, moonlit room that is empty save for a one-person bed on a metal frame and a baroque chest of drawers built long after Sophia was interred beneath the cathedral floor. A lancet arched window overlooks the Moscow River and the Kremlin's domes. Stone tiles cover the floor. There is no place large enough to hide a painting the size of *Leda and the Swan*.

We return to the outside grounds. I turn my back to the crime-scene lights and punch a number on the speed dial of the Nokia.

"Anything?" the General says.

"No."

He says nothing. His rattling inhalations make him sound as if he has a cold.

Frustration and sleeplessness cause me to blurt out the question that is troubling me the most. "How did Maxim's man know to wait for me here?"

"I was about to ask you the same thing," the General growls.

What can I say to that? He's lying. He sent me to Strahov, who worked for Maxim; he and Maxim used me to eliminate the politicians, one each, so they both had something on the other; and the same nun who let me into the convent also opened the door for the Ukrainian frog and Posnova. Those are the connections I know of, meaning there are doubtless many others. I am utterly alone.

"I'll find the paintings," I say, but the General is already gone.

chapter 46

The sight of the broken elevator at Masha's building is almost enough to make me weep. The climb takes an eternity. I drag my injured leg along the polished hallway past the colored sound dampeners to her door. Rest my head on my arm propped against the jamb while waiting for her to answer and then nearly fall inside when she opens the door.

She catches me. "You look terrible," she says, leading me inside to the wicker chair.

I tell her what I want while she boils water for her thick Russian tea. While I'm talking she chops leaves and throws them along with an unrecognizable powder into the kettle.

"You need a doctor, not a reading," she says.

"I've been hurt worse. I'll live."

She sniffs. "At least let me clean your leg."

"No. That's not the kind of help I need right now, Masha."

Her jaw tightens as she returns her attention to the tea. She drops another leafy substance into the pot.

When the concoction is ready, she fills a mug and hands it to me, watching while I take the hot liquid in five blazing gulps. It tastes sweet and sour at the same time, and it leaves a burning residue in my mouth. She removes the drained mug from my hands and returns it to her tiny countertop.

"Nothing's happening," I say a few minutes later.

She ignores me. She refills the kettle with water. Dumps more herbs inside. Billowing clouds of sickly sweet steam fill the tiny apartment. The humid warmth is comforting, like a hot towel wrapped around my body. She turns out all the lights save one next to the bed, which she covers with a brownish blanket that allows only a thin glow of ocher light to pass. Her shadow performs a steamy dance, seeming to merge with her wavering form so that I can no longer make out where she ends and her ghostly companion begins.

I think my injuries must have overtaken my brain. A hissing roar like a distant ocean fills my ears. Perversely, the scrape of her wooden shoes sounds thunderously loud, as does her voice, as if she is talking from a place inside my head.

"A reading is unlikely to reveal the thing you seek."

I struggle to keep my eyes open. She is wearing a shapeless tangerine shift that rustles with a sound like crinkling tissue when she moves. The shift flows into burnt-orange marmalade, then turns to poured gold, pulsing in syncopation with the roar in my ears.

"I will only be able to see what is already in your mind. Even then . . ."

Her voice seems to trail away visibly, like a rippling snake winding into the mist that surrounds her. The realization that I've been drugged worse than the addicts on the street below penetrates the fog of my mind, but the thought generates a languid mental response bordering on indifference. The drugs are like sorcery tendrils seeping into the crannies of my brain. I feel as if I am floating along a slow-rolling river.

The skin on her hands reminds me of dried corn husks—brown, wrinkled, wicked of moisture by the workings of sun and time. But her palms are soft when she holds my right hand in hers—twin petals wrapping an oversize hunk of meat is the image that comes to mind, just as it did during my first reading months ago. Soon I feel radiating warmth, as if the recessed coils of a hidden heater are glowing like burnished copper beneath her skin.

"Alexei," she says softly, dreamily.

Her normally rutted timbre is smoky soft, as if coming from the throat of a young woman, not that of a waning, chain-smoking babushka.

She strokes my hand. "So much bad has been done to you." Seconds tick past, or maybe hours. Time is a concept without meaning. "And *by* you."

She swells in my steam-clouded vision. Her eyes are closed. The lids are crevassed, blued by faintly applied, flaking shadows. Her fuzzy chin droops to settle to her chest, and then she seems to shrink inside herself, almost as if, I realize sluggishly, I am looking into a shape-shifting mirror.

"So much evil leaves a terrible mark."

She falls silent again. Divination is hard work, or so it seems. I struggle to orient myself. The flat teeters, rocks, sways. Ivory blades of light pierce my narcotized mind. The light changes to shafts of violet, then twisting red, and, finally, soothing green frosted with a glaze of ice. My limbs fall limply to my sides. The back of the wicker chair embraces me comfortingly. The chromed greenish glow envelopes me. My mind wanders frivolously. The glow fades.

And then the brightness returns without warning. Iridescent images scorch my mind, too powerful to escape . . .

Lissome Valya floats in a tungsten sky, beckoning. Leda shimmers amid the bulrushes. Posnova writhes under my torturing hands. Maxim speaks, low and deep. *Volk—he is the man for this.* A cargo plane spins out of control, exploding in the fiery red sands of the Iranian desert while the General watches solemnly, sadly. Sophia howls frustration and rage behind a lancet arch framed by stone piers.

A black cross nestles on a bed of blazing, crystallized frost. A man with a flame-scarred face and amber eyes flies against a wheeling backdrop of gold and cobalt blue, dead with heartbeats still left, his outstretched arms spreading his wind-rippled coat to form fruitless wings.

Everything swirls as if I am in the bowl of a giant whirlpool, and suddenly I am one with the caretaker in his nauseating plunge. The sky spins, indigo-bright, paint-splashed with gossamer clouds, then filled by the golden dome of St. Isaac's Cathedral. The onrushing ground swells, looms, grasps. I glimpse the face of Christ, composed and peaceful in his moment of ultimate remission of sin.

My head thumps against the wall behind me. The cramped flat reforms. Rumpled bed, TV with foil antenna, cramped ceiling, and Masha, eyes wide open, peering not into my soul—that part of the experience is over—but rather straight into my face, looking concerned.

"Are you all right?" Her scratchy voice has returned.

"What time is it?"

"You've been here an hour."

I rub my eyes, trying without success to recall the passage of time.

"You see now?" She cocks an eyebrow.

"No."

Her lips thin. "Open your eyes, Alexei."

My head aches. My leg throbs. I love Masha, but I want to shake her until answers fall out.

"I saw what you saw," she says. "It is enough." She settles back onto the mattress and closes her eyes. "It is enough if you are not blind."

chapter 47

I ride the train to the loft. It is barren, soulless. I can't stay there, and I can't handle the loneliness of the apartment on Solyanka Street. I take the fire escape back down to the street. My stump and the fleshy wound below my knee join in an agonizing cluster of pain as I trudge toward the café. Enter quietly through the back way, plop into my chair, close my eyes.

Vadim wakens me. Gauze, bright steel instruments, a steaming basin of water, and a yellowish jar of balm are arrayed on a cloth spread over my table. He uses a scalpel to slice away my clothes. Washes me with a sponge and inspects the hole in my leg.

"You need a shot?"

His tone implies the answer should be no, not for a mere flesh wound. It's not his leg. The pain is such that I want something. But drugs? Can my body survive more drugs?

"No."

He cleans the wound the way you clean the barrel of a gun, running a tool like a bore cleaner wrapped in soaked cloth through the tunnel made by the bullet. Vadim is no doctor, but he has lived life in war and prison, so this injury is well within his expertise. I clench my teeth to keep from whimpering.

He finishes with the leg then cleans my face where Peter battered it. That done, he gathers his things and sets a plastic pouch on the table. "These are for the pain and infection," he says grudgingly. "I'll be upstairs if you need me."

"What's wrong?"

He shakes his head without making eye contact. "I talked to Valya." He starts up the stairs. "You're a fool, Alexei. The hole in your leg will heal. The one in your heart will bleed forever."

After he leaves I curl in the corner behind my table with a box for a pillow. When I close my eyes the room spins, an aftershock from the session with Masha. My interlude with the plunging caretaker does not reprise itself. But Valya floats at the edge of my vision, growing smaller, imploring with enormous charcoal eyes.

I need to derive meaning from my visions, not weakened resolve. I focus on business. On the General, on Maxim—a matched pair. And, finally, I drift into a restless sleep.

The answer accompanies my usual nightmares filled with the faces of the dead and dying. Sophia Alexeyevna sleeps restlessly, filmed with sticky sweat. Starlight glows through her window and gleams off the polished stone floor beside her bed.

I don't know what time it is when my eyes flap open like pulled shades. The basement is dark. I hit the speed dial on the Nokia.

"What?" The General sounds tired.

My watch glows 3:30 A.M. I'm shocked that I might have actually awakened him. "I need all work orders related to Novodevichy Convent."

"Going back how long?" If I did awaken the dwarf, he has regained his wits with remarkable speed. Now his voice is clipped, alert.

"Two months," I answer.

He disconnects. I sag against the wall. Recall my visions with real-world fuzziness. No drug-induced clarity this time. But what I see is enough. The five domes of the Smolensk Cathedral. Sophia glaring out from her prison in Novodevichy Convent. A circular blade edged in diamonds abandoned on the floor of Orlan's gallery. He must have been the first to figure it out. Right before he died. Ten minutes later the Nokia buzzes.

"I've got the requisitions on the computer," the General says. "What are we looking for?"

"A job big enough to conceal the paintings."

Computer keys click. "June twelfth," he says. "Nine days after the caretaker rode the train to Moscow. A section of floor in the convent near the Pond Tower was replaced."

A jolt of electricity stiffens my back.

"A drawing shows the precise location," he says.

"Send Dubinin and a team of men to the convent, with the drawing. Tell them to bring digging tools and something to cut stone."

chapter 48

Dubinin and five soldiers wait under jaundiced lights outside Transfiguration Gate-Church. As soon as I've eased out of the passenger seat of the Mercedes, Vadim takes off fast, not wanting the soldiers to see his face.

Dubinin leads the way into the convent. The same wizened priest shuffles along with us back up the same impossible steps and into the same room with the baroque chest of drawers. Dubinin pushes the chest aside to reveal a section in the corner where the thick grout between the stone tiles is darker than the surrounding area. He pulls a folded blueprint from his tunic as one of his men sets up a generator and a light. The bulb snaps on, hurting my eyes.

"Here," he says, pointing to the spot on the drawing with his free hand. "This is where the work was done."

I stare at the wizened priest. "Who requisitioned the job?"

He stares back at me defiantly. "I did."

"Why?"

"As a favor to my friend, Felix Kuvaldin."

"You knew, then. The whole time, you knew."

He doesn't answer, which of course is answer enough. His lips tremble, but his eyes remain defiant.

I settle onto the bed and lean back against the wall. Regard Dubinin, who is standing ramrod straight in front of me, positioned to block the priest if he is silly enough to try to run. The mustachioed captain is smaller than I am, doubtless more polished as well. The aggression I exude like a black aura makes people nervous, so my job is more difficult than it should be sometimes. He is, I know from his bearing and the canny glint in his eye, one of the General's entourage of handpicked lieutenants—probably one of several candidates being groomed as my replacement. Prepared for the day when I am stomped under Maxim's boot or garroted by the next Kamil or dispatched into the Moscow River from a watery landing beneath the arsenal, when I am no longer useful to the General.

"Cut away the stone," I tell my younger doppelganger.

The keening wail of the metal blade slicing stone barely registers on my consciousness. I'm reclined on the bed in Sophia's chambers, pensive. Dubinin squats next to me, watching the soldiers work. The blade screeches to a stop. A stolid sergeant strips off his blouse, spits into his palms, lifts a pickax.

"Gently," I warn.

The sergeant cringes at the sound of my voice. He proceeds to tap with the pick like a tired paleontologist. Others join him with their own tools. I pop Vadim's pills, a pile of slick shapes and colors that fills my cupped palm. Dubinin's features stiffen into a look I read as disapproving. "Fuck you, Captain," I say, and he regards me with open-mouthed surprise. Maybe I was wrong about the look.

The circle of men undulates with picking brushstrokes of distorted motion, fading in and out of my fevered vision. Suddenly, the sergeant's sharply drawn breath stops everything. Dubinin rises lithely on two good feet and marches across the room to stare over the shoulders of the kneeling men. At his gesture they clear away more debris with their hands. When he is satisfied, the men settle onto their haunches to await further orders.

"It is a metal box," Dubinin tells me. "Long, wide, and flat."

"Remove it. Carefully."

The box slides out. Its flat metal sides gleam in the places where the soldiers' hands have swiped away the dust. The box is still nearly new, although scraped in places. It looks like an oversized portfolio, held closed by a metal clasp. Black rubberized weather stripping seals the joints. One of the men uses a fine brush to wipe away the remaining grit, taking care not to miss a spot. Dubinin queries me with a raised eyebrow.

"Open it," I tell him.

The top falls away.

Dubinin's sharply drawn breath indicates that she has captured him too in her five-hundred-year-old spell. I pull myself off the bed and squat next to the open box. *Leda* glows her ethereal beauty. Maybe the frothing drugs cruising my arteries have altered my perceptions, but her eyes seem to beckon me hither into her bulrush glade, as if a step into the chiaroscuro abyss will envelope me in warm peacefulness.

"Ah-hmm." Dubinin clears his throat, breaking my reverie.

Sophia's chambers swim in kaleidoscopic colors that refuse to go away no matter how many times I blink my eyes. So I close them tightly and slide my fingers along the gnarled oak frame, trying to feel my way back toward familiarity.

I recall the first time I felt along the coarsened edges, in the catacombs beneath the Hermitage, thinking then, as I do now, that the frame is much thicker than it needs to be. I open my eyes. Squint. On close inspection I see that extra material has been shimmed onto the back part of the frame. The added material is not noticeably different from that of the original frame, and it has aged in a way that blurs its edges together with Da Vinci's oak, but now that I know what to look for, the difference can be seen. Perhaps the concealment of the *Leda* behind the Mignard required the extra thickness. Or perhaps more than the *Leda* still resides within the double frame. Whatever the case might be, a sophisticated facility and specialized technicians and tools will be needed to learn the truth of it.

I gently close the metal top and snap the clasp closed. "Call a car," I instruct Dubinin.

He taps numbers into a cell phone. "Where are we going?" he asks around the mouthpiece.

"The Pushkin State Museum of Fine Arts."

chapter 49

The Pushkin Museum is a hop southwest of the Kremlin. Like the Hermitage, secret hoards of art appropriated from Germany by the Red Army are occasionally revealed there after long periods of hiding behind cloaks of denial and quintessential Russian misdirection. Gold from ancient Troy, first discovered in the nineteenth century by a German archaeologist. Works by Degas, Renoir, Goya, El Greco, and Tintoretto. And others we continue to keep hidden—a treasure trove to be raided when more money is needed. The Pushkin is the logical place to bring the *Leda* and, if it exists, her hidden companion. Doubtless that is why Dubinin looks openly shocked when I signal the driver of our panel van to continue past the museum.

"Where are we going?" Dubinin says.

I ignore his question and call the General. "We're almost there."

The Rerikh Museum sits along Maly Znamensky Lane, lonely compared to the more celebrated Pushkin. Nikolay Rerikh was a Russian mystic who lived much of his life in the Altay Mountains of Siberia, painting landscapes and mythological scenes. Years after his death, he has developed an international following, but his iconic museum is unpopular enough to be a suitable place for the General's artistic spoils headquarters.

I tap the driver's shoulder and point him into a space between two metal doors that are just beginning to slide apart as we drive up. Dubinin's surprise at our true destination comforts me in a childish way.

Once we are inside, I gesture the driver to a stop near a door guarded by one of the General's adjuncts. Dubinin and the driver slide the metal box from the van and carry it between them, following my lead. The door lets onto a stairwell that takes us down two flights to a basement that is, I know from previous visits, separated from the main museum by a brick wall. The basement is starkly lit. Special lights shine over an angled drafting table that serves as a prop for items under study, a lab table holding a microscope, Bunsen burner, slides, and scattered papers, and a cluttered desk pushed into the corner. Several other rooms are hidden behind closed doors.

The General stands before the drafting table with his arms behind his back. Medals glint among the colored ribbons that decorate his outthrust chest. He points his bluff chin toward a man in a white lab coat standing next to the desk in the corner. "This is Sulyan Fedun. He will help us to analyze the painting."

Fedun's long, skinny face twitches. He easily stands two meters tall, uncomfortably towering over the General. I'm positive the General is indifferent to the discrepancy in height, too used to power to concern himself with such trifles. Fedun's pale skin is blotchy red, whether from birthmarks or nerves I can't say. His long fingers worry the lapel of his lab coat. He is right to be afraid. How many people will be allowed to live with this secret?

"Clear the table," I tell him in a voice graveled by weariness and pain. The sound of it startles the lanky man into frightened action. He hurries to move items from the lab table, drops a rack of glass slides with a crash, and then stands there, holding an empty carriage, waiting for someone to tell him what to do.

"Move, man!" the General bellows, and Fedun scurries to comply. When the box is safely on the table, Dubinin opens it to reveal *Leda*.

"Sss," Fedun draws his breath, goggling.

The General merely glances at Leda. "How long before we know if anything has been hidden beneath this one?"

Fedun gathers himself in a gulping breath. "I don't know. Hours. Maybe a day or two."

"Stay with the paintings," the General tells Dubinin. To me, he says, "Get some sleep."

I address Fedun. "Do you have a cot?"

"Yes."

"I'll sleep here."

Dubinin shakes me awake. "Fedun has found something."

My chronometer shows 3:30 P.M. I have slept for more than ten hours. I lever up and off the rickety cot to follow the captain into the main room. Fedun stands sweating before the angled drafting table. A cloth has been draped over the table to conceal whatever rests on top of it. Another cloth covers the desk in the corner.

"The General is on his way," Dubinin says.

I lean against a wall that seems to move. The bandage that Vadim had wrapped around my leg is frayed and damp. I pull up the loose cotton of my trousers, heartened to see that the wetness is sweat, not blood. Fedun swims in and out of focus, scarecrow tall.

The General arrives, trailed by two lieutenants. He shakes his head at the sight of me and turns to Fedun. "What do we have?"

"A Trojan horse," Fedun says in an echoing voice that bounces bass reverbs along the tangled pathways of my befuddled brain.

Lost months dance in my mind's eye. *All for nothing!* the psychic cripple residing in my head screams. Dead police, tortured caretakers, lost Valya—all for fakery.

"A phony?" the General says.

"More like a *matryoshka*—a nesting doll," answers Fedun.

Then he slides away the covering of cloth.

chapter 50

A voice reverberates inside my head, droning incessantly. It is Fedun, I think, lecturing.

The Last Supper shows Christ relaxed, he says, resigned to the evil that courses through the arteries of men. Inner peace glows from his form, carried on the curves of his outstretched arms, which cradle the surrounding clutch of shriven apostles in a harmonic convergence that other renderings of the scene somehow fail to capture. The limitations of size subtly alter the scene, resulting in slight differences between this painting and the three-paneled masterpiece in the Milan monastery, although some of that may also be because the Milan painting has been subjected to such great trauma and so many changes over time.

Experts long suspected that Leonardo did not paint the face of Christ on the refectory wall, that what we can see there now was done later, by a less talented artist. Their suspicion was correct—the endless restorations failed to capture the glory Leonardo was able to impart. More sublimely than does the faded face on the wall, the canvas version shows a profound nobility of expression in Christ, on a par with the grace of his gesture toward the bread and wine laid out before him, all balanced by the exquisitely drawn figures of the apostles.

Blues and reds predominate, played against the pale whiteness of the horizontal tablecloth. The painted canvas makes a gradual, nearly imperceptible transition between areas of different color, a softening of edges and forms, a well-known veil-like quality of the surface, a technique called *sfumato,* from the Italian word *fumo* for smoke—a technique with which Leonardo was the greatest master.

"How has it fared against time?" The General's voice sounds like crackling ice, shattering my drugged reverie.

"Remarkably well, considering," answers Fedun. "It has been damaged, but even so . . ." He spreads hands, indicating that the point is self-evident. "One more thing," he adds. "Look closer."

The General leans over the canvas.

"Do you see the lines? The grid on the canvas beneath the paint?"

"Yes."

"Beneath the paint is a preparatory sketch, drawn first, before the painting. Leonardo then used this painting to transfer the design to the much larger mural on the wall of the refectory—to the version of *The Last Supper* that was already fading within decades of its creation."

"Does that diminish the value?" The General is nothing if not pragmatic.

Fedun's long face casts a thin shadow against the wall that shimmers when he shakes head. "No," he says gravely. "On the contrary, no value can possibly be placed on this work. It is priceless."

"What proof do we have that this was Da Vinci's work?"

"In October 1499 the French king Louis the Twelfth saw the wall painting in Milan. He was so smitten that he tried to purchase the wall to take back with him to France. All of which is well known to historians."

"So?"

Fedun walks like a man on stilts to the desk, snaps on a retractable lamp, pulls it closer over the desktop, and whips away the cloth covering. A flat panel sits on the desktop. The panel is nearly covered by three yellowed documents placed under a pane of glass. One of them looks from a distance to be the transmittal invoice Lipman showed to me in the Neva Café. The other two are handwritten as well, but they appear to be pages from an ancient legal document.

"You know about *Leda and the Swan*," Fedun says, looking at me. "These other pages are a contract—a contract for King Louis to purchase the preparatory painting of *The Last Supper*. Sophia Alexeyevna must have been able to purchase it from the French court at the same time she acquired *Leda*."

Fedun's mouth continues to move like the exaggerated lips of a character in an old-time movie, but no sound escapes.

Dubinin's hand on my arm startles me. *How did he get so close?* I wonder. The General spins to face me. His arms are outstretched like those of Christ in the painting, but the image that comes to my mind is that of Judas, wearing a look of feigned surprise as Christ announces that he has been betrayed. And as I pitch forward I wonder how many pieces of silver are enough to purchase the General's betrayal.

chapter 51

I awaken alone in my bed in the loft. The intricately painted nesting doll on the cantilevered ledge descends into ever smaller versions until it seems to disappear altogether. I wonder who brought me here. If it was anybody other than the General or Vadim I will have to make a new home. I may as well do so anyway, I decide, because this place is haunted by memories of Valya.

I splash water on my face and go to a window. Predawn light shines through. The alley below is strewn with trash but empty of people. I decide to walk to the Rerikh Museum.

The trip takes nearly an hour, but the pain is cleansing, and my wounded leg holds up well enough. On the way there I dial the General's special line, but get no answer. I call Vadim.

"So you're still alive," he says without preamble.

"What's going on?"

"Nothing," Vadim says, then waits quietly while I consider the implications of silence from the General.

"Meet me outside the Rerikh," I tell him, and hang up.

The outer steps leading down to the lab in the basement of the Rerikh Museum provide a comforting, railed nook in which to wait for Vadim. Dawn has arrived, and with it more people. A searing burn licks the cratered hole in my leg. The rest of my body feels icy cold.

A policeman struts along the sidewalk across the street. I'm reminded of Yuri, swinging his baton, so proud of his status, now so irretrievably dead. Another police officer joins the first—a woman, I surmise from the sway in her walk. They glance in my direction, then look quickly away.

My internal radar sounds an alarm that sets my heart racing and sharpens my senses. I shift my weight to my good leg, slide my right hand into the pocket of my overcoat, and grip the Sig. Two large men in belted brown overcoats cut a swath through the crowded street to my left. Unlike all the other pedestrians, they stride erectly, looking straight ahead, with no regard for anything happening around them.

The door behind my back is locked. At least four police cover the streets. Like cockroaches, where you find four there are undoubtedly many more. I vault the rail, land hard with a grunt of pain, and lurch for the nearest corner. The overcoats cut in my direction like twin sharks carving a school of tuna. The policewoman opens her mouth in a round *O*, ready to shout. Too late. I'm rounding the corner, almost away—and then I bump chest-first into rock-hard Viktor, the police commander.

"Hello, Volk," he says, twirling chrome handcuffs on the end of a long, pointed finger. His lips are pulled back, smiling victory. One tooth is stained a dingy cigarette yellow.

The brown overcoats arrive. One with red hair claps the cuffs on my wrists and grinds them closed tightly, metal crunched to bone. Viktor takes my elbow and leads me into a waiting police van. His breath fogs from his mouth when he talks. It smells like Lucky Strikes.

"You are under arrest for the murder of Gorgon Yakovenko," he says.

chapter 52

They take me to the same Kosygnia Street station that housed Gromov during his interrogation and throw me into a cinder-block holding cell, maybe fifteen square meters. The side facing out looks onto a dank stone hallway through floor-to-ceiling bars slick from prisoners' warm breath condensing in the early morning chill. The population here represents the dregs from last night's arrests.

A boy with a cobra tattoo wrapping his neck kneels in the urine-stained corner, his hands pressed against the walls, puking. A bony transvestite sporting a five o'clock shadow, high heels, and a cockeyed, matted blond wig huddles against the bars. A smirking gangster in an open leather vest laced with silver chains leers at her, massaging his crotch.

The other side of the cage hosts a sprawled drunk, out cold. He groans when I roll him away with the toe of my boot and squat on my haunches with my back to the wall. Cops roam the hall outside the bars, but nobody offers me a phone call. Viktor must be feeling powerful.

I consider my situation with all the objectivity I can muster. The General, Maxim, Lipman, Posnova, Peter, the politicians—nearly all of the connections have become disturbingly clear, although questions remain. The most important one I have no answer for is why the General allied himself with Maxim—an alliance so strong that he was willing to sacrifice both Valya and me.

The blond transvestite mewls. The gangster has pushed her to her knees on the concrete.

The bars remind me of the prison where I spent my formative teens, three years caged with animals far worse than these. The times when I was helpless are long past. I may be imprisoned again, but I can still change what happens here now. The gangster unzips his leather pants. I cover the distance between us in two giant strides. His hair feels slick in my fist. I snap his head back so hard that his feet leave the ground and he slams backward onto the concrete.

"What the—"

"Shut up. Don't move."

He settles onto the concrete.

"Leave her alone."

"That's no woman. I—"

I cut him off with a vicious kick to the ribs. He screeches and tries to curl into a protective ball. My next kick snaps a bone in the hand he is using to protect his groin. His screams change to a higher pitch.

"She is a woman if that's what she chooses to be."

This time he's smart enough not to answer.

"Volkovoy!"

I don't need to turn around to recognize Viktor's voice. "Leave her alone," I tell the gangster again before I turn around.

The guards cuff me. Viktor leads me to the same windowless room where Gromov was interrogated. With practiced ease he unsnaps the cuffs from my wrists, threads them one cuff on either side through cutouts in the metal chair, and scrunches them closed again. He settles into a scuffed wooden chair opposite me and leans forward with his elbows on his knees, furrowing his brow.

"Too many dead guys out there, Volk," he says in a serious tone. "Dead cops. Dead crooks. Splattered all over, from here to St. Petersburg. And now I got two dead politicians, at least one of them yours—I know it. And your ass isn't covered this time."

I don't see any cameras or microphones. The cuffs are tight but not unbearable. I wonder who is on the other side of the one-way glass.

"You're everywhere," he says, "like a bad smell." He picks his nose and studies his prize thoughtfully. "Been that way for years. But then the shit would come down and—*pow*!" He claps his hands. The sound echoes like a rifle shot on a cold night. "Somehow you were always taken care of."

The wound above my stump is burning again. I shift my weight and feel the warm slide of blood down the upper part of my calf—the part that's still there. I should have gotten more pills from Vadim.

"Why am I here?"

Viktor smiles victory. "I told you. For the murder of Gorgon Yakovenko."

"Who the hell is he?"

"You know goddamned well who he is," Viktor says. He leans close to my face and blows stale cigarette fumes. "Nobody's coming this time, my friend. Just me. Work with me, and maybe I can make things better for you."

So the General hasn't made his usual call. I'm on my own for now. Maybe for good. I am as happy as I have ever been about anything that I used Vadim's throw-down to kill Yakovenko.

"Go fuck yourself, Viktor."

He jumps up and looms over me. I brace myself for a punch. But instead of hitting me, he pirouettes and bangs on the door, which opens to reveal one of the brown-coated men from the street. The one with red hair. "Watch him, George," Viktor says, then slams out of the room.

George takes up his station in front of the door. He looks everywhere but at me. I don't know what impulse makes me want to say it, but I tell him, "I'm sorry about Yuri."

George locks his surprised gaze onto mine. All the cops think I'm nothing more than a half-tamed wolf. I know that Yuri was regularly assigned bagman duty to me in Gorky Park because the more senior officers were afraid to do it.

"He was a good man," I say.

His jaw drops. He's still foolishly staring at me when Viktor slams back into the room and pushes him outside.

Viktor is gripping rolled-up sheets of oily fax paper. He steps to the side of the bolted chair and fans the smeared pages in front of my face. All I can see is the Federal Security Service letterhead. "What the fuck does that say, Volk?"

He sounds out of breath. Too many cigarettes, probably.

"I can't read it."

His fist shakes. He wants to smash the papers into my face. I know that from his frustrated growl, but he still fears me enough not to do it.

"It says that your prints were found on the Colt .38 that was used to blow three holes in Yakovenko's head. How the fuck do you explain that?"

"My prints are on lots of guns. Most of them provided courtesy of the Russian army."

Viktor leans forward and sends more of his foul breath into my face. He's breathing hard. His teeth are clenched. "Listen, you fuck. My phone's not ringing. Get it? That means your fucking ass belongs to me."

He's an idiot. He was so sure he had me nailed that he never bothered to run a ballistics test on the bullets that killed the politician and compare them to the gun Maxim undoubtedly gave him.

"Listen, Viktor, the gun doesn't tie to the dead guy. Check it out and then let me out of here."

For a long time he just stares at me, clenching and unclenching the fax paper in his fist. He knows I'm not bluffing, that he is one step behind. The realization is plain on his face. Then he slams out of the room.

George comes down to release me a few hours later. Paperwork takes another hour before he escorts me to Kosygnia Street. At the door he puts his hand on my arm and leans close. "I liked Yuri, too," he whispers.

chapter 53

Strolling through the grounds of Alexandrovsky Gardens is not a pleasant experience in these days of lost pride and tourism, but the feel of freedom blunts my anger at the things I see. A week has passed since my release from the jail, and I am still glad to be a free man.

Dusk has yet to give way to night when two boys—German tourists, I think—strip to their underpants and wade into the diverted, frigid river water, which gurgles around and over man-made escarpments and gently falling plateaus carrying candy wrappers, cigarette butts, and empty cans of Budweiser. The boys' friends toss bottles at them. A girl strips to bra and panties, much to the delight of the crowd watching from the balcony adjacent to the restaurants atop the underground Okhotny Ryad shopping mall, and steps daintily into the water, a half-smoked cigarette dangling from her lips. The boys grab her and threaten to throw her in deeper while she squeals and giggles.

I pause next to a squat woman standing on a garden walkway next to her wire basket on wheels. She pulls her shawl closed over her breast. "Half-grown Nazis," she says. Her voice is deep like a man's.

"The evil cubs come to finish what their grandfathers started and couldn't do."

She doesn't seem to expect an answer, so I don't offer one. The truth is different, I believe. In the end the Germans chose the winning side in a war of culture. Russia picked a different path and now is being conquered in an unexpected manner by a cultural onslaught it was unprepared to defend against.

"We should have crushed them under our boots," my new acquaintance says. I assume she is referring to the Red Army in Berlin, longing for a chance to travel back in time and push artillery and air-power west all the way to the Atlantic. She spits onto the walkway. Yanks her cart with a grunt of disgust and wheels away.

I follow her, moving more slowly, angling to the right and pacing around a circle of closely cropped turf and manicured flowers. South of the Tomb of the Unknown Soldier is a row of dark red urns filled with earth from each of the "hero cities" that stood against Hitler's best. Dubinin seems lost in their midst, standing there with his hands buried in the side pockets of his sea-green tunic, staring at the marble tomb.

I stop at his side. We stand together enveloped in our own cocoon of silence amid the clamor of passing tourists, rowdy teens, and schoolchildren being taught lessons different from the ones their parents learned.

"Forty-one kilometers," Dubinin says, still not looking at me. He is facing the tomb. "I wonder sometimes if things might have been better if the Nazis had bridged the last gap."

I recall the hedgehogs on the road outside of Moscow, the ones marking the point of Hitler's deepest incursion. The tomb contains the remains of a soldier who died there, under an inscription reading "Your name is unknown, your deeds immortal." Hopeful words, belied by the coarse crowds surrounding us. The deeds of the soldier have long been forgotten, except perhaps in the fading memories of the old woman towing her basket and a few others like her.

"Things would have been the same, probably," I say.

Russia is always the same, whether she toils under the tsars, the Communists, or the republicans. Vast quantities of vodka are required just to endure the unleavened sameness of it all.

Dubinin continues to stare at the tomb while he lights a cigarette and takes a deep drag. "I know you don't like me, Colonel," he says.

He pauses, perhaps waiting for me to disabuse him of the idea, but I don't take the bait.

Smoke wreaths through his bushy mustache. A ghost of what might be a small smile plays underneath the bristles. "The General tells me that you are too valuable to lose. I wouldn't know about that."

A group of schoolchildren in blue blazers and overstarched white shirts marches past, trilling in high-pitched voices. They wind around the curled form of a beggar without sparing him a glance, although one of the girls wrinkles her nose.

"I am charged with the General's protection," Dubinin says. "So I need to know your state of mind."

I wonder if I am in the crosshairs of a sniper's rifle. The shot would be taken from a spot inside the Kremlin's walls to give the shooter an easy escape. "Did the General ask you to come?"

"No. He still trusts you. He thinks you will understand why he had to do what he did."

I suppose the captain is obliquely referring to betrayal. "What did Maxim have on him?"

Dubinin drops the butt of his cigarette, shifts his weight to stub it out with the toe of his shiny boot. I have never seen him smoke before. If he starts to light another one, I will do my best to kill him before a bullet rips my brain.

"A plane loaded with weapons went down in Iran," he says.

I recall the scene of damask-hued desert beauty captured on the screen of Leonid's television, and remember the dead soldiers' assignment to a "transport operation" in Vladikavkaz. Now I know why the General made his alliance with Maxim. He must have sold the plane and its cargo to Maxim—and promised delivery in Iran. The plane went down not long after Lipman made off with the paintings at the

Hermitage. So the General suddenly became indebted to Maxim, which is yet another reason why the big Azeri seemed to be a step ahead of me at every turn.

"Seventy-five million dollars, prepaid by Maxim, and lots of men who became invaluable when Maxim made the final accounting," Dubinin continues. "The General had to make good. He could either blow your cover or let Maxim believe that you are what you pretend to be—and that they were both using you to track down the paintings. Maxim knows the General occasionally uses you for some of his more unpleasant tasks, but if he finds out you're still military, not just some ex–Special Forces gangster—well, let's just say the political fallout would be too much for the General to bear."

"The General sent Valya and me straight to Strahov."

"Strahov was Maxim's man. The General didn't know about Peter Vyugin until it was too late to do anything for the girl. I don't think Maxim did either. Strahov didn't stop Vyugin from hurting her because all Strahov cared about was that you be motivated to find the paintings."

This has the ring of truth. I doubt that either Maxim or the General would have let Valya be chopped up if they could have prevented it without compromising their aims.

"Maxim nearly hung me with Yakovenko's murder."

Dubinin smiles. "The General knew you were too smart to be trapped so easily."

Maybe that was the case, but I doubt it. I remember the General's terse reply to my e-mail about the hit. He could have easily warned me about what was coming.

"None of us is irreplaceable, Volk," Dubinin says, as if sensing my thoughts.

"So Maxim gets *Leda* and *The Last Supper*?"

Dubinin shakes his head. "No. That's where the two soldiers come into play. Maxim killed them to cover his tracks. Turns out he'd bribed them to add a special container holding enriched uranium to the cargo. They knew what they had loaded, and who they had loaded it for, so Maxim decided they needed to die. Once we pinned the murders on Maxim's man, Gromov, the General was able to uncover the uranium plot. That gave the General some leverage, because Maxim can't afford to let *that* leak to Putin. So the General and Maxim are stalemated."

I don't bother telling him the murderer was Leonid, not Gromov. From his point of view it makes no difference anyway because they were both Maxim's men. From mine, well, Leonid fought for Russia and Gromov didn't.

"So the General keeps the paintings and pays Maxim back with more weapons," Dubinin says. "But no tactical nukes. Not yet, at least. The paintings are being . . . held. Others are responsible for them now."

Leda still cradles me in her amorous embrace. Christ's outstretched arms reach toward me just as they do to his apostles in *The Last Supper*. I resolve not to permit anonymous *others* to decide their fate, even as I realize that it is a resolution easier made than kept.

"Are they real or forgeries?"

Dubinin pulls up his collar and seems to crouch behind it. "I was going to ask you the same question."

chapter 54

Late in the night Dubinin leads me through the tunnels to the stone cells adjacent to the underground banks of the Moscow River. He whispers instructions to a pale corporal, then leaves. The corporal avoids my gaze as he jangles heavy keys to unlock the battleship gray door of the cell farthest from the front and pull it open.

Lipman's eyes widen when I enter the room. The door clangs shut, leaving us alone. He's lying on a steel bunk bolted to the floor, covered with a blanket. The blanket bunches under his feet as he backpedals, trying to put some distance between us. Without giving him time to recover from the shock of seeing me, I slam my fist into his slack jaw. The force of the blow cracks bone and thwacks his head against the wall. He sags onto his bunk, unconscious.

The ceiling is low, barely two and a half meters. I grab an exposed pipe running along its length and hang for a moment, testing its strength. It holds. I loop a short length of rope over the pipe, cinch one end around both of his ankles, then pull the free end of the rope until he is hanging by his feet with the top of his head swinging less than ten centimeters above the stone floor.

I tie off the rope to the steel frame of the bunk and settle in to wait. Light a Robusto. Puff appreciatively while he gradually comes to, moaning. When he tries to talk through the blood in his mouth, I set the cigar on the edge of the bunk, then squat next to his head to make sure he knows it's me, just in case the blow addled his brain. When the light of recognition dawns in his eyes, I slide out my knife and show it to him. Stark terror blooms in his eyes.

"Why did you give the paintings to Lieutenant Passky in St. Petersburg?"

"What?"

"You heard me. Why didn't you keep them, or turn them over to Maxim?"

"I was working for two politicians. Yakovenko and Dudayev. They told me to give them to Passky." Lipman is still swinging upside down, but he's gathered some of his wits, obviously glad to still be alive and talking.

"I know that. I just don't know why you stayed loyal to them when Maxim was far more dangerous."

"My brother," he says. "My brother is in a Siberian prison with a life sentence. He was caught running heroin. I agreed to trade the paintings for a pardon and a share of the profits."

Now that I have my answer I raise the blade in front of his eyes. He flails with his hands and arms, trying to ward it off, and gurgles, "No! No, wait!" as I slowly drag it across his exposed throat.

I wipe the knife clean on the thin cotton of his prison-issue pants, then settle back onto the bunk with the Robusto to watch him die.

chapter 55

I hold Valya close, willing my body to melt into hers, but willpower is not enough. A month has passed since my meeting in Alexandrovsky Gardens with Dubinin. Over her shoulder through a plate-glass window I can see the birches around the Sheremetevos-2 airport terminal bending in the wind.

"I love you," I say.

"I love you as well, Alexei."

Before the Chechens chopped off my foot they crushed it in a homemade vice made from the filigreed gears of a 155-millimeter howitzer. That was the beginning of six months of torture after my surrender in the Ingushetia forest. I begged to die. I did things that still burrow under my skin and curdle my pride and make me wish for the easy release of a hollow-point exploding in my skull. The same gut-wrenching agony is focused here, on this moment—my last with the love of my life. I would give all three of my limbs to have her stay here. But neither this place nor I deserve her.

She still has an hour before her flight. The first leg of her journey takes her to Rome. She told me that was a jumping-off point, but did not say where she was going from there. When she opened her clutch on the way to the airport I glimpsed a train ticket—Rome to Florence to Milan, where *The Last Supper* graces the wall of the refectory. I try not to draw unwarranted conclusions. Let all of those enigmatic connections stay in Masha's world of potions and sorcery.

Time rushes past, but I'm not going to last the hour. I'm too weak. "I have to go."

"I know."

And I do—walking slowly at first, then faster, as fast as my wrecked heart will allow.

chapter 56

The elevators in Masha's building still don't work. They probably never will again. I creak up the stairs, nine dragging stories, wishing foolishly to have my real foot back, to be made whole once again. I came here straight from the airport. Valya is probably airborne by now.

Masha's floor is busy with police, and for a moment I fear that she has died. But they are not here for her. They have come to arrest a wizened woman whose cataract-clouded eyes brush past me without seeing as they escort her away.

The door to Masha's flat is cracked open. She waves me in. The TV is turned off. I take my seat in the too-small wicker chair. She bends over the sink in the kitchen, scraping an iron skillet, close enough that I could reach out and touch her from my chair.

"I burned the cake," she says, running water into the sink. She tries to angle her lined face so that I won't see the tears rolling in and out of the creases.

I point toward the outside hall. "Why?"

"That was Svetlana." Lathered soap bubbles up to her elbows.

The pan is so clean that her furiously working hands are sanding raw iron. "They say she was selling radioactive lingonberries."

Chernobyl nuclear fallout has led to glowing fruit, atomic food inspectors, and, now, arrested babushkas—all part of everyday life in twenty-first-century Moscow.

"I'm sorry, Masha," I say uselessly.

She hangs her head. "They should arrest the shippers. Not a poor woman trying to sell fruit to live."

They won't hold Svetlana for long, I know. Just long enough to send a warning to the other gap-toothed grandmothers doing the same thing. Whether Svetlana is sufficiently sturdy to survive the lesson is another question.

Masha dries her hands on her apron, pulls it over her head, folds it with care on the tiny ledge of the counter, and settles into her usual position on her bed. Her quavering hands fumble with the straps on her prosthesis, so I gently nudge them aside and finish the job of removing it. My fingers work the fascia and muscles to relieve the aches I know she feels in her leg. Her eyelids droop.

"Only one pair remains," she says cryptically.

I recall my first palm reading. How many lifetimes ago did that occur? *Two,* she had told me. *Two of everything.* And now I see the truth of those words. Two brothers—Kamil and Tariq. Two sets of false lovers—Lipman and Arkady, Valya and Posnova. Two glorious works of art, maybe. And two kings on the chessboard, the last pair still standing—Maxim and the General. Stalemate.

The aroma of burned cake fills the room. Masha's breast rises and falls with the deep breath of sleep. I adjust a crocheted afghan blanket so that it covers her body to her downy chin. She continues to breathe deeply, and her eyes remain closed, but her lips flutter.

"The final pair rules you," she says, and then she sighs and seems to sink into the lumpy comfort of the mattress.

As I quietly close the door to her flat, I know the truth of her words. My cage is so large that the bars are invisible, but even unseen I know they are there, and so I am no less a prisoner.

chapter 57

Dubinin leads me to the General's crying-stone room later that night. The only source of light, a shaded lamp on the General's table, makes everything beyond its circle perversely gloomy. The heavy, protruding ridge of his brow shades his eyes like a veil, so all that is visible is the prowlike jut of his chin and thick lips pursed in concentration as he reads my report. Or rereads it, more likely. The General is nothing if not prepared. If he is disappointed, it fails to show. The walls weep river water, the ceiling drips the discharge of loose arsenal pipes, I choke back a lump in my throat for my lost love. And the General remains as impassive as whatever synthetic being occupies the glass case of Lenin's tomb.

Finally he looks up and says, "What of you and Valya?"

"We're over."

His head inclines toward the tabletop. It is impossible to gauge his feelings. "She was a part of you," he says finally, echoing my own thoughts. "Better perhaps to lose your arm."

I change the subject. "Why didn't you tell me about your troubles with Maxim?"

"Because you didn't need to know. You needed to do the things you do best. I risked your life, Colonel, just as I have done in all manner of ways since your first days in Chechnya. The fact that you are still alive is proof enough that the risk was well calculated."

It is one thing to suspect that you are a pawn in a vast game, quite another to hear it expressed so bluntly.

"What do you know of the Imperial Easter Eggs?" he asks, easily shifting gears.

chapter 58

Maxim agrees to see me a few days later. His room in the Metropol Hotel overlooks the Bolshoi Theatre and Karl Marx Square. The juxtaposition of new-breed capitalist Maxim Abdullaev drinking tea while he admires his view of the stone bust of the great Communist Marx would strike me as ironic except for the circumstances of the meeting.

I'm standing behind and a little to one side of him. We're alone. His usual flotilla of armed guards is nowhere to be seen.

"I've had you watched," he says. "You vanish, they say. *Poof*, gone."

"Rats have many holes."

He blows air through fleshy lips like a warhorse. "Sometimes you disappear near the Kremlin."

"Soldiers are good business."

"Maybe." He sets his cup of tea on the windowsill and clasps hands the size of shovels behind his back, contemplating the view—or perhaps eyeing my reflection in the window. "Tell me about you and the General."

I choose my words carefully, the way a technician with a twitch disarms a bomb. "He commanded my division in Chechnya."

He waits, unmoved, but I add nothing. My parched lips scream for moisture, but licking them would be a deadly giveaway that Maxim is on the right track.

"What does he want from you?" Maxim says finally.

I must take care to answer the question without revealing something he does not already know. "He loves his soldiers the way good parents love their children. Sometimes he asks me to do things to help them. And sometimes he asks me to do things an army general can't do, not if he hopes to survive politically."

Maxim nods. I wonder what he has taken from the words. I limp to his side for a better view of the crowded square. Vendors proliferate. Tourists swirl in peacock reds, yellows, and blues. Old women pensioners implore with pained faces and homemade trinkets and baked treats. Sharp-eyed pigeons dive for crumbs and drop whitish streaks of feces down the stern granite visage of Karl Marx, doomed to suffer in this capitalist perdition until the forces of time and nature wear him away—or until the next revolution, whichever comes first. Maxim points down with fingers shaped like a gun.

"You know what I see, Volk?"

"No."

"Opportunity." He regards me thoughtfully. "I wonder what you see."

I stare down, considering. Decide the truth can do me no further harm. "A different kind of opportunity."

His brow furrows while he considers my answer. He seems to reach a decision. "The General is a good man. Foolish, no doubt of that. But . . ." He shrugs, then wheels to face me full on, studying me. "You. You are a dangerous man. Sentimental and strange, but even more fearsome for it."

He stares for a while longer, then shakes his head as if he can't make up his mind about something.

"I have a line on two Impressionist paintings. Pissarro." The way he says the name makes the first syllable sound like a drawn-out, sibilant pronunciation of the word *piss*. "Like the ones in the Hermitage, but not so well-known. Maybe we can work together."

I recall Pappalardo's conversation with Posnova in the New York gallery. "They're fakes."

He wrinkles his nose and snorts at my naïveté. "So? So is all art. Artists are phony, so what they make is phony. They smear paint. Pound stone. Scribble worthless words. Live miserable and die hungry."

He grimaces and aims a meaty fist at the red walls of the Kremlin three blocks away, slowly extending his index finger. The finger points to Red Square, where thousands of executions have been carried out before cheering throngs. Then it aims at the Konstantin and Yelena Tower, also known as the Torture Tower for the suffering it housed. Then it sweeps to take in the Annunciation Tower, which Ivan the Terrible used as a political prison for the doomed. Finally, it angles down to the subterranean bowels, where buckets of Russian blood have been spilled for sadistic sport, running in red rivulets of sorrow and pain into the Moscow River.

"Tourists," he says, almost spitting. "They snap their pictures. Drink and eat until they are so fat they can hardly move. And they admire those walls. How Russian, they say. How historic. How beautiful."

He drops his arm and snorts disgust. "What fools. This place is fucking death, inside those walls and out. Invaders, patriots—they all die suffering. Nothing changes. But for now, in a nothing time, the blood is washed clean, and the herds of cattle see art."

He scratches between his legs. Uses the whittled nails at the ends of the same fingers to pick his teeth. Waves his other hand toward the tourists in a gesture that seems to take in the entire world.

"Those people with their money and their soft lives. Always warm. They look at the pictures and talk art to show how smart they are. To feel important. The ones who can pay buy what they can. The more money they pay, the more important they feel. Then they piss on the picture for their friends." He spreads his thick thighs, grabs his crotch, and swivels to pantomime a man spraying urine in arcing curves, marking territory. "See what I possess? See how tasteful I am?"

He settles back into the chair. His piercing gaze cuts like a laser. "*That* is what we sell, Volk. Not canvas and paint."

A sound like a loaded freight train rumbling over trestles emanates from somewhere deep inside his massive chest. He is laughing, but his smoldering gray eyes burn with contempt.

"Art?" he says. "It's art to them."

chapter 59

I make the short walk from the Metropol Hotel to the loft last for a long time. I already miss Valya, and I still long for Leda in the same way I have since the first time I saw her. I dread the night. The dead will haunt my dreams. They always do. The guilty as well as the innocent, strangely enough, each one another cairn on the landscape of my memory, marking things that were lost and things that were never really possessed. Now I will have to confront them alone.

So what do I know about art? Art is like the two-faced diplomat buried in Novodevichy Cemetery—parts that can be seen and parts that can only be sensed. Men like Maxim and the General see the colors and the shapes and the market value but not the meaning. Others are able to perceive the symbolism created by the greatest artists, those few who transcend mortality, whose genius allows the rest of us to feel the heartbeat of humanity—and, perhaps, to touch a piece of the good that resides in our own hearts.

acknowledgments

I'm grateful to my mother, Jan, for giving me a love of reading. I can't think of a more important gift.

Many thanks to Lisa Ghelfi, Al Ghelfi, Lee Ludden, Adam Tuton, Scott Isham, and Patrick Clark, all of whom offered encouragement and suffered through various drafts of the manuscript. Keith Gazda, Bob Ghelfi, M.D., Gregg Ghelfi, J. D. Ghelfi, Keefer Meranto, and Jessica Barranco provided invaluable insight. Paul Thayer helped whip the original manuscript into shape and gave much-needed support. Sinclair Browing generously gave her time to a new writer in need of advice.

I greatly appreciate all those in Russia who guided me through her good parts and bad. Special thanks to "Galina," who revealed some of the hidden places in the Hermitage and elsewhere.

Thanks to my agent, Scott Hoffman, who believed in Volk from the beginning, promoted his development, and took him to the right person—Sarah Knight, my editor.

Thank you, Sarah, for the many things you've done to champion the book, shepherd its progress, and make it better—and for letting me win one or two of our semantic arguments. How did you manage to nail that one, best line the first time we talked?

Valentina Troufanova tirelessly showed me the Russia she loves. In many ways, she personifies her great country. There is much of her in Valya, Volk, and, especially, Masha.

All mistakes are mine.

Read on for an excerpt from

Volk's Shadow

Coming soon from Henry Holt and Company

chapter 1

A man like me is not supposed to have doubts.

Especially not at a time like this, poised in the open fuselage of an Mi-24 assault helicopter, carving a tilted arc around a black square in the grid of lights on Moscow's south side. This is the worst time to be asking myself questions that can't be answered. But lately they're always there, corroding all those things I once believed so intensely. Defend the motherland, secure our southern flank, protect the innocents. Gripping a canvas strap to brace against the force of our turn, I whisper the words in a soundless incantation.

The AMERCO building rises from the darkness, a fiery, open wound torn midway up its south face. Smoke glows in chemical-pink wreaths against the night sky as the helicopter swoops, flares, drops to a hard landing. I leap out while the rotors are still thumping the air in a dying backbeat rhythm.

A policeman jumps in front of me. He shouts something about Chechen terrorists. The blast happened less than an hour ago, he yells, but I already know that and more. I circle my finger in the air impatiently, and he points the way to an improvised command center. Charging away from him toward the burnt skyline, I think that what he should have said is that the *first* blast is less than an hour old. More explosions might come, because at least two terrorists remain alive.

I am here to change that.

The General's orders, issued over a scrambled satellite phone, ricochet inside my mind. Do not delay. Do not negotiate. Attack. Dead hostages, destroyed property—whatever the costs, they will be less than the price of capitulation. Orders birthed by hard experience fighting a shadowy war against a faceless enemy. Orders that mean I don't have the luxury of doubt.

My path brings me within sight of the blown-out half of the sixth story of the targeted high-rise, the Moscow headquarters of an American oil company. Its southern side gapes like a screaming mouth, bent steel beams and metal studs for a tongue, belching smoke. The damage appears worse from here than it did from the helicopter.

Moving faster now, I rush past a staging area for the dead and wounded, set back about a hundred meters from the edge of the zone where rounds from the building might reach. Many of the wounded are missing pieces. Limbs, eyes, and, in the case of one shrieking boy, part of his jaw. Each step drives nails into my left foot—the foot that is not there—a phantom pain, the product of being this close to my old adversaries, entering a world of horror, knowing what is to come.

The millennium Moscow bombings in Pushkin Square left 150 dead, the takeover of the House of Culture Theatre 130, just two among so many others I can't bear to think of them all. The worst for me was the Beslan school massacre, during which 344 died, including 186 children. The architects of many such attacks are dead, some of them killed in operations memorialized by secret medals I've tossed into a cigar box, but others have risen to take their place.

The makeshift command post has been established in the first floor lobby of an office building three blocks away from the one that was bombed. I cross a wide street emptied of traffic. Slam open the steel-and-glass door. A small group huddled around a folding metal table all turn to stare at me.

"Who's in command?" My voice sounds loud even to my own ears.

"Who wants to know?" Tall, thin, and spectacled, he looks like a haughty professor, although too young to be one. I know his kind at a glance. A staffer, privileged from birth by his family's social position in the old Soviet order. His uniform and red beret identify him as a special forces officer of the internal troops of the FSB—the principal successor of the KGB—but his kind can be found throughout Russia's military, political, and bureaucratic elites.

I throw off my overcoat so that he can see my rank on the tunic beneath.

He turns his back to me.

"I'll get with you later, Colonel." He spits out the words as though he's trying to rid his mouth of a bad taste.

"Now."

He whirls to face me, lips twisted into a snarl. "You'll not speak again until I address you. Is that—"

And I am upon him, wrenching him onto the table. It collapses under his weight and the force of the blow. A laptop crashes to the floor with him as he smacks the marble facedown. I plant the heel of my combat boot on the back of his neck.

"Who is second in command?" I say, so softly that everyone in the room leans forward to hear me.

A florid-faced policeman snaps smartly to attention. "I am, sir. Inspector Barokov."

The FSB officer under my boot struggles to rise. Or to reach a gun. I pull my Sig, bend down, and crunch it against the side of his head to knock him out. Then nod to the inspector to go on.

Still saluting, he tries to draw himself straighter. "The Chechens took the AMERCO offices on the sixth floor. We didn't have time to contact them before a bomb blew. We're lucky the whole building didn't come down. We don't know how many are dead, and we can't get inside."

He waits for a response. I'm not surprised the building still stands. Its bones were erected during Stalin's heyday, when labor was forced at the end of a bayonet and buildings were made of steel, brick, and mortar laced with blood. I flick my right hand toward my brow. He drops his salute, but remains at attention.

"Two terrorists are left on the north side of the sixth floor with maybe ten hostages, depending on how many from the office are still alive."

"How do you know all that?"

"They released a hostage to communicate their demands."

I could not possibly care any less what the terrorists want. In my mind's eye I can see the General's granite features, like a craggy Neanderthal's, his heavy lips moving. *Do not negotiate.*

Barokov points with his chin to a woman sitting in a reception chair, doubled up with her hands cupping her face. She appears to be crying. All I can see of her is ash-blond hair and a soot-stained pantsuit with a long rip running down the sleeve. Another uniformed FSB officer, a lieutenant, stands stiffly beside her, but he does nothing to question my authority. He roughly jostles her shoulder to get her attention, and she looks up at him, then turns to face me. She has shell-shocked green eyes wet with tears. She's overwrought, nervously fingering a blue pendant swinging from a chain around her neck and looking back and forth from me to the officer.

"You heard what he said?" I ask her. "Two terrorists, ten hostages, sixth floor. That's correct?"

She glances at the officer. "Yes. There were two of them. Both on the sixth floor." Her Russian is bad, with a heavy American accent.

I turn away, gathering my thoughts. "Show me the building layout."

Inspector Barokov unrolls faded, tattered blueprints while others set the table upright and then stand aside, looking everywhere except down at the professorial FSB agent oozing blood onto the polished floor.

"They're here," he says, pointing to a wing of offices toward the middle of the building. "We might be able to get in here." His finger lands on a stairwell that I can see is accessible only by entering the building directly below where the terrorists are thought to be.

I grunt and pull the plans closer, searching for a likelier path, sliding my finger along the crinkled paper to an exterior door on the west side of the building. The portal is tucked beneath an overhang six floors below and roughly thirty-five meters from where the hostages are being held.

"That door will be locked," Barokov says. "And getting there will be a problem. But there are only two of them, so if you can make it inside, the stairs probably won't be guarded."

The lock doesn't bother me. But he's understating the difficulty of getting there. The path to the door will be a scramble through the terrorists' field of fire. The darkness might provide cover, but not if they have night-vision goggles, which they probably do. The American military hands them out in Iraq the way it handed out sticks of chewing gum in France after World War II. Except that in Iraq the goggles are then sold to the people trying to kill American soldiers—free enterprise as practiced by Iraqi insurgents.

I page through the plans to the structural sheets. The main building is twelve stories high. It narrows six stories up, the center column rising like a thick candle in the middle of a cake. The sixth-floor ceiling is dropped, with a crawl space above it. Less than one meter of clearance. I roll back several pages of plans to find the one I want, then consider for a moment, trying to burn the drawing into my mind like light onto a photographic plate.

Barokov clears his throat and steps back. The former hostage is still quietly crying. Back at the helicopter a team of five combat-hardened commandos awaits my orders, and the chatter in my radio, mostly confused shouts, tells me that a separate Vympel antiterrorism unit is deploying nearby. But I can hear the General's voice in my head, urging me forward. *Do not delay. Attack.*

I turn away from the group and radio my squad leader, talking in a low voice into my hand-cupped mouthpiece. Instruct him to deploy around the perimeter, storm the building at the first sound of fighting, save the hostages if he can, worry about me last. Then I set aside the radio and strip down to black paratrooper pants and tactical body armor over a long-sleeved, collarless shirt made of a body-hugging synthetic. Slide the Sig into a nylon holster. Adjust the knife hanging below the back of my neck. Take one last look at the plans, and then I'm out the door, where I wait for a moment while my eyes adjust to the pinkish gloom.

"Who the hell was that?" I hear Inspector Barokov say behind me.

chapter 2

Chunks of blasted concrete and scattered building materials offer the illusion of cover on my approach to the blasted AMERCO building. I avoid the islands of light where the fires still burn. Crouch, crawl, slither, and slide—all well-practiced maneuvers. Street fighting is in my blood from three years of little else in bombed-out Grozny and the surrounding villages. After Grozny I spent most of two years in the icy forests of Ingushetia and the snowcapped mountains of Dagestan. Right up to the moment of my surrender—and six long months in a zindan, a mud pit, where time was measured by the shivering intervals between torture sessions. Within minutes I make it to the smoking building, my back against a brick wall, sweating despite the chill air, but breathing easily. No gunshots, no shouts. Nothing.

The door is locked from the inside, the lock well made. I spend nearly ten minutes picking it by the light of flickering flames, probing with small metal tools, alert for a cry of discovery. When it finally tumbles, the mechanism sounds like a reverberating gong. I wait another minute, my breath fogging the air. Still nothing except for wailing sirens, crackling fires, and distant crowd-control instructions amplified by a megaphone. I wedge through the heavy door and close it gently behind me.

The stairwell seems as deserted as Barokov thought it would be. Another surprise, because I thought he had underestimated the danger here as well as on the approach to the building. Outside sounds are muted. A dull roar fills my ears, accompanied by popping flames that have grown louder, magnified as though the inside of the building has become a giant hearth. The steps are made of concrete edged with metal toe-kicks, the walls lined with tubular handrails slick from condensation.

I ascend the stairs slowly, quietly, pausing at each landing while the structure groans around me like the hull of a sinking ship. Reach the sixth floor and squeeze through another door into an abandoned hallway filled with smoke and drifting paper. Slide along a wall beneath portraits of smug executives to an oak door leading into the room we identified on the blueprints. Inside is a wide area partitioned into cubicles. I place a chair against the wall closest to where I think the hostages are being held, nudge aside a ceiling tile, and peer into the dark crawl space.

In the light of a handheld torch that barely penetrates the smoke, the heavy I-beams disappear into the grayish haze, crisscrossed every five meters or so by steel braces. Suspended below them is a strip-metal grid that holds fiberboard ceiling panels identical to the one I just removed.

I sheathe the torch. Hoist myself onto the top of the wall at the level of the drop-ceiling grid. Straddle a beam, gripping with my thighs for balance. Creep along the sweating steel, moving noiselessly, making good progress, the darkness so complete I can't even see across the span to the parallel girders I know run along both sides of the one I am on. I worm forward for about three minutes, counting each transverse brace to measure the distance, choking on unseen gusts of ashy air, blinking away particles of soot and dust. When I've covered thirty five meters I think I am directly over the hostage room. Except for the muted snarl of popping flames on the other side of the building and the distant clamor of sirens, everything is deathly quiet. Too quiet if the hostages and their captors are below. Not even a murmur or rustle of movement comes to me.

And then an eruption of light from the beam across from me stabs my eyes.

"You're dead," says a muffled voice.

The shocking glare strikes so suddenly I lose my grip. I let myself fall, not in a planned dive or some other well-executed evasion, but just a clumsy tumble that takes me straight down through the flimsy ceiling tiles to crash onto a desk in the room below. All of the air blows from my body.

Five meters away the second terrorist, his vest bulging with explosives, mouth covered by a swath of black cloth, stares wide-eyed at me. The muzzle of his Kalashnikov droops uselessly as he struggles to process my sudden appearance. Above us, his partner fires blindly through what's left of the drop-ceiling beneath him. The stitching of bullets races toward his comrade and explodes his skull. All the while I lay writhing on the broken desk, helpless, while random bursts from the man on the beam spray more bullets. One or more slugs must strike the dead man's vest, because an explosion rips through the room.

When I was a boy assigned to the work farms I pretended to be a Stakhanovite, a shock worker like the famous miner who always exceeded the norms. On rare days off, I imagined I was Ilia Muromets, the legendary protector of the Russian people, battling invaders with my giant, gentle strength. But when things were really bad I tried to disappear, to detach from my body and float away. That's the sensation I have when the explosion hurls me through the air in a long, weightless tumble. Everything after that is a confused haze—searing pain, shouted curses, rough hands, a jolting ride.

I open my eyes to find a ring of faces staring down at me. "He's alive!" someone says, and they begin cheering. The red-faced police inspector Barokov drops to a knee next to me and probes my body for injuries, pausing when his hands encounter the rigidity of my prosthesis.

"Nothing appears to be broken," he announces. More cheering and clapping, but not enough to blot out the sirens or the crackle of flames that are now burning with renewed intensity. "You saved them!" another voice says.

I sit up and rest my elbows on my knees. I'm on a stretcher on the street outside the ruined building. I can't seem to draw a full breath. Everything hurts. My face feels as though it's been washed in acid. Wetness on my forehead turns out to be blood, which looks like chocolate syrup on the end of my fingers. The fabric of my shirt and pants has burned through in the places not covered by armor. Scorched flesh on my arms and legs triggers licks of pain. Standing is hard work.

"What happened?" I ask Barokov.

"Fifteen minutes after you left, the building blew again. We thought everyone was dead. Your men stormed in and found all ten hostages, alive. They'd been moved to the first floor, on the east side. They say the terrorist holding them vanished after the second explosion. Three of your men retrieved you after they rescued the hostages. The Vympel unit found parts of two dead terrorists."

Disturbing questions slosh around in my mind. Why did the terrorists bother to move the hostages away from the danger? If a third terrorist was guarding the hostages, how many more were there? And how did they know where to wait for me?

I stride off toward the improvised command post. No shuffle, no limp, nothing to reveal weakness except for the slight roll caused by the rebounding spring in my prosthesis. The inspector jogs beside me to keep up, weaving through rescue workers and soldiers, who are everywhere now. Eyes shining and wearing a broad smile, he claps me on the back like an old friend. "You're a hero!" The voices in the trailing crowd echo his sentiments, but they barely penetrate my consciousness.

We arrive at the command post, where I enter and shut the door on my admirers. Pull my overcoat back on. Wrap the clothes I removed earlier in my tunic and throw the bundle over my shoulder. Glance down at the forgotten FSB officer. He's curled up like a child, his face ghostly white against a canvas of pooled blood leaking through a makeshift wrap of torn cloth. I wonder why his lieutenant left him this way, then shake away the question and take a moment to gather myself.

The setting was urban, not rugged mountains the way it was in the past, but the attack bears familiar hallmarks. During the time he had me in the pit, Chechen rebel Abreg liked to talk about everything—philosophy, religion, global politics—so I have a window into how his mind works. He knows the psychological value of soft civilian targets, and he would argue that a strike such as this is a justified response to the devastation in Chechnya. But too many things don't add up. Why this building? Why trigger the bombs in the early evening, a bad time for a high body count in an office building? Why protect the hostages?

Inspector Barokov and the others are still waiting when I step back outside, probably so they can offer more unwarranted congratulations.

"What happened to the woman—the hostage?"

They exchange uneasy glances. The inspector's ruddy features appear even more flushed as he squirms under my gaze. He's short and roundish, but now he tries to stretch himself taller. "We don't know. She and the FSB lieutenant disappeared right after you left."

"Who is she?"

Barokov looks to his comrades for support that fails to come, takes a deep breath. "Everything happened very fast. She spoke English, very little Russian. The only person she talked to was the FSB man in there. The one you hit." His jaw hangs open for a moment, then snaps closed. "I'll take him to the triage area now, but we're not going to get any information out of him for a while."

"The hostage—did she work for AMERCO?"

"That's what she said."

"What happened after I left the command center?"

"Nothing. We waited."

"Did anybody talk about how I planned to get inside the building?"

A shadow ripples across his face. "We looked at the blueprints and guessed at some things." He shifts his weight from one leg to the other, then looks me full on. "Lots of people were talking on their cell phones. Everything was happening so fast, anyone could have—"

He steels himself, like a boy about to deliver bad news to his father.

"I'm sorry, Colonel. I didn't think to lock everyone down."

Five minutes later the ground falls away and I'm airborne through flurrying snow, arrowing north in the Mi-24 helicopter back toward the Kremlin to brief the General. During the bumpy ride a medic stitches my head then strips me down to the waist and applies salve to my burns. He's wasting his time. The pain is nothing to me, and I don't care about scars. These will only add to the road map of conflict already carved into my body—a decade of Russia's military hot spots memorialized in scar tissue.

My chronometer beeps. I was on the ground for less than an hour.